Joshua Hummus Humphrey moon on the traditional lan... ... ... w u. u..uj... people in the year 2528 BE. He was highly educated at La Trobe University, where he read Postcolonial Feminimism. He spent two years writing and performing in comedy plays and doing stand-up before deciding that he should be writing very serious novels about the difficulties faced by migrants on their journey to bourgeois liberalism. So he has spent the last few years volunteering at orphanages in Southeast Asia. After he realised that he's nothing but a beneficiary of heteronormative white male privilege, he dressed up as a non-binary mer-person and published *Exquisite Hours*. That novel sold out six print-runs in seven weeks and allowed him to volunteer with especial sincerity. In 2016 he attended a wellness retreat in Bali. While unlocking the magic of the sacred feminine he learnt that all of his opinions are always entirely correct. Banana seven? His greatest concern now is how phrases like, 'Man up,' are unhealthy. He knows the soul of history not as much as the facts and frequently informs people that Christianity has caused every war ever *and* that the very idea that he exists means there was a universal demand for his heart—two of the wildest truths the moon has ever whispered to him. Banana seven! As someone who dislikes gender classification, he holds space to honour everyone's androgynous potential while at the same time loathing things that offend his feminimism. He refuses to have children until people can legally marry trees and hopes one day to make boom boom with the earth in order to save it. He was integral in getting Bosnia to adopt bestiality appreciation week and has spent most of his family's fortune on getting cupcakes recognized as a masculine baked good. He has been retweeted by Stephen Colbert, Ricky Gervais, *and* Lady Gaga and—seeing that free speech has an atrocious impact on minorities—he recently sold the rights to all his books to the Chinese Communist Party and converted to moderate Islam. His spirit animal is the pangolin, his body animal the bonobo, and he has suffered from ingrown balloons since 1937, when a fortune-teller told him that in 2021 he'll travel to Nepal where his best friend will be his breath. Woke son of the labouring people and citizen of the World Republic, he hereby vows to promote equality, diversity, and inclusion in all his work. Also, he believes in the wonderfulness of your dreams. *The Creative Art of Wishfulness* is his fourth comedy novel.

JOSHVAHVMPHREYS.COM

BOOKS BY

JOSHUA HUMPHREYS

WAXED EXCEEDING MIGHTY

EXQUISITE HOURS

GRIEVE

TO SAVE A FOREST VIRGIN

IMAGINED TREASURES

THE CREATIVE ART OF WISHFULNESS

THE CREATIVE ART OF WISHFULNESS

A COMEDY NOVEL BY

JOSHUA HUMPHREYS

#103

Dear Louise,

In the hope that Godfrey's travails might prove more enjoyable in the reading than they ever did in the living, I present to you these pages!

Yours,

BANANA SEVEN

· MELBOURNE · UBUD ·
· MADURAI · LONDON ·
· 2019

CONTENTS

I.	*A Portrait of the Artist in Bangkok*	1
II.	*A Selfie of the Artistpreneur in Bali*	37
III.	*The Creative Art of Wishfulness®*	74
IV.	*Madurai, Athens of the East*	159
V.	*Their Year of Living Wishfully*	270

Every text will be scripture that people choose to think so, and all gods gods to them that worship them. All will conceit themselves equal with Brahmans, and cows will be held in esteem only as they supply milk.

THE VISHNU PURANA

Fear never hast thou felt, and wouldst from the wood go forth to the world? Thou shouldst not until thou hast learnt fear.

RICHARD WAGNER

I hope you don't think I'm obsessed with money. Because I am.

ALEXANDRA WISHART

·abite nvmmi·

ACT ONE

A Portrait of the Artist in Bangkok

I

Godfrey Lackland's alarm was now his own sweat.

Very tediously it was waking him at 8, when so abounding as to puddle in his eyes and threaten to drown him by the nose.

Without air-conditioning (he two months ago removed the batteries from its remote and so himself from temptation) the risen sun from 6 warmed the windows which by 7 heated the curtains which by 8 were drapes of magma. Kneeling as though in his afterbirth, Godfrey drew them quickly and beheld in sloppy nude the remnants of the vista which had awed him into giving six months' rent upfront to secure the 27th-floor apartment with the temple views.

Of road, of car park, semi-jungled—a canal came up around the patched brown rooves of the river-houses and straightened beside the burgundy and saffron peaks of the closer temple—its bonsai garden running to the water tended to, as Godfrey squinted from the sun, by bare-shouldered monks in orange robes. Its three white-walled salas had for a time been his sketching halls at dusk. In March the greenery on the opposite bank had been cleared by machines; the rebar and concrete frame of a condo complex would soon obscure entirely the further temple—in front of whose shimmering dragon scales the gherkin waters narrowed, turned, and disappeared.

Godfrey wiped his sweat towel over most of his body then put on a t-shirt and his shower shorts; passed in one step his bathroom and crossed his living in three and took the sweat towel to the elevator. He put his keycard to the reader and pressed 8; descended; stopped—it reopened at 21. There seemed nobody waiting but him. He pressed the door-close button; before they could shut entirely they jarred open.

In the bay of three elevators a Thai girl, in hotpants and Peter

1

Pan crop-top, was flopping her head from side to side. Last week it had been a nighty covered in glittery swastikas. She now, as then, had a peace-making hand to her cheek while the other reached high to take photos with her phone. Godfrey tapped the close button and the doors drew across her wobbling neck. She reached back and pressed the call—his view of her reopened. He pressed close, she opened, closed—and so began a steel-chrome shimmy-sha—open, close, open, open—which ended only when the girl found that a human was disallowing her more photographs of herself without having to wait for the next elevator. He watched in the opposite wall's reflection as she admired an endless scroll of the same peaceable image.

Alighting at 8 he emerged onto the black decking which from the toilets rose to the swimming pool. Beside the glass-enclosed gym he passed the male changing rooms and waited at the door of the female. For where the men's soap smelled like rotting lemons, the women's flowed as Laotian plumeria, principal scent of a shower gel he had used when last he was gainfully employed, making—never earning—twenty-seven dollars and seventy-eight cents an hour for giving suggestions on how to market pregnancy tests to hopeful rather than fearful mothers. When after a time no sound, he tip-toed in and squirted a handful of yellow into his hand and strode back out—ascended the wooden steps to the bay of showers which overlooked one end of the pool.

Twenty metres long and tiled in azure, its raised ledge all day in the sun had been the second enticement to beguile him into handing over six months' rent plus a bond.

And he bathed.

In the pair of red polyamide shorts in which he could no longer go running—their mesh pockets long torn to passageways rather than receptacles—Godfrey stood under the middle showerhead and lathered and scrubbed, himself and then the sweat towel.

He wrung it and hung it over the back of a brown plastic sun lounge then reclined to air-dry. As he turned onto his front he thought of how slowly he would drink the 150 millilitres of his Carabao, keeping it between sips in the shade; how much he missed coffee; hoped that his banana would be sufficiently not-green.

He put his t-shirt back on and left the towel to dry and returned to the elevators; passed the portrait of the long-dead king in the high lobby of imitation marble and iron chandelier. And on the wooden bench outside the front doors he sat and waited for the tuk tuk whose breeze would minimise the sweat brought forth between shower and breakfast, lowering thereby the chances of ruining his thrice-worn t-shirt and saving him, hopefully, from having to do a wash for another day—giving him by June about an extra $1.30.

And he sat, and he waited, and still the tuk tuk did not appear. He set off for the bridge; the gate guards clicked to attention. As he rounded the first corner the tuk tuk—an elongated golf cart— came off the bridge loaded with passengers. Godfrey grimaced and grunted. Here he could either walk back and hope the driver would wait no longer at the bench than for him or he could assume that the driver would, as he often did, park beside it for twenty pointless minutes and he could walk on and waste no more of his morning. He walked on.

His feet stamped onto the black steel of the bridge's footpath and his t-shirt began its soak to translucent. Shortly the tuk tuk zipped past him with not a single passenger and the driver gave a smile and a wave—malicious gloat of a combatant who had again won this infuriating daily contest. Godfrey smiled and shook his head and slowly declared: 'Clovnul magar,' as the tuk tuk turned and disappeared.

He looked down at the water as emerged from the bridge the garlands on the prow of a longtail boat before the blue and orange and green of its canopy motored along. The sky a perfect, hot, azure, Godfrey jangled his wet t-shirt at his chest as he descended to the 7-11 beneath the condo complex that was the eastern namesake to his own. He took a Carabao from the fridge and a plastic-wrapped banana from the stand and was given two baht change. He clinked the coins between his fingers as he recrossed.

He sipped once, ate the banana in three bites, finished the Carabao with its second and thought how fleeting were the pleasures of the earth. Elevated to his apartment, he changed into the blue polyamide shorts with the intact pockets and took his dry towel and his notebook and his sock-stuffed running shoes to the pool.

The gym was empty. He searched around the sun lounge for his sweat towel and quickly let it go as lost as stolen—how temporary the treasures. He sat on the white marble slab in the centre of the gym and sighed as he turned inside out then put back on the socks from two days ago. A large and old Westerner opened the gym's glass door for his young and small girlfriend. Each stepped up to a treadmill and placed their water bottles on their platforms and strolled.

Godfrey kicked out his left foot to finish putting on its backwards-ticked Niek and thought upon the clear tranquillity that exercise would bring—kicked his right and looked forward to the one kindness he did his body, otherwise so over his mind neglected. Looking down at the holes forming outside his pinkie, at the fraying fluorescent where the shoelace began, at the minute tear through which his big toe soon would poke, he remembered as a child having to go barefoot in the summer in order to have decent shoes in the winter. He took out the music player whose silver body also flashed him back to the Laotian plumeria and put in his earphones and on came *Boogie Children*. He stood and turned and—

All five treadmills had been seized. A woman in her pyjamas swung bent arms in a melodramatic strut; a young man in full workout gear wiped, in the overcooled room, his brow with the sweatbands at his wrists; a pigeon-toed girl hunched over her phone as she dawdled. Godfrey watched them for a time, as a young man humped a sit-up bench behind him, then stood on the decking and scowled at them through the glass, taking note of their idiot faces—he would use them later—thinking, 'Why don't you just walk outside?' though he would never say it, embarrassed at again choosing the use of a treadmill before the washing of a shirt.

He left his dry towel and notebook on a sun lounge and re-descended, and walked the twenty-three minutes to the canal which was his preferred running track anyway. He passed the glittering gates of the temples which made pleasant the view from his apartment and stepped off the road and held his breath as he leapt over a putrid sluice up onto the raised path. He took off his shirt and inserted his earphones and to the resonator of Bukka White's *Fixin' to Die* he set off.

An extension of that which could be seen from his apartment, the canal was on both sides lined with a concrete gangway two metres above the water. He ducked beneath the jungle overhanging the first leaf-littered corner, passed the high copse of bamboo which almost concealed a cage of macaws he suspected were illicit. The run opened to its first straight, lined with mangrove palms, and a bloated mongrel carcass floated down, stiff and slow in the current. Magenta, white, pink, peach arms of bougainvillea bent over fences as though reaching to touch him before he crossed the bridge where the southern bank's footpath ended. He resumed his run beside houses gated off as though suburban, above a half-submerged mattress and a dead turtle, beside what seemed some sort of farm, the water-taxi shelter off which three chubby children jumped into the blue-grey translucence of the almost-water.

The dog had been floating the other way, Godfrey thought as he ran past the old lady in her lampshade hat, ferrying people in her sampan—they must have swum with it. He passed a glittering temple and its flower-framed portrait of the queen and came at last to the end of the footpath and the peace of the secluded bank opposite what he called The Orange Temple. Burning golden and yellow in the—it must almost have been midday—sun, above and behind a thin screen of jungle, a robed monk read barefoot on a concrete bench at the water's edge. Sitting between the two-storeyed bell-tower and the white-walled prayer hall, all was reflected at his feet in even more brilliant blue and tangerine and green.

A dog barked violently in the jungle beside Godfrey, frightening him rather, and he turned and ran back, the wet children saying 'jog-ging' to him as he passed, water monitors scrambling to the water from their camouflaged rest—sweating as few had sweated before—an ancient woman in a grocery-filled longtail keeping pace with him for much of the return.

His dry towel unstolen, he placed it at the pool's edge beside his notebook and a Singha then took off his shoes but not his socks and dived into the pool—as Godfrey believed that chlorine cleaned what was vitally unso from his clothing. It didn't, and he had had since moving to Bangkok two rashes from knee to infected knee. (The long way from knee to knee, just as an aside. It wasn't as though he had ever had a fungal rainbow arcing across his lap.) Bathed, he wrung his shirt and socks and draped them over the sun lounge and walked back into the pool and around to its raised ledge—dried his hands and closed his eyes and held his face to the sun. Then he uncapped his pen and opened his notebook and found the page headed, 'HIMMAPAN'.

A book of musical notation, it was at first an affectation only rarely displayed, and then with provincial diffidence. As the work accumulated and the sacrifice endured—as the glimmers of talent grew irrefutable and at last as Godfrey embraced the irreversibility of his path—this hard-backed 230-page 11-staved epitome became to him an inextricable part of how he worked and of therefore who he was. It had been with him now for two years, its softening yellowing pages scribbled with grand conceptions and sentimental flourishes and projects whose execution he had not yet grown into. Its last fifth was composed entirely of calculations, budgets, and of lists—that most stared at of the things that would no more be once he was not destitute. Among its em dashes were 'Lettuce sandwiches', 'Asking for the cheapest beer in a pub', 'Never wearing underpants', 'Showering in public like a hobo', 'Inexplicable fungal infections'.

Beneath the half-page of yesterday's notes he now wrote in, two lines to a stave, the recollections of his run: children swimming among dead animals, the old outpacing the young, beauty existing only in hidden cages, a privilege even. He opened the beer with his back teeth and drank half in one go, finding as it touched his lips that the temperature gradient between it and the city was already disappointingly close to zero. As he added in the faces and probable character of those who had seized the treadmills a voice said, 'Cannot beer here.'

'There's nobody else around!' Godfrey wailed to the building attendant standing over him. He suspected these minions of being in cahoots with the tuk-tuk driver, that together they watched him on CCTV and came out to torment him whenever he attempted to enjoy himself. 'You cannot beer here,' he in a black polo repeated.

'There's—.' Godfrey growled and finished the beer then flicked his hand and said, 'You take.'

He connected his music player to his small dome speaker and the pick-axes of *I Be So Glad When The Sun Goes Down* clinked as Godfrey thought upon what other frustrations he could turn into iniquities before adding them this evening to the mythical forest at the base of Mount Meru.

Presently a skin-bald middle-aged man, whom Godfrey knew by overheard phoneversations to be Italian, came up onto the decking with his girlfriend, whom Godfrey knew by the same to be Dutch. In tight blue jockey shorts he readied a sun lounge. '*I ain't all that sleepy but—ah ha—I wanna lie down.*' When he had coconut-oiled his sak yan tattoos he approached Godfrey at the pool's edge. 'Please-a. Could-a you maybe turn off-a the music, because I want-a to…'

He pointed to the sun lounge and his girlfriend. Godfrey assumed that they wanted to relax in silence. It was a desire to which he was uniquely sympathetic. He apologised and pressed pause and returned to his notebook as the man reclined. Presently a very loud clicking noise sounded from the occupied lounges. Godfrey's head lifted to it. The Italian had his hands behind his scalp and the Hollander was swiping at her phone; somehow they emitted the sound of a piano under a woman rhyming as many words as possible with Havana. When shortly the woman began to say, 'Oo,' a lot Godfrey said, 'Huh?' Yesterday it had been the unceasing shutter sound of two Chinese girls' phones as they took turns on an inflatable unicorn. 'Hergh,' and he gave up the pool as lost as occupied and hung his wet towel and his clothes on the rail of the balcony outside his kitchenette and soon it was time for dinner.

Venturing fully out to the road beyond the bridge reminded Godfrey always of his childhood. Canopied with powerlines and lined with overflowing wheel-bins—always choked with traffic—an afternoon haze bathed everything in apricot light made visible, made tangible, made edible, by a swirling swarm of dirt. For Godfrey had grown up next to a dust factory. Not soil, not gravel; dust—conveyer sorters nestled among hills of grey and red sending crushed stone skywards at speed, the larger pieces dropping off their ends while stone-dust blew high into the air to rest and heighten the hills but much more to blanket the surrounding suburbs. When the factory was in production Godfrey's mother would enact a series of measures to protect her children from bronchitis, emphysema, asphyxiation. The table set upside down, the wet towels at the windowsills, the moist cloths over his nose—were memories that should have recoiled Godfrey from Bangkok. He did not know such places existed on earth.

He had chosen the city because he had a year ago read in a pre-war travel book by an aristocratic madman, that a pigment was made in Siam from the neck of the imperial peacock. Wanting its lustrous jade as his Veronese's viridian or Brueghel's gamboge, after a month of asking Bangkok's art suppliers and inquiring in its amulet markets—of being offered in Chinese medicine shops the bird's ground feathers as aphrodisiac—Godfrey was told in writing by Chalermchai Kositpipat that no such colour had been manufactured in Thailand for 100 years.

He coughed and put his forearm over his nose and squinted to with an accumulation of pedestrian cross the road. Godfrey dropped two coins into the bucket of the woman with the skinned-over eyes—always singing insufferable karaoke through an amplifier—then placed the same into the tray of socks which hung at the neck of the cross-eyed man who wandered around saying over and over again in falsetto, 'Do you want to buy?' Then came the alley which in late afternoon brimmed to congestion among the full rotation of the scents and smokes of Thai cuisine. Godfrey knew exactly where he was headed: since his first shower he had salivated repeatedly in anticipation of today's only meal.

The dish was called khao mok gai, which he had figured out meant rice-something-chicken. At 40 baht—$1.74—he could conceive of no meal bringing more pleasure for less money. A deep-fried chicken breast cleavered over curried rice and sprinkled with fried shallots, it was served with a sweet green sauce that he would one day bottle and have on everything. Sitting as it did in the sun from lunch, in selecting an open polystyrene container from the woman's shelf Godfrey played a kind of diarrhoeic roulette, and that with a Colt Single Action Army, as he reckoned it one in six that got him.

He inspected the eight meals already prepared and looked for signs of freshness and of age—glistening good, dull bad—before pointing to one. The woman added the shallots and the extra packet of green sauce for which he always asked and handed him his plastic bag in exchange for two green notes.

In the manchester section of a huge white-aisled Tesco he took the tag off a towel and slung it over his shoulder. In the alcohol section he surveyed the smaller bottles of liquor. Mekhong, 211 baht; Cavalier Brandy 170; Hong Thong, 139—the same price and a larger bottle but its hangovers made him a temporary quadriplegic. It would be as it always was. Sangsom, 139 baht. $6.16. He had tried the spirit—not quite rum and not quite brandy—with every possible mixer, including the multitudinous Fantas of Asia. Only Dr Pepper made it barely stomachable, and at $1.98 a can was one of the few luxuries he allowed himself.

So at 183 baht and the towel casually declared his own, on top of the 40 baht for dinner, Godfrey had 3 baht left over for the day. If he only drank half the Sangsom he in the morning would have 3 baht and half a bottle of booze, giving him tomorrow a spare $6.29—a sum that could be exchanged for any number of small indulgences.

He collected a glass and some ice from his apartment then ascended the emergency stairwell from his own to the 42nd floor, then up one more flight. With his shirt soaked again he came out to the rooftop—the third and final clincher that had convinced him to start the year with a 53% reduction of his only bank account.

Bordered on both sides by a hedge of jasmine and guarded by

leafless pink frangipani, emerging from the corridor to the raised lawn brought Godfrey a breath-halting vista of the entire City of Immortals, an enormous golden sun glinting off the Chao Phraya, and out halfway to the sea. He lifted a chair and a table from the sunken concrete patio and stood at the hedge for a long, joyous, moment: watched the 6-lane expressway and the red-craned port; Sukhumvit and its traffic and blue-and-white skytrains; the being-built condos of Khlong Toei—foreground all to a bend in the river beside the whole primate city—Sathorn and State Tower and the twisted Maha Nakhon building in the furthest distance pricking like unbent staples into a mauve haze. Below, the puddled vacant block and rotting rooftops of Watthana sprawled across to the long street which Godfrey called Pridi Song—the very view which had formed the desolate landscape to his first anarchic Bangkok work.

He sat and relaxed into the chair and mixed his first drink—half Sangsom, half Dr Pepper. He took a sip then unwound the elastic bands from the little bags of sauce; drizzled it over the chicken and down the sides of the rice. He held the polystyrene container at his chest as he dined. The sun nearing to set—an aurora of yellow and orange holding a canopy of platinum cloud over the tiny skyscrapers—Godfrey knew, having watched every sunset here but four since January, that the ubiquity of colour, the intensity of the gold, the pinks threatening reds and the menace of rain in Sathorn—meant that he was in for a show. He returned the empty container to its plastic bag and made another drink and squatted on his chair so as to be able to see as far as possible over the hedge. He looked up and back to the soft blue of the east then again ahead—to swirling seahorse-clouds promenading before a papaya corona, a widening core of pulsing candlelight soon to turn by smog vermillion—a blazing variation on his favourite, solemnising, prelude to work. Then a chair was placed beside him.

An old Thai man in shirt and trousers asked Godfrey how he was. Godfrey dismissed him with a suspicious, 'Go-od,' and pointed to the city.

'Here can not drink,' the man declared.

'Ah, come on!' Godfrey moaned, tired instantly.

'Here can not drink.'

'Who are you?' he pleaded as their faces glowed as though beholding an eruption.

'It say clearly on sign: rooftop can not drink.'

'I don't know who you are!'

'I am on condo board.'

'And I am pay rent. So I can drink whatever and wherever I want.'

'Here can not drink,' the man smiled then calmly shook his head.

'I'm the only person up here, guy! There's no consequence at all of me drinking. Who cares but you?'

'Sign say cannot drink.'

'I don't care what sign say.'

'You are khi mao.'

'I'm not ki mao!'

'Ugly man you.'

'What!?'

'You ugly man.'

'You're ugly man, I'm not ugly man!'

'You must stop drinking now,' he smiled on.

'You must stop telling me what to do now!'

The old man smiled still. Godfrey felt as though the sky had been blanketed with volcanic cloud, their faces flickering with thin arcs of moltenfall that soon would dull to cinders. He said, very kindly, 'Well, I just hope your aunties all get chlamydia, all right?' The old man lifted his chin in an almost-laugh then nodded as he smiled. Godfrey raised his elbow then moved his glass to his mouth. The old man grinned and intercepted; put four soft fingers at Godfrey's wrist. 'Sign say no.'

'Man say yes.'

'Can not.'

'Unhand me, donkeyclown, goddam it!' Godfrey strained to lift his glass to his lips. His wrist was held down. He clenched his neck and thrust forward his chin. Still they would not meet.

'Can not.'

'Can!' said Godfrey, as ruby liquid dribbled down the grooves of his throat.

And grinned at by a boardmember he gave up the sunset as lost as policed. He kicked his chair over and took the elevator to his floor and paced to his apartment and rushed to the bathroom, where whatever therein transpired could be heard from the hallway three apartments down. He made liberal use of the bumgun, an amenity from which he would never happily return, and immediately after flushing heard an email notification trumpeted by the 23-year-old system which operated the laptop that was always plugged in on the low table in his living room.

It was from someone called Jezebel Dulrich. He sat naked on the couch and leaned forward and read.

Dear Godfrey,

I saw your 'Epic Elevated Pastoral' in Café Transylvania and I really love your style! I've been looking for an artist to do a portrait of my Dippy, he's a chug, and I've attached photographs and I was thinking you could paint him with the captain's hat but not wearing it (Dippy loves to sail), and with his bowl filled with salmon roe on gruyere (his favourite food). Adrian told me your going rate for commissions is $1000 and I'm more than happy to part with such a small amount in exchange for Dippy's immortality.

If your not to busy and would like to take on the work I'd love if you replied with sketches, ideas and your bank details!

Super excited to hear back,

J-Dul.

Godfrey closed his eyes and held his fists to his temples and growled: 'Fuck yes.' At $570 for rent and $425 for food he would have $5 to spare—another month of work and thanks to Dippy the chug his first July wash would be free. How bountiful the rewards of the earth! He typed a reply accepting the commission, told Jezebel Dulrich he'd get sketches to her the day after tomorrow then copied and pasted his bank details. As he hit send a knock came at the door less than a metre from him.

'We're celebrating,' Godfrey said to the girl whose Western name was Twinkle but whose name at her American university had been Amanda but whose actual name was Maladee Howang.

'Why are we celebrating?'

'I just got more work. Yadong?'

'I like your dong.'

'Shoosh, we're celebrating.'

Hand in hand Godfrey and Twinkle descended the building and walked under the highway to the beginning of Pridi Song and the makeshift bar opposite the vacant block. Here a Laoatian couple sold moonshine from a wooden shack, its two dim lights hanging inside a plastic basket and a carved coconut. The bronze potion in two large jars on a green plastic tablecloth, yadong was noxious all the way down and Godfrey suspected it of being mildly hallucinogenic. It also cost forty-five cents a shot, but he was celebrating. He smiled and ordered four. They were ladled and he looked Twinkle in the eyes and said, 'Lechaim,' and they downed their first before sipping at the second.

'Can I sleep over tonight?'

11

'You cannot.'

'Why?' she whined and tilted her head.

'I have to work.'

'Painting the chug?'

'The Himmapan.'

'Oh, I love that one. Can we go to Thonglor for a bit though?'

'Too far, too expensive.'

'It's not that expensive! I know girls at Iron Fairies, I used to go there in my slut phase. They'll give us discount.'

'In your what phase?'

'It's not important now.'

'Rovers for a beer then I have to work.'

'Rovers is awful! It's for fat old white guys. You're not a fat old white guy yet.'

'Yet. The beer is cold and the snacks are free and you can sit and watch the street. What else could you need?'

'Well I'm coming over later anyway.'

He stepped up into the bar and said hello to the regulars whose names he did not know and bought two Singha and two shots of Sangsom.

Twinkle still pouting with dissatisfaction, they sat at the long bench on the streetfront. 'Big spender,' she said, then gave an unheard recollection of her long day at work pitching team-building workshops to assistant managers. From behind a screen of potted ferns Godfrey watched the pink taxis and the decorated trucks loaded with workers and the orange-vested scooter-taxi drivers and the men riding garbage trucks as though stagecoaches. He ate peanuts and pork scratchings by the complimentary handful and said 'Mm-hm' to Twinkle whenever he sensed he ought to. Though he knew not the strength of the yadong he felt quickly the approach of the limit that would render him unable to work: the colours of the street intensified, the smoke sucked up from the gizzard grills began filling with dragons, the scooter-taxi drivers seemed as ewoks dodging trees on speeders. One more shot, he knew, would souse him to perfection.

'I'll see you later then?'

Godfrey nodded and returned to the underpass and began scratching out of his mind's silvery muck the picture he wished to exist as complete—the sections already painted clear to him as though never covered, those sketched filling with colour from their edges, those he would draw tonight growing in grey lines as he ascended to his floor and drifted to his apartment and put his notebook at his right hand and centred his pencils and removed the cloth that covered his sketchbook and sat at his kitchen table.

He stared off into the distance and silenced the dozen vulgar melodies playing through his head. He began to see corners of the paintings that had come before his—Rackham's Frolic, Piero's Cetus, Bilibin's Expulsion—invoked in one long vision the predecession of Guardi, Crane, Ezekiel. He saw as his head began to sway the forest to which he would any moment open and hummed the waltz from Tchaikovsky's Sixth. As his throat reached and held a quavering note—he never knew which would do it—his eyes shot open and he lifted his sketchbook's hardcover and looked as on an antechamber at the blackletter words of the title page, 'ABITE NUMMI'—taken from Burton's Melancholy, for money would have no power here.

In one swift movement Godfrey Lackland took up a 2B and leaned forward and drew one, drew two, flicked a third curve above the apsonsee stuffing children into sacks to take them to Spain—and began the outline of a putrid canal. So recommenced work on his Himmapan, the enchanted forest at the base of Phra Sumen, the Buddhist's first encounter with the source of all life.

Home of the Nariphon tree, which sprouted virgins and was raided by sprites, Himmapan was by Godfrey's brush being hybridised, updated, elevated into a kind of *selva oscura*—the Dark Forest which in the centre of his left page divided Dante from hell's vestibule and the ordered world from unlikeness; the high-rooted wood into which Lancelot and Alice had alike ventured and now struggled to extricate themselves; malachite wilderness wherein Robin Hood nested gaily in the bright green leaves and buff oak trunks of freedom and righteousness, first casualties of industrialisation.

The work's sectioned layout was taken from its vast likeness in the sermon hall of Wat Suthat, those exquisite murals whose line and form Godfrey was assimilating as he worked. Soon they would be unconscious aspects of his style—the kranok a standard curve in the vocabulary of his brush, Mara's Assault a foundational stroke in the architecture of his mind. Its groves were populating now, in cinnabar and turmeric and kraam, with girls in inflatable unicorns and garuda protecting ivory elephants as they bathed in teal waters, with sindhava horses white as the clouds—and, this evening, with children bathing downstream of a dead chug, their cleannocence guarded from lion-legged apsonsee by overweight redcoats on treadmills and with iron-legged macaws being gang-banged by kinnaras—all surrounding the crenellated walls of the cheese fortress within which a naga-enthroned millennial Christ leaned an ear-budded ear to the temptations of Mehmed the Wonkarer.

For five hours Godfrey performed with hunched shoulders and a stiff back—the minute skin strokes, the garuda-feathered eaves, the flowing gherkin and circles of sak yant—taking no food, no drink, no breaks—finishing entirely a new eighth of a page, sketching another, polishing three episodes to almost-done—until the space behind his eyes ached and he could not see his own figures from fifteen centimetres away.

He sat back and stared dumbly into space—out over his balcony to the high black of night, across to the hypnotising arrangement of pot and fork handle protruding from his sink. He remembered none of the process, had no recollection of paint to paper, could recall the mixing of no colours nor see the sketches made whole or the enchanted forest for its trees. But there it was. More complete than it had been, still far from finished, its rest unknown.

He thought momentarily upon his new commission, how nice it had been to drink ice-cold beer without subtracting its cost from a budget—of how tomorrow he had $6.29 to spare. He could get a fruit shake and a coffee for breakfast; have a beer on the rooftop; even eat lunch. Lunch! He would have a salad—they made his runs faster and his toilet shorter—and a cantaloupe Fanta. 'Fantaloupe,' he thought, but was too tired to make a note of it. He chuckled at these last propositions and said, 'Abite nummi,' as he slid into bed and closed his eyes in the thin sheen of Twinkle's hair.

II

The risen sun; the heated windows; drapes of smelted iron.

Alone on his knees, Godfrey patted his body dry with his new sweat towel. As a longtail boat sliced across the smokey reflection of the sun he thought upon the sumptuousness of the day ahead— a fruit shake, coffee, lunch—a salad! He rubbed his eyes and sucked his tongue as he opened and closed his teeth and watched the watering monks below. Then a familiar ding sounded from the living room.

A new email from Jezebel Dulrich: *Sincerest Apologies.*

Good Morning Godfrey,

So long story short my aesthetician has just started treating a Hemsworth and of course this means that his botulinum prices with his reputation have doubled overnight. You can imagine my excitement! I wondered if we can negotiate a slight change in the fee for the little painting I was going to get you to do. I'm still very keen on having Dippy immortalised, would you be able to do it for $550? I'll skip my Nefertiti neck lifts for a couple of days so I can afford it and he's only a small dog so maybe with the fee we could halve the canvas? You'd save on materials etc. and of course I'll recommend you to all my friends and everyone at the clinic.

Looking forward to hearing back, and have an incredible day!

J-Dul.

Godfrey momentarily disbelieved. Quite out loud he said, 'Is this bitch for real?' Then he remembered that the last two years had taught him the supreme reason of believing atrocity before goodness. It simply led to fewer disappointments. And he had before him an atrocity. To her a single meal at a fabric-clothed table; to her a night's stay in an air-conditioned hotel; a tiny handbag or single shoe, a Nefertiti neck lift, a thermal jacket for a fur-covered aberration of nature, a flight to goddam Bali and back. But to him!

252 meals. 222 cans of Dr Pepper. 24 nights of accommodation. 32.4 days of sustenance; more than a month of life. Her revocation meant that in July he would be homeless or starving. How fucking dare she. He typed out a reply.

Dear "J-Dul",

I'm an artist, and agreed to paint your "chug" only because I am, literally, a starving one. To have you request a reduction in my very reasonable fee feels like a slap in the uninjected face. Imagine I asked you to work for me and said, 'But I'm going to pay you half of what you're usually paid, which is less than half of what you should be paid anyway.' But inferring from your vacuousness I can only assume you've never actually worked a day in your life. Fuck your imitation dog and fuck your Nefertiti neck lift and fuck you. I hope Dippy gets run over by a dump truck and your newest dress gets ruined by the bloodsplatter. You are the reason that art without me is dead. You are the reason the West is dying. You're the all-consuming unwrinkled sphincter of the irretrievably decadent world.

I hope you don't have a nice day and that you chance upon the eating of a dick,

Godfrey.

He had fulminated rather, but it was much of what he had for so long wished to say in response to just one of the three emails he received each week requesting his labour in exchange for as close to nothing as these demi-patrons dared ask.

With his glans on the coarse fabric of the couch, Godfrey hit send. Immediately he remembered last night. Two beers and two shots of Sangsom, six yadong. $15.17. By a single spurt of revelry he was $1.28 over today's budget. Minus the half-bottle of Sangsom, he had $4.25 for the day. With the can of Dr Pepper, $2.99. 65 baht. He again had to leave Bangkok in two months and today would be a Gourmet Market day.

'Fuck.'

He sniffed three shirts before finding one sufferable then with sunglasses on and notebook in hand he descended. Beyond the concrete soccer fields of the underpass he crossed paths with a monk and his pink-jumpered pig then weaved through the street dogs lazing on the bridge over a milky-white khlong to Pridi Song—that street whose controlled mayhem and crammed squalor, whose infinite variety and harmonious insanity—he so loved. He saw it as a kind of elongated garden of yellow and blue and pink and wires and 7-11 green; a Hogarth's Lane of chipped paint and rotting concrete and grill-covered balcony—scooters as missiles, trucks as obstructions, taxis as strolling companions. The food carts, the goldfish soup bags, the smoke sucked by bathroom fans from hot coals, the smell of sliced cantaloupe and fried dough and stuffed fish and milk tea—the other, lesser, chicken rice lady. An old woman leaned almost to horizontal in pushing her charcoal cart past an elderly monk who was blessing in exchange for food a kneeling woman beneath a canopy of powerlines climbed by men in balaclavas. Satellite dishes like red sunflowers were turned all at the same angle on the upper storeys. Miniature restaurants dangled with beige ducks, their metal stools and plastic tablecloths shining grey and wet. Boat-noodle broths floating with innards filled the hot air with thick, sweet, cinnamon; the blasts of cold from the open doors of convenience stores, the shops set back from the road: massages and t-shirts and barbers and photocopying and offerings.

Soon he came to Sukhumvit, that Edomite street already the setting for two of the more disturbing paintings in his Bangkok book. His shirt twice soaked to dark blue, he felt redouble the heat off the standstill traffic—one long barbecue pit of engine and smoke, entirely full, nobody moving—a painted-for-him allegory of liberated mankind's future. He followed under the concrete spine of the BTS, huge sounding lid to the constant rumbling of truck-idle and the roars of ill-exhausted motorbike, shelter to buses that looked firebombed. Puddles of black water dyed the ends of his toes and warm drips fell inexplicably onto his neck as he passed the hairdresser that had been his first non-self haircut in three years and the grocery store that sold Belgian tequila and sometimes had Sangsom for 10 baht cheaper than Tesco. Heritage Condo was still under Neo-Art Deco-Codussian construction and past four banks and a cluster of ATMs a grotto of plastic fern rotted around a spirit temple, its four-faced gods turned and bowed to by every passing Thai. Laotians sold pomegranate juice and shamans lottery tickets; a Thai girl wore a t-shirt that read, 'Own your awesome' and French tourists photographed fruit—then the mildewed ceiling of the driveway and the water-garden promenade set back from the road, a thick mist rising from its long pond. At its end, red and orange fake-flower peacock tails dangled from jungled balconies outside each of the six levels of EmQuartier.

Inside, beyond metal detectors and glove-saluting guards, came the descent of muzak and the smell of warm cake. At last, the reason for Godfrey's sixty-seven-minute stroll through the internal combustion engine of Sukhumvit: Gourmet Market. As Kevin McAllister entering his own toy store, Godfrey Lackland passed its black trolleys and beheld with a sweaty back the wall of grapes that greeted him. To his right was the reason for his voyage; that would come in good time. He read their names: Californian Globe, Midnight Beauty, Witch Fingers—and stood over the black trays bristling with toothpicks. He took two of each, bit down on their juicy coldness, noted that 200 grams of any would wipe out a good day's budget. Beside the grapes a young Thai woman in a kimono held a tray of single Japanese cherries; Indian pomegranates were individually plastic-wrapped; Israeli envy apples had been sliced into wedges and pre-stuck with toothpicks.

At last Godfrey looked to the cheese case. Today, again, it was as a glass fortress, something to be assaulted, boldly. He scanned its garrison. In black aprons and hair-nets, none of its sentries were familiar to him so nor—much more importantly—would he be to them. He made another round of the grape plates then broke off, crossed to the side of the fortress closest to the entrance and would soon have all the che—

Dancing.

Overhead a keyboard and drum preceded a boy's voice and instantly the grape-tending staff stepped in front of Godfrey and began to wobble. He halted. The cheese-guards came from behind their battlements to join the musical defence. He was baffled. Behind him the checkout girls did likewise as the boy's voice urged everyone to clap if they felt feel like a room without a roof—which Godfrey thought made no sense—but so they did, leaving their soup warmers and their sample stands to line up beside one another and sway and clap and flop their arms about their bodies. Surrounded by dancing and suspicious, he called off the offensive and went to graze the rest of the store.

At the salad bar he used separate carrot sticks to sample all seven dressings, Miracle his favourite, Raspberry his least. He took coffee from beside the chip aisle, regurgitated a drink called Mansome and then came the kimchi corner—his single toothpick rounding tubs of fermented cabbage, cucumber, potato. The music stopped and the employees and Western customers applauded. Godfrey turned to the kindly meat outpost—Thai ham, Chinese sausage, German-branded bacon: all distasteful. He took a shot of coconut water as the front returned to quiet and again turned to the fortress of cheese—cheese! His most longed-for luxury, missed sensation, deeply craved foodstuff. A successful scaling of its glass walls was the only thing that would allow him to walk back to his apartment feeling in any way satisfied. He would try again.

He reconnoitred. The happy song had brought an unwelcome

change in the guard: he recognised the woman rearranging the cheddar blocks at the eastern gate. She had yelled at him before. But this, he quickly convinced himself, did not necessarily mean she would recognise him. Had not his chicken rice lady taken two months to remember his face, he having each day to ask for the extra bag of green sauce? So he went for it—strode to the shorter western wall and looked innocently into its glass case. One of its defenders strafed as Godfrey pretended to peruse the selection. He returned a volley of, 'Sawadee khap,' and faked the discovery of a sample tray. He pointed to it in surprise. Its defender nodded, invited, turned away. The coward.

Grana padano, gruyere, brie, smoked red pepper, manchego, aged cheddar. Six little bowls of cubed dairy and a holder brimming with toothpicks. He jabbed at the cheddar and savoured it for as long as he could. He searched among the smoked red pepper for the largest cubes and skewered two at once and swallowed them almost instantly. Not wanting to be seen as overstepping his privilege he lowered his eyes to the display case and pretended to consider which he would be purchasing. Unconsciously he took note of the prices. Few were less than 300 baht per 100 grams. Abite nummi. On a good day he could afford a sliver of Wensleydale. How Godfrey hated his monetary autism, and, having none still, he was increasingly concerned that it defined him—he, an artist. One distant day he would eat nothing but cheese. After breakfast he would add, 'Only ever eat free cheese,' to the list at the back of his notebook.

He returned to the samples and took a cube of gruyere then, losing control, made what he thought was too noticeable a dent in the grana padano. He discarded his toothpick and moved slowly to the longer northern wall.

Wyke Farms mild colored cheddar, Parmigiano reggiano, brique du nord, asiago, comte, Old Amsterdam. There it was. Golden cubes brimming in a porcelain bowl. He would be sated.

He leaned in and pulled a toothpick and his hand moved to—

'You no more!'

'What?'

'You all the time cheese but no buy! No more you!'

'What are you talking about?'

'I see you before! Sample for customer, not for you!'

Godfrey put his palms in the air and backed away; turned in mild shame to the sashimi kitchen and went to the other side of the melons. He had seen the Old Amsterdam, had almost touched it—that aged Gouda whose sweetness and hardness and flakes of salt he could almost taste and had to have. He would regroup, let the defender's temper soften, her vigilance weaken—perhaps she might soon move stations and tyrannise over the paté boards. Then he would return. He was offered and sipped from a paper cup of almond milk. He winced and turned to survey the morale of the cheese garrison. She was glaring at him. He looked away, up to the ceiling, and slowly returned to pretending to browse among yellow-fleshed watermelons and envy apples.

'You're going to think this sounds strange,' came a voice to Godfrey's left, 'but I just had a feeling I *had* to talk to you.'

'Wha?' said Godfrey, impatient of strange interruptions.

'Doesn't this place have the most *intense* hummus?'

'Huh? Oo!' His eyes livened. 'Will you do me a favour?'

'OK?'

'See the cheese fortress?'

'The what?'

'There are free samples, you see them?'

'Yeah?'

'Prick as many cheese cubes as you can and bring them here.'

'What?!'

'The lady recognised me, they won't let me try anymore,'

'Are you famous?'

'In much of Romania.'

'Wait, what do you want me to do? This sounds crazy.'

'When was the last time you did something that made you feel alive?'

'I don't know. I guess…' Her eyes widened. 'That's an amazing question.'

'See? So go and steal me some cheese.'

'Steal you cheese? Why am I stealing you cheese?!'

'Because I can't afford to eat today. The world is upside down and art goes unrewarded, and if I don't have a mouthful of aged Gouda very soon, I will starve.'

'Are you an artist?'

'The aged Gouda's on the right, it's called Old Amsterdam. Bring as much of it back as you can.'

She inspected his clothing and noticed his collar fraying behind his neck. She saw his filthy feet and the dirt-darkened seams of his short pockets. 'You're a starving artist.'

'Could you...?' He made a cheese-pricking gesture with his thumb and first finger and moved his stabbing hand towards the display case.

'My God, this is so exciting! I feel like I'm about to rob a bank!'

'I'll be right here,' he said as with a push at her back he set her off like a paper boat on a lake. He watched from behind the barricade of melons; ducked as recogniser reckoned with greenhorn. When she returned with the loot he said, 'What's this?'

'That was so exciting!'

'This is Wyke Farms mild coloured cheddar. The Gouda was on the right, no?'

'I get mixed up with left and right.' Godfrey groaned as he shovelled. 'I poured like the whole bowl in my hand! Like a thief. Or a gypsy! Thank you! What kind of starving artist?'

'Hm?'

'You're an artist. What kind?'

'Painter,' came from among chewed cheese.

'That's amazing.'

'Neh.'

'You're really a starving artist.'

'Famished,' Godfrey smiled, lipping cheese from his palm like a horse.

'Now you do me a favour.'

'Wha?'

'Show me your paintings.'

'Huh? What for?'

'I might buy one, where are they?'

'In my apartment.'

'Which is where?'

'A sixty-seven-minute walk.'

'We'll take a taxi.'

'A taxi? What are you, rich? What's your name?'

In the taxi Alexandra asked questions.

'Why are you starving?'

'Because I'm an artist.'

'I hate—*hate*—that narrative. It's not the way it should be, you know? Do you have a Patreon?'

'I just had a woman commission me to paint her dog. But I celebrated too hard, then she withdrew the commission, so not only her money disappeared, but most of mine as well. Hence the free cheese. Thanks for that.'

'No, thank you! It was so exciting. Why Bangkok?'

'Because it's cheap.'

'But not cheap enough?'

'Nowhere's cheap enough for me.'

'Governments should *pay* artists, artists heal the world, like doctors. They replenish its soul. I want to create a support system for creators. What are you painting right now? Is that too private? Hemingway said if you talk about it you lose it. He was talking about our pain *and* our art. Where does your work come from? What's your pain?'

'My pain?'

'Yes! What inspires you?'

'Art's an expression of man's delight at his subordinate place within a life-allowing order. True artists can only be joyous—where does pain come into it?'

Alexandra's eyes bulged. 'You should be a millionaire on that sentence alone! It's one of my passion points: true artists *shouldn't* be poor.'

'I don't mind the poor, painting's my destiny.'

'You believe in destiny?'

'And if it gives no material reward, then so be it. To follow your destiny does not mean happiness, Alexandra. But once it's been revealed there's no happiness if you *don't* follow it. So here I am.'

'My God, who said that?!'

'You're a bit of a clovnul magar aren't you?'

'A what?'

'A clown for donkeys, in Romanian. A donkeyclown.'

She paid for the taxi. Godfrey warned her about the state of his apartment.

'This is where you live?!'

'Where I work, yeah.'

'It's so authentic. My God, are they temples?' She saw then went to the view from his bedroom window. 'There's so much… *I* want to be a Buddhist. There's so much inspiration here. Is this what you look at while you're creating? Show me what you're creating right now?' She followed Godfrey to the kitchen. He swivelled his sketchbook and uncovered it and opened its black cover. 'Can I touch it?'

'Touch what?'

'Your book of art.'

'If you want to.'

She put a palm to a blank page and closed her eyes. 'Can you *feel* that?'

'Paper?' Godfrey smirked.

'Artspiration.'

'Here.' He turned to his Himmapan—the three worlds of Wat Suthat by Godfrey translated to one in subdued reds and greens and yellows. Alexandra's mouth widened and her palm went to her chest.

'Oh my God, I have goosebumps. I'm going to cry. This is so amazing! Who's that?'

'That's Savonarola in hotpants. And an orange transvestite, Calvin with unalome tattoos. I painted them last night.'

'We should *get* tattoos! Why is he, or she—he-she?—what are you supposed to say? Why are they orange?'

'If you don't know I can't tell you. But right here's where I'm going to put that dog lady. With her stupid face looking up at Mara while it's injected with snake oil by Angelico angels with barely detectable horns.'

'Horns? Why horns? What does it all *mean*?'

'Anyway,' he said as a hopeful preface to an imminent cessation. 'This is my Bangkok book, the necessary precursor to my India book, which I'm finally ready for, but I just need the money.'

'India! I've always wanted to go! Yoga in Varanasi, can you imagine?! My God, you should make colouring books!'

'What?'

'There's so much detail! This is amazing. How do you even create something like this!? Look at the... I mean, how do you... Tell me: what are your top seven creativity techniques?'

'My what?'

'Leonardo da Vinci used passionate curiosity. He was an alchemist you know? Picasso used to paint blindfolded. Tolstoy wrote in the village square.'

'Oh *those*!' And Godfrey realised that he had met her before— they who deified what to him was little besides toil, who thought that 'art' sprung from a mystical pond easily reached, that talent gushed from the Fountain of Learnable Ease—that within the objectionable forest of routine and normality there grew a kind of magical tree flowing with genius-sap to anyone accessible, and that if only one went there they'd be handed a bottleable elixir of limitless inspiration forever. 'Backwards man.'

'What?'

'You put your clothes on backwards and walk around in reverse. It helps you see things from a different perspective.'

'My God, that's brilliant.'

'Sometimes I put a chair in the sink and look at things from up there. Tap-dancing songs. Y'ever heard of them?'

She could not have.

'Songs that people tap dance to, but without the music. Just the clicking.'

'Stripping life back to its true essence.'

'Some days I dress up as a carrot and carry around an eggplant. Then I throw it off the top of the building.'

'Letting go of your life's *un*-genuine soul.'

'Letting go of the eggplant, yeah. Prank calls pretending to be Norwegian fishermen. Nothing's as creative as a misunderstood conversation. And sand. If you can get your hands on cheap bags of sand, you put it all over the floor and you just… create.'

'Like you're on a beach?'

'Like you are on a beach.'

'The infinite ocean goddess. The ineluctability of rebel waves.'

'The what now?'

'You're a creative genius. How have you come into my life right now? We *have* to collaborate.'

'There is no collaboration in art, Alexandra. There is only compromise.'

'No, on creativity! We should collaborate on creativity! My God, yes! Have you ever taught it?'

'Creativity cannot be taught.'

'No, it can! Show me your website.' Godfrey looked at her as though the command were obviously preposterous. He began shaking his head. 'You won't?'

'I don't have a website.'

'How do people see your art?'

'It's right there.'

'But how do they commission you? How do they *pay you* to create? Are you joking, you don't have a website?' Godfrey pouted and shook his head. 'You're not a real artist if you don't have a website! And, that's only six.'

'Six?'

'Creativity techniques.'

'Alcohol.'

'You drink alcohol while you create? Hemingway did say Write

24

drunk, edit sober. You wanna know something about me?'

'Obviously.'

'I've never been drunk before.'

'You what?'

'Do you drink a lot?'

'You've *never* been drunk?'

'It's not a part of my life.'

'I've never not been drunk. Art's like committing a crime, and tyrannicide's a lot easier under the influence. You've never been drunk?'

'Will you take me drinking?!' There seemed no limit to her enthusiasm. 'I'll pay!'

Alexandra wanted to get changed first. They took a taxi to her Siam apartment. 'Jesus, what are you a stockbroker?' said Godfrey upon entering it.

Three times the size of his, it had pine floors and French windows and dimmable downlights and an oven. Alexandra said, 'Ha, are you kidding? No way!' as she crossed to the bedroom. Two MacBooks sat open on a low coffee table in the living room. One had stickered over its logo a purple devanagari om, the other an Eye of Providence in a green triangle. The table alone was larger than Godfrey's kitchen. He looked out over the private pool that was her balcony. '*What* do you do for work?'

'I run a bunch of online stuff,' she called from the bathroom. 'Workshops and courses and retreats. I'm in Bangkok just to create, but I've barely had time to selfie since I landed.'

'You know I never understand what people do for work.' Godfrey opened the refrigerator and found a shelf of cartoned coconut water. He slid one out and unscrewed its cap and mumbled. 'Maybe that's the key, my job's too simple. People only pay you for jobs they don't understand. Oh, you sit at a canvas and paint? I did that when I was four, why would I pay you for that? Ah, you run a bunch of "online stuff"? I don't know what that is or how it works. Here's five thousand dollars. Thanks!'

'What's that?' said Alexandra, reappearing at the bedroom door with a brush running through black hair to her shoulders.

'Nothing.'

'What kind of out are you taking me?' Her large, dark-lined eyes bulged again with excitement. 'Black dress?'

'No, no, nothing fancy. Just drinks on the street and a ping pong show.'

'A ping pong show? What's that?' She smacked persimmon lips together and switched brushing hands.

'We sit and watch people play ping pong. They're very good at it.'

'Why would we sit and watch people play ping pong?'

'It's a Thai thing, very authentic.'

'If you say so. Isn't this exciting!? Tomorrow I'd *really* like to go to a bookstore and look at books on secret societies. Will you come with me?'

She closed the bedroom door before Godfrey could make sense of the invitation. 'Can you play this?' He ran his fingers across the guitar, upright at the end of one of the couches.

'No, but I really wanna learn!'

After fifteen minutes of listening to lids pop open and applicators click onto a sink Godfrey said he would wait downstairs. He took the coconut water and finished it before it got too warm and threw the carton in the lobby's bin. He was squatting outside when an hour later Alexandra came out of the building's front doors.

'What the hell took you so long?'

'Oh, I had to post.'

'This way,' Godfrey said and pointed to the street to their left.

She turned to him as she bounced. 'Isn't this so exciting!?'

'It's fucking hot today,' said Godfrey as they walked.

'I'm going drinking with a real artist! An artistpreneur meets an artist!'

'A what?'

'An artistpreneur, and you're like van Gogh, and I'm this young naïve dancer who's never been drunk!' Alexandra skipped ahead as she enthused: 'And he's going to initiate me into the secret forbidden rights of all his creative inspiration!'

'Turn right up there,' Godfrey called out. He caught up with her as she stopped to consult her wrists. 'What are you doing?'

The word 'left' printed on one and 'right' on the corresponding other, she said, 'I get them confused.' She held up the arm that matched Godfrey's direction. 'Right, right?' and she followed it. They walked up a main road in blazing sunlight. As they crossed a bridge over a canal Godfrey said, 'Can I talk to you about something?'

'Anything!'

'That hat.' He pointed to her white fedora.

'Isn't it incredible?'

'Can I?'

'Oh, of course!' Gently he lifted it from her head. 'I bought it in Bali off this woman who—' And he flung it into the canal. 'What are you doing!?' she laughed, half shocked. 'Are you crazy!?'

'Sorry. But that hat was almost as pretentious as the camera.'

'My camera?' she said, pointing its lens up at her face. 'I'm a photographer. This is my content Canon. It takes the *best* most easiest pictures and shoots video in 4k, and it's *so* easy to use. Which reminds me, wait a second.' She lifted the strap from her neck and took off the lens cap. 'Let's take a picture together.'

'We have to cross here.' Godfrey looked to the traffic ascending to their left and hurried through a thin break; slowed to allow its other side to go round him.

'Oh,' said Alexandra, fiddling with the digital menu's buttons. When eventually she found the right setting she pressed record and turned the camera to herself and fixed her hair then narrated as she walked. 'So I'm here in Bangkok with this amazing *painter* I just met. I don't know where he's taking me, but I think he's showing me the secret drinking holes that inspire him in this totally awesome inspiring city!'

Godfrey watched her ignore truck horn and scooter beep as she somehow crossed the eight-lane road without either looking at the traffic or being killed.

'This is so authentic,' she said as she followed him down a concrete staircase. 'Like Frodo going into the jungle!' Through a walkway lined with dirty umbrellas they stepped onto a rusted steel platform fendered with tyres. It jutted out onto a canal of opaque gherkin fluid that smelt of musty sewerage. Alexandra's eyes bulged with fascination as she looked around. Shortly a chugging sound loudened and a prow approached.

'Are we going on a boat!?' she said, squeezing Godfrey's arm. 'I *love* being on boats. I think it's because I'm a water sign.' The longtail slowed and rocked in and Godfrey held down the guard rope with his foot and helped her onto the wooden orange deck. 'Such a gentleman.' She sat and refiddled with her camera then rested it on her leg and took out her phone and started filming— the passengers behind her, those in front, then the passing view of mouldy concrete wall and gated garden and graffitied house.

'Thank you *so* much,' she shouted, the covered engine screaming beside them.

'What for?' Godfrey shouted back.

'This is so real, so authentic.'

'It smells like shit.'

'But this is *real* Bangkok—a breathing, pulsating, living city. It's so real. Life is life,' she said as she filmed. 'You can't *replace* life!' She pushed down the plastic sheet which the Thai woman in front of her had raised to protect her from mist and splash. With the last note in his wallet Godfrey paid the 18 baht to the masked ticket dispenser swinging and clambering outside the boat. 'Do people live in these houses?'

'They're river slums.'

'Can I take a photo of you?'

'What?'

'Say hi.' She turned her filming phone to him. He looked at its lens and raised an eyebrow. Then she leaned back into him and turned her screen and took a picture of them both. 'I didn't come this far to only come this far!' she shouted. Again she bulged again her eyes: 'At the end of the ride we should burn this boat, like Cortés! Then we're stuck in Bangkok and have to create here forever or die! What do you think? Oh, my heart's so full! Is yours?'

'What?'

'Is your heart full?'

'It's kind of full I suppose. Then my atria contract and it's empty. Then it's full again, and so on. It's the circulatory system.'

'Come on, get excited! Look at where we *are*! Thank you *so* much.'

A boat sped towards them from the opposite direction. Alexandra again held down the plastic wall and leaned over the wooden side to with two hands film its passing. The water, a kind of radioactive-looking spinach-and-yoghurt tea, churned high against the slime-rotted concrete. Their own hull slapped into the other's wake and splashes came over the gunwale and into Alexandra's open mouth. She gagged and threw up and held onto Godfrey's arm. 'It's so authentic.'

He walked her through Khao San Road, slowing when she stopped to take a photograph, staring whenever she filmed herself, waiting whenever she backtracked to do a retake. The day was all but gone, the colours saturating, when they passed the Phra Sumen fort and the oily-olive river and the fire-twirlers in fisherman pants on the lawns—then came onto and under the red paving and green leaves of Soi Rambuttri.

'Oo, that place has khao soi,' said Godfrey, remembering the dish from January.

'I'm starving, we'll eat here?'

'The meals are six dollars.'

'So?'

'Instead of two.'

'Are you even serious? Dinner's on me! What's six dollars?'

'It's a lot of money.'

'Come on! You deserve this. I deserve this!'

They sat at a low bench overlooking the narrowest section of the street. Yellow fairy lights glowed around wisteria roots rising with the restaurant's unpolished shutters to dangle over the street. A fan was turned to them and on and Godfrey ordered khao soi and a large Tiger. Alexandra asked if it could be made vegan but it couldn't so she ordered vegetable fried rice with no fish sauce and Godfrey ordered her a beer.

'Vegan, uh?'

'Meat's so bad for you, it's like putting poison in your body. It's one of my *dreams* to live in Bali and eat great healthy food all the time! Do you not look after your body?'

'I feed it.'

'You should *totally* look after your health! Health is eighty percent of your wealth.'

'And eighty percent of zero is zero. A long life's a gamble, it's like the Middle Ages again. You either get lucky and live till you're 90 or you get terminal cancer at 35. I grew up next to a dust factory and I've drunk every day since I was 16. What the hell's the point in eating tofu and drinking coconut water and next year I'm told I have an inoperable growth in some part of my body I've never heard of?'

'Who *are* you?' He drank two thirds of his beer in one go and poured hers into a glass. 'You're like an artist out of the eighteen hundreds or something. You should have syphilis!'

'What?'

She held up her beer and said, 'To us?'

'All right.'

'Doesn't this place fill you with life?'

'Ask the bears.'

'What?'

'Ask the bears.' He pointed casually to the street. A tall young man in purple shorts and no shirt was slouching as he lurched beneath a head of dreadlocks the colour of geriatric bananas.

'What bears?' she smiled. 'What are you talking about?'

'Dreadlocks.'

'You're not making *any* sense.'

'Dreadlocks. Dread-locks. A dreadnought, and Goldilocks. A ship, and three bears. Shippin' three bears. Shippin' three bears to where? Ship three bears to wear what? I don't know, ask the bears.'

'Hhhuh!?'

'It's something my brain does, it kind of skips ahead.'

'Who *are* you? Are you like a genius or something?'

'Uh-oh,' he said as Raymond Babbitt. 'Ninety-seven-X, baaaaam! The future of rock and roll. No, my brain just kind of skips a few steps. I used to think it was like being a prophet, but... Now I'm not sure.'

'You make a profit from it?'

'Huh?' He shook his head as Alexandra stared into the green galaxy of the fairy lights.

'My God, think of how lucky we are. Most people never get to even *see* this place, let alone meet someone here. And we're free! So free, free to create. Did you know that there are more slaves right now than there have been in all human history—people who live off less than $10 a day? But we—.'

'I live off less than $10 a day.'

'You do not!'

'My daily budget is thirteen Australian dollars and eighty-nine cents. That's less than ten US dollars.'

'You deserve so much more!'

'Nobody *deserves* anything. To be human is to suffer.'

Instantly she became forlorn. 'I know what you mean.'

'Do you?'

'I suffer from abundance every day,' she said as their meals were placed in front of them. A potted orange orchid stood beside a length of bamboo propping up one of the shutters. She rubbed one of its petals between her fingers as Godfrey slurped and spooned in haste. 'It's one of the pain points I'm working on but—. My God, you're like a homeless man!'

'I haven't eaten since yesterday,' Godfrey said between spoonfuls. 'God, I love palm oil.'

'Or a lost puppy. Well don't worry, little puppy. I'll take care of you.'

After finishing her beer Godfrey reached for his wallet, which he knew to be empty. Alexandra put her hand on his and said, 'Please, I'm paying.'

'Why?'

'Look at everything you're doing for me.'

'Drinking your beer?'

'I would never have seen *any* of this if you weren't showing it to me. All this life, this wild authenticity. I *need* human contact, I *love* human connection. And you make me laugh! I haven't laughed in so long. So let me pay you back with something you need, which is food, right? And something you love, which is beer.'

Hot and sticky night had fallen. They walked around the corner to the open Volkswagen and whirling disco ball of My Friends Bar. They sat at a fluorescent drum, flanked by a Chihuahua and a man wearing a pirate earring staring into grimey space.

'What'll it be, lady?'

'I have no idea,' she said as she read the menu. 'I don't know what any of these are.'

'Have you *really* never been drunk?' Godfrey was more suspicious of the claim than he had been of any other, ever.

'Never.'

'How does that happen?'

'What did van Gogh drink? What are *you* drinking?'

'Small Singha and a tequila shot,' he said to the child waitress.

'I love it when a man orders for me.'

'She'll have the same.'

'What?' and he winked at her. 'So do you *have* a girlfriend?'

'I do not.'

'What do you think about love? Do you think love is a kind of fantastic madness?'

Godfrey stared at her for a time, waiting to see if the questions were, as he hoped, a pair of jokes. The unceasing bulge in her eyes soon told him they were not. 'I think it should not be talked about.'

'But it's the only thing *worth* talking about. I just want peace and simplicity,' she declared. 'I prefer spending my energy on creating. Relationships should be the cushions of life, not the centre, know what I mean?'

'Up to a point.'

'Perfect love to me is just for someone to be *in* the cave with me. I want a caveman creator, someone who'll lavish *and* ravish me.' Their drinks arrived; Godfrey reached for his wallet. 'This is on me, remember!? You take me drinking, I pay.'

'You're actually rich, right?'

'No,' she said, again disappointed as she gave the child a bank note whose size and colour Godfrey had not seen since February. 'I'm so close to creating the life I want but I don't have passive income yet. My next course will be my first 100k launch though, that'll change everything.'

'A hundred k? A hundred kilograms?'

'We can talk about *that* in India. No, dollars!'

'Jesus, a hundred thousand dollars!? I could paint for ten years with that. A hundred thousand…' and Godfrey tapped the tequila onto the barrel then downed it. When he had finished most of her beer they passed the barricades and entered the blue light and the thumping bass and the whole crocodile on a spit and the skinheaded Brits in bird shirts and the face tattoos and the Chinese dressed as toddlers and the roasted tarantulas and the French as hippie planteurs and the tailor touts and Russians dressed as Buddhists and all the scorpions-on-a-stick of Khao San Road.

Godfrey led her to the improvised seating outside a street bar. 'Two buckets of red bull vodka.'

'Buckets?'

'Tradition,' Godfrey sang. 'Tradition! And after here we'll go to the ping pong show.' He raised a hand to a balloon-inflating child. He was again intercepted when he tried to pay then handed one to Alexandra.

'Tell me more about this ping pong show! What's this?'

Godfrey demonstrated as he instructed. 'Put it to your mouth. Yep. Now inhale just a bit. Then exhale.'

'Is this drugs?'

'Happiness.'

'What do you *think* about happiness? Do you think it's a phantom menace or a God-given birthright? Or maybe a path, rather than a state? Can you *be* happy?'

'Then inhale more, and exhale the same; then in and out. Stop, now hold it.'

She held for a time then blew out a wide-eyed, 'Woah!'

'Told ya.'

When the tingling eased she said, 'I want to go to Peru to do an ayahuasca ceremony! Wouldn't that be awesome? I think you can do them in Bali now.'

Godfrey leaned back in his tiny plastic chair and stared out to the darkness of the street—the neon signs, the sweet smoke, the strolling throng of tourists—their singlets and bumbags, elephant pants and hemp shirts, bandanas and topknots. He took a large sip from his bucket then urged Alexandra to drink from hers. She did, and grimaced, and said from the back of her throat, 'How do you drink this stuff?' When she recovered from the sip she said, 'Tell me about your life, your story. Where have you even come from? Have you always painted?'

'If you talk about it you lose it?'

'But your work is your life and your life is your art, and our lives are our *biggest* works of art! Tell me about yours!'

'What's an artistpreneur?'

'An artistpreneur,' she said, repositioning herself in her tiny chair. She straightened her back and tucked her hair behind her hears. '…is someone who creates abundance through creation. Someone who takes the starving out of artist, and whose art *is* their life. A rebel. An alchemist. A wildly authentic Renaissance woman.' Then she said, as though having conceded something in exchange for a privilege, 'Now what's the India book?'

'Definitely can't talk about that. But I have a very grand conception, my biggest and best yet, that I've been wanting to do for years. A kind of medieval Hindu Nuremberg Chronicle, but I have to get to India to do it. Which takes money. Which I don't have.'

'My God, who *are* you?'

'Why do you keep asking me that?'

'I find you in Bangkok lost and starving, creating these amazing paintings that nobody sees and you don't even care! You take me drinking and on adventures and all you want to do is travel and create? It's like you don't even know what fear is! You're living the life that everybody wants to live, but you're actually living it! And you wear shirts! Nobody wears shirts! What century are you from!? What pirate ship brought you here? What space shuttle have you landed from?'

Godfrey pouted and ordered tequilas from the child tending the front tables. He raised his glass and said, 'To Botticelli then?'

'The shoes?'

'If that helps.'

Alexandra followed him in downing her shot. She slammed it, and her palms, onto the table as her mouth flew open from the burning. She gasped for her straw, thinking it would alleviate the horrible sensations. As she sucked at it her body rejected the tequila and into the bucket went a round gush of vomit.

'Woah!' Godfrey chimed and stood back from the table to distance himself from mist and splash.

'I think I have food poisoning.'

'Come on, donkeyclown. I'll take you home.' Alexandra swayed as she rose then leaned her slender frame onto Godfrey's shoulder as he walked her through the throng to the main road. He stood with her at the kerb and hailed a taxi. She ran back to a potted tree and with an exposed neck fertilized its soil.

'Alexandra?'

'Mm?'

'You can't throw up in the taxi, OK?'

'I won't,' she moaned. 'It's food poisoning but it's all gone. I'm so sorry. I'm so embarrassed.'

'Don't be embarrassed, it's your first time, it's totally normal.'

Godfrey helped her into the taxi and closed her door. 'I feel awful,' said Alexandra as he slid in from the other side. 'Now tell me: how does it feel to be a real creator?'

Godfrey looked across the backseat and grinned and said in deep Alabaman: 'I gotta pee.'

He held her up just long enough to get her into her bedroom. She clambered for the pillow-end of her bed and fell face-down into it.

'Take money for a taxi,' she mumbled into the sheets.

'It's OK, I'll walk,' said Godfrey then prepared her room for the coming of drunken ejection.

'Are you crazy? What's money? It doesn't matter! You showed me so much cool stuff. We had an adventure! Let me pay for your taxi home. I never would have seen so much… authenticity without you. Thank you for the connection, thank you for the human contact. It means so much to me, so much. We're going to have a r-… Ha. I love… your job. You're a real artist! I'm so sorry. Please! Take taxi for the money.' She slapped at the duvet to find her handbag; slid her fingers into it and flung a 500 baht note into the air. Godfrey turned her onto her back and pulled up the duvet. 'Godfrey?'

'Mm?'

'What's your last name?'

'Lackland.'

'Godfrey Lackland… and Alexandra Wishart,' she said, then seemed to hum a tune that suggested they were sitting in a tree.

He put a carton of coconut water next to the lidless rice cooker and told her they were down next to the bed. Then he picked up the note and turned out the lights and went home.

III

With his sweat towel over his shoulder Godfrey opened the lobby's glass door for Twinkle and at the wooden bench kissed her goodbye on the cheek. He sat and waited for the tuk tuk as she crossed the drive to the carpark. Presently there appeared a newly familiar figure, saluted as it bypassed the boom gate.

'Well, well, well. Don't you look awful.'

'I do? Oh. … I think I have food poisoning.'

'Food poisoning?'

'Do you have a girlfriend?'

'Walk with me, I'm getting breakfast.' They set off for the bridge. 'What brings you down to Phra Khanong?'

'I couldn't call because you don't have a phone, and you have no social media so I couldn't message, which is crazy. And you don't exist on Google—which means you don't exist. What *happened* last night?'

'Do you not remember?'

'I remember throwing up and being on a boat and an orchid and lots of lights. I think I lost my favourite hat. I've never had food poisoning like this.'

'Food poisoning?' Godfrey smiled.

'Thanks for putting me to bed. Can I pay for your taxi home?'

'Y'already did.'

'Oh good. And thank you again. Not just for getting me home, but for the human connection. And for not raping me. Connection's so important.'

'Thanks for buying me dinner,' said Godfrey as they stomped onto the steel of the bridge and walked towards the sun.

'Oh, that was nothing. Especially compared to why I'm here. I have a proposition for you.'

'Oh have you one?'

'My biggest event for the year is my retreat, The Creative Art of Wishfulness. Me and four other facilitators lead an *amazing* week of art therapy and yoga and meditation and empowering life design.'

'It sounds ridiculous.'

'You don't even know what it is!' she said, smiling at his dismissal. 'Just listen. My creativity guy pulled out last week and I

35

was going to run it without him, which would have meant more money for me, but I'd prefer it to be a fuller experience than the money. And then somehow I meet you?! I mean, universe! It would be so *so* amazing to have a real artist with first-hand insight into the creative process, my God, yes! I can see the blurb already—and the testimonials! It looks *so* much better this way! And that's why I'm in Bangkok, I'm on my way to Bali for The Creative Art of Wishfulness.'

'Bali's for fuckwits.' Godfrey wiped a sheet of sweat from his forehead.

'You've never been! Just listen. I'm an artistpreneur. I take the starving out of artist.' She threw her hands out at her sides. 'I want you to come to Bali to be my creativity facilitator.'

'I don't know what that means.'

'I want you to teach creativity to the people on the retreat!'

'I told you, creativity can't be taught.'

'No but it can! We'll be there together, and I'll help you craft your workshop and you can plan India and we'll go on adventures and work *together* on creating an amazing inspiring experience.'

'You have absolutely no idea who I am. Or what I do.'

'No but I do! I've seen your work *and* your life. Most people only *talk* about doing what you're doing, what you're living! I've seen your eyes light up when you discuss about art—passion's the most valuable thing you can have, we're already moving towards a passion economy! You have so much to give. Come on, teach creativity for me. Come to Bali with me. Please?'

'And I'm supposed to do what there? Tell a bunch of housewives and corporate buttholes they're all Rembrandts repressed? That art'll lead them to a more genuine authentic version of themselves? I can't tell people what they want to hear, and what they want to hear is that art is beautiful and amazing and filled with butterflies and happy-making rainbows. Art is a cunt. It's a reverser of the divine order, and most people do *not* have what it takes. No. Absolutely not. I want to stay in Bangkok. I simply want do my work as an artist.'

'I'll pay you five thousand dollars.'

ACT TWO

A Selfie of the Artistpreneur in Bali

I

Alexandra Wishart, in a white dress bursting with violet columbines, stood over four floral dresses laid flat on the end of her teak four-poster bed.

'Too maideny,' she looked down at herself and thought, then changed into the yellow with the blue carnations. Outside, suitcase wheels rumbled over stone-stuck concrete. She hurried again to the bathroom mirror and with her index fingers cleared her forehead of hair then pouted and puckered her lips. The suitcase wheels loudened; she went through to her balcony, overlooking frangipani and traveller palms, and put her hands together on the balustrade and leaned up onto her bare toes and looked over and down and announced, 'Welcome to Bali!'

Two saronged young women stopped on the footpath and looked up. The heavier of the two, holding a suitcase handle, said, 'Thank you?' germanically. 'Who are you?'

Alexandra went back inside. Upon reflection the yellow dress had not been absolutely perfect—carnations weren't really tropical enough. She tapped at the overhanging mosquito net. Soon she said, 'Geniuses pick green.' She changed into the green dress with the big white buttercups and looked at herself in the mirror. 'Yes! Geniuses pick green!'

Her phone was charging on the dresser beside the bed. Biologically addicted to passing time on it, she scrolled and swiped and liked and tapped through several of its applications.

Soon suitcase wheels rumbled over stone-stuck concrete. Alexandra went to the end of the bed and held up the red dress with the yellow hibiscus. 'Was there time?' she thought, minding the wheels that soon would reach the pool. 'Red *is* the colour that people notice first.' The wheels loudened. 'No, but geniuses pick green.'

The bathroom mirror, a forehead cleared and lips still large enough—and out to the balcony and bare tiptoes and over and down and, 'Welcome to Bali!'

An empty footpath.

On the ground floor at the furthest end of the row of adjacent bungalows a Mediterranean couple were trying to get their key to turn in their door.

'Maybe green's too much,' said Alexandra at the dresses. Then came to her something of a revelation. 'Orchids!' Instantly the blue and orange dress made perfect sense. 'From the restaurant. He would remember the orchids!' She changed into it then went to the dresser and filtered a dozen photographs of herself; deepened the persimmon of her lipstick in a hammock close-up then removed a blemish that had been bothering her for mon—. Rumbling wheels?

She turned an ear to the balcony. Rumbling wheels. Mirror, forehead, lips—hands on the balustrade and tiptoes and with undiminished enthusiasm, 'Welcome to Bali!'

'Thanks!' said a lone man unknown to her. 'I'm Roger.' She returned to her bare heels and sighed through her nose. 'I like your dress, they're orchids, right? What's your name?'

'Alexandra?' Godfrey came out to the balcony.

'You're here?'

'I'm here!' said Roger with open arms.

'When did you arrive?'

'Just now! Wanna go get a kombucha?'

'I was in traffic for three hours.'

'Welcome to Bali!' She returned to her tiptoes and hugged him. 'Isn't it amazing here? Look at this place!'

'It's not bad,' Godfrey said, looking out to the traveller palms and the royal blue of the pool and the miniature split gate which led to it—thatched huts and fern-forked trees and the necks and orange crests of birds of paradise.

'I didn't hear you arrive.'

'I literally just dropped my backpack onto my bed. Three hours I was in traffic. I hate traffic.'

'Isn't it so wonderful here?'

'I like the view over the valley.'

Alexandra followed him through his bungalow. Their shared rear balcony was partitioned by a blind of wooden slats. Rising and rolling and turning and jutting, half in shade, half bright-lit—all glistening with humidity—countless canopies of bamboo leaf and palm frond spread across and along a valley like an Escher field of stairs, broken into by enormous coconut palms stuck into the undulations like green and golden pinwheels. A tiered shrine, lichen-covered, was without offering on the ridge directly below them. Alexandra put her hands together on the balustrade and closed her eyes and inhaled through her nose. She smiled, ignoring the smell of rubbish-fire. 'I'm so content here.' Temple music wafting from the distance was silenced by a chainsaw.

'You're content here or content?'

'Which did I say? But don't you love how alive it feels? How peaceful, how beautiful it is—how old!—how real? I'm *finally* feeling normal enough to take a good selfie.'

Godfrey nodded half sideways as he stared out over the valley.

'There's so much we have to do! The monkey temple, the temple of happiness, the artist's market, the waterfalls! The rice terrace swing—you can take photos of me and I'll take some of you—*so much* content here—a cooking class, the sunset walk, and the most *amazing* vegan food—I'm going to make you get healthy while you're here. It's getting late today though so maybe we'll have to do most of it tomorrow? But today there's—'

'You've done all that before, right?'

'No,' she said, bouncing with enthusiasm still.

'You've been here a week though? And you've been here before?'

'I've been working my *ass off* on a new thing and updating my website, posting like crazy, and I don't love doing any of that stuff alone. And we are *definitely* getting inked! My God! For every milestone we reach we get a tattoo, even if it's just a single word, to celebrate, you know? Tattoos, I think—don't you?—represent the permanence of each experience, each adventure, how they touch our soul—the pain of being transformed. They leave a mark, because so does each milestone.'

Godfrey stared at her. She smiled and blinked and went on.

'The other co-creators get here Sunday. But till then you and I have one big jungle adventure together!'

'The other?'

'Co-creators.'

'The facilitators?'

'Mm hm.'

'They get here Sunday?' Slowly Godfrey was piecing things together. 'It's just you and me for two days?'

'Our two-day jungle rendezvous! Oh, and I'm going to help you.'

'Help me what?'

'With your online stuff.'

'I don't have any online stuff.'

'Exactly.'

'Well, I'm going to take a swim I think. I'm dripping with sweat.'

'You idiot, no!'

'What?'

'Do you realise where you *are*? There's still a few hours of sunlight, there's so much I want to show you, so much we have to do!'

'I can't go for a swim?'

'No! Temples!'

'Temples?'

'Temples!'

'All right, well, I'll just take a shower.'

'Me too, I should freshen up, I've barely had time to poop I've been working so much.'

Godfrey went back inside. His bungalow was as hers—a mosquito net tied back at the bed posts, dark-polished floorboards, a wooden staircase rising steeply to a dusty loft with a reed mattress and innumerable musty cushions. He unzipped his backpack and took off his shirt and took out a pair of shorts. He looked to Alexandra, standing at his doorway. She darted her eyes from his body and stared at a rug.

'Could you?'

'Could I...?' She looked up, ready to do anything he asked of her.

'I'm going to take a shower.'

'Uh huh?' she said, almost excited.

Godfrey pointed his shorts at the bathroom, then at her, and back to the bathroom.

'Oh, yeah. Sorry. I was thinking about the view. Isn't it so so beautiful here?'

'Downstairs in fifteen?'

An hour later Alexandra descended the stairs beside her bungalow and wound the footpath to the pavilion that housed the resort's lobby.

'What took you so long?'

'Oh, I had to post.'

'There's a motorbike out the front. They give them to you for free, that's pretty good.'

'We're going on a motorbike!? It's exactly as I thought it would be.'

'Technically it's a scooter.'

Two feet planted firmly on the drive's grass-seamed paving stones, Alexandra clipped a strap under her chin and said, 'Your helmet?'

'Neh,' Godfrey exhaled.

'That's dangerous.'

'Yes.'

'My God, you're right!' and she almost sang: 'I went to the woods to live deliberately and suck the marrow of life.' She unclipped its strap and pulled herself towards him and clasped her hands at his stomach. Godfrey looked momentarily down at the clasping then turned the scooter about and sped across the stones. As they wound down the resort's drive Alexandra nestled her head into his back.

'What are you doing?'

'Hm?' she moaned.

'What are you, taking a nap?'

'Oh. I just… I haven't had human contact in so long. It feels so nice, you know?'

They came out onto the main road and turned into loud traffic. Alexandra lifted her head from his spine and raised her chin as high as it would go and leaned back. Then she howled. 'What are you doing?' She gave three high-pitched barks, the third of which returned into a long howl. 'What the hell are you doing?'

'We're running with the wolves!'

'We're driving with the traffic.'

When they came to the first corner they were doing neither. A t-intersection overwatched by a towering white statue of Arjuna, the Conqueror of Sloth had been encircled by minibuses and trucks. Still and idling, they splurted black smoke onto the helmets of the scooter drivers and into the lungs of the children as passengers between their knees. Godfrey planted his feet and stepped through a descending capillary of van mirror and rear bumper. When soon he found an outside line he lifted his feet and meandered around rubble and open sewers. Alexandra, her head resting and eyes closed, missed what was already to Godfrey a familiar procession—a narrow road of moneychangers and SIM-card stands, of piles of garbage bagged and loose, of flip-flop emporiums and piles of rubble both swept and un; pet food stores and machine-gun soldiers outside banks and dream-catcher stands and Ralph Lauren shops and a Dairy Queen and Chinese tourists in fluorescent tennis clothing smoking with one hand and ice cream cones in the other.

Godfrey veered to pull into the temple to which Alexandra's pre-nap directions had sent him. A traffic officer waved him to the opposite side of the street. He parked and woke her up. As they approached the entrance to Pura Saraswati they were offered free samples of caramel pudding frappuccino, for in Ubud, Bali, the Temple of Knowledge shares its grounds, literally, with a Starbucks. Both declined and walked on to the split gate. A man in a blue plastic chair chimed nonchalantly, 'No photo,' as they passed. Beyond a long wooden souvenir stand they beheld the black waters of two lotus ponds, running still up to the closed tower-gate of the inner sanctuary.

Alexandra leaned her shoulder into Godfrey's arm. 'I love that we're about to share everything we know.'

'What are we about to do?'

'On the retreat.'

'Oh, yeah. I'm looking forward to it.'

'Think of all the fires we're going to light. The rivers we're going to reroute, the souls we're going to save!'

'I did have a few questions actually. How long does my workshop need to be, like a full day? And can it be a lecture or…? What form should it be in? I have absolutely no idea what—'

'My Godfrey, look at these *buildings*!' She put her palms together at her chest and bent her wrists and raised her elbows and spun on one foot. 'Do you think they'll have temples like this in India? Will you?' She handed him her phone and walked the concrete path between the ponds. She stood before a sunken snake fountain and put her hair behind her ears. Then she turned and kicked a foot back into her hand and slowly leaned forward. She reached out her other hand and closed its fingertips and smiled and said, 'Ready.'

'The, ah…' said Godfrey. 'The guy said no photos.'

'That doesn't apply to us!'

'Does it not?'

'We're creators! You're an artist, Godfrey!'

'Yeah but… this is a temple, I don't want to, I don't know, disrespect them.'

'Oh my Godfrey!' She opened her eyes and rotated her head to look at him. 'The gods of now don't *care* about the gods of yesterday.'

'What does that mean?'

'These temples are dedicated to us, to now! The gods of today *love us* using their space to create.'

'Well I'm not sure about that, but there are signs everywhere. No one else is taking pictures.'

'Because they're not artists, they're just tourists! Fat obedient tourists!' She reclosed her eyes and returned her chin to reaching for her outstretched hand. 'Go.' Godfrey raised the phone and centred her figure and hit the take button once then turned the phone sidew—

'No photo!' was yelled very gruffly from the entrance.

'I fucking told you,' said Godfrey, lowering the phone and hurrying along the path. He turned and waved in silent apology to the man in the plastic chair. 'I fucking told you.'

'Look at these carvings!' said Alexandra. 'Have you ever auscultated a piece of art?'

Godfrey took a long time to say, 'Huh?'

They stood at the trunk of one of the trees which grew out and up beside the naga-balustraded staircase. The gate's base was of ascending blocks of yali head and corner-defending garuda, each side under the watch of a fanged rakshasa. Two golden umbrellas, shading the demon guards, glowed hot and yellow in the late afternoon heat. The lava-stone sprouted with fern and was patched with moss, the gate itself of blush stucco, Kala-lintelled—grey-stone finials everywhere encrusting as cooled, harmless, flame.

'I've never seen anything like it,' said Godfrey. 'It's almost robotic. Blocks, no curves, no points. Blunt. Passive. Base? It's cluttered with ornament, carved mould, like a Portuguese church.'

'Wait, stay right there.'

'Hm?'

'Don't move. The light on your shirt. And through your hair.'

'You can't take photos here, Alexandra,' he almost laughed.

'Don't be ridiculous. Look at me? You're *actually* auscultating art, do you realise that?'

Godfrey ran his hand over the stubbled moss on a twist in the balustrade then leaned in to inspect the finish of the carving. He tilted his head to follow the curve in a—

'No photo!'

'Would you stop?' he said to Alexandra, photographing him still.

'No photo!' loudened but calmed as it neared. The man had upped from his plastic chair to stride the lotus ponds. 'You leave please!'

'Oh, I'm sorry, I didn't know,' Alexandra sweetly and softly pleaded.

'You know, I tell you.' The man stood wide-footed in his red sarong and white udeng and almost growled at them: 'Now you leave. No photo I say, but no listen. Saraswati Temple sacred place.'

'I told ya,' said Godfrey, and they were escorted in silence to the Starbucks.

Back across the street they passed a second scooter parking lot as Alexandra led him up the gentle slope of a street market—a crowded walk of open-fronted shops selling dreamcatchers and calaveras and maschere and Superman marionettes and bottles of snake oil and statues of Buddha in wood and gilt and stone; and Bob Marley singlets and dreamcatchers and boomerangs and snake oil and didgeridoos and Bob Marley singlets. And bongo drums and ukuleles and elephant pants and dreamcatchers and bamboo wind-chimes and Superman marionettes and Bob Marley singlets and snake oil and boomerangs and statues of Buddha in wood and gilt and stone. Alexandra ran her fingers along the racks of floral sun dresses and brushed the dangling feathers of the dreamcatchers on their way up and down to dinner.

Godfrey walked in astonishment through the patrons of Healing Foods Café. He said, very slowly, 'What the hell?' as he sat opposite Alexandra. It was as though he had put them there himself, painted at dark benches and round tables in purple and patchouli-leaf without exaggeration or embellishment, his Balinese canvas instantly more alarming—far more amusing—than anything in his Bangkok or his Bucharest book.

'This place has the most *intense* hummus.'

From speakers overhead a chorus rejoiced in nursery rhyme about the sun combining with the rain to form a twelve-coloured rainbow. Its menu on tie-dyed paper informed its patrons that the Healing Foods logo meant the source or essence—nothingness, and that everything is interconnected in a chain of co-becoming and that here was a place where all could be the shine.

Godfrey flapped through it. (The menu, not the shine.) 'What the hell's shilajit?'

'Oo, that's an ancient concentrated earth mineral found on rocks in the Himalayas! How does the eggplant steak reuben sound?'

'Ridiculous.'

'What about pizza? I'm *so* hungry.'

'The… pirate tonic pizza? With jin nourishing kidney tonic for highest potency,' Godfrey read slowly. 'Eucommia, jujube dates, astragalus, and hizandra berries which help anti-aging and longevity.'

'And libido,' said Alexandra, smirking as a waitress came to the end of their table. 'What about the sushi lasagne!?'

'Can you hear yourself? Sushi lasagne? I'll have a beer.'

'You will *not* have a beer! You're taking care of yourself now, I need my investment healthy.'

'I am sorry sir, we do not have beer,' said the waitress. 'But we may encourage you to try the double reishi warm elixir with chaga mushroom? It have a calming effect, maybe for you like beer.'

'No.' Alexandra suggested a cleanse juice. 'Would you *shut* up?' said Godfrey in a kind way. 'What the crap is coconut bacon? Zucchini wrap,' he said to the waitress as he handed her his menu. 'Fuck me.' He looked around with disbelief, condescension, detestation. He eyed in one wide neck-turn a shoeless bearded redhead, a muscle shirt, a tuft of armpit hair over sideboob. 'All right, seriously, what am I in for on this retreat? Are they all these people?'

'No!' said Alexandra, almost insulted. 'These are Bali hippies, they don't have money, I'm a businesswoman. There are seven people coming from all over the world. And you and me facilitating, with Hennifer, Venerika, and Bradley. It's going to be *such* an amazing week,' she said, rolling her eyes to the ceiling. 'Hennifer's a yogini and a healer, and Venerika's—'

'You mean Jennifer, right?'

'No, it's Hennifer! She pronounces it with an h. She's such a beautiful woman. And Venerika's a life coach and a writer, and then Bradley's a photographer and a poet. I'm actually not sure you'll like him.'

'I'm quite sure I won't.'

'But him I'll tell you about later.' The waitress returned with their food. Godfrey looked into the ends of his wrap and was not excited. Alexandra put the palms of her hands an inch above her buddha bowl and straightened her back and closed her eyes.

'What are you doing?'

'We form a relationship between our food and our spirit before we eat it.'

'You didn't do that in Bangkok.'

'You're on my turf now.' When shortly a relationship had been sufficiently formed Alexandra opened her eyes and picked up a spoon. 'So, the first day is my introductory seminar. That's called Wishful Alchemy.'

'Oh, I just got the ah…'

'What?'

'Wishfulness, wishful. It's your name.'

'Yes! I created everything out of nothing.'

'Alchemy, right?'

'Wishful Alchemy. It's the core workshop, Hennifer's and Venerika's tie in with it perfectly. Yours will too.'

'Alchemy's a fake science, you know that yes?'

'It's a *misunderstood* science! My Godfrey! About creating something out of nothing, about endless pursuits and miraculous goals, obsessive determination—creating the life you *want*.'

'It's a fake science used to con people out of money, pretending to be able to turn crap into gold.'

'It's absolutely *not* that! You don't understand it at all! Alchemy's about transmutation, turning what's messy and worthless into something pure and life-affirming, with a clean space in your heart and powerful intentions.'

'Oh, powerful intentions!' said Godfrey as though the explanation had clarified everything.

'*Wishful* Alchemy is about finding the elixir of a *purposeful* life, discovering your own organic panacea—what sets your soul on fire—and working on your magnum opus, your life! Because—'

Her eye was caught by a gecko on the teak pillar beside their table. She broke off as she looked at it. Then she watched it. Then she stared at it.

'Alexandra?'

'It's so beautiful, so delicate. Like an innocent snake burdened with legs. I haven't seen a sunflower in six months. I'd like to be a cowboy's jungle, you know what I mean? Hm.' Soon she looked again at Godfrey and picked up where she had left off. 'Because your art is your life and your life is your greatest work of art, like your India book. My life is your India book. Each day you *create* your art *through* your life. Oh, this hummus is so intense!'

Godfrey stroked, with some force, a fingertip at an eyebrow. 'And people pay you for this?'

'Mm hm. Oo! At the end of the year I want to do a retreat in Europe! Maybe Paris, the inspirational home of Hemingway and Picasso.'

'And they pay you how much?'

'The regular price is five thousand. But we always get a few early-bird sign-ups, they're only forty-five hundred.'

'Dollars?'

'Mm hm.'

Godfrey intoned as a deepening trio: 'Nikolai Konstantinovich Roerich. How did you come up with this idea? I've never heard of a retreat.'

'Are you serious? Retreats are huge! I went on one in Ubud, that's where I met Hennifer. Then last year I was living here for a few months working on a writing course and I was messaging my friends to ask if they'd come visit—they all said it was too far and too expensive. I even told them I'd pay for their flights and they could stay in my homestay—but still no one would come! So I thought, What if—you know? What if I ran my own retreat? Your life is your art and your art is your life, right? And you create your art, so you create your life. And now my life is Wishful Alchemy. I launched it and people came!'

'So wait. You're paying people to—no... People are paying you, to be their friend—no. People are paying you to be your friend.'

'They're paying for an *amazing* week of art therapy and yoga and meditation, and empowering life design!'

'But the idea came from people paying you, then coming to Bali, so that you have someone to hang out with.'

'My Godfrey, you look at things the wrong way! The aim of my life is to make myself happy and The Creative Art of Wishfulness does that. And rich, which is great!'

'It is a weird little world you inhabit.'

They walked back through the artist's market—dreamcatchers and didgeridoos and dreamcatchers and snake oil—to the scooter. Alexandra clasped her arms at Godfrey's waist and howled twice at the rising moon then pressed the side of her head to his back until they reached the drive of Zen Resort.

'Oo, I want to show you something!' she said after being woken.

'I need a beer.'

The night was hot and wet and strangely blue—the long pool glowing a frost of turquoise onto the high foliage and the bungalow walls. Alexandra put a MacBook on the front balustrade. 'You ready?'

'Ready for what?'

She leaned in, and with the white glow of a webpage in her eyes she read:

'Story-painter, troublemaker, daring Renaissance man.' She spun her beaming face to Godfrey and back again. 'Van Gogh-quoting danger-explorer, shirt-wearing whiskey-lover and pipe-smoking ship-sailing imagination warrior.'

'What the hell is that?'

'Hi, I'm Godfrey Lackland,' said Alexandra. 'And welcome to my soulspedition.'

'Huh?'

'Combining the technical skill of the Old Masters with my own real-life wanderlusting travels, I add the spark of my own vision in the hope that I can bring the world, and you, back to life.'

'What are you reading?'

'I wish for my life as an artist-adventurer to remind you that there's a creator inside everyone and that all it takes to revive your inner-van Gogh is a bit of audacious living and purposeful artspiration. Come with me, as I paint the world one lifeful landscape at a time, and let's renaissance the Renaissance together!' She leaned back from the screen. 'What do you think? It's modelled on mine, but you get the picture, right?'

'What picture?'

'It's you.'

'What's me?'

'And look.' She pointed to the address bar at the top of the page. Godfrey read his own name dot com.

'OK?'

'Do you like it?'

'I don't know what it is.'

'It's you, it's your website.'

'What you just read sounds like the dating profile of an idiot who goes around telling people he loves colours. I don't smoke a pipe, Alexandra, and I don't drink whiskey.'

'But you *should* smoke a pipe! Imagine how good it would look on your socials.'

'What are socials?'

'My Godfrey, this is what I'm trying to tell you!' she moaned as though for the hundredth time. 'You can't just be a painter!'

'I can, and I will. Thank you for all the effort, but this is your world, it's not mine.'

'This is who you could be,' said Alexandra, looking out to the spikes of the traveller palms, powder-blue against the night. 'To them.'

'To who?' said Godfrey, leaning out of his chair to look down at the glowing and trickling pool.

'Your followers.'

'I don't have followers.'

'Because you don't have a website.'

'Because I am an artist,' he said in clear and adamant monotone. 'I don't pander, I don't compromise. I do not want or need followers. I draw because I have to and I simply want to do my work as a painter.'

'Oo wait, let me add that.' She read as she typed: 'I paint not for money nor fame, but because I *must*. My fire comes from above, and you should never apologise for having limitless artspiration. ... Maybe don't mention the fire being from above. Christianity doesn't sell. My fire comes from within,' she said as she retyped.

'I am one word away from pushing your laptop off the balcony.'

'Why?!' she laughed. 'You need to have an online presence. If you don't you're not an artist, not today. No one will buy your work if they think you're just "doing your work as an artist",' she said, puffing out her chest and lowering her voice. 'They want to feel like *they* could be the artist, they want to *be* with you on your journey.' Then she said, slowly, as though it were the single most important revelation and known from long experience: 'They want you to make them feel as though you might make them feel as though they might feel alive.'

'I'm going downstairs to get a beer. Do you want one?'

'They don't have beer here.'

'Then I'm going to bed. No pipe, no whiskey, no boat, no ship. Just bed.'

'It's so early.'

'I've had a long day in traffic. And I have to work tomorrow morning, 6am. I always work in the early mornings.'

'Oh. ... OK. ... I thought that...'

'What?'

'No nothing. I just had this image of us watching the stars and talking about art, and you'd show me more of this person who makes the complicated so simple and make me laugh some more and talk to me of India and other things. And we'd imagine together what the end of the world smells like on a warm November breeze, overlooking the mountains of Northern France where we've gone to die like our heroes.'

'Huh?!'

'You're right, we have *so* much to do on our jungle adventure tomorrow.'

Godfrey stood and said goodnight. Alexandra closed her laptop and put her ankles on the balustrade and turned an ear and then an eye to Godfrey's door.

He lay on his bed and looked down to his feet. Where the straps on his flip-flops had been they were black: grime fading to dirt along his toes before redoubling to opaque gunk at the corners of his big toenails. He thought that probably he should get up and wash them; for some reason he wanted to stay still. He saw, up under the drawn mosquito net, an air-conditioning unit. He found its white remote on the dresser. He pressed its largest button and the unit beeped and an icy breeze soon fell on his thigh. 'Fuck yes,' he muttered, and pressed the down arrow until it would beep no more. He folded his hands at his chest and closed his eyes and said, 'Ahhhhh yesssssss.'

'Yes?' came instantly from the balcony.

Godfrey reopened his eyes. 'Hm?'

'Did you say my name?'

'I said yes, there's air-conditioning in here.'

'Oh. … Goodnight.'

'Night.'

II

Sweatless, Godfrey woke shivering at 10.

When he was nine, on the only overseas vacation his family ever took, Godfrey had stayed in a similar resort in Sanur. He thought that probably there would be a buffet breakfast downstairs. He put swimming shorts over his boxers and slid on a black t-shirt and turned as quietly as possible the handle of the door to the rear balcony. On the table outside lay a wooden tray under wire-framed netting; upon it a plate of fruit and two cups of juice and one of coffee.

'Fucking yes,' he said, and brought it into his room. He had so missed coffee, even cold; momentarily he contemplated a life without flat Red Bull. Then he surveyed and ate the tiny bananas, the crested watermelon pips and all, the zig-zagged pineapple—ignored the papaya. He could ignore fruit. Glorious ignorable fruit.

He took his notebook and a pen from his backpack and returned to the rear balcony and for a moment beheld the valley, its rolling carpet of fern and ficus, red leaves here and golden there; listened to the echoing bird calls and disconcerting insect buzz—and nodded in approval. He set the glass-topped table at the balcony's edge and brought the chair out from the dresser. He clomped it so loudly onto the wooden decking that it roused the attention of his closest neighbour. He was watched through sheer curtains as he thumbed through his notes with the last of the coffee at his knee.

Alexandra came out to her half of the balcony and for the third time that morning unrolled there a purple yoga mat, one end almost touching the bungalow-to-balustrade screen of bamboo slats. She turned her back to Godfrey and kneeled in a red razor-back and black yoga pants. She pressed her butt into her heels and bent her pinkie toes and arched her shoulders. She rolled her wrists for a time then leaned forward and slid her hands down the mat as far as they would go. She held the position, breathed, brought herself back up. As she puffed out her chest she looked very quickly over her shoulder.

Godfrey had turned to the group of pages in his notebook headed, 'INDIA'. Accumulating now for eighteen months, since first he had thumbed through a colour facsimile of the Nuremberg

THE CREATIVE ART OF WISHFULNESS

Chronicle, his notes were a series of ideas attempting to combine that medieval history of the world with the forms and styles of its oldest religion. A kind of Hindu biblical paraphrase, the Dharmic Bull would by Godfrey's hand soon morph with the Golden Calf, the Tower of Babel grow as a gopuram—the symbolic grotesques of his naturalist ideal be sketched and painted upon the walls and colonnades of south-Indian temples.

Alexandra lay on her back with the bottoms of her feet facing Godfrey's chair. She brought a knee up to her chest and breathed audibly in. After exhaling through pursed lips she clasped her big toe with two fingers and slowly straightened her knee until her leg was upright and her foot pointed down at her forehead. She inhaled, exhaled, relaxed—released the big toe and lowered her heel to the yoga mat then raised her other knee to her chest. She clasped her other big toe and straightened until her foot pointed at her forehead. She inhaled, and added to her outward breath a loud squeal of release. Then she gave a loud 'Yoik' and looked down the length of her lowered leg to the figure behind the bamboo screen.

His India notes had long been channeling into six distinct works. There would be an Inferno, an Age of Kali, a Garden of Earthly Delights, a Four Ages of Man; the others would materialise in the drafting. Having conceived loosely of his India Book—how the forms and myths of Hindu religion and the arts of Tamil Nadu would merge, somehow, with 15th-century European woodcuts and the civilising premonitions of medieval prophecy—he had already made notes for the disappearing legs of his Cow of the Four Ages and for the rajagopuram whose tiers would take the place of the circles of hell. He now took up where he had left off in December, after coming via Huxley to the Vishnu Purana.

On a page with five blank staves left he wrote, as usual, two lines to a stave:

'A Flood, but instead of water a drought—all's because of man reversed.
At its rear an elephant graveyard, with Ganesh and Airavata:
the elephantine forms of religion; Mufasa and Dumbo too, dead—
a barren Disney Elephant Graveyard.'

Alexandra stood at the balustrade and hunched over her phone. At breakfast she had posted a picture of her breakfast; she scrolled now through the comments on three platforms—liked the flattery she found, deleted what misaligned with how she wished herself to appear, responded to those containing questions, affirmations, congratulations. Soon she locked her phone and turned her back to

Godfrey. She bent over straight-legged until her fingertips touched the mat beneath her. She stepped her right foot back then wrapped the inside of her forearm around her left calf. She took a deep breath and leaned forward, inhaled, lifted her right toes from the mat. When one leg had almost formed a straight line with the other she walked her right hand towards her planted foot and wrapped it around her ankle. She inhaled, exhaled, quietly coughed. Then she moved her head to the side and looked passed her shin to the bamboo screen and coughed again, this time a great deal louder.

'Good morning,' Godfrey chimed as though surprised. He closed his book on his pen.

'Good morning!' said Alexandra, red-faced and upside down. Slowly she returned to upright and breathed calmly out. 'You weren't working at 6, ay?' She pushed the screen aside and ducked around it.

'I wasn't, no. I didn't have a pool of my own sweat to wake me up.'

'How was your breakfast? I thought you'd like to eat in your room while you worked.'

'You brought that up?'

'Yeah I went down at 6 and just put some fruit on a plate.'

'So nice of you.'

'Oh, no, I'm just grateful to have you here. And! Today's the day of our big jungle adventure! You excited? I thought we'd start off at the sacred monkey forest.'

'Monkey forest?'

'It's *so* amazing there, so spiritual, you can feel the gods of tomorrow whispering to the gods of today. And the baby monkeys are so so cute.'

'Monkeys, Alexandra, I can't. I'm really afraid of monkeys. Like phobia afraid. I start shaking, my heart beats faster, I sweat and hyperventilate. I can't.'

'What? Why?' said Alexandra, intrigued and concerned.

'I was attacked by a monkey when I was nine.'

'Whaaaat?!'

'It was awful. This guy a few houses down from us had a pet chimp. James. The guy, not the chimp. The chimp's name was Caesar. And James would walk down the street with this monkey like they were friends—he'd talk to it, teach it backgammon. Then one day I was talking to James and I played, you know, You've-got-something-on-your-shirt. And James looked down, and I flicked him in the nose, but tapping a chimp on the chest is a sign of aggression. So this monkey thought I was being aggressive and he broke out of the house and jumped across the front yard and pinned me down and started pounding at my head.' Godfrey flailed his arms high as though beating himself with his wrists. 'Luckily there was a garbage can lid right next to me and I grabbed it and smashed the monkey in the face and he ran away. But I am *so* afraid of monkeys. Primates in general really—chimps are apes— but definitely no monkeys. I can't.'

'My God, that's terrifying! I'm so sorry that happened to you.'

'That's OK. I just have to… I gotta stay away from monkeys.'

'Of course, my Godfrey! We can go straight to the rice terraces. They have a swing there that swings you out over the valley, the photos look *amazing*. At the waterfalls we can get a profile pic for the retreat's website. Isn't it amazing?! People are coming to learn from *us*! And we'll get an artist's portrait for you for when you get your website up and running, which you will. I know you're resisting, but you'll see how wise your queen is.'

Godfrey tapped the notebook at his knee. 'I ahhh… I'm probably just going to work for most of the day. I've just started on my seminar for you and I really do want it to be revolutionary in what it tells people. Thanks again for this opportunity, honestly. I really feel like I can convey so much of how I work and create, you know?'

'Oh,' she said, clearly disappointed. 'OK then.'

'What's up?'

'Nothing, it's OK.'

'What is it?'

'I value truth above everything else.'

'Mm hm.'

'If you don't want to spend time with me you should say so.'

'What makes you think that?'

'I don't know, I guess I had this image of us spending all this time together here. Our days and nights, and going to see all this amazing stuff and being content together.'

'Ah,' said Godfrey, 'the image. But we're here to work, no? I work all the time, it's all I do. Your brain's a muscle and it has to be exercised or it becomes flabby. If I don't write notes or paint every day I get out of practice.'

'I understand, I'm the same. Will you at least watch the sunset with me?'

'Of course! I just—work's paramount. If I don't work I'm not myself.'

'I know, I'm the same. I guess your work is your art and your art is your life.'

'Exactly! But sunset, right? Five o'clock?'

'I've heard of a great place to watch it.'

Alexandra rolled up her yoga mat and went inside and Godfrey opened his notebook and added into its staves the term 'monkey forest'. Instantly he was struck with, and transcribed, the idea of Hanuman in a toga, laurel-wreathed, riding a horse even—but did Hanuman figure as heavily in Indian mythology as in Thai?

Alexandra returned to the balcony with large sunglasses at her eyes and her camera around her neck. 'I'm heading out for a massage and a stroll.'

'Yep,' Godfrey yapped. 'I'll see you at 5. Meet you at the pool?' Would Hanuman get massages? As Caesar he would, Godfrey thought, and wrote down the idea. 'Rafiki in the graveyard with the elephants too, and those green gorillas in Animalia,' one of his earliest memories of being enthralled by a painted image. 'The Jungle Book, King Louis playing the cornet—were there elephants in that movie?' He hadn't seen it but he knew that Kipling's setting was India.

He flicked through to the end of his notebook and at the top of the closest blank page wrote his bank balance. $850. His bond was on its way back to him: +$570, as was the five thousand for the retreat: $6,420.

The flight to Madurai was 250 and food and accommodation were taken care of here. The visa for India was 120 so he would land with 6,050. Last week he had looked briefly at accommodation and found a hotel about which he was almost excited. $100 a night, but he would talk them down to 70, sing for his dinner, exchange paintings for a reduction—he had seen as much done in a film. Six times seven was 42 nights, times 70, was – 2940 for accommodation.

A motorbike, surely not more than $600, and he could sell it when he left and was prepared to lose $200. –200 for a bike, and – 5 a week for petrol: –$230, then food. The hotel had a buffet breakfast. He thought that two extra meals could easily be stashed, stolen, preserved from a buffet breakfast. With a booze budget of ten a day—was India a beer country or a liquor?—he would spend money only on the roof over his head, which would be his office, his bedroom, his restaurant—and that pool! It looked, in Alexandrian parlance, amazing. He would live like a king in India, *and* have $2,460 left when his work was finished. In his last week he would figure out where was next.

$2460. Three times he underlined the number—it looked sturdy on the page, gave him confidence—and drew a box around it twice. Then he drank the last of his tepid coffee and returned to his notes.

He could see it all: six weeks in India, six paintings, a painting a week, four A3 pages to a painting—his largest and longest worked out project. He would at last be able to put into effect what had for so long been expanding and filling in the centre of his mind, to expel in Indian colour the accumulated prophesies of ten years of indignation, of alarm, of life. And in Madurai! Athens of the East! Towering with gopurams and running with mighty rivers, its very name the sweetness of the nectar which Siva rained upon its high towers. 'Siva taking a shower,' Godfrey wrote. 'Would the blue wash off? Siva showering with a diva,' he mumbled as though it were the beginning of a rhyme. 'Beyoncé, covered in blue; a smurf Beyoncé. Siva and a smurf Beyoncé.'

Madurai with its 13th-century Meenakshi Temple—the architecture he would see!—possessed of a shrine in the hills where the waters descended from heaven, first Abode of Murugan—audacious god of war and love and youth—the very place where he slew Surapadma and took him as his vehicle in the form of a peacock. 'Beyoncé riding a peacock,' Godfrey wrote. 'Driving a jade peacock? Or the eyes of a peacock tail as webcams. Or just all of them are closed: blindness, voluntary or forced.'

And on the notes accumulated.

At 5 Alexandra was lying in a red bikini on the sandstone edge of the pool, the yellow-topped rice fields—fern and unkempt ficus and palm frond—descending beyond her to the rear of the adjacent resort. One arm was across her forehead while the other held a book.

'Watcha readin'?'

'Oh,' said Alexandra, turning to its yellow front cover as though she had no idea. 'It's the most amazing book, it's like scripture.'

Godfrey angled it to himself. 'What the donkey kinda name's Glovindria?'

'You don't like it?'

'Sounds like a lesbian wizard.'

'She *is* a priestess!'

He read the book's title out loud: '*She The Warrior: how to stop doubting your greatness and get everything you've ever deserved.* Well I guess you know what you're in for.'

'She says it's because my soul-life reaches further than most people's, that's why I feel alone more often than others.'

'Of course she says that, it makes you buy her book.'

'What do you mean?'

'It's not written *to you*, is it? It's written—' He tapped at its front cover. 'There you go, New York Times Bestseller. It's written to millions of women, and you think all those women have "soul lives" reaching further than most? What the hell's a soul life anyway? You realise the invalidity of her claim?'

'But this book is like scripture!'

'She is blowing smoke up you arse.'

'Up my ass?'

'Arse, Alexandra. Where I come from, bullcrap like that blows smoke up your arse. You read it, you feel flattered, so you agree with everything she says and you tell your friends to read it and they feel flattered too. So spreads the denial of original sin, the plague of completeness passed on by coughs of flattery. Flattery. Flattered. Flat-head. Flatt-ed. Flatter. Flitter, flutter, flatter. The earth is flatter, my dear. Flatter-y. Flackery Donglad. Flat-hairy Donglad. Fat hairy coughs of Donglad completeness.'

'When's your birthday?' She asked as though the question inspired her. 'You're a fire sign, I can tell.'

'Oh yeah, how old *are* you?'

'I'm thirty-seven.'

'I'm thirty-seven, I'm not old—well I can't just call you "man." Well you could say "Dennis".'

'You OK?'

'Sunset, you ready?'

'Yes! Just let me put on a dress.'

45 minutes later they set off. Soon they were beyond the city, strolling up a gentle hill, along a paved path lined green with waist-high grass. It wound and barely rose, turned and softly fell, along a ridge between two shallow jungle-walled valleys.

'Isn't it breathtaking?' said Alexandra.

'No, it's not.'

'My God, are you serious!?'

'It contains not a single element of the sublime. Your standards

57

are too low. Just because it's elsewhere doesn't mean it's beautiful. Discern, Alexandra.'

To their left the sun gave plain white light from behind a dark tree line. A single tuft of cloud had moved into, and was presently moving out of, the shape of a genie's lamp. Gently it wafted north to leave the dusk entirely bare.

'Every sunset feels like a promise,' Alexandra declared.

'Every sunset,' said Godfrey, about to match her depth, 'feels like a sunset.'

'Isn't it romantic up here? Like our stage is set for a new transition.' A clearing had recently been made in the grass by a rubbish fire. Alexandra tucked her red dress with the yellow hibiscus under her legs and sat down and held her forearms around her knees. She closed her eyes and raised her chin to the horizon. 'Can you see the colours of the wind?'

'Mm!' said Godfrey, standing with folded arms at the edge of the char. To his right two people interrupted their walk to stand in a single file beside him. They were making way for a couple strolling hand-in-hand and side-by-side from the opposite direction. Godfrey stepped onto the black grass and looked back and excused himself as both couples kissed and strolled on. He turned to look to the distance of the hill he had just walked down. He saw there three other pairs of people—young, old, Balinese, tourist. In the other direction the same. No single person was ambling; all had found or brought or bought someone to stroll with.

'Won't you sit?' said Alexandra, her eyes closed again. She opened them and shimmied over a few inches.

Godfrey scratched the side of his face and almost shook his head as he sighed and sat. Alexandra shimmied back those same inches then tilted her head until it rested on his newly adjacent shoulder.

'Do you think there'll be stars tonight?'

Godfrey scratched the back of his head. 'Probably, it's the sky.'

'You know I'm proud of the fact I've never seen a shooting star? Because when I do I know it'll be for something world-shattering.'

'Mm,' said Godfrey in high sarcasm and moved his eyeballs as far down to her as they would go.

'I'm so looking forward to after this retreat.'

'Mm,' said Godfrey in even higher.

'We can run away to India.'

'Mm,' said Godfrey, now gone very low. 'What?'

'Never mind.' Alexandra lifted her head and looked defiantly out to the sunset. It was giving off at its inception a little orange here and some grey haze there. 'Have you ever heard a wolf cry to the blue corn moon?'

Godfrey mumbled, 'Run away to India.' Then: 'Alexandra, I have a question for you.'

'Your questions are always so good. What is it?'

'What's your ideal man? Describe him to me.'

'My ideal man? Why do you ask?'

'Just curious.'

'Hm. Well, he's sensitive, he knows how to cry. But manly, too, like he chops his own wood. With an axe, like a Viking. Not muscly, that's gross, but big, you know? Strong. He can talk about phases of the moon and creativity and fighting. And he likes politics and nutrition, but not sports or video games—they're dumb. He's known the best of life and its worst, his face was in the gutter but he looked up at the stars. And now he has money. He appreciates cacao but he's happy eating chocolate. He's good at animals and babies, probably he's my age and wears shirts, he doesn't dress like other people. Is this too long, too specific?'

'No, no, it's perfect. I can almost picture him. Anything else?'

'He has a big social media following, so we can travel the world together and post our amazing lives, and the posts *pay* for the travel! And of course I'd like if he was good-looking, I need him to be *in* the photos. If I'm going to let him colonise my ovaries he can at least know how to use a selfie stick. I guess that's it, what about you?'

'What about me?'

'Do you have an ideal woman?'

How glad he was that she asked. 'Ideal's a loaded word I think. But there are probably a few prerequisites. Let me think… She'd be blonde, I have a thing for blondes.'

Alexandra's black hair bounced as she turned her gently nodding face from Godfrey to the sunset.

'She'll be buxom. I like larger girls, you know? Full-figured, wide hips but a thin face. Small eyes. And curvy because she drinks too much—beer—I love the idea of being with someone I can get drunk with. And eat meat. She eats a lot of meat, *just* meat, and we can sit down together and have a whole roasted lamb and drink beer. She'll probably be British, I like the way they talk, I don't like it when people speak like the movies, if that makes sense. What else?' He scanned through all that he knew of Alexandra Wishart, wanting to leave no aspect of her being preemptively spurned. 'A non-creative job, I need that normality, like an office job. And like me she has no phone of course, she sees the world rather than photographs it. I think that's about it. But yes, when I imagine myself with someone, she's always blonde, curvy, about my height, a heavy drinking meat eater with an office job and no phone. And she's British.'

'I hope you find her.'

'Maybe we can all chop wood with your Viking.'

'Where shall we eat dinner tonight?' she said, attempting to recover some of her enthusiasm.

'I was just going to eat on the street.'

'No!' she scolded. 'You will not eat street meat while we're here. You're being healthy!'

'I can't afford healthy food here. I saw the bill at that retard restaurant.'

'Everything's on *me* while you're here, my Godfrey! *Especially* the healthy food.'

'I don't want you paying for my meals, that's too much like…'

'You don't want to spend time with me.'

'What?'

She chinned one of her knees. 'I can feel it, you don't want to spend time with me.'

'I spent most of yesterday with you. And I'm here now.'

'Is that enough?'

'What do you mean, enough? Is there a critical quantity?'

'You're free to do whatever you want, you don't *have* to hang out with me, but I had this image of—'

'Ah yes, the image. Alexandra, that's your image. I never—. Can we—. Here.' He pulled a flask from the pocket of his trousers and unscrewed its cap. 'Rum. Can we watch the sunset without you trying to make me feel guilty?'

'Guilty? I would *never* make you feel guilty! My God, I'm the most open-minded and understanding person you'll ever meet! But I can tell you don't want to spend time with me.'

'I'm spending time with you right now.'

'Just the sunset and that's it?'

Godfrey squinted at her and showed her the backs of two fingers. 'When did I say that?' he said, and lowered his middle. 'And so what if I do?' and he made a loose fist.

'You said you didn't want to eat dinner with me.'

'I said I wanted to eat street food. You're very welcome to join. And I'll come to dinner and watch you eat fungus and listen to rainbow songs but I can't afford—'

'You don't want to.'

Godfrey put three fingers at each of his temples and pushed circles into the sides of his head.

'I'm sorry.' Alexandra tightened her arms around her knees. Then suddenly she released them and swiped her fingers like windscreen wipers before the valley. 'No I *won't* apologise for feeling too deeply! I felt myself coming back to *life* when you arrived! I wrote in my spoken word diary today that I was in love with Buddha and chocolate and with homeless people and I wanted to go shopping and read philosophy! I *wanted*, you see? Because here's someone in the same place as me who gets me and who I get, someone I can create with, who feels equally alone but we don't have to be and our journeys—'

'Alexandra.'

'What?'

'Shoosh.'

'What?'

'Can we watch the sunset like you wanted to? Have a drink like adults. Sit in silence, and watch the sunset?'

'You hate it here and you don't want to spend time with me. If—'

'Shut up, Alexandra. Just shoosh.'

'My Godfrey! I—'

'We're here to watch the sunset, right? We do not need to talk all the way through it. Especially if what we're talking about is just a misunderstanding. I don't not want to spend time with you. You said every sunset's an opportunity, right? Take this opportunity to farewell the day and watch the night begin and just… shoosh.'

'Well…' Alexandra tilted her head until it came again to rest on Godfrey's shoulder. His eyes fell closed again. 'That's a bit better.'

With his teeth clenched and jaw askew he offered her the flask. 'Drink?'

She grinned and drank and said, 'Blergh.' She shimmied over another inch then tucked her arm under his and from blue to white, at last to pallid ash, the dark of night came on, and, starless, descended.

'I can't believe you shooshed me.'

III

As the sun rose hot on the valley behind Zen Resort—the tropical birds whooping their morning songs over dancing temple drums, the sweet showers of prayer bell—a woman in a white tunic sashed with orange stepped up to her family's spirit shrine and placed into its niche a little square basket weaved of palm leaf.

From the tray at her left hand she poked smouldering incense under the green offering. From a water bowl she took a pink orchid in the ends of her fingers and sprinkled the shrine twice; closed her eyes and circled the flower among the sandalwood smoke. When gently she opened them she found at her right elbow an iPhone, upright in the hands of a blonde woman in a sarong tube dress whose hair was from the humidity frazzled.

The device wristed closer to the shrine; the blonde woman widened her smile then accompanied it with a raise in her eyebrows that made her look deranged. Her canines sprung fully over her bottom lip as her deep-set eyes met the Balinese woman's, whose oblation interrupted—whose shying away from her family's spirit shrine—was filmed by Venerika Odorono—Word Weaver, Bleeder of Ink, New York Times Bestselling Poet.

'Vagablonde, Smile-Maker, Qualified Joyologist,' said the purple-fonted text at her name dot com. 'After publishing under the handles Thug Unicorn and Rainbow Wordslut, Venerika now writes proudly under her own truth. Purposeful Creator of Write Yourself Free© and author of *Holy Howl: an homage to women with swords* (across whose exemplarily sparse centre were printed the words, "Sometimes I smell my grandma on my verbs & I weep."), leader of writing workshops from Morocco to Minnesota, Fierce Wellness Seeker, Immigration Enthusiast, Life coach.

'Today my favorite words are:

'Vibrant, urethra, spellbound, gentrify, turmeric, vagarious, amethyst, consent, fissure, liberationist, plop, tinder, barren, Paris, boggle, balcony, winter, doggy, rhythms, pulsating, galaxy, squirt.

'What will be yours tomorrow?

'Sign up for my museletter and get a discount on my master-course – Inspiragination – where I'll teach YOU the brave art of splendacious descriptiveness and marvelous metaphoritude.'

As the midday sun took its tyrannical seat overhead and the resort cats stretched and yawned across the reed mats on pavilion floors—as the hotel guests already checked out took lounges by the pool to await their shuttle buses and Godfrey Lackland snuck in a swim while Alexandra Wishart got a massage—a young woman in a white tunic sashed with orange crossed a long dry lawn to the open corner of her family's house-protecting shrine.

Its low-walled grounds were kept quiet by a thickness of juvenile coconut tree. She placed into its niche a small round basket weaved of palm leaf and from the tray on her left hand jabbed a stick of incense between the newest offering and the old. She took from a water bowl a white and yellow frangipani between the ends of her fingers and sprinkled the shrine once, twice, a third time—wafted the flower among the sweet smoke as though making the sign of the circle rather than cross.

'And here we have the exact ceremony I was *just* talking about!' was rather yelled than said. The reiteration was made for an iPhone recording the coincidental discovery. The young woman startled from her ritual and looked to the narrator, who turned her back on the shrine and raised her elbow to bring herself into upright frame. Presently the yelling, from this tall and wide brunette woman in a halter-necked tube sarong, restarted.

'These offerings are called kanang sarri,' she enthused loudly and slowly at her screen. 'They symbolise sacrifice *and* routine, things I strongly encourage you to include in your daily morning gratitude journey!' and on went Jennifer (with a soft j) Toogood: Gratitude Facilitator, Follower of The Bliss, Third Eye Optometrist—as expanded the captions over the self-narrated video which played automatically upon visiting her name dot com.

'500-hour Certified Yoga Teacher, Fempowered Cacao Shaman, Founder of The Academy of Authenticity, (walking now with eyes closed through a canola field, her two dachshunds playing at her feet), Abundance Amblissador, Mom of Twins, (twirling in the kitchen with toddlers in her arms) Anti-vax Influencer, Honorer of Gender Creativity, Declutterer, Salsa-maker, Freefarter, Life coach.

'Ask yourself: Where will *your* authentic revolution take *you*?

'Sign up beneath this video and receive a *FREE* introductory eBook, *Follow Your Bliss: how to become your own Life Amblissador.*

'Or download my #AbundanceThroughAuthenticity app for daily inspiration: ↓ YES PLEASE!'

At the end of Zen Resort's drive a statue of Ganesh, eyes closed and right palm up, garlanded from ear to belly to ear with orange flowers and tied with white silk at his waist, sat cross-legged atop a mossy pedestal. As the day neared its quiet close the youngest of the family within whose grounds lay Zen Resort neared the bottom of the drive bearing a tray stacked with smaller offerings. Soon she turned to face the trunked remover of obstacles.

Godfrey Lackland had set off to find the nearest store that sold booze, any booze. After a long and confusing day of working through the trifles, incidents, and grotesques that would next week be the first of his India sketches, he could barely concentrate and hardly see and hoped above all to find cold beer.

Down the straight road which led to the drive's entrance there now sped upon a skateboard a lanky man in a loose green shirt, its neck and sleeves unhemmed. A ukulele strapped at his back and miniature keyboard under his arm, the white feather in his felt sun hat fluttered in the wind as he pushed a foot to the pavement to hasten the vehicle beneath him.

The girl placed three small palm-leaf baskets at the base of Ganesh's pedestal and balanced one upon his left knee. She took four incense sticks from her tray and lay one across each of the offerings. Squatting, she splashed the water from a lotus bud over those on the ground then rose to sprinkle the higher as Godfrey Lackland rounded the drive's final corner. 'Komang, sawadee khap, no! Salamat pagi.'

She stopped mid-sprinkle and raised her bowed head and whispered, 'Salamat Pa—.'

Godfrey leapt forward and wrapped his arms around the person on the skateboard; twisted his body so that both fell onto their shoulders. The man squealed as his hat rolled onto the road. 'My feather,' he said, rising to find it gone. He hobbled down the hill to retrieve his skateboard. Coming back up he found that the tie on top of his head had come loose. He slid it off and down his back cascaded a grey-brown sheet of wavy hair.

'You crushed my ukulele.'

'It was either your ukulele or Komang.'

'Gratitude for saving me, bro. I always try to connect with three new people a day. My name's B-rad. Brad. Lé. B-rad-lé.'

'Ahhhh,' said Godfrey, receiving his long limp hand. 'I'm Flackery. Flackery Donglad.'

'Nice, bro, nice. That's Ganesh, right? I'm a Buddhist but I love all manifestations of the divine.'

'*Just* on my way out. But you have a very evening.'

'Love and light bro, you too! Wazzup!,' he said to the girl in the white tunic, returned to the offerings on the ground. She circled the lotus through the screen of incense smoke, bright white in the deepening dusk, and slowly wound infinity knots with its petals as she was photographed from five angles by Bradley Arshat Farquwheat. 'After last year's event exploded my heart and tattooed a rainbow on my soul,' read the paragraph dedicated to him on the retreat's website, 'I knew I had to be back for 2019's Creative Art of Wishfulness.'

'Spoken Word Poet, Photographer, Vegan,' read the as-typed words on the landing page to which his hyperlinked name led, 'Mindful Buddhist, Content Coach, Chaser of the Light, Healthy Masculinity Facilitator, Kindness Pirate, Brotox Advocate, Never Giver Upper, Enthusiastic Uke Player, Deepthroater of Burritos, Betrayal Trauma Survivor, Life coach.

'And here's a list of some of my favourite shit:

'Podcasts, Dung Beetles (these guys literally turn shit into their home, how cool's that!?) Wayfarers, the Bobs (Dylan and Marley), Waterfalls, My Own Poetry (I fucking love what I do), Ethiopian Food, Quitting Your Job, Trying New Things, Original Nintendo, Single Malt Whiskey, Uber.

'Uber's *so* rad! If you sign up and use the code BRADLÉOFTHELIGHT, you'll get $20 worth of FREE rides. AirBnb. AirBnb is super awesome. I've stayed in some amazing places for way less than a hotel and if you sign up using my last name as a code you'll save $50 off your first trip! Do it, it's a badass experience. And remember:

'I believe in the wonderfulness of your dreams.'

Arranged in a groupchat, the three co-facilitators met under the resort's reception in the first, unhot, hour of night. They caught up on how they had lived, on how precisely they had laughed, and on just how much they had loved since last they had seen one another. They said how excited they were for the upcoming week and again and again commented on how amazing it was to be back in Bali— expounded upon both its vibes and its energy and awaited then welcomed the descent from her bungalow of Alexandra Wishart, dot com—her landing page's header a black-and-white image of her pouting over the lifted collar of a trench coat.

In courier font beside and between pictures of typewriters and old libraries and Balinese sunsets and herself in yoga poses: 'Artistpreneur, Renaissance Troublemaker, Creative Artspirationalist.

'Unleasher of Genius. Surgeon of Souls, Redesigner of Lives.

'Head Alchemist on The Creative of Art of Wishfulness© and Warrior-Poet-in-Charge of The Artspiration of the Self©, an online course giving YOU the power to rewrite your life. Join us now by clicking here and share in the artspiration of a whole society of soulful rewriters.

'200-hour Certified Yoga Teacher, Branding Priestess, Love Insurgent, Emotional Freedom Liberator, Birther of Abundance, Brave Soul Midwife, Wild Soul Pilgrim, Photographer, Vegan, Life coach.

'I hope that my journey touches you in some way, and reminds you that you are NOT alone in your journey to self. I believe there are people all over the world who have been apologizing for too long for seeing too far and feeling too deeply and it's the aim of my work to bring those people together as part of The Revolt of the Soulful—a growing movement dedicated wildly to the transformation of the Soul Self.™

'Chances are we've been revolting in a café near you already so why not join us? Walk beside me! While we sound the war-drum of creativity and alchemise the ammunition of our happiness.

'Click here to join this secret society of 50k+ subscribers and receive FREE life prompts, word alchemies, and authentic revolting advice.'

Told to be at dinner at 7, Godfrey walked into the restaurant almost on time and ordered a beer from the waitress at the entrance. He found Alexandra at the balcony overlooking the southern end of the artist's market. With her in high-backed chairs were the other co-facilitators, to whom she proudly introduced him.

'Not Flackery Donglad!' said Bradley, pointing his finger like a gun. He again gave Godfrey his limp hand. 'So nice to create beside you, bro. Love and light.'

'Bradley's our photography expert and he'll be running the Darkness Experience.'

'What's the darkness experience?'

'The Darkness Experience is...' Bradley began then stared. 'When was the last time someone ran their fingers through the knots in your soul? You know?'

'Nope. But it's an interesting question.'

'And Hennifer.'

'The life coach with a soft j!' said Godfrey.

'Yeah, my grandfather's second wife was a mestiza of the Apache people.'

'Cool.'

'Well it's not cool, it's who I am.'

'Who your grandfather's fourth wife was.'

'Second wife. His fourth wife was African American. But I identify with her, so that's who I am.'

'All righty then. It's *very* nice to meet you, Jennifer with a soft j.' His beer arrived with a frozen handle and he ordered another.

'We all know each other already,' said Venerika. 'Tell us about you, Alexandra's been talking about you so much. You're an artist, is that correct?'

'A painter.'

'Do you ever suspect that your voice is a butterfly trapped in the cage of your soul?'

Slowly Godfrey began shaking his head. 'Do you?'

'Sometimes I wish I had no wings,' said Alexandra. 'Just so I'm not scared to trust them.'

Godfrey scrunched his nose and wrinkled his chin.

'Trust the perfection of your wings and you *will* fly,' said Bradley.

'I've lived on the banks of the Ganges River since the turn of the century,' said Jennifer with a soft j. 'Emotions are not weakness.'

'D'you know what a tautology is, Hennifer?' Godfrey said.

'I'm a doctor of joyology,' said Venerika.

'Joy-ology?'

'Have you ever suffered self-love-shaming from an enemy of inclusion? Ever wished that you'd wake up one day amid the gentle hurricane of paradox? So I'm a joyologist.'

'And the wordsmith, right? A tautology's a phrase that says the same thing twice, superfluously. A waste of breath.' He pointed an index finger to Jennifer with a soft j. 'You said you lived on the banks of the Ganges River.'

'Since the turn of the century. We each create our own enoughness.'

'You don't have to say "river", you see? There's no other

Ganges. You can't live on the banks of the Ganges Equine Psychiatrist's. Can't be curing horses of low self-esteem there.'

'So let's play an ice-breaking game,' said Hennifer, hoping to retrieve the conversation from Godfrey's frivolous, and frankly quite insulting, hands. 'This game I call Acknowledging Confidence. I want everyone to walk around the restaurant and to bring to our table the person you think is the most confident person in the room. Then we're going to introduce our person to the rest of the table and talk about *why* we thought they were confident and discuss what we can learn from them, OK? Ready?'

All except Godfrey nodded.

'Go.'

Four chairs slid out and Godfrey darted his head around as they dispersed about the restaurant. As his second beer arrived a familiar sound came through speakers. He recognised Big Bill Broonzy's guitar, jumping as it was finger-picked.

Soon Bradley brought over a young woman with her hair in a bun, almost his height, wearing a green dress with a low unhemmed neck, a trio of white feathers tattooed onto her shoulder. 'I promise it'll be fine,' he said as he implored her to take his seat. Overhead the guitar gave way to an interlude of rising voice: '*Long as there's just the two of us, have the world and its charm,*' as upstairs Alexandra convinced a young woman to come down to her table. Venerika brought over and invited to sit an older man with grey stubble, very visibly wide-shouldered underneath the strings of a grey kind of barely-there shirt.

'*Baby now, win just a little, lose a little, sometime have the blues just a little, but…*'

As Alexandra's young woman crossed the restaurant's floor the music changed without pause or break to jazz, Benny Goodman's clarinet taking up and over the melody. Olive-skinned, her curly dark hair streaked with caramel, its thickness tied behind her head—round-cheeked and big-eyed, thin and muscular beneath a loose and flowing dress—her movements and posture dampened by the shyness of youth—the girl sat and looked at Venerika's man, at Bradley's woman, and at last at Godfrey, to whom she raised a very suspicious eyebrow.

'Who have brought you here?'

'I didn't, ah… Nobody. I'm actually at the table.'

'You are not joining in the weird game?'

'I ahh…' Godfrey looked straight ahead and mumbled at the

side of his mouth: 'I'm being held against my will.'

'Should I call your embassy?' the girl whispered. Godfrey nodded with bulging eyes. 'Where are you from? If you're Israeli I can have a helicopter here in fifteen minutes. Blink twice if you're Israeli.'

Godfrey held his eyes open wide and quivered his head as though refusing pie.

'British? Maybe James Bond is nearby. He can come and sweep you off your feet. No? Don't tell me Australian.' Godfrey looked down to the table and nodded. 'One of those, huh? Why come you are not wearing a vest shirt and no tattoos?'

'Because I'm civilized,' he whispered across to her. 'Why aren't you in fisherman pants eating a tofu burger?'

'Because I'm not American.'

'All right!' said Jennifer with a soft j, returning alone to the table. 'Today's World Hijab Day.'

'Romanian?'

'You think I am a gypsy?' the girl whispered.

'Your accent is strange,' Godfrey informed her.

'So *I* didn't bring anyone over, because I wanted to watch how everyone else interacted. But now that we do have our confident persons here I'll just ask Godfrey why he's the only one alone at the table.'

'I umm… I'm probably the most confident person in the room.'

'Australian,' the girl whispered, Alexandra holding excitedly on to the back of her chair.

'Well, as much as it deflates the exercise, Godfrey's right. You *all* should be the most confident person in the room. The exercise is designed to help you recognize the symptoms of confidence and to be able to describe them *so* you can absorb them. Alexandra, why did you bring this lovely young lady over?'

All eyes turned to her, the girl put her hands in her lap and lowered her head then looked up and across to Godfrey.

'I saw her up there from a distance, alone, but she had this ancient air of dignity, like it was her *choice* to be alone and she would *only* allow company if it was exceptional. As I got closer I saw she wasn't on her phone like everyone else but she was reading a book, and when I said hello I could tell instantly that she's smart and confident and a really strong woman, you know? It's in her eyes. Her cheeks look like she was always smiling and she has this gorgeous Mediterranean hair like a Greek poetess. But she doesn't flaunt any of it, she just knows.'

'Oh, our food's here!' said Jennifer with a soft j. 'That's annoying. Umm, well I guess we can talk about confidence without you lovely people. Thanks so much for playing along, and for coming over. Sorry to disturb.'

Bradley's woman and Venerika's man pushed their chairs back and stood.

'I can go now?' said the girl to Alexandra behind her.

'Thank you so much,' said Alexandra. 'I hope I didn't interrupt your dinner.'

'No, it was a compliment I guess. Thank you?' As she stood she whispered to Godfrey, 'Good luck with your escape,' and returned to her table. The music was again a frolicking guitar as she sat back down. She looked down to Godfrey, still watching her, and smiled and shook her head.

'Godfrey,' said Alexandra.

He uncraned his neck. 'What's up?'

'We're…' Alexandra rounded her chin from bowl to identical bowl. The co-facilitators had closed their eyes and held their palms an inch from their dinners.

'What am I eating? I didn't order anything, I just want beer.'

'These are the best abundance bowls in Ubud. Ready?' Alexandra closed her eyes and put her hands over her food and with the others sat upright and silent. Godfrey looked up at the girl. With his palms up and joined at the pinkies he shrugged his shoulders. She lifted her chin and smiled. He closed his eyes and put his hands an inch above his beer. Then he watched Alexandra's closed eyes as he licked his finger and slid it under her hand, over the edge of her bowl and into her hummus. The girl's hair came up and over as she bent forward with laughter. Her forehead almost hit the tablecloth as Godfrey sucked his fingertip.

'Retreat selfie?' Bradley eventually said. Alexandra looked at Godfrey. He snapped his rejoined hands to over his abundance bowl. Bradley twisted in his chair and extended a stick so as to be able capture the whole table in his phone's screen. 'Say cashew cheese!'

Godfrey shook his head and again smiled up at the girl.

'Really?' said Alexandra.

'You picked good.'

'Ha,' Alexandra feebly moaned. She stuck the end of her spoon into the intensity of her hummus and folded her smashed avocado into her quinoa.

'I could barely concentrate.'

Alexandra pressed her tongue into the back of her bottom lip and stabbed at her maca with enough vigour to clunk her cutlery into the bottom of the bowl. 'Haa,' she moaned again, softly and slowly.

After a brief discussion about how they could all always be their best and most awesomest selves they again returned to inquiring of the one facilitator with whom none had previously worked.

'Do you *like* Alfreda Primrose?' said Venerika.

'Is that a person?'

'Her fractals of consciousness? Those pillows!'

'Oh my, those pillows!' said Alexandra with her hand at her sternum.

'What's a fractal?'

'You've never seen an Alfred Primrose pillow?'

'She sounds most uninteresting.'

'Alexandra says you're a real artist,' said Jennifer with a soft j. 'But how come I've never heard of you?'

'Strong question. Real art's been forced underground, to lie dormant until the state ceases to be its biggest patron while also its chief cause and censor. Art's dead for the next little while.'

'What about Teng Hi Hien though?' said B-rad.

'Never heard of him. Is it a him?'

'He creates these installations that—'

'I'm not interested in these artists so-called, they don't exist to me.'

'This sounds like hatespeech.' said Jennifer with a soft j. 'Did you know chickens can count to five?'

'Their graffiti is pointless novelty or propaganda and they're nonentities so far as real art is concerned. They're interested in comfort and rights and democracy. Art is fascist, it relies on subjection, it's a bastard, and any artist who talks about rights is a communist, consciously or no.'

'Bro, you're not famous. How can you say what is and isn't real art?'

'It *is* Bradley, right?'

'B-rad. Lé.'

'You a drinker, B-rat?'

'I love single malt whiskey.'

'Shall we have one? Two?'

'Sounds awesome, brah.'

Godfrey ordered five rums from the waitress. Alexandra declined hers and Venerika and Jennifer, outraged by opinions contrary to their own, excused themselves to walk back to the resort.

'You seem so authentic,' Bradley said.

'It's refreshing, right?' said Alexandra, excited that he saw in Godfrey one of the things she most liked about him.

'Authenticity's the only logical decision, you know why? If you're not authentic, you have to spend so much time on your mask. By being authentic you free up so much space to fill with love and beauty and fun and giggles, and all kinds of sparkly and glittery sunshiney things like rainbows and unicorns.* Cheers to authenticity.'

'Wow,' said Godfrey and drank. He caught the movement of the girl upstairs as she rose from her table. She lifted her hand to Godfrey in a slight wave as she descended. Godfrey held up his second rum to her and tracked her exit with his lowered forehead. When very soon Bradley passed out Alexandra asked the waitress if she could call them a taxi.

'So I should mention…'

'Uh huh?' Godfrey tapped at Bradley's outfacing cheeks.

'I have one rule while we're co-creating.'

'Uh huh.'

'No romantic relationships, inside *or* outside the retreat.'

'Uh huh.' With a fist he tapped Bradley in his vertical jaw. 'He's fast asleep.'

'I need you focused on your work, on the product, on giving the people starting with us tomorrow *the* most awesomest retreat they've ever been on. Are you listening?'

'Always.'

'I especially need the testimonials to be exceptional. I just wanted to get that rule out in the open and onto the table. Hopefully the stars have heard so it it'll change the vibrations I've been feeling.'

'Speaking of onto the table, let's get him off it.'

They lifted Bradley out of his chair and put each an arm around their neck and wet-noodled him down the restaurant's front steps and into the taxi.

---

* This is something that one of the many males upon whom this character is based has said. In real life. While sober. Without a sense of irony, sarcasm, or with any intended derision whatsoever.

'Where do you think she was from?' said Godfrey as immediately they settled into traffic.

Alexandra's face was white-lit by her phone screen. 'Four are there already,' she read, 'two arrive at the same time in an hour.'

'Did you ask her?'

'The last guest arrives tomorrow at four am and we have soul profiles at nine, so… Oh, he's going to be tired for our first day.'

'Alexandra?'

'Mm hm?' she said without looking up.

'Where do you think she's from?'

'What?'

'The girl you brought to the table.'

'Can you give me one second? I have to read this.'

'She had this energy. You felt it, right? Like everything came alive when she was there. Younger even.'

'Ha,' said Alexandra in that slow and feeble way.

'She *was* young though. I wonder where she was from. Greek? Sicilian? Those cheeks, I couldn't concentrate when she spoke. I could just hear music. The sounds of the city baby,' Godfrey sang. 'Seem to disappear, oh-o and…'

In a single swift movement Alexandra locked her phone and put it in her handbag and opened the car door and repeated her feeble, 'Ha-a,' and disappeared into the market.

'I can hear music… Looks like it's just you and me, donkeyclown.' Godfrey slapped the back of his hand into Bradley's dangling head. 'Hope you've got money in your pockets, because I do not.'

ACT THREE

The Creative Art of Wishfulness®

I

Alexandra Wishart, in the red dress with the yellow hibiscus tied at her neck, hurried down the aisle which divided the long-occupied chairs of Zen Resort's taupe-walled conference room.

'Sorry I'm late, sorry I'm late. I just had to make a last-minute change to your Dreambinders. Good morning everyone!' She pushed a stack of thin plastic-bound booklets into Godfrey's hands and said, 'Could you pass those out for me?'

She sat in the plastic chair vacant at the front of the room and sighed with relief at having at last arrived; looked to the red lanterns hanging from the teak roof then turned to inspect the banner draped across the back wall—a pink and red picture of a hilltop split gate with, 'Your Life is Your Art, Your Art is Your Life,' in enormous capital letters. Godfrey passed the booklets out to the larger semicircle of chairs then had his co-facilitators pass them along. Her breath caught, Alexandra cleared her throat and leaned her elbows onto her thighs and began from her seat.

'Welcome to The Creative Art of Wishfulness, in Ubud, Bali. We're now in the Abundance Hall. Most of you will have eaten breakfast in the Spirit Restaurant and later today I'll show you where the Pride Pavilion is as well as the Sanctuary of Truth and the Life Enema Closet. Isn't Zen Resort so beautiful?'

The seven people facing her moaned and sighed and tilted their heads in concurrence. She put her palm to her chest and continued.

'I'm Alexandra Wishart, artistpreneur, renaissance troublemaker, creative artspirationalist, and head alchemist at The Creative of Art of Wishfulness, which is a registered trademark. Thank you *all* for coming to Bali to take the first steps in re-inspire your souls, and for trusting *me* to unleash your genius, to birth the creator inside you, and to revolutionise your life.

'This morning I'll introduce our co-creators then get you guys to introduce *your*-selves, then our astonishing week begins with our very first workshop, Wishful Alchemy.'

Alexandra swung out her right wrist. 'First we have Venerika Odorono. Word weaver, vagablonde, and New York Times Bestselling Poet. Some of you may know her as Rainbow Wordslut or Thug Unicorn, she's the purposeful creator of Write Yourself Free, and this week she'll be giving a seminar on Wishful Words, exploring how changing our language can awaken our brave soul lives.'

'Alexandra, can I just say?' Venerika slid forward in her chair.

'Of course.'

'It's a registered trademark, Write Yourself Free. And I'll actually be awakening our brave soul muses, this week, not our brave soul lives.'

'Oh that's right,' said Alexandra. 'Awakening your brave soul muse, through the spoken and written word. Here we have Hennifer Toogood. 500-hour certified yoga teacher and founder of The Academy of Authenticity, which is a registered trademark. Hennifer's going to be our yoga instructor for the week—we have yoga every morning at sunrise in the Pagoda of Perpetual Peace— and on Wednesday she'll give her workshop on creating abundance through authenticity.'

Gentle applause as Alexandra swung out her left.

'And Godfrey Lackland, Godfrey's a story-painter, a daring Renaissance man and a noble-risk-taking creativity counsellor. His art is truly amazing and very soon he'll be world famous, he has an agent showing his work to Zac Efron. Godfrey's usually travelling the world with his art so we're *very* honored to have him here, to teach us how to turn our pain, our ambition, all our wild imaginations—into authentic purposeful creativity.'

'Thanks, Alexandra!' said Godfrey, his unexpected volume startling the entire room. 'Super excited to be here. And to have Zac Ephraim looking at my paintings. Which we all know is the first benchmark of creative success.'

'And last but not least, Bradley Farquwheat: spoken word poet, photographer, and purposeful creator of The Darkness Experience.'

Dim-eyed and in a great deal of pain above his David Bowie t-shirt, B-rad lifted a hand and grinned and waved.

'Bradley leads a workshop called The Art of the Selfie and he's here to give you any coaching you might need on Buddhism, life, content, or the ukulele—and on Wednesday afternoon we have his Darkness Experience.'

'So grateful,' he said, and put his joined palms to his nose.

'All of us here are highly qualified life-coaches, except for Godfrey, who's thinking about getting his certificate?'

'Thinking about it certainly!' Godfrey yelled as though responding to orders.

'And this week we're going to lead you *together* on an amazing adventure of art therapy, yoga and meditation, and empowering life design, so let's get started! The first thing I want us to do is for you guys to introduce *your*-selves. This part I call our Soul Profiles. We're about to go on a journey together, and if you briefly introduce yourselves and give a short Soul Profile of yourself, a bit about your life-adventure so far and why you're in Bali for this self-creation experience—would you like to go first?'

The man in the chair closest to Alexandra's right wrist nodded twice and said, 'Sure. Hi everyone.' He leaned forward to make eye contact with his own semicircle, then with Alexandra, and at greatest length with Godfrey. 'I'm Donny Vossehol. United States Marine, First Sergeant UAV Pilot. I think I'm in Bali because I never got the mental health support that I needed in the service. After four recurring bedsores I was medically discharged with debilitating sciatica and I went to Tibet and to Thailand and explored I think a dozen nature-based feminine-led belief systems? But I've come to Bali to find a guru. I've been following Alexandra for a long time now and I figured Bali, and 2019, was the perfect time and place to find that guru.'

'Thank you, Donny. I hope we can set you on the right path to finding your guru.'

Though Donny had been thanked by Alexandra, he stared still at Godfrey. With subtle gestures of head and neck Godfrey implored him to look elsewhere.

'And you, would you like to go next?'

The woman to Donny's right opened her eyes very widely and drew her chin into her neck. 'OK, I guess that's me! Hi all, I'm Michelle Trinity Dillika. You can call me M.T. I guess I'm here on a soul vacation. Or a vacation from my soul,' she smiled. 'I've spent the last ten years in the same job, forestry management, and in my spare time I try to follow all the things that bring my heart happiness. Lately though I haven't been hearing much at all from God, in the way of direction, or kind of… warning me against large purchases. So like Donny I follow Alexandra, and I just, when I saw her Bali promotion I knew that if I followed my heart's will, just like Alexandra said I should, then I'd come to this amazing beautiful country, and I'm hoping to re-find some direction. That's…' She nodded as she looked around the room. '…I guess that's it.'

'Thank you, M.T., that was lovely. I hope we can reconnect you with the Divine Energy you mentioned. Maybe you can work with Hennifer this week on your soul map? A soul map reorients the self, directs it to creating the voices you *want* to hear, rather than those that want you to hear *them*.'

'That would be so awesome.'

'I'll go next? Hi all, I'm Nancy Dwight-Blamey,' said the next woman along, though she seemed not to pronounce the 'd'. 'I use my grandmothers' maiden names. I'm a sociologist, I have a PhD in patriarchal structures of pre-invasion rape-cultures. I've already led two lives that I know of for sure. In one I was a concubine, drowned by my owner, and in the other I was a witch, burned at the stake by Christianity. A lot of my work goes into healing the human race *from* the devastation of the witch-hunts, and I lecture actually in Melbourne on treating intergenerational trauma. I guess I'm in Bali, I follow Hennifer—I didn't know it was a soft j, sorry—I follow Hennifer, and I just felt like now's the time for me to discover and start living my *third* life.'

'So nice to have you, Nancy,' said Jennifer with a soft j. 'I've looked into my past life regression. I was burnt at the stake too.' She seemed excited by the shared immolations. 'After being subjected to trial by water.'

'We have so much to talk about.'

'Fairchild McMonnies is my name,' said the next person along. 'I was raised in the jungle, I'm one of those real-life Mowglis you hear about. My parents lost me to a pack of wolves when I was three, and after the wolves got me through infancy I was found and adopted by a band of gorillas. So by eleven I'd lost most of my English, except of course for the words 'I want' and 'I need'. But yes, eventually I was rediscovered by a group of tourists on safari and—'

'Sorry, can I just ask?' said Alexandra. 'This is an incredible story, you ran with the wolves?'

'They were pack-stalks mostly, but there was a bit of running towards the end. I was only with the wolves till I was six though, so I couldn't really keep up. I'd stay back more and have the kills brought to me.'

'I can't believe you ran with the wolves!'

'Shall I go on?'

'Of course, please.'

'So yeah, I was rediscovered by a safari and brought back to human civilization. I went to Cambridge and Princeton but I got expelled from both, actually, for stealing. I'm a recovering kleptomaniac, 12 years. I'd steal, and I'd take and I'd deceive but I would always blame externals—my upbringing, my eight years with the gorillas, my superior intelligence. But anyway I got scouted just before I left Princeton by London's biggest vulture fund and that's still where I work, I've just taken a month off for Bali to take a closer look at my kleptomania and to I think reconnect with my creative side, which I associate with childhood, which I missed out on, being raised by so many tribal, predatory mammals.'

'I just can't believe you ran with the wolves!' said Alexandra. 'But welcome. We're so glad to have you here and I think Godfrey's insights into creativity, and into how his imagination works, will be really really helpful for you.'

Godfrey looked up from his notes and clicked his tongue between his teeth and winked at Fairchild McMonnies. Usually he would have been holding in a succession of wide and desperate yawns. He disliked people talking about themselves and could think of few things more tiresome than expounding upon the agglomeration of excuses which most seemed to think made a personality. Eleven people in a circle enthusing over one another's soul journeys should have sent him striding out of the Abundance Hall with muted screams of fury. This all had the glimmer of discovered gold. He was practically having his pictures painted for him, and had been hurrying to take notes since Alexandra's introduction of Venerika Odorono.

The scribbling of, 'A gangster unicorn at the trademark office beside Rocksteady,' was quickly followed by, 'Typewriter alarm clock,' which somehow led to, 'Che Guevara liberating people's emotions,' and, 'A yoghurt teacher? Teaching yoghurt, or yoghurt teaching kids. About what?' then a quick sketch of a Lenin shrine to perpetual peace. Soon were added a drone coming for the Dalai Lama and a bulldozer shaving God's beard then Lancelot shouting 'More Witches! Gorillas standing behind guitars and sitting at drums as the Beatles,' and, 'the Monopoly guy suckling at the

Capitoline Wolf,'—as Godfrey's Dreambinder became a quickly filling extension of his 11-staved notebook.

'And you?' said Alexandra to the man in fisherman pants and white t-shirt. He looked by far the youngest of the group.

'My name's Felix Piddling, hi. I'm a painter, actually—Godfrey, I'm sure we have a lot to talk about. I'm extremely successful, my work's hanging in Zac's entrance hall, actually, above the statue of Zac himself. I'd be more than happy to talk to him for you. As a painter I love colours, colours are the smiles of nature. I especially love colours that change colour but they're still the same colour but different. Zac has a painting of mine called Green and Brown in his loggia. Hugh, too, has my Wenge Pink Purple. Umm... and I guess I'm in Bali *for* the colours. I have a level now of financial freedom that means I can travel in this way where each experience is an opportunity to stay at a place like this and connect and grow with lovely colourful people.'

'Colours?' Godfrey yelled without looking up.

'I just love 'em, you know? When I started painting, I thought, paint what you love, and people would be drawn to that. And I *love* colours, they're the smiles of nature. Pink, green, yellow! I mean, blue! Godfrey, am I right? And when I won the National Endowment for the Arts award with my Red and Red and Yellow, I got some exposure and half a million in prize money and that's how Tom found me, then Hugh, and then Zac. So yeah. I'm looking forward to all the workshops and connecting with everyone's hues. Especially you Godfrey, a kindred seafoam spirit.'

'Thank you, Felix,' said Alexandra.

'You're greenly welcome!'

'And you? I love your dress!'

'Thank you!' The young woman beside Felix Piddling grabbed at her yellow sun dress printed with blue lilacs. 'So I'm Ne'cole. N-e-apostrophe-c-o-l-e, Shartz. And I'm here today with you, because I am worn out. I'm spent. Exhausted. I run, or I did run for years, wellness retreats, two of them here in Bali actually and one in Morocco, and for years I just emptied myself. I gave so much time to helping others that the aloneness—you know?—ended up getting to me. And what I realised after I tried to off myself the second time was that I'd actually started out *with* nothing to give. I was already empty—you see?—when I started the retreats, and I know now that I started them for the wrong reasons, and running them for all those years I gave away so much that I went into the red. And the loneliness of that space, never realising that I was already empty, led me to self-harm.'

Her hand had for a long time been at her chest. So had been that of Ne'cole Shartz. 'Red's not a good colour,' said Felix.

'Right!? So I'm in Bali. I started following Alexandra just after she started following me. I love what she does, I think she has *so* much to contribute, her authenticity shines from every word, and I thought, why not go on one of these retreats myself!?'

'I feel like I'm going to cry,' said Alexandra.

'Oh, me too,' said Ne'cole, a single tear amassing at their eyes.

'…Summers in Rangoon, luge lessons—in the spring we'd make meat helmets. Mowgli as a vulture in a three-piece suit and Jack Ephraim as Canova's Napoleon—Who *is* Jack Ephraim?' and 'Secret Rainbow Man—a superhero with eyes and palms giving ecstacising beams of refracted light,' then, 'Someone sharting into a headless neck…'

'Thank you, *so* much,' said Alexandra. 'I really hope we can rejuvenate you and fill you all the way back up with—'

'Shit,' Godfrey mumbled, scribbling over the severed head in his Dreambinder.

'What?' said Alexandra.

'Sorry, just taking notes. I forgot something I was thinking about earlier.'

'And you? Sorry to leave you till last.'

'Turbot Slurritrend,' said the woman without fuss. 'I'm the son and daughter of Gandhi and Sylvia Plath. I believe we all have the right to choose our parents. My name used to be Sluggy La Trine, but I didn't identify with by birth names. We all have the right to choose our own names. I'm from Freedonia. Some of you might not have heard of it yet, it's a young country. We all have the right to choose the country we're from, so I fly on three passports, one's Incan, I really connected with Machu Picchu when I was there, and one's Freedonian. I recently had my vagina reconstructed. I was misgendered of course, from a young age, and did *not* identify with the genital configuration I was born with. So eight years ago I transitioned. Got the clitoris, the hormones for the breasts, a very curious boyfriend and went to a few raves. But then four years ago I started to really get back in touch with my birth gender. I consulted some lawyers and exercised my right to choice, and I had a penis located from an organ donor and had that reattached. Prosthetic testicles, et cetera, et cetera, and started shaving again, and it just felt so good. For a while. I realised it was actually gender norms and social constructs that were forcing me into wanting to regress. So I made the first steps again and I'm having my vagina reconstructed as we speak. It's a process. Foreskin to clitoris, shaft into labia. It's a battle, and yes, my current genital configuration isn't pretty, not in a conventional sense. It looks kind of like an oyster inside a tomato growing a midget's thumb. But I guess that's why I'm here.'

For the first time since Fairchild's Soul Profile Godfrey looked up from his notes. He detected no one else alike tensing their stomach in order to hold back laughter.

'I feel like, being so privileged, that I need my privilege checked. And I thought Bali and this resort would be the perfect place to be reminded of that privilege, and to work on my self-confidence and to really fall back in love with my genitals. I've actually just started reading Glovindria's new book after Alexandra recommended it.'

'My God, isn't that book *amazing*?' said Nancy Dwight-Blamey and Ne'cole Shartz and Donny Vossehol and Felix Piddling and M.T. Dillika.

'Really I hope this retreat helps me to stop doubting my greatness.'

'I'm sure it will,' said Alexandra. 'Thank you so so much. My heart's already so full having only just met you, I can't *wait* to connect with you more and to take you on this amazing adventure of art therapy, yoga and meditation, and empowering life design.' She stood and held her booklet in the air. 'So you all have your Dreambinders. This morning I'm going to introduce you to Wishful Alchemy.

'What *is* alchemy?' A seriousness now seemed to overtake her. Standing, she became stern and meticulously animated.

'Alchemy is you touching my arm and it setting fire to my soul. Alchemy is you owning your awesome, and howling to the moon that you are *not* too much. Alchemy… is a tsunami of authenticality that washes away the creative blocks in your life and leaves you standing there as your true self so the universe can find you!

'This week I'm going to teach you how to honour your hunger, how to not be a creative person but a creative *gladiator*. We're all going to show you how to redraw the map of your soul's adventure and start living vicariously through yourself. We'll show *you*, that the self is the guide to the self, and through direct perception we can all work out our own salvation.

'From now on I want you *only* doing things that you're

passionate about, things that so ensorcell you that you forget to eat and sleep. Let other people do what they want! If you're doing what you love, it doesn't *matter* what anyone else does. You should be doing what *you* love, and what you love should be yourself—so in love with yourself that you forget to eat and sleep! Narcissism is not a disorder anymore, it's healthy! We used to think smoking was good for us and narcissism bad. Well there are new doctors in town, doctors that speak *our* truth, to *us*.

'We *all* have pain that we live in our truth. But you *write* your truth *when* you live it. You create your freedom, when you give it freely to others, and then the universe gives it back to you abundantly. So where does that pain fit into your freedom?'

None seemed to know. Perhaps that was why they were here.

'*This* is alchemy.'

'Ah,' said Ne'cole Shartz.

'Your pain is not your problem, your pain is your purpose. And alchemy… is turning your pain into your purpose and your purpose into your life. Wishful! Alchemy, is creating your art *from* your life and your life from your art. Wishful Alchemy, is taking the rich Virgin Earth of your story and imbibing it sprinklingly with dew gathered from the greenest fields of your summer heart!

'So we come to our first exercise. I want you all to turn to page one of your Dreambinder and you'll see seven headings. Spiritual, Mental, Vocational, Financial, Familial, Social, Physical. I want you to write, in each of those areas, because writing things down *initiates* action—if you write it, you *will* live it—I want you to write under each of these headings what you want to *have*, what you want to *do*, and what you want to *be,* in those areas. For example, under spiritual I would write that I want to *have* contentment, that I want to *do* more yoga, that I want to *be* at peace.'

Godfrey interrupted his note-taking and turned from the middle of his Dreambinder to its front. He wrote almost without thinking: 'HAVE it all, DO Monica Bellucci, BE elsewhere.'

'And these will become your passion points. What you've written, by Wishful Alchemy—'

Very shortly Godfrey was unable to control his sniffled giggle. 'Sorry,' he said to Alexandra, stopped mid-sentence to inspect his enjoyment. 'Just remembered something funny. Sorry.' He pointed his pen down to the Dreambinder on his crossed leg and straightened his face and returned to the booklet's middle.

'What you've written, by Wishful Alchemy, *becomes* what you live.'

'Groucho Marx at Machu Picchu,' Godfrey's notes ran on, and, 'A midget trying to catch an oyster in a tomato, the fruit stuck upright on his thumb like little Jack Horner who'd pulled out his plum.' There followed the written fact that you'd die if you only did things that made you forget to eat and sleep and a question mark beside both sets of genitalia in the same groin and Narcissus watching himself smoke cigarettes and, 'What the fuck does ensorcell mean? She really doesn't want us to sleep,' then, 'a pain porpoise beating the shit out of a depression dolphin.'

Godfrey had been nervous of impressing on the retreat and had come to Bali prepared to work. Always dedicated to the task at hand, he also always excelled at it, even when that task was giving suggestions on how to market travel insurance to young men with low rather than high self esteem. At his own introduction he saw in a flash what this all was. Unrelated to logic or reason, even to language, ungrounded in anything approaching reality—Godfrey Lackland was relieved to discover that he would not have to pay very much attention at all, that his usual concern for structure and subtle-threaded theme—those aspects of his art whose planning and execution required nothing short of a trance of concentration—had no comprehensible place in the Abundance Hall of Zen Resort, Bali. He would simply have to pass the time.

He glanced at the prospectus behind the Dreambinder's title page. The Creative Art of Wishfulness, five days. Two doses of Wishful Alchemy, one of Wishful Words, yoga he could avoid, the Art of The Selfie he would attend as research, Abundance Through Authenticity he'd be sick for and he could write his creativity workshop—how much could these people know about it?—the night before he was to give it. 'The Darkness Experience,' nope. A Creation Day, whatever that was; a Day of the Elements, a Water Purification Ritual, a Fire Ceremony, and done. He would simply have to pass the time.

'And now that you've written your Have's, your Do's and your Be's, I'm going to introduce you to something called The Ten Demandments.'

Then India, and his work as an artist.

'You'll see the first one's already written for you. It's the beginning of Wishful Alchemy: Love Thyself.'

Perhaps Bali would some day be a joy recalled.

'The inner peace that *I* experienced after acknowledging that I *am* complete,' said Alexandra, her voice fading from consciousness as Godfrey returned to his notes to write, 'Hulk Hogan elbow-dropping a Decalogue.'

'Right now, exactly as I am, radically changed my world.'

To endure, and keep himself for days of painting.

At a long table draped in red velvet and upon folding wooden chairs, unable to enjoy the evening air for the white of the spotlights beaming from the restaurant's eaves and unable, for the sound of rattling cymbals and shaking bells and shrieking bamboo whistles, to hear either the trickle of the infinity pool or the rustling of jungle beyond it—the facilitators and newly wishful alchemists of The Creative Art of Wishfulness held each a flowered ear to the stage set up in front of a hotels restaurant's empty dining pavilion.

Overlooked by five floors of golden-lit balcony, two dancers in pink saris gilded at their hems and overwrapped in yellow, whirled and spun and shuffled back and forth between two red umbrellas. With their left hands bent unnaturally backwards and fingers held to an orchid-point they occasionally strewed flowers from a bowl onto the stage.

Seemingly mid-performance they ducked and scurried backstage and the music began to slow. When it was replaced by enthusiastic applause two columns of waiter came down from the pavilion to cover the length of the table in vegetarian Balinese food—cones of rice and fringed leaves and skewers of lemongrass and lime wedges and red chillies and floretted cucumbers and wet brown and shining yellow.

'Now in Bali,' said Alexandra, standing as though to give another presentation, 'it's tradition to form a relationship between your food and your spirit before you eat. If you'd all hold your hands together just an inch over the dish closest to you… And close your eyes… Very good, and breathe in, and *feel* the sacrifice the earth has made to feed you.'

Godfrey, the only with his eyes still open, wrinkled his chin and frowned.

'And breathe out… Grateful for the abundance you've created—breathe in. Excited for the greater abundance you *will* create.'

Still the only with his eyes open, Godfrey now watched the entrance onto the restaurant terrace of the girl from last night. A waitress led her down a parallel row of red-clothed tables. Her high-collared white shirt floated at the intricacies of her neck; a long grey skirt printed with brown feathers made her look taller than she was. Invited to sit in the chair nearest the pool, as she rocked from leg to leg along the aisle she looked the restaurant over. Quickly she caught sight of Godfrey, leaning out from Alexandra's upright body three tables and five chairs distant. She lowered her head and smirked, impressed at seeing again the captive among his captors. He paraded a hand to his left, imploring her to take in the eleven people forming relationships with their food. She smiled and pointed to him and shook her head; put her hands together over the tablecloth and closed her eyes; pointed and shook her head again as a question.

Godfrey shook his own; she mouthed, 'Why not?'

'Stupid,' said Godfrey as Alexandra opened her eyes. She bulged them at him as she sat. 'Beer, Alexandra?'

'Alcohol's a fool's poison.'

'Is it!? When did we decide that?'

'Please participate.'

'I am farticipating!'

'So Alexandra,' said Ne'cole Shartz, across and two seats down from her. 'Tell us! When did you first come to Bali? What made you decide to hold a retreat here? We all wanna know!'

'I actually first came here on one of your retreats.'

'Oh my God, you did?'

'Do you remember the one you were too stressed to come to? But you sent out the nicest email explaining why and you gave us Stevia Flunt instead. She was so amazing. That's where I met Hennifer too actually.'

'Oh, of course! And you know, pulling out of that retreat inspired my fourth demandment? To stop giving so much of myself when there's just so little to give.'

'Such a beautiful demandment,' said Jennifer with a soft j. 'No amount of earthing is too much earthing.'

'It's a true one,' said Alexandra. 'I can feel it. I'd rather write one true sentence than get a degree. How about you, Nancy? Would you like to share one of your demandments?'

Nancy read from a small notepad kept always in her khaki breast pocket. 'I demand to stop running around in circles at the edge of a volcano, only to fall into the crater when I trip on your virginal sacrifice.'

'Wow,' said Venerika, comprehending her precisely.

'To struggle *and* to sparkle,' said Turbot Slurritrend.

'Is that one of yours?' said Alexandra.

'I think so. Or to sparkle *and* to struggle.'

'I will demand to live a fulvous life after the strawpocalypse.'

'So Felix,' Alexandra said. 'You *are* demanding. It's so much more powerful in the present tense.'

'I *am* demanding to live a fulvous life after the strawpocalypse? Oh, I see!'

'Love will be a pair of scissors that you're begging me to run with,' said M.T..

'I know that,' said Bradley, smiling and pointing at her.

'You should! I've been following your spoken-word poetry for years. Your truth touches me in the eyes, but in a way that it's like my eyes are the nipples of my face.'

'What can I say?' said Bradley, grinning and pointing the ends of all his fingers upwards. 'I'm fluent in silence.'

Endure, for days of painting.

When forks and spoons were lowered all and alike wishful alchemists and facilitators began excusing themselves to begin the uphill stroll back to the resort, Godfrey ordered five rums.

'No, no,' said Donny Vossehol beside him. 'That's enough for me tonight.'

'You had a beer,' said Godfrey, lifting his empty bottle from the table.

'Alcohol's not included in our shared dinners,' said Alexandra.

'Don't worry, I'll take care of it,' Godfrey said in mock de Niro, tapping his temple with the side of his fingertip.

'Trying to impress your bimbo?'

'My what?'

'I see you looking at her.'

'I'm looking at you. Or do you mean the smart, confident woman with the ancient dignity and the hair of a Greek poetess?'

'I have to use the ladies'.'

'I'm gonna hit the hay,' said Donny, standing to push his chair in. 'Today was empowering but exhausting. I'll see y'all for yoga, 6am?'

Donny walked beside Alexandra towards the pavilion until she veered into the restaurant and he disappeared into the alley which led to the main street.

Their fields of vision unobstructed, Godfrey waved his arms in two crossed arcs. Quickly he had the girl's attention. He waved her over; she shook her head. He nodded and insisted—tapped at the vacant space beside himself and said, 'Have a seat,' as she neared. He stood and told her his name.

'Or.'

Godfrey turned his head sideways then looked back at her. 'Or what?'

'Idiot, my name is Or.'

'Like o-r-e? Is your dad a miner?'

'Like aleph, vav, resh, you moose.'

'What are you talking about?'

'O-r. It's Hebrew.'

'Israeli! I was wondering where you were from.'

'Detective Godfrey.'

Alexandra returned from the bathroom. 'Oh. Hello again.'

'I'm selected for one of your experiments again.'

'They're not experiments, they're soulcersises. But I think we were all just leaving actually. And we are kind of together.'

'The Creative Art of Wishfulness,' Godfrey announced as though it were a bout.

Alexandra drew with one hand an oval around the table. 'As in, a private group.'

'Oh, I'm sorry, I didn't know.'

'That's OK, Godfrey should have told you. It's just, we're talking about private and personal things and it's a safe space of non-judgment.'

'Wait, what's the problem?' said Godfrey. 'Donny left, Turgid's not here. It's just B-rad and Venerika.'

'Yeah, you're fine,' said Venerika. 'I *like* your name. Or. It has so much potential, you know? Like the divine choice. Mine's Venerika.' She held up and out her hand.

'No,' said Alexandra, feigning reluctance. 'It's kind of not OK.'

'Alexandra!' said Godfrey dispensing shot glasses. 'Surely our very long table can momentarily accommodate such a smart and confident woman, with an ancient air of dignity and beautiful eyes and exquisitely curly hair. Your words, not mine. Plus we have this extra shot of fool's poison.'

'My hair is wavy, it is not curly,' said Or and smiled. Godfrey noticed that her two front teeth pointed slightly in to each other. 'What?' she said, spotting his lowered gaze. He pouted and shook his head.

'Poison's one of my favorite words today,' said Venerika.

'If you truly are a poison,' said Bradley to the night sky, 'I would make myself immune for you.'

Or looked suspiciously at Godfrey. He turned his head to the pool and pretended he had a scratch behind his ear. He shortened his throat and ejected his tongue and rolled his eyes, catching and matching her smile as he turned back to the table. 'To poison!' he said, holding high his shot glass.

'Lechaim!' said Or.

'To life!' said Godfrey, very pleased to hear his own toast.

'Is this single malt?' said Bradley.

'It is!' said Godfrey. 'Smoked with volcanic peat from the remote Balinese highlands.'

'Aren't volcanoes amazing?' said Alexandra to the diminished group. 'Like windows into the earth's soul.'

'More like pimples, no?' said Godfrey.

'I feel like I'm finally exploring my wolfitude here. You know I hadn't eaten a real corn chip in so *long* before Bali? My god I love this song.' Alexandra was responding to a piano, begun anew from the speakers behind the spotlights and loudening as the restaurant emptied of people. Soon a female voice:

'*I wish somebody would have told me babe…*'

Alexandra closed her eyes and put her hand at her collarbone and swayed to the beat of the piano. Shortly Godfrey and Or recoiled together at the commencement of a male speaking voice. Then Alexandra said, 'Dance like nobody's watching in a rainstorm *everyone* can smell.'

'Petrichor,' said Venerika.

'I fucking love that word!' Bradley shouted, and held up five fingers to the waitress. 'You guys wanna see me do a cartwheel?'

'Petrichor's the smell of rain,' Venerika informed Godfrey and Or. 'It was one of my favourite words last Friday.'

'You guys are really in touch with yourself, huh?' said Or.

'The self is the guide to the self,' said Alexandra. 'My goals are my stations—my train, desire.'

'What brings you to Bali?' Godfrey said to Or.

'What brings *you* to Bali?' she replied, outmatching his curiosity as she glanced down the table. 'You are a poet, a healer, or a yogi?'

'Do I look like any of those? I asked you first.'

'I broke up with my boyfriend. He paid for a trip here, and I told him I was still going, alone.'

'You go girl!' said Venerika.

'I can see why you'd break up with him,' Godfrey said.

'Why is that?'

'He picked Bali for your vacation.'

Bradley distributed his rums, keeping for himself those declined by Alexandra and Venerika. Or said again, 'Lechaim?'

'What does that mean?' said Alexandra.

'To life,' said Or.

'*I got life, mother*,' Godfrey sang.

'Oh, life, oh me! On the questions of these recurring,' said Alexandra with her hand again at her collarbone. 'Life's the only thing that matters, don't you think? You can't *replace* life. Living life to the fullest is the *only* way to live it, so you can't even *hold* the memories in.'

'Lechaim,' said Or, and she and Godfrey drank as Alexandra swayed and mimed the female voice: '*All these reckless nights you won't regret!*'

'You should sing if you know the words,' said Or, smiling gently.

'Oh, I'd love to, but my voice would scare people I think.'

'Sing, come on! Singing connects you with different energies, rare energies. Even religion calls us to sing with God, not to speak.'

'Please don't talk about energies,' Godfrey said. 'Why don't you sing?'

'I don't sing anymore.'

'Anymore?' Or raised her eyebrows. 'You don't sing and I don't dance. We'll have a ball together.'

'Why you don't dance?'

'Because it's so stupid. Why don't you sing?'

'Because I don't feel like it. I sang opera when I was younger. But now I don't know, it's left me.'

The music beginning to carry her quite elsewhere, Alexandra interrupted her miming and her swaying to say, 'I'd love to just twirl through the streets while howling at the moon!'

'You should!' Or smiled. 'Stand up! Sing so we can hear you!'

'No, it's late. Bradley, are you OK?'

'Hm?'

His forehead was on the table.

'We should get going. Venerika?'

'I should get to going too,' said Or. 'I have to be up for a sunrise hike or some crap.'

'Some crap?' Godfrey smiled.

'It seemed like one of the only things to do here. But what, I should drop my pants and fire a rocket?'

Godfrey ignored the strange question and said, 'I'll walk you home.'

'I'm a big girl.'

'We have yoga at sunrise,' said Alexandra, emphasising the a in yoga.

'I know!' said Godfrey as though speaking to a surprised toddler. 'But I can't let a young woman walk home by herself. It's against my code of chivalry. You're not staying here are you? Good, I'll walk you home.'

'Bradley?' said Venerika into his ear.

'Mmnm! I should be writing a listicle.'

'Well it was nice being involved in your little group again,' said Or to Alexandra.

'It's not little and it's not a group.' Alexandra bent over beside Venerika and draped Bradley's arms at their necks. 'Please don't repeat anything you heard tonight, it's a safe space of non-judgment.'

'Cross my heart and hope to die.'

'Well I hope so.'

'See you tomorrow,' Godfrey called as they walked Bradley to the alley. 'No? Can't hear me? Okay. Yep, see you tomorrow. She's like a child, I can't win. ... Shall we?'

They walked a sidewalk of red tiles, as many broken or absent as whole. Overhanging with vine and leaf and powerlines—metal roller doors locked down or lights off in the store windows—the one-lane road was lit only by an occasional yellow streetlamp outlining the cubed and angular portals and draped and crazed guardians of the entrances to low-walled temples and high-walled homes.

'You can smell the petrichor?' Or smiled.

'Don't get me started on these people,' Godfrey smiled back.

'Your friends, right?'

'They wish. These people, I can't—. I mean it is a long story but I am in the *wrong* place.'

'No! You seem to be as deep as they, as them.'

'If they are deep, consider me as shallow as my bank account. If that's the deep end, put me in the shallow end of the pool where all the kids are pissing. I'd rather kids' urine than to be like them.'

'You just have met me and you're talking about children peeing on you?'

'I'm working with them.'

'You work with kids who pee on you?'

'With the donkeyclowns you just had a drink with. And I've tried to tolerate what they talk about but I just can't. I can't get—. Phh. I just can't get…'

'No satisfaction!' Or blurted, rising to her tiptoes and grinning.

'Exactly.' Godfrey smiled. 'I can't get no satisfaction.'

'But do you try?'

'Oh I try,' Godfrey assured her. 'And I try.'

'And I try,' Or lilted.

'And I try,' Godfrey loudened.

'*And I try!*' Or sang, completing slowly the crescendo. '*I can't get no!*'

'Dah der deow,' Godfrey buzzed. 'Now now now now now—neow neow—neow neow neow.'

'*When I'm!*' they sang softly together and smiled across the sidewalk, '*Driving in my car, and a man comes on the radio.*'

'*And he's telling me more and more,*' Godfrey yelled as the heels of his flip-flops tapped against the asphalt.

Then Or took up the song in a husky voice: '*About some useless information, supposed to fire my imagination.*'

'*I can't get no!*' they yelled together. '*Ah no no no.*' Godfrey stamped a foot to the remembered beat of a tambourine. '*Hey hey hey!*' Or sang as his other foot stamped too, then both feet strutted in front of the other. '*That's what I say!*'

Or's voice slunked and snaked as she closed her eyes and sang at fullest volume. '*I can't get no…*' Godfrey turned and lifted a shoulder and strutted backwards as he pointed at her. '*Sa-tis-fa-ction. I can't get no…*' she repeated in notes longer and sweeter than their originals. '*'Cos I try… and I try…*' Godfrey joined the crescendo as he alternated the raising and lowering of his shoulders and the shuffling off and onto the balls of his feet.

And they danced and sang down the one-way street, coconut palms spiking blue in the dim light against the black sky—strutting, wailing, kicking, yelling, nodding, chanting, and prancing—'*A no, no, no!*'—air-tambourining up the verdant hill.

'*No satisfack-shun,*' they harmonised at the split gate in front of Or's hotel and yelled together in conclusion: '*No satisfaction!*'

They relaxed and smiled and drooped with sweat. 'How did that happen?'

'You started it I think.'

'Oh, you were *dying* to sing.'

'And you weren't dying to dance? Though I don't think anyone would call what I just saw dancing.'

Godfrey's mouth opened in mild offense.

'You're quite sensitive.'

'Neh,' he exhaled. 'But… I haven't done this in twenty years.'

'Twenty years!? How old you are?'

'It's from Willy Wonka. Why, how old are you?'

'I am old enough.'

'To party? Well, old enough woman, I don't want you to miss your sunrise thing. Good night?'

'And I don't want you to miss your yoga.'

'What even is yoga, honestly? I actually have no idea, what do you wear?'

'Not this,' she said, pulling at the centre of his shirt.

'*Not* this? Well I'm screwed, I was planning on going straight to yoga from here.'

'Were you now?' she smiled and almost laughed. 'You know I hate hiking? I do know some yoga poses. I could show you them, teach you for preparation to your first time.'

'Is anyone really prepared for the first time?'

'If they have a good teacher.'

'Or you're an eager student.'

'I am?'

'I don't know, are you?'

'Wait, what?'

'You gonna show me your classroom?'

Ever so slightly, as though it were a secret signal among constant surveillance, she flicked her head backwards and to the side. They walked through the jungled entrance beyond the split gate and wound a lantern-lit and pond-lined path.

'It's hot yoga, do you know what this is?'

'I don't. But I very much like the sound of it.'

II

Three baskets in the dawn shadow of Ganesh.

The young woman offering them to the moss stayed flat-footed and squatting as she took three smouldering incense sticks and lay them over the white and violet petals within. She turned and said 'Salamat Pagi,' to Godfrey Lackland as he came through the split gate at the entrance to the drive of Zen Resort. She offered him a hand of green bananas from her tray. Godfrey thanked her and snapped off half the bunch and peeled one as he walked the gently winding rise.

Soon he came to the collection of low buildings that were the family home: long swallow-tailed pavilions roofed with dark tiles, palm trees towering between them, televisions tucked up on shelves against wooden columns. Two girls in white dresses sat on the marble steps of the largest pavilion, spooning sweet yoghurt from plastic tubs. Staghorn ferns bloomed halfway up winding tree trunks and at the narrow gate which separated residence from resort Godfrey was silently greeted by two green-wrapped apsaras in high niches, shaded beneath umbrellas sun-faded to mauve.

He entered an open-topped grove of frangipani and fern, looked upon a standing stone frog spouting water into the fishpond opposite reception. Ahead was a high enclosure of palm trunks and heavy fronds and the curved and pointed rooves of the bungalows. Through another gate the pool—water trickling at its distant rear from a jug poured by a crowned white Lakshmi tall upon a lotus flower. Through the smallest gate he wound the path to his bungalow and soon would have a desperately needed shower and a tooth—

'What are you doing?' said Alexandra as her bare feet slapped onto the pebbled footpath.

'Honouring my hunger.' Godfrey chomped his last banana in half.

She had timed her descent so as to make it almost an ambush. 'You weren't at yoga.'

'I wasn't.'

'Why not?'

'I'm not really a yoga guy. A yoguy.' He was tired almost to the point of delirium. 'Not a yoguy. A yogi. Yo-Guy de Lusignan. Yogue haahh. I don't really make the yogas, Alexandra.'

'Where have you been?'

'Like how many countries have I travelled to?'

'Where did you sleep last night?'

'In the pines.'

'What?'

'My girl, my girl,' he sang to her in a deep voice, 'don't you lie to me, tell me where did you sleep——. In my room, I slept in my room.'

'You didn't.'

'I did.'

'I went to your room, you weren't there.'

'How do you know? Why'd you go to my room?'

'To get you for yoga. Where have you been?'

'I've been yogging.'

'What?'

'Jogging.'

'In a shirt and flip flops?'

'I always run in a shirt, it helps me sweat. Detoxification. And I take my flip flops off and carry them, it's called minimalist yogging, Alexandra, you should try it.'

'Godfrey.'

'Alexandra,' he said in his deepest voice.

'You're free to do whatever you want here.'

'You keep saying that.'

'But I need to know where my co-creators are at all times. I'm the sanest, kindest, most understanding person you'll ever meet. But I do have the one rule.'

'You do *not* talk about Wishful Alchemy,' said Godfrey in Alexandra's voice.

'No romantic relationships while working for me on the retreat.'

'Working *for* you now?'

'*With* me. Working with me and the other co-creators. Think of yourself as an elite athlete. You need to be focused one hundred percent on what's going on, I need focus.'

Godfrey looked up to her bungalow and thought upon the gecko in the rainbow restaurant. 'You sure that's why you're asking me where I've been?'

'Yes.'

'There's nothing you'd like to confess? We're both adults. Get it out in the air and we can resolve it.'

'Resolve what? You're free to do whatever you want, but *all* my co-creators know there's just one rule.'

'Don't do to your neighbour what is hateful to yourself.'

'No romantic relationships.'

'The Abundance Hall is a sacred space of non-judgment,' said Venerika Odorono with manic eyes and twiney hair. 'Where we can share, laugh, cry, and write—and be completely, authentically, genuinely, truly, veritably, undisputably, honestly, truthfully, avoraciously *you*, good morning! Formally Rainbow Wordslut, I'm Venerika Odorono, hi. Word-weaver, inspirationalist, vagablonde, and New York Times Bestselling Poet. My current favourite words are throbbing, ovary, throaty, twinkle, captivated, avocado, bourgeois, usurious, symptoms, chimerical, exploit, anal, aplomb, revolutionary, undulate, unsterile! Istanbul, backseat, reverse cowgirl, sprung, change.

'And change is the first thing we're going to work on today: changing your language to change your life. Ne'cole, you have beautiful hair today.'

'Tha-anks!'

'No, say not Thanks. Say, I'm so grateful.'

'I'm so grateful?'

'Doesn't that feel better?'

'It does!'

Venerika strolled back and forth at the front of the room. 'Did you know that we each have 50,000 thoughts a day and eighty-five percent of them are negative? Eighty-five percent! But what if instead of going through your day thinking, "I'm not enough," you went through your day thinking, "I deserve more"? *These* are Wishful Words. The modern impersonal fast-paced world is so focused on quantitative value. Isn't it? I have *this much* money, I work *this many* hours, I know *this much facts* about penguins. Well instead of valuing someone for what they *know*, why shouldn't you value how happy *you* are? See?'

Most saw.

'If I ask you a question you feel is unimportant, even though you know the answer, wouldn't it be more powerful in the space of the universe to say, "I'm perfectly happy, and so grateful you asked that question"? Nancy, can I ask *you* a question?'

'Of course.'

95

'Do you have knowledge of the patriarchical rape structures in your past lives?'

'I do. I do have that knowledge.'

'No!' said Venerika, waving her finger like an upside down pendulum. 'You don't have knowledge in those areas, because saying you do might make you doubt your greatness. But you do have…?' She raised her eyebrows in anticipation of their delighted understanding. 'Happiness.'

'I do?'

'Of course.'

'I do.'

'Exactly.'

'I *do* have that happiness, *and* I'm so grateful.'

'Perfect, Nancy, you get it! Fairchild, this one's perfect for you. If I said to you, I've got a secret deal, where you can make a million dollars, but you have to lie to a group of strangers about being an energy expert—how would you feel?'

'I'd feel excited. How do I get in on it? Who do I speak to?'

'No, you'd feel guilty!'

'Oh. OK.'

'But! What we call guilt is just the real world trying to tell us that we are *not* enough. What we call our guilt we *should* be calling our *wildness*. Fairchild, I've got a secret deal where you can make a million dollars just by lying to a group of strangers. How do you feel?'

'I feel… wild?' His concerned look turned to one of jubilation. 'I feel wild! The deal speaks to my wildness! I'm so grateful you've told me…' He slowed in order to modify and exchange such long-learned concepts. 'And now I *have* that happiness!'

'Oh my Gosh,' said M.T. Dillika, 'this makes you so unafraid of life, right?'

'You've brought me to our next Wishful Word! Opportunity. All of you have nothing to fear, not even fear itself. What you call fear is actually…? An opportunity!'

So Godfrey returned to his Dreambinder. Under the heading instructing him to unbind his wild he again found The Creative Art of Wishfulness forming an abundance of preparatory notes for his India paintings. 'Throbbing ovary' needed no inflection, and 'throaty twinkle' was written twice, the second time in capitals with an interrobang. Then a captivated avocado and a sketch of a chimera—fire-breathing lioness with a serpent's tail and goat's body; a very confident anus and a remembered outline of the

Nuremberg Chronicle's Constantinople and babieless Byzantine brides and facts about penguins! 'What the hell was that? What would a penguin expert *look* like? Would they look like a penguin? There's no way this woman,' standing now where Godfrey would tomorrow, 'has 42,000 thoughts a day that are negative—vastly more likely that she has 42,000 thoughts are scattered, flatulent, idiotic, dumb, stupid, completely authentically genuinely retarded—a few of my favourite words today. She's worked with Alexandra before?' Godfrey wrote. 'This, is exemplary?' Yesterday had been strange, but this... How comforting it was, how illuminating of the intellectual standard expected of his tomorrow—how necessarily elevating to whatever he was going to that evening make up and in twenty-four hours present.

When eventually Venerika had turned aloneness into fun and work into love—doubt into freedom—she gave everyone a 15-minute break before moving on to part two of her workshop.

'Writing yourself out of mediocrity!' she announced with a raised fist. 'And into depth, fun, and radical growth. To write is to exhaust the limits of the possible. To write well, from the pulsating centre of every second, is to unbind your wild and write yourself free! Today, we're going to awaken our brave soul muses and write ourselves to freedom. Like Martin Luther King, and Gandhi, and Bukowski and Hemingway and Rumi and Buddha—you are all now freedom writers.'

Here the world was; this, the people. For so long removed from society, the extrapolations which placed Godfrey's paintings at the modern end of an unbroken sequence of organised symbolic now seemed worse than correct. Mild in conclusion, gentle in warning—he had been giving mankind the benefit of the doubt. His, after so much fulminating, were underpremonitions. As knowledge became happiness and Venerika the Wordslut told everyone to be the rainbow—dared them to shine—Godfrey had from the enchanted wood come forth to the world and this is what he found. He ran out of room in his Dreambinder before Venerika had finished her next sentence.

Late afternoon was The Art of the Selfie with B-rad-lé Farquwheat.

Filing along the mildly scenic ridge upon which they had two nights ago watched the sunset, Alexandra heard the breaking of a crown seal. She snapped her neck around to glare at the bottle in Godfrey's hand. 'What are you doing?'

'Exhausting the limits of the possible.'

'You drink too much.'

'Candy is dandy but liquor is quicker.'

'Pay attention, you might learn something.'

'I doubt that very much.'

Bradley asked the very wishful alchemists to form a circle around him as they walked. Every twenty metres or so he said: 'Now stop! Aaaaand selfie.' All obeyed, their phone screens facing them, rotating and squinting and tilting and smiling as they were taught the tips and tricks of successfully photographing oneself. The process and the result, Bradley said, were two of the keys to authentic happiness and a loyal following.

'*Especially* when it comes to sunsets! This is the golden hour, when the light on your faces is the best of the whole day and the light of nature the prettiest and *most* amazingest. Look to my left. Remember you want the sun going onto your face, behind the camera, with as little negative space behind *you* as possible. That's good, M.T.! Heart that one, you might be able to use it later.'

'My phone's running out of battery,' said Felix, tapping away at the thing. 'Is there anywhere around here to plug it in?' Phone in one hand and charger in the other, he stepped off the path and inspected the legs of a bench that looked out to the length of the eastern valley. Presently he yelled, 'Snake!'

'Oh my God where?' yelled Ne'cole Shartz. Most of the wishful alchemists jumped as Godfrey's co-creators huddled.

'Kill it! Kill it!' screamed Nancy Dwight-Blamey.

'Where?' said Godfrey with impatient calm.

'Right here!' Felix squealed, pointing to the grass beside the bench.

'Kill it!' screamed Nancy. '*Kill* it!'

'Relax!' said Godfrey, unclasping Alexandra's hand from his elbow. He strode to the centre of B-rad's selfie circle. 'If there's a snake, it's just a frightened animal and we're in its home.'

'Snakes are evil,' said M.T..

'They're not evil at all,' said Godfrey.

'So gross,' said Ne'cole.

'Snakes really creep me out, guy,' said Nancy. 'That's Adam and Eve right there. Guilt. No wait, wildness. The oppression of women since the beginning of time. God, they're creepy, kill it. Kill it!'

'Nancy, take one step back. And we all walk on, and we leave the animal be. OK? Do you know about the Naga? … Do you know anything at all about the island that you're on? Mucalinda was the king of the Naga, a race of snakes. And just after Buddha reached enlightenment—'

'I'm a Buddhist,' said Bradley.

Godfrey lowered his eyelids and nodded. 'Just after he reached enlightenment a great storm arose and Mucalinda coiled around the Buddha—'

'Eww,' said Ne'cole. 'That is *gross* gross.'

'Just kill them,' said Nancy, though they had walked on from the animal.

'And sheltered him from the rain with his seven cobra heads and raised him above the flood. The naga, snakes in Bali, are a symbol of our closeness to nature, symbiosis with it. They're not slithering devils.'

'Hm,' said Nancy. 'I didn't know this.'

'I didn't know that, bro, and I'm a Buddhist. Wow, look at the sunset! Everyone come and stand beside me. Yep, just like that. Now we're going to photograph *just* the sunset, because remember—there's no better place than under a picture of a sunset to tell everyone how your heart is.'

'Does he need to be here?' said Godfrey as Alexandra stood beside him and looked out to a sunset very much like their last. 'I mean, I'm sarcastic but what I'm talking about's vaguely important. He's literally just teaching people how to take pictures of themselves.'

Alexandra gave a high-pitched sigh and rested her head on Godfrey's shoulder. 'I try not to let him do what he does.'

'What does he do? You mean the talking all the bullcrap?'

'No,' she sighed again. 'He ah… Well, he kind of manipulates me I guess.'

'Go on.'

'Whenever I drop a hint of a new retreat or a new course, he always messages, tells me all the amazing vacations he's been on, and then he kind of starts…'

She hesitated. 'What?'

'He sends suggestive messages.'

'Suggestive of what?'

'Like there's a chance… that maybe *one day*… we could…'

'Bang?'

'You're so immature!'

'I am. Beer?'

'Nn-nn.'

'Come on! Live a little.'

She unfolded her cardiganned arms and took a swig. 'That is *disgusting*, how can you even drink that!?'

'It's better when it's cold. So B-rad's a sexting manipulator, uh?'

'He says we'll do all these things together, and he tells me how much debt he's in, and how he doesn't really have much work right now. But it's always interspersed with winking emojis and shirtless selfies and dot-dot-dot maybe-we-could-do-this-and-that. So I invite him, even though he doesn't have *that much* to offer, and as soon as I invite the messages stop.'

'You shouldn't let him do that to you,' Godfrey chuckled, 'that's pure manipulation.' Then he sang: '*There's no life, I know to, compare with pure manipulation.*'

'I'm just grateful.'

'Huh?'

'Thank you,' she whispered as though the words were taboo.

'For what?'

'For *not* doing that to me.'

'I don't have a phone, so… And now look, my beer deserves more!'

'What?'

'My beer is empty,' Godfrey whispered.

'You *were* paying attention.'

'More than you know.'

'Are you ready for tomorrow?'

'I am going to blow your mind.'

When the meagre colour had faded from the sunset Alexandra said she had reserved a table for twelve at Healing Foods Café. 'Not everyone has to come of course,' she said to the assembled group. 'If you'd like to go back and prepare for tonight's ecstatic dance, or eat elsewhere, but for anyone who wants to join we'll be there from seven-thirty.'

As they walked down the steps which returned to the main street Godfrey said, 'I'm going to excuse myself from dinner if that's all right. I want to go over my notes for tomorrow.'

'But you'll come to Vibración after right?'

'Come to what?' She had pronounced every vowel and lisped the c.

'Vibración, ecstatic dance. Vibrational alignments, electro

shamanic grooves, the most *intense* cacao shots. My Godfrey, it's amazing! You *have* to come! You said last night you hadn't danced in so long, this is the perfect opportunity!'

'No. Dancing is ahhh… stupid. But thank you. I really do want to sparkle and twinkle and excel tomorrow. I am after all your employee and you are my boss.'

'I'm not your boss.' She nudged him with her shoulder. 'Stop saying that.'

And while the wishful alchemists and co-facilitators dined and enthused, then as they took part in a form of dance so far removed from the responsibilities of the novelist—suppos'd repositor of what is still vaguely remarkable in our vanishing little civilization—and as they and their evening warped to very far beyond his powers of description, Godfrey Lackland sat on his balcony overlooking Zen Resort's night-lit pool—his ankles up on a cushion on the wooden balustrade, swatting mosquitos against his thighs and his neck—and worked up to beginning to prepare tomorrow's creativity seminar.

He knew that he would have to give it a name. There had been Wishful Alchemy and Wishful Words and Write Yourself Free and The Art of the Selfie. This, he knew, was branding, however weak. What then would be called his seminar?

'Creative Creativity,' he wrote, and crossed it out. 'Alchemic Creative Fullness. Loppy-Dop Creativity With Godfrey Hackshand. … Myths of Creativity. Creation Myths. Dinosaurs and Humans—Fred Flintstone—Wilmaaaa! Through the Mists of Create-ivity. The Mysts of Wishful… Palchemy. Palchemy! The art of turning lost rich people into one's friends and benefactors. … Creative…' What had she called him in that blurb she wrote? 'A joy pirate? Creativity spelunker? Exploring the Caverns of Creativity! Adventures in Creativity,' he wrote between staves. 'Privateering in Creativefulness. Private-tearing. Private Tears. Public Tears, when you realise you're not creative. Adventures. Creativentures. Trademark copyright patent pending. Ventures are like dentures but for virgins. Toothless virgins. Creative… Toothless virgin blowjobs. Yikes.' Though he was trying to concentrate, the standard he knew was expected of him made it difficult to take tomorrow seriously. It would be like giving a lecture on the faculties of colour to an auditorium of blind and handless Kiwis. It simply did not have to be all that good, and would be above all a matter of pleasing Alexandra—which, he surmised, could be done by spectacle rather than substance, and by the insertion of a few Wishful Words. 'The Creative Fart of Wishfulness!!!' he returned to scribbling. 'Wishful Creativity? Creative…' He tapped the end of his pen against the top of his head. 'Wishhhhhh… A-fishy-fish. Quabbity Assuance. Wishy… Wwwwww…. Wish-dom.'

The name would come through the writing of the seminar, Godfrey thought, and threw his notebook onto his bed and turned the A/C on and propped up his neck with two pillows.

'In order to be creative!' he announced with his notebook reopened. 'To be creative is to…' And he crossed it out. 'Creativity is… It puts you… in… hospital. Creativity makes you… horny. Creative Horniness, because of toothless virgins. Creativity comes not easily to those who would walk through life in happiness.' Too morose. Plus he had lost track of all the words that they were substituting for or with 'happiness'.

'There's no such THING as creativity!' he wrote, then thought for a time about how he would give a two-hour seminar on the hypothesis. 'Cre-a… zee. I'm going to help you put the *crazy* into crea-zy-tivity! Crea-fuckin'-tivity! Wishhhhhhdom…'

And on he wrote until shortly he fell asleep.

III

Reassembled in the Abundance Hall, all sat rejuvenated and purified after discussing in a kind of call-and-response yoga session whether or not the ocean spoke to them, and if it did then what did it say? The wishful alchemists awaited with fanatical eagerness the beginning of their third day of empowering life design. Alexandra Wishart, hopeful that her discovery would rise to the occasion and excited for what calibre of genius he was to offer her most courageous followers, fixed her wide eyes on the hall's entrance.

Shortly appeared there the front of a pair of khaki trousers, and a buttoned shirt below the rear of a young man's head, its hair impressed with sunglasses.

Godfrey stepped back slowly and carefully, balancing an invisible phonebook on his head in keeping to the very centre of the aisle between the chairs. When eventually the semi-circle of wishful alchemists came into view he turned to face Alexandra. He gave two flashes of his eyebrows and said, 'Good morning,' flapping his neck backwards with the syllables. 'And welcome.' He slid the sunglasses back and off and turned to face the alchemists. 'To Godfrey Lackland's School of Wishcraft and Creativity.

'This morning, I'm going to reconnect each of you to your *most authentic* creative soul self. Yes, I'm a painter.' Godfrey threw up an elbow and reached behind his shoulder and pulled a paintbrush from his breast pocket; waved it like a wand as he spoke. 'But the actual act of putting brush to canvas is just a tiny part of what the creator does. Almost all my creative process is behind the scenes and takes place in the days that *lead up to* the act of creation. And what I do, that short and very easily teachable process, I call... Creative Wishcraft.'

With a tingle diffusing through her body, Alexandra looked left and right with what she hoped was a twinkle in her throat. The look on her co-creators faces, the confidence in Godfrey's voice, the fascination in the wishful alchemists' eyes—brought her ever closer to a jubilant, proud, tear.

'Creative Wishcraft is no shortcut to genius or dirt road to success. But it *is* everything I know about creativity, straight from the mouth of a painter who's not just walking the walk backwards, but painting the paint all the way around *and* who has Jax Enron looking at his work as he speaks. Backwards Man is a technique I've used for a *decade* to give me a different perspective on the world and to see things from uniquely wonderful angles. Putting chairs in the sink, dressing up as a carrot—these *are* effective methods for seeing differently. But what about methods for *feeling* differently? Methods for expressing *truly*? Methods for genuine creative wishcraft? How many of you, when you're working, work naked?'

His question was met with pouts and shaking heads.

'And you tell me you want to be creative,' Godfrey said with an upturned nose. 'You say you want to bear your soul, splatter it onto paper, ejaculate it unto canvas, moisten it into potteries—but you keep layers of polyester between heart and medium? How fucking goddam double clog dare you!? How, my dear Neckhole, how my good friend Donny, my sweet sweet Turgid—'

'Turbot.'

'Sweet Turbot, how! can you be your best creative self with clothes on? Inside each of you is a moistening womb yearning to birth your genuine creative soul self muse. It's difficult enough for that muse to come out—she's shy, there's a big judgmental world out there, with standards and commonsense. But she wants to come out and you smother her with clothes!? Clothes! There's only *one easy way* that your genuine creative soul self muse lady can crown and be crowned. And that is by working naked. Always.

'I've been arrested nineteen times for naked wishcraft, all over the world. Slack Apron's looking at my paintings right now *because* I don't let arrests deter me. If you stop creating because your scrotum melts on Bangkok asphalt, do you think you *deserve* to meet your genuine creative soul self muse lady painter baby goddess? Of course you do! But if you won't melt the plums of creativity how can you enjoy the flan of artistic success? I *know* you all feel that throaty twinkle saying, "I *am* creative!" I want you to listen to the throaty twinkle. Can you hear it?'

Some appeared to be able to.

'I *am* creative,' whispered Donny Vossehol, dressed as Godfrey in reverse.

'You are, Donny, you are! Listen to the throaty twinkles! And in today's day and age everybody has access to a wheelbarrow. Right?'

Though unsure what wheelbarrows had to do with throaty twinkles, most nodded.

'Not everybody owns one, but you can always get one. Ask a neighbor, go to the hardware store, fashion one out of a used canoe. Wheelbarrows still exist, is what I'm saying. And you might ask, "Where would I get a used canoe?" But what you *should* be asking, is can I put a midget in my wheelbarrow.

'The genius, said Michael Donatelangelo—one of the truest creators of all time—the genius always remains in part a child, sees with the wondrous eyes of children. You've built your wheelbarrow out of a used canoe, but how many of *you* can engage the services of a midget? I can't, right now, there's no rent-a-midget in Bali, or dwarfhire.com. But if there were, I guarantee you we'd all be creating by twenty past ten this morning. How, you ask? Well let me tell you a story. You all know Picasso?'

Widespread nodding.

'But do you know Enano Carretilla?'

Universal shaking.

'Picasso's midget. And whenever Picasso was coming up with a new painting, he'd push Enano around in a wheelbarrow and ask him what he could see. And the midget would look around and say: "I thee a bull with hith eye in the thide of hith head." Picasso would write it down. "I thee a green woman with a tree-angle for a noth." Picasso puts the wheelbarrow down, slaps his midget in the head. "Midget! What do you thee?" "I thee a woman with a red hat and a trathparent hakerchief." And so Picasso would paint— Guernica, his crying woman, his *other* crying woman. He had the eyes of a little person, a child, and he saw through them. This, is Creative Wishcraft. Walk around naked, pushing a midget *in* a wheelbarrow, and you'll *feel* the creativity blow.'

And on Godfrey went, the back of his shirt loose at his chest, resting his hands in his front rear pockets, for a full two hours.

'Wishcraft!?' said Alexandra, beaming with excitement as his applause died down. '*Where* did you come up with Wishcraft!?'

'Holding onto that one for a while.'

'My God, it was instaperfect, they *loved* it!' She almost doubled over with excitement as they walked out of the Abundance Hall and onto the Slope of Artspiration. 'That was the best workshop I've ever *seen*. I'm *so* excited for you to see Hennifer's this afternoon, you're a natural at this! She's going to help you *so much* with your online persona—can you come a bit earlier and we can give you an intensive?'

'Actually,' said Godfrey, almost wincing. 'A lot of what I just said was ad-libbed, I want to get it written down before I forget it. *Then* I'll have to start work, I might actually have to miss—what is it? Abundance on Authenticicality? But that's OK right, attendance isn't compulsory? I don't have any online stuff for her to abundanate anyway.'

'Oh. … Yeah, that's OK I guess. I'll just see you at The Darkness Experience.'

'Definitely not coming to that.'

'What? Why not?'

'I don't want that freak touching me in the dark while he whispers in my ear to try new things.'

'That's not what he does!'

'I guarantee you that's what he does.'

'Well can you make sure you're done for the full blood wolf moon ceremony? It's 7pm and Mercury's in retrograde.'

'Is it?' said Godfrey, vacantly surprised. 'I thought it was in Gatorade. Or seventh grade. But you said it's in Kool Aid? We gonna drink some?'

'You're sure that's where you're going?'

'Huh? Of course.'

'I value honestly above all else, you can tell me.'

'Tell you what? I know I'm here working for you—'

'With me.'

'Well, for you. But I do still have to do some work as an artist. If that's all right?'

'I hold space for everyone to live life their own way and you're free to do whatever you want, but please remember my rule.'

A low-walled pair of pavilion shrines swivelled in the short grass of an uneven ridge as Godfrey and Or hummed past it, her hands holding down the hem of his shirt, the warm breeze waving the ends of her hair under the squeeze of a helmet. The square-carved lotus pedestal of a roadside shrine, its volcanic-stone altar—white smoke rising over yellowing leaves in the unseen depth of the valley behind it—all flashed by as they drove a rising boulevard of towering coconut palms. A bend of concrete flood-drain opened to long and deep terraces of drowned paddy, brown and brightest green with mud and rows of seedling; distance a rising and falling run of valleys shown by the rolling heights in their trees; a fossilised waterfall of garbage stuck into the steep dirt of the roadside from the high bamboo-line to the gutter.

Soon they slowed off the main road and were stopped by a man who asked them to pay for parking. A slab of cloud rolled in, squared off at one end and thinning out to ripples of white and blue, diffusing the afternoon light into a warm softness that bathed everything in tinctures of bronze.

Godfrey pulled up outside a grey split gate and opened the seat to let Or put away her helmet. They paid; Godfrey was wrapped in a sarong; descended—a long and winding walk of concrete steps lined with open-fronted shops selling dreamcatchers and calaveras and maschere and dreamcatchers....

'*What* were you doing this morning?' said Or, not quite grasping his first explanation.

'I gave a talk on creativity.'

'You told them how to paint?'

'How to create.'

'Create what?'

'Exactly. I have no idea, I just had to teach them how to create.'

'So how do I create?'

'You walk around naked with a midget in a wheelbarrow.'

...Superman marionettes and bottles of snake oil and Buddha statues in wood and gilt and stone and Bob Marley singlets.

'This is what you do, this is your job?'

'Good God, no. I'm a painter, I told you.'

They passed the descent's first plateau, a rice field littered with cloven coconut husks. In a short rock-cut passageway they were informed by a plaque that they were entering Gunung Kawi, the path now lined with pink bougainvillea petals and lilac. As they came to a turn the pink changed to magenta and the lilac to white as ahead and below two Balinese men sprinkled them from large plastic bags against the edges of the walkway as they shuffled down.

'You called ahead?' said Or.

'Ha, not quite. Smooth if I had though, right?'

They emerged from the passageway and were almost at the floor of a valley crossed to their right by a bridge. The sound of a river gushed loudly as behind them, on a plateau unreachable by their path, a single-toothed mask-maker turned a tiny bamboo windmill. To their left a path curved around smooth rock.

'And this scary woman is your friend?'

'She's my boss, but this is the first thing I've ever done for her. And I am genuinely worried she's followed me here.' His head and eyes darted from side to side.

'She would follow you here?'

'Oh God, is that her!?' He pushed Or aside and slammed his body back onto the rock. 'No, it's a tree. Phew. And yes, she would definitely follow me here.'

They rounded the stone wall and came to a paved terrace of flowerless plumeria—grey trunks and chubby branches; further around there rose four huge niches cut out of the rock face, an enormous tiered shrine almost worn to smooth in each.

'Not bad,' said Godfrey, taking in the grassy roof of banana palm and the white lichen covering the stone. 'She keeps saying over and over again, "You're free to do what you want, you're free to do what you want." But I just think, Yes, I know I am. Why are you telling me over and over again? Is it because I'm *not* free to do what I want? And if I do something you don't like you'll stab me in the eyes?'

Or laughed. 'So why you are working for her?'

'*With* her, Or. I'm working *with* her, not *for* her, as she keeps telling me. Money. I am doing it for money. I have a new set of paintings I want to do and she came along and said, Teach this stuff for me—and from one week of torture I can spend two months painting.'

They stepped onto the thin bridge which crossed the valley. Up and across they could see more niches and more towering shrines; below, the river raced white over rocks towards them, emerging from a curtain of vines hanging like long tassels from creeper-covered trees.

'You know she's in love with you?'

'Ha ha, no fucking chance!' Godfrey said, then momentarily saw Alexandra asleep on his back—her hands clutched at his stomach— her head on his shoulder watching the sunset. 'No way. She's just lonely. Or needy. Leedy. Nonely. Loneedy. Looney. She might actually be the loneliest person in the history of solitude. And she can't be in love with me, I described my ideal woman to her—and I literally described the *exact* opposite of her in every way. She can't possibly think there's any chance that I like her in that way.'

'You don't understand women at all.'

'I know they like eating cupcakes,' he squinted off into the distance. 'And wearing make-up and scrunchies. But apart from that…' Godfrey returned his eyes to the bridge and to Or. 'I do know they look very pretty in blue and white dresses, with auburn streaks in their hair.'

She returned his gaze and he lifted auburn from her cheek and ran it behind her ear. 'Is that a true fact?'

'That is a true fact,' Godfrey smirked and waited to see if Or intended to move from the bridge. Then he took the backs of his fingers from her hair and leaned in.

And she moved. 'None of you understand women. And if you'd seen the way she looked at *me*.' Or hooted then across the bridge and up stairs of stone ascended the river-valley wall. Godfrey caught her up as she balanced on a stone slab to look over a slope of rice terraces, flooded by protruding plastic pipes.

'And you flew from Israeli to go on vacation alone?'

'I'm on my way home from Japan.'

'Nice, I've never been.'

'I was working there a while after Travis turned to a asshole.'

'I hate to tell you this, but Travis didn't turn into an arsehole. His name's Travis. He always was one.'

'Yes, I should have known this. So when that happened I went to Japan to work to make money for my startup. And then the time came for together vacation, so I'm on my way home. But, I don't know if Israel is where I want to be.'

At the top of a stone-cut stairway, broken through with roots and slippery with moss, they strolled beside a wall of dark niches, blind windows, and short doorways—all cut out of and into the stone, a human-worked valley glistening with water, vines falling thin and straight from the wet soil above, single stems like slivers of crystal sprouting from bright green moss, yellow lichen and orange fungus exploding and bursting—all upon stone purple here and ochre there.

'What kind of a startup?'

'A fitness club, but like health *and* self-defense. Krav Maga, which I was instructor for, combined with Pilates.'

'Not you too.'

'Me too what?'

'I can't stand yoga.'

'Pilates is not yoga! Thank you.'

'But you stretch.'

'You stretch when you yawn, yawning is not yoga. And if I do Pilates and Krav Maga,' said Or as Godfrey ran his fingertips over the unrecordable shades of green, 'it means I look beautiful while I kick your ass.'

'That you do and would.'

At the end of the wall Godfrey thought he could discern a path worn out of the jungle. He opened his sarong and lowered his flip flops onto the dirt and helped Or down after him.

'A lot of wellness is inner strength with no outer,' she continued. 'But the psychology of self-defense and the beauty that comes from kicking your ass... These make a whole person.'

'As opposed to half a one?'

'I wanted to do it right after my IDF but I knew that doing it now would not be the best time.'

The mud track led to a small waterfall. They crossed its slippery stone and the path quickly lost definition as they stepped up a rising series of grassy bulges. The valley almost turned back on itself before bringing them out to stand upon the middle level of a fallow rice terrace. They held their arms out as they balanced along the soil of its squared edge.

'What happened with Travis was kind of perfect because I could go to Japan, and I got there to work in Soapland and—'

'Work where now?' said Godfrey, almost losing his balance as he turned back to look at her.

'What?'

'Where did you work?'

'Soapland.'

'That's what I thought you said. Is this a land of soap? How clean. And sudsy. They just sell soap?'

'Yes,' she said, condescending to what she thought was a joke. 'They just sell soap. And I can go back when I want to start the centre, because I have the money from working.'

'At Soapland.'

The terrace left the contour of the valley and jutted out to an open vista. The grey slab overhead had in parts broken through; a warm mist sprinkled their faces as though sprayed from a bottle. At the terrace corner they looked out over nothing but green—a slope of waxy banana palm and drying weeds running down to the river, improbably thin trunks soaring over the valley walls, the steep and faded forest opposite, triple canopy at both ends of the river. Crickets whirred in the tall grass at their feet, frogs glurped in the mud—and out across the valley the birds howled and lerped and whistled to one another over the whooshing of the river.

'Soapland!' Godfrey announced to it all 'Where the bars clean you. Come to our land of soap!' he said in a kind of Kenyan accent. 'Where you are washed against your will. Bathe in the scent of plumeria!' he returned to American. 'Eat suds, drink washing liquid, rub laundry powder into your hair. Bring your homeless to Soapland today! Wash one homeless, get one free! Soapland! Arrive in your dirtiest, leave in your cleanest! Not to be confused with Soupland, where the spoons are *always* full. Soupland! Sorry sir, we have no salad, only soup, it's Soupland, land of soup! Would you like to take a ride on the soup-slide? Lobster bisque all the way down—sit in a bread basket, soak it all up. So-planned! This mission's so planned, man,' he changed to a Dennis Hopper. 'It's like more planned than any mission I've ever been on, man. Have you even *been* to Unplanned, the land of Unp, man? Nowhere near as good as Soapland, man, you can't find the place, that's how unplanned Unplanned Land is. Unplanned Land's kinda bland…'

'You are insane,' she declared as a realisation.

'Frand,' said Godfrey and looked across the valley. The mist thickened to a drizzle; his shirt darkened with rain.

'And you are going to kiss me or not?'

'I wasn't going to, no. Should I?'

'You're a moose! You bring me to this beautiful old temples and take me through waterfalls on secret paths to rice fields to what? So you can show me how funny you are? I'm Israeli, we don't laugh.'

'Do you not?'

'Only at stupid Australian people.'

'An endless fountain of hilarity.'

'I haven't have been kissed by a man in a sarong. It's my fantasy.'

Godfrey smiled and turned upon the packed dirt of the terrace edge and put his hand at the small of her back. He stepped in as he pulled her towards him. Or groaned from the back of her mouth and Godfrey put a thumb in the groove of her cheek and they kissed; and they kissed; and kissed, and kissed—until rain dripped from the front of their hair and their clothes soaked to heavy.

'You're not going to howl like a wolf are you?' said Godfrey.

'I might purr like a kitten.'

'Your pool is amazing! That's the problem with my place, no pool. I'm going swimming.'

'Huh?'

'I'm going swimming,' Or said and stepped up past the miniature pavilion with the reed mat covered in cushions.

'You don't want to see the paintings?'

111

Her dress was already a circle at her ankles. 'They'll still be there in half an hour,' and she dived in. In the pool's blue lighting her hair was a straight length of darkness running to her bikini bottoms as she glided underwater.

'Well?' she said, floating backwards.

'Well what?'

'Are you coming in?' Her grin—those cheeks—meant that to Godfrey there was no way he was not. She drifted towards the fall from Lakshmi's vase. Godfrey looked up through the traveller palms to his bungalow then to Alexandra's. The lights were off. 'Give me a second.'

He was told at reception that it was seven o'clock pm.

'7 o'clock. Do you know how long a bullshit full blood wolf moon thing goes for?'

'Moon ceremony? Moon ceremony is taking about one hour and a half, sir.'

'Hour and a half. Thank you.'

'You're very welcome, sir.'

He ran up the steps beside the pavilion and crashed into the cold light of the water. Or lifted her chin to the cascade and ran her hands through her hair. 'It's *so* nice at night.'

'It feels like I'm swimming in pee.'

'What is with you and pee? This is all you talk about?'

'Well! Two weeks ago in Bangkok I was running along a canal and a dead dog floated downstream.'

'What is wrong with you?'

'What?'

'You talk only about kids peeing and dead dogs?'

'Wait, you haven't heard the whole story! Upstream, these kids were jumping in and out of the water, so they must have seen the dog floating, right? But they were still swimming, in dead-dog water.'

'This is not a nice story, why you tell me this? Bangkok is gross.'

'Yeah, Bangkok's gross.'

'You were there why?'

'To paint.'

'For inspiration?'

'Please don't talk about inspiration. There is no such thing, there's only work and madness.'

'So you are a mad clown?'

'A donkeyclown.'

Or lowered her shoulders into the water and again threw her

head back; ran her hands along its sides to straighten and neaten her hair. 'Don't you get lonely in huge Asian cities?'

'Neh.'

'Never?' she said, daring him to tell the truth.

Godfrey rested his neck against the edge of the pool and spread his arms behind him and raised his legs until his toes were out of the water. 'Neh.'

'Then why you are hanging around me so much?' Now in the shallow end, Or kneeled until the water was at her chin.

'I told you.'

'Because you have nothing better to do,' she said, creeping towards him.

'Because I like you.'

'You better not.'

'Why's that?'

'Because in four days you go one way and in six days I go mine, and we never see each other again.'

'You're right. It's just because you're a tiny bit attractive. Very mildly. Your mouth is like a gentle flower, and its tremors charm fear from my heart. And when you're around I can't concentrate. And when you're behind me on the motorbike I nearly have accidents just from the smell of your skin. And when you're in the swimming pool... Well, let's just say I can't get out of the swimming pool right now.'

'And why is that?' She pushed his legs down at the knees and walked her hand to his stomach. 'Ohhh, I see. Well, so as long as it is only physical.'

'Only and very.'

Godfrey could feel how cold were her lips before even they had touched his own. Water dripped down her face as he filed his fingers through the weight of the waves in her hair. She floated in and breathed into his mouth and put her right leg beside his left. He squeezed her waist with his hand and she bit his lip and pulled it from his mouth as her other leg floated over.

'Get out,' came a soft voice from the split gate behind him. It was unheard.

Water splashed against Godfrey's neck as Or moved her body along his. 'Get out,' said the voice, rather louder, though unheard still. Or put her hands on the pool's ledge and pulled herself forwards and lowered her neck to—'

'Get, *out!*' and at last it was heard.

113

Or pushed off the wall and Godfrey turned his head. 'Ah, what are you doing back? Did the wolf moon turn into a—'

'You should leave.'

'Huh?'

'Leave.'

'I'm going to go,' said Or, already putting her dress back on.

'You don't have to.'

'Yes she does. You too.'

'Have a nice night,' said Or from the miniature pavilion. Dripping, she set off for the front of the resort and Godfrey walked after her, through the apsara doorway and past the family pavilions. 'Good luck surviving that.'

'She is such a bitch. I'll see you tomorrow, right?'

'You sure that it's wise?'

'Why wouldn't it be?'

'This is your job. She doesn't want you to see me.'

'So who the fuck is she?'

'She's your boss.'

'Yes, and not my girlfriend.'

'Well if she doesn't stab you in the eyes, then sure.' Or smiled. 'Now go back to your firing squad.'

'Take this,' he said, holding out his shirt.

'I'm fine.'

'You'll be wet on the bike, you'll freeze.'

'Thank you.' Or closed her eyes as Godfrey kissed her cheek. She put on his shirt as she crossed the paving stones to her scooter.

Through the first doorway Godfrey was yelled at from above at the second. 'You shouldn't stay here. You should leave.'

'What the fuck is your problem?' Godfrey strode the pebble path and bounded up the steps and put on a shirt. Alexandra's hands were on the balustrade of their front balcony, her jaw clenched and eyes closed, her breathing enlarging her body more than Godfrey thought possible. 'What the fuck's your problem?'

'Don't turn this onto me.'

'Turn *what* onto you?!'

'Please leave,' she said flatly.

'I'm not leaving. Tell me what I've done.'

'I come back to get you,' she said between sharp breaths. 'To see if you're still working, to see if you'd like to participate, in the full moon ceremony, and I find you fucking your bimbo.'

'Woah!' said Godfrey in a parabola. 'Nobody was fucking anyone. We were talking, Alexandra, and we kissed.'

'You disgust me.'

'Excuse me?' Godfrey squealed.

'I want you to leave. I'm paying for the bungalow, you should leave. I can't even look at you.'

'And where do I sleep?'

'At your bimbo's hotel.'

'I don't want to sleep at her hotel. I like my bungalow and I have work in the morning.'

'Oh yes, work. Work! I forgot your work. You're working right now, ay? That's why you couldn't come to Abundance Through Authenticity? Because of your work. But your work is actually fucking your bimbo.'

'Please stop calling her that.'

'She's a bimbo.'

'She's not a bimbo, she's a nice girl.'

Alexandra turned to him and growled as though tearing the words in two: 'And she does not look *anything* like your ideal woman.'

'Wow,' Godfrey nodded.

'I can't get the image out of my head, you make me sick. Your love decisions make me sick to my stomach. Please leave,' she said plainly. 'Respect that I want you to leave, and leave.'

'I'm not leaving, I haven't done anything wrong. Will you just be professional?'

'Professional!? Me, professional!? I'm sorry, I'm not the one who's missing the wolf blood moon ceremony so that he can stay here and spray his sperms into a pool.'

'We just kissed,' Godfrey groaned.

'Don't even say it, it makes me sick, you make me sick. I can't get the image out of my head!'

'Are you drunk? I hope you're drunk.'

'I'm not an alcoholic like you, I had two shots of cacao. You lied to me.'

'When did I lie? Does cacao make you drunk? Because you are not making any sense, you sound insane.'

'Oh yes!' she boasted sarcastically. 'You say I'm insane so that what you're doing looks normal, and *I* look like the crazy one, right? I was burnt at the stake, I know how your people work, I'm *not* insane. I don't spend this much time with someone for

115

nothing.'

'What does that mean? I'm here working for you.'

'With me.'

'*For* you, I am working *for* you. You are my boss and you brought me here to do a job. And yes, I've spent a little bit of time with Or, but is the work I'm doing not good enough? Was the best workshop you've ever seen, not good enough for you?'

'I have one rule.'

'And I broke it, because I think it's stupid. Don't you create your own freedom? Don't *you* hold space for everyone to live life their own way? D'you know who said that? "I value freedom above everything else."?'

Alexandra calmed herself before reasserting: 'You *are* free to do whatever you want. But—'

'No, I'm free to do whatever *you* want me to do. And what you want me to do, is you.'

She scrunched her nose and bared her top teeth. 'I am *so* disgusted by you. Disgusted by what I witnessed earlier and not at all attracted anymore.'

'Attracted!' Godfrey shouted. 'The word comes out! I asked you yesterday if there was anything you wanted to tell me.'

'And what did I have to tell you?'

'Godfrey, I'm attracted to you, and it makes me uncomfortable to see you with other women.'

'You are so full of yourself.' Alexandra walked into her bungalow and yelled. 'And she is *not* a woman, she's a little girl, and even if I was, and you *thought* that I was—the fact that you bring that bimbo here and parade her in front of me? What kind of person are you?'

'I thought you were at your bullshit moon ceremony till nine.'

'And I came back to get you because I wanted to share it with you.' That long-welled tear now slid down her cheek. 'I just—. Please go. I need time. To go over the instances where my neurons believed there could have been more.'

'When did I *ever* give you an indication there could have been more? More what?'

'Are you *even* serious?'

'Tell me.'

'Don't tell me you're not taking responsibility for this? Bangkok? The boat ride, dinner? You took me drinking! You took me *home*! The motorbike and the temple, and dinner and the sunset, you shooshed me.'

'Oh my God,' said Godfrey, now concerned. He held his fingers at the bridge of his nose. 'You just listed every second we've spent together.'

'Together, yes!'

'No, just every second that we've spent in one another's company. That's not together.'

Alexandra thrashed her head from left to right and smiled: 'I can't believe you're pretending.'

'Pretending what!?' Godfrey yelled. 'Goddam it!'

'That you didn't know *why* you were coming here. That you don't know *why* you were spending time with me. For two years I've been building my fempire and all these people have come in, and I find out all of them have spoken and flirted and spent time, just because I could give them *money*. And I'm in Bangkok and I finally find someone with the same lifestyle as me, someone with such a rich inner world that I feel superficial next to him but I also feel happy in his presence—and I think *maybe* I can help him and we can spend time together and just see what happens.'

'And this is what happens. You flail around like a crazy person.'

'Don't you call me crazy,' she said, extending a fist across the bungalow to point a finger up at his chin. '*Don't* you call me crazy.'

'If I knew that part of working *for* you was going to be to have to—' He broke off and clenched his teeth and growled and retreated.

'To have to what?'

'Nothing.'

'I'm not paying you to fuck me!' she yelled, her offence pre-empting the insult.

'Well that's so goddam nice of you to say! Thank you, Alexandra Wishart, for not treating me like a prostitute. No, not thank you— I'm so grateful!' he almost screamed. 'So grateful, universe goddess of authentic tomorrows, that Alexandra Wishart isn't paying me for sex!'

As Godfrey lapsed into sarcastic oration, Alexandra's eyes, larger than most, now became larger than all. Her head tilted back and her neck seemed to freeze as she stared past her nose. Godfrey startled at the configuration of eye-white and rigid throat and the new silence unsettled him. He leaned, then stepped, back. She jabbed her bare feet into the floorboards as she growled across the room.

'You can *not* pretend that you haven't had a part in this!' Jab.

'You lied to me.' Jab. 'I asked you where you were going today and you *lied*.' Jab, jab. 'I value truth above *everything* else and you lied. Do *not* pretend you haven't had a part in this!'

'A part in you going insane for no reason?'

'Do not call me insane!' She flailed her head from side to side as though pulling flesh from a ribcage. 'You can *not* pretend that you haven't sent me signals and you *haven't* been spending all this time because maaaaaaybe you felt what I felt too.'

Godfrey removed all expression from his face and looked the very short distance into Alexandra's distended eyes. He said without tone or inflection: 'I did not feel it and I never have. I *was* going to work today, but you know what? Then I thought, if she's so controlling and contradictory, why should I respect her stupid rule?'

'Controlling!? I'm the most open-minded and freedom-loving person you'll ever meet!' Somehow her eyes grew larger still. Her neck unfroze and her head began to roll in figure-eights as she spoke. 'Two years, Godfrey! I haven't had sex in two years! Two fucking years! And I thought to myself, here's an artist I can give an opportunity to and some bread money.' Her voice now whirled like the dips and climbs of a rollercoaster. 'And yes, he's good looking and I don't know what planet he's from and he's so passionate and intelligent and I feel superficial beside him and I'll bring him to Bali and we can ride motorbikes and watch sunsets and the least I was *hoping* for was—'

Her head and the roller coaster stopped mid-air.

'Say it.'

She inhaled deeply and her eyes rebulged.

'Say it,' he urged again, daring her.

'The least I was hoping for was to get a good fuck out of it!'

Godfrey's mouth flew wide open and his eyebrows furrowed most deeply. 'You would make of me a prostitute.'

'I *need* the closeness, Godfrey. And I'm not sorry for feeling this deeply. I'm not sorry for yearning so genuinely. I'm *not* too much! I *need* the human contact, and I spend this much time with someone to lie awake at night and listen to him breathe but I have to watch him fuck some bimbo instead of me?'

'You lie awake listening to me breathe?'

'I can't even talk to you. I can't look at you. I can't listen to your voice tell lies, lies, lies anymore. Standing there pretending it's me, that it's *only* me, that *I'm* the crazy one, and you had no part in this.'

'I did have no part in this. And *this*, is fucked. I'm going to bed. You had better apologise to me in the morning. I'm going to sleep.'

'Oh, I'll apologise. I'll apologise for bringing you to Bali. And for taking pity on an artist, for thinking I could get him some exposure and stop poisoning himself with meat and beer. I'll apologise for thinking maybe he would take my advice and build his website and get a following and join the *real world*.'

'The real world?' Godfrey turned back from the door and stuck his forehead forwards in condescension. 'Do you really want to talk about the real world?'

'You don't *know* the pain I carry.'

'I do know, because you tell me about it all the goddam time.'

'And you want to make it worse?' Alexandra was almost squinting. She seemed to be daring him to respond. He relaxed, breathed lightly, shook his head once and opened out his hands. She tilted slightly her head, the dare standing firm.

Godfrey clapped his hands together and nodded. 'Good night.'

IV

Alexandra Wishart opened her eyes and took in her early-morning audience.

She had requested that this, the morning of their Creation Day, be the one yoga session she led instead of Jennifer with a soft j. So before her sat cross-legged all her wishful alchemists and her three co-creators and in the furthest corner, hunched over and rocking back and forth on his pelvis and holding together the bottoms of his feet, Godfrey Lackland.

'And breathe in,' said Alexandra, and did as she scanned the room. 'Aaaaand create your freedom as you breathe out,' she exhaled. 'Let other people do what they wish—breathe in. Hold it... If you give yourself radical permission to live your truth—and out—it doesn't matter what other people do, keep exhaling. Now breathe in... You create your life. And out. Your life is your art. In. Your art is your work. And breathe out, and say it after me. And so,' she exhaled loudly as she began her conclusion.

'And so,' all intoned in response.

'Breathe in... Work makes you free.'

'Work makes you free,' all mumbled in a chant. Godfrey stopped rocking and looked at the backs of the calm and obedient heads of those following her.

'This morning,' said Alexandra, putting the backs of her hands at her knees and touching her fingertips together. 'I got to twenty-seven thousand followers.'

'Woah,' said Venerika, and most under the pagoda followed her in applauding.

'I want you now to channel,' said Alexandra, running the side of a hand down the centre of her body, 'the divine being coursing inside me. Can you feel it?'

Ne'cole mumbled a yes. Jennifer with a soft j moaned in the affirmative. Turbot looked around to see if everyone else was nodding. They were. She nodded too.

'One more time: breathe in. ... And out, work makes you free! And relax.' She shook out her fingers. 'Today is our Creation Day. We've learnt how to turn our pain into our purpose. We've learnt how to change our language to change our life. We've discovered the simple keys to abundance through authenticity and Bradley has shown us how to use our abundance to get as many followers as possible. Today we're going to *really* begin creating our art from our lives and our lives from our art. You all remember Godfrey's workshop on Creative Wishcraft. Well this morning I want you to spend three hours implementing his creativity techniques, and to work hard at birthing your genuine creative soul self muses. Today I want us *all* to unleash our crazy!'

Godfrey clenched his teeth and drew the corners of his mouth back as he remembered, and saw, Alexandra's frozen neck and her dilated eyes and the rollercoaster of her screaming head.

'What will *your* magnum opus be? What will your life look like after The Creative Art of Wishfulness, after Bali, and beyond? Each day is yours, you create your life, your life *is* your art and your art *is* your life—now go and make today the greatest work of art ever painted!'

Slowly the wishful alchemists descended the Pagoda of Perpetual Peace and wandered to the nooks and corners of Zen resort. Only Donny Vossehol stayed behind. He wanted to talk to Godfrey, and headed him off as he walked after Alexandra.

'I *have* chosen you,' he said as he unbuttoned his shirt.

'You what?'

'I've chosen you.'

'For what?'

'You're my guru.'

'I'm not your guru, buddy.'

He unzipped his fly and said, 'Your unwillingness to be my guru tells me with even more certainty that you're my guru.'

'I'm not, I'm just a painter. Wh—. Are you dressed like me?'

'Not anymore.'

'Why are you taking your clothes off?'

'No layers of polyester between your heart and your medium, remember? When do you go to the bathroom?'

'What?'

'I'm gonna go whenever you go. Morning and night, or morning and afternoon? Or no morning, just a once a day guy? And I wanted to ask—what brands of paint and brush do you use? I want to paint like you.'

'Taking a shit when I take a shit does not make you an artist.'

'It might. I don't know who I am. I have post-traumatic stress disorder.'

'That doesn't exist, sport.'

'What doesn't?'

'Donny, I really don't have time for this. Could you spend the morning creating and we'll talk later? Use my other creativity techniques, dress up like a carrot, it'll change your life.'

Godfrey broke free of Donny's grip and descended the pagoda's steps to look for Alexandra among the wishful alchemists spread out like melted pocket watches across Zen Resort.

Fairchild McMonnies was balls-naked on the Lawn of Authentic Growth. As it turned out there were midgets for hire in Bali, and Fairchild booked for the morning one that spoke only Bahasa. So he hired through the same company a translator and now pushed his stolen wheelbarrow to the edge of the lawn. He asked his hireling to describe for him a tree. He put the wheelbarrow down, waited for the translator to relay the question and for the midget to describe what he saw. He wrote down the translator's response, was asked by Bradley Farquwheat if he wanted to see him do a cartwheel, pushed the wheelbarrow to the next tree.

Felix Piddling's phone had died during yoga. He for a time walked around the Love Grove charger in hand, saying over and over again to the gardening, the cleaning, the kitchen staff: 'Power? ... Power. ... Power?' He was met with shrugs and pouts and dismissive points and soon moved on to the Tipi of Fanatical Tolerance where, after being asked by Bradley Farquwheat how long he could do a handstand for his charger became entangled with his genitals and he struggled to find any at all.

Nancy Dwight-Blamey, prostrate in the shade of the Pride Pavilion, was halfway through reading a book on the Dutch East India Company. During Bradley Farquwheat's Darkness Experience she had confided to him (after he whispered into her ear to try anal sex) that she was beginning to suspect that in fact she was searching for her fourth life, and that her third had been lived as a Balinese slave—stolen from her jungled existence to be exchanged for opium by the King of Boeleleng and later forced to participate in a puputan. The spine resting on her bare sternum, she could feel her creation growing in her hands, felt a twitch in her abdomen where her suicidal knife had probably entered, longed to return to the more natural existence of her most recent self.

With a resourcefulness usually reserved for aides-de-camp and those people who can procure sharp things in prisons, Turbot Slurritrend had requisitioned for the morning a wheelbarrow, a chair, a carrot costume, an eggplant, and a bag of sand. Quickly she ran into difficulty making up her mind as to which would lead to absolutely the most creativity. She tried sitting on the chair in the wheelbarrow, then put the wheelbarrow in the sand and sat in it without the chair but dressed as a carrot. She told Bradley Farquwheat she wasn't sure if she wanted to see him do a totally awesome cartwheel, then no wheelbarrow, no chair—just herself as a carrot cradling an eggplant turning her toes in the sand. But she fretted that the carrot costume went against Godfrey's first creativity technique; soon she left it in the sand and pushed the eggplant around in the wheelbarrow for a while. She found most unhelpful its inability to describe what it saw.

Though appearing to wander aimlessly, M.T. Dillika was in fact strolling the grounds of Zen Resort with her left breast out (that closest to her heart) in order to listen to what everyone else was saying. She had eavesdropped on Donny's toilet entreaty and thought Godfrey's response invaluable. She took straight to bare heart much of the conveyance of Fairchild's midget's translator; briefly thought about helping Felix untangle his scrotum; thought Ne'cole Shartz and Alexandra Wishart precisely as wise as each other as they sat cross-legged in bikinis in the Zone of Incredible Vibes, discussing how each had come to attend the other's retreat.

'No, I ran the launch for three mouths,' said Alexandra. 'And there's no way you could tell that you were being marketed to because I was just saying how I felt, you know? Or how I *would* have felt in a way that people connected to.'

It was a method to which Ne'cole was unused. 'Wait, not how you *could* have felt if you'd have known that people would have responded to it?'

'No, that's the thing! It's always how I feel I should feel. I think: What kind of people would come to Bali, and what kinds of feelings would those people have? And *that's* how I say I feel.'

'Wow, you are so so amazing,' said Ne'cole, putting a heavily bracelleted hand to her chest. 'Really you've taken things back to their most authentic soul essence.'

'You're the amazing one, truly,' said Alexandra, and put a left-tattooed wrist to her chest.

'Alexandra, can I talk to you? Sorry, Neckhole, I just need to talk to Alexandra.'

'We have nothing to talk about.'

'Oh yes we do.' Godfrey squinted at M.T.'s exposed breast.

'I'll leave you two to it,' said Ne'cole, and used her crossed legs to scissor-lift herself up. 'Walk with me M.T.'

'We need to talk about last night.'

'There's nothing to talk about.'

'Are you serious? You screamed at me for an hour.'

'Oh, that,' she said, waving a right-tattooed wrist in dismissal. 'That was just—. That was nothing.'

'Nothing? Do you remember what you said to me?'

'I focus on the laughs. You're focusing on the caca.'

'What laughs, Alexandra?'

'The laughs we've had together. You should go, I know you don't care about these people. We'll just get through the next two days and we'll never have to see each other again.'

'You're so goddam dramatic, there's no talking to you is there? Fuck this, I'm going to do some work.'

'Still calling your bimbo your work?'

'What's your problem? How can you sit in front of these people and preach about freedom and choice then try to make me feel guilty?'

'Guilty!? I'm the most open-minded and empathetic person you'll ever *meet!*'

Godfrey glimpsed the forming of a pattern. It was one for which he had neither the energy nor the desire to repeat. He breathed in, smiled, breathed out.

'You guys wanna see me do a cartwheel?'

'Fuck off, Farkwit, goddam it! I'm going to work, Alexandra. To write the notes that will become the sketches for the paintings for India. OK?'

'Just be at the Afternoon of Silence. I'm paying you to be there.'

'She was so maaaad,' said Or as she took their tickets from the girl behind the counter.

'Furious, you have no idea. An hour she was screaming at me. Like a crazy person. She's giving me painting after painting.'

They walked a wide path raised over cleared forest, here and there grey decking cut out for the shooting up of a thin tree trunk.

'You take your inspiration from your real life?'

'Real life? Ha ha. That is *not* what this is.'

'So what do you paint? Where do your ideas come from?

'I don't know.' Godfrey stared down at the walkway and thought for a moment. He looked across to Or and half-squinted an eye.

'Woe unto the prophets that follow their own spirit and have seen nothing. Israel,' he said, and pointed to her, 'thy prophets are like foxes in the desert and cows will have the same value as goats and many *will* profess false knowledge to earn their livelihood as alchemy is you touching my arm and it setting fire to my soul.'

'Is this Soapland again? What even are you talking about?'

'It's one of the India paintings.' He counted on his fingers: 'Ezekiel, the Vishnu Purana, Alexandra Wishart. It'll be a painting, I already have the notes: Jackals, cows, a flaming arm, a desert background.'

'I have no idea what you do for work.'

'I'm Salvador Bali!'

Their tickets were checked by a wide woman in blue silk and between garudas they descended into a stone passage carved on one side with a procession of monkeys and on the other with an army of them.

'But you seem I think to care for her?'

'She's helped me,' Godfrey admitted in the dark. 'No one's ever helped me before. Plus I do just think she's lonely. If she wasn't lonely I wouldn't dread her so much but there's no lightness to her, no frivolity. She sees the whole world through how lonely she is and how much money she can get from other lonely people. Loneliness must be a multi-billion dollar industry. But two more days. Two more days and I'm done and in India. But in the meantime, dread and fear. I am actually afraid of her.'

Emerged into a manicured jungle of low scrub and high canopy, they came to a pedestrian roundabout encircling an enormous Banyan tree, its trunk and adjacent lingam tied both with a red and black checked cloth. The falling roots had been pulled out and staked at each of the four paths which led to it.

'Why scared? Does she know krav maga?'

'Because I've looked into her eyes. And because she said that her only rule here is no romantic relationships while I'm working for her.'

'This is romantic to you? I hate to break it to you, moose, but…'

'While anyone's working with her,' said Godfrey. 'We have to be focused like elite athletes she said.'

Parties and pairs and classes and families of tourist all wandered the forest, some looking at their phones, some at the screens on the backs of their cameras, some eating bananas, some feeding them to the macaques, others, not small in number, bent around the Pond of Mystical Carp and waving at monkeys in the hope that they'd wave back.

To three of the vines hanging near the tree's centre there clung people with arms tensed and ankles wrapped while their partners took photographs of them. One said, 'Aspetta, aspetta,' and leapt into the trunk and kicked off it with his sneakers. He said, 'Dai!' as he swung out.

'Hmm,' said Or. 'I think the rule is made up. Just for you. She likes you, she saw that you drool when you're around me and she made up the rule to keep you for herself. Did you have asked the other employees?'

'But even the fact that that's a possibility, Or! Who is this woman!?' Godfrey turned for a final look at the banyan tree before they stepped onto a rising path. 'But no, I haven't, that's a good idea. Wait is that—'

With a pinkie and thumb extending from a fist, and his tongue protruding from his mouth—in his feathered felt hat and an extremely long singlet printed with a wheel of life—Bradley Farquwheat hung from one of the vines, waiting for a picture to be taken of him. He seemed now to look beyond the young woman who was poising his phone. He returned his tongue to his mouth.

'Fuck.' Godfrey turned and hurried on.

'What?'

'Quick.'

'What's wrong?'

'That's one of the facilitators.'

'The what?' Or turned as Godfrey ushered her on. 'Oh, I've seen that guy, he looks like an asshole.'

'That arsehole cannot see me here.' Godfrey took Or by the forearm and pulled her gently to the bend in the path.

'Why not?' she began to cackle.

'I told Alexandra I couldn't go to the monkey forest because I was afraid of monkeys.'

'Why did you tell her this?'

'Because I didn't want to go with her.'

'I helped you overcome your fear.'

'If he saw me I'm a dead man.'

'You're afraid like a child of its mother.'

They came to the top of a thin stone path which descended into dense forest and disappeared into the roots of a banyan tree. Upon an upright stone slab carved with, '← Holy Spring Forest,' and, 'First

Aid →,' a large female macaque sat upright and looked to a Balinese man in green uniform and udeng. The monkey watched and waited as the man held out a banana in his open right palm. He said, 'Kiri kanan?' then closed both hands and put them behind his back. Then he offered the monkey the top knuckles of both fists.

'Kiri kanan?' he repeated, 'kiri kanan?' Shortly the monkey leaned back and reached out to tap twice on his left hand. He turned it over and opened both and there the monkey had her reward. She peeled it as Godfrey and Or stepped down.

Stone balustrades carved as snake scales rolled out and down to a paved terrace packed with people. Or looked over and down and found that they were on a bridge. A stream flowed far below, the bottom of a steep and coldly-shaded valley.

'It's like the staircase to the chocolate room,' said Godfrey as they ducked beneath the aerial roots.

'To the what?'

'The chocolate room, from Willy Wonka.'

'You've said this before, is it a movie?'

'What kind of a childhood they give you in Israel?'

'I was too busy hiding from Lebanese rockets to watch movies.'

'Sing this,' said Godfrey, looking out to the lower wooden bridge which allowed tourists to photograph the higher stone one. 'Ding dong dung,' he chimed slowly. 'Ding dong dung.'

'Ding dong dung,' Or sang, replicating the notes.

'Hold your breath,' said Godfrey as an American. 'Make a wish. Count to three.'

Or closed her eyes. 'Echad, shtaim, shalosh.' He turned her to the end of the bridge and she opened them as he sang.

'*Come with me, and you'll be, in a world of pure imagination.*' Or went to step down; Godfrey swung his arm and blocked her from doing so. '*Take a look and you'll see, into your imagination.*' Quickly he took three steps down then one back up. With a hand on the larger scales of the dropping balustrade, Or smiled and stepped down after him.

'*We'll begin, with a spin.*' He turned to her and found a smile immovable from cheek to smoothest cheek. '*What we'll see will defy…*' Again he blocked with his arm her casually elated descent; looked up into her eyes and sang slowly: '*Exp—*'

And she finished his line singing: '*Planation.*'

'*If you want to view paradise, simply look inside and view it.*' Three steps down, he crouched, then jumped two back. '*Anything you want to, do it…*' He put his hand in Or's hair and flopped it across her head.

127

'*Want to love the world?*' He looked down at the crowd of tourists in a packed arc of singlet, camera, fluoro. '*Too many tourists.*' He raised his voice and began rather to belt: '*If you want to view para—*'

'All right Johnny Depp, get off the bloody stairs.'

'We want a photo of the bridge.'

'So take one,' Or said.

'With us on it.'

'I'm sorry, fat sir,' said Or at Godfrey's back. 'But God did not have made the world so you can take photos in it.'

'Get off!' was whined by another tourist. 'Come on, go away,' was commanded by another.

'My God, these people!' said Or. 'You are barbarians!'

'Oi, calm down,' Godfrey laughed, and they pushed their way through the tourists and walked the wooden walkways which jutted and rose through the forest, white clouds overhead glaring occasionally through the high canopy.

Hanging onto the closed gates of what a signboard told them was The Great Temple of Death, Godfrey said as though concluding: 'But yes, I'll finally be able to live the life I want, instead of the life I've *had* to live, even for a short time. And dread her or not, she's given me that.'

'You want to live in India?'

At their feet, square paving stones were grown over entirely with bright green moss. Their luminescent covering diminished as the tiles ran up to the complex's first bale, two-tiered and covered in neat and thick black thatch.

'I want to paint without having to worry about dying from starvation. And the one great work of my youth has to be painted in India. Six weeks it'll take me, in Tamil Nadu.'

'Tamil Nadu?' Or asked, the words unknown to her. The moss cleared as the stones, revealed as purple, ran up to a red gate with steps covered in families of monkey, its tiers rising in carved grey stone. Behind it the tree line opened to blue sky. 'Who is Tamil? And what do you do together?'

'What?'

'Tamil 'n' I do. … Tamil and I do, believe,' she said, rolling into a muddled Texan accent. 'That you're goin' t'India to paint. Tamil and I do, feel sorry for ya there, but Tamil and I do *not* have no desire to go t'India. Tamil Nadu not! Tamil not Nadu.' For the first time since having to learn it in high school she was pleasantly surprised at the flexibility of her third language. 'Tamil nuttin' to do. Tam'll have nothin' to do in India, unless Tam's a painter like you, Godfrey Lackland, next door to Soupland, which is just a few clean bowls of marak from Soapland.'

'Well, well, well. Alike an insane donkeyclown.'

'And trained in psychological warfare. You better watch out.'

'You should come to India.'

They stared on in silence, their hands gripping the iron bars of the gate, watching the monkeys pick bugs from each other's fur. Soon Godfrey turned his head and leaned across.

'Don't kiss me at the temple of death.'

At the gate to the Temple of Knowledge, Alexandra Wishart stood between her co-creators in front of all her wishful alchemists except Nancy Dwight-Blamey.

'We can't wait much longer,' she said to Jennifer with a soft j, looking at the time on her phone.

'Caramel pudding matcha latte?' said the young woman at the steps of the Starbucks. She offered a black tray of half-filled paper cups to M.T. Dillika and Turbot Slurritrend, the closest alchemists.

'No thank you,' said M.T..

'I'm not sure,' said Turbot.

'How about caramel pudding frappuccino?'

'Hm,' said Turbot, and put a fingertip to her chins as she looked into the paper cups.

'Please could you leave us alone?' said Alexandra. 'Thank you. We only have the temple for two hours and our time's about to start,' she said to Jennifer with a soft j. 'OK, if Nancy arrives, could you hang around the entrance for when she arrives? And give her a birthing tablet and chalk and tell her very softly what we're doing?'

'Of course. Sugar is the alcohol of the child.'

'K. So good afternoon Wishful Alchemists! Welcome to the Temple of Knowledge. Today is our Afternoon of Silence. We have the temple booked just for us, for the next two hours, so that we can spend our afternoon not talking, but *thinking*, about *how* we're going to put our creation morning into action—how work will set us free. And though silence is a fractal in the consciousness of source, communication is the *most* important thing, since *none* of our ideas should *ever* go unborn. So we have these birthing tablets to hang around our necks—'

'Blackboards,' said Godfrey, very quickly.

'Birthing tablets.'

'What's a fractal?'

'And chalk, so that if we have an idea that *needs* to be brought into the world, we can write it down and share it with our fellow alchemists.'

Godfrey went to the centre of the complex, in front of the sunken snake fountain, and watched with wrinkled forehead as the group arranged themselves around the temple—as they patrolled the path in front of the gate behind him, sat with fists at chins on lichened ledge and mossy step. Donny Vossehol stood beside him, his forehead wrinkled and clothes on backwards. Venerika paced up and down the walkway between the long lotus ponds. Godfrey scrunched his right eye closed and pushed his bottom jaw across from his top and limped towards her. He wrote, from upside down and in capitals, 'Am happy,' then groaned and tapped his chalk against the board as Venerika neared. He groaned again as Venerika, her mouth ringent, wrote, 'My grandfather had a stroke.'

Godfrey growled and bulged his open eye then growled in a higher pitch and wrote, 'Of luck?'

'No,' wrote Venerika and Godfrey relaxed his face and stood up straight and nodded his head as she stormed back down the path. 'There'll be no more talk of wars in this house!' Godfrey shouted as loudly and as gruffly as he could.

'Shh!' came sharply from the direction of Alexandra, her back straight and right foot pressed against her left knee at the pavilion nearest the entrance.

'Damn it!'

'Sshh!'

Godfrey moaned in the direction of Bradley Farquwheat. He was staring at the sky in the northeastern corner. 'Mnm!' Godfrey tapped him on the shoulder and whispered, 'I have a question.'

Bradley put the side of a finger from his nose to his chin.

'Question…' Godfrey wrote on his blackboard.

Bradley wrote: 'I'm fluent in silence.'

Godfrey shook his head and ignored him. 'Romance on retreat. Y or N?'

'Go for it bro!' Bradley wrote, then angled his birthing tablet at Godfrey.

'No rule against?' Godfrey hastened to write.

'?' Bradley shook his head and pouted.

'A.' Godfrey pointed to her with his thumb. 'Said no romance on retreat.'

'Love is only rule here,' Bradley wrote, then added a chalk love heart in the bottom corner.

'You?' Godfrey wrote and pointed at Bradley. 'Romance on retreat?

'Alexandra!'

'What about?' Godfrey shook his head in uncertainty.

'Bali '18.' Then was birthed in chalk before Godfrey's eyes: 'Me and her!'

Godfrey wiped his blackboard with the side of his fist and wrote over white smears: 'You & her what?'

'Connected hearts to souls,' wrote Bradley.

'Hm!?' Godfrey squeaked.

'We hooked up,' Bradley struggled to fit in at the bottom of his tablet.

'Are you fucking serious?' Godfrey whispered furiously and was from three directions shooshed.

''Twas beautiful,' Bradley scrawled on his cleared tablet. Godfrey shook his head. 'Deep connection.'

'You,' Godfrey wrote, 'are a wanker.'

'Impossible,' wrote Bradley in reply.

They stood beside one another and held their blackboards adjacent. 'No have dick?'

'I no do.'

'No do what?'

'Masterbate,' Bradley wrote.

'Bull,' wrote Godfrey then underlined it. 'Shit.'

'Only connect. Sex to ♡, and ♡ to ♡.'

'Do not believe you.'

'Swear… to… Buddha.'

Godfrey spat on his blackboard and rubbed it clean. His chalk wrote wet: 'Full of shit.' He held it up to Bradley's face.

'Of gratitude always.'

Godfrey pointed around the Temple of Knowledge—at Alexandra and Ne'cole conversing wildly in chalk, at Donny with his clothes on backwards, watching him from a few feet away, at Jennifer with a soft j cradling her birthing tablet, at Venerika strolling like Wordsworth through a fen—at the rest of the wishful alchemists with their fingers tapping at their chins and their heads tilted to the side. Godfrey threw his arm around in a wide circle and thrust his blackboard in all directions and tapped it with his chalk.

'Authentic change,' Bradley wrote.

'Full of shit,' Godfrey rewrote over his words then added, '!!'
'Disappointed.'

Godfrey again cleared his blackboard and wrote in cursive over smudges of white: 'Look! I'm writing myself freeeeee!'

'Jokes are death of feelings,' Bradley wrote.

'You,' wrote Godfrey, 'are the death of intelligence.'

'Insulted. ♡ hurts. Wish you were more fluent in silence.'

'Fluent in bullshit!' Godfrey wrote. 'Full of it!' and he flanked the accusation with, '♪' and '♪'. He coloured in the notes' circles as he mimed in tenor: 'Full of shit! Full of shit! You and you and you and you, full of shit!' Again he rubbed the side of his fist back and forth at his blackboard. 'Where were you today?'

'Where you?' Bradley returned in chalk.

Godfrey tapped at his original question. Bradley shrugged his shoulders.

'Keep mouth shut monkey boy,' and Godfrey underlined the 'shut'.

'You bad man,' Bradley wrote.

'Bitch rat, what?'

'You no understand...' Bradley wrote, 'healthy... masculinity.'

Godfrey breathed one calm breath and smiled and rubbed his board clean. Then he wrote as neatly as he could: 'I shall give you healthy masculinity.' He drew the y's descender slowly across the blackboard then raised the object over his shoulder and leaned into Bradley, who flinched and cowered and crouched and held his birthing tablet with both hands behind his head.

'Oh no,' said Alexandra, and dropped her birthing tablet. She cupped her mouth with her hands. 'Oh my God.' The sole of her foot fell from the inside of her knee. 'Alchemists! Alchemists! Take a break,' she announced in a panic. 'I have horrible news.'

'What is it?' wrote Jennifer with a soft j then began to write, 'Pangolins won't...'

'!?' wrote Bradley Farquwheat.

'Nancy's been bitten by a snake. Someone from the resort just came to tell me. She went to the Temple of Happiness instead of here and tried to pat a cobra. I'll come with you,' she said to the man from the resort, his scooter parked hastily at the temple gate before running to bring Alexandra the news. 'I have to go to the hospital. You guys keep birthing. You're doing so great, I can *feel* the universe coming back to life. Can't you? Oh my God.'

V

As you very well know, because you've been paying the carefullest of attention—haven't you?—the final day of The Creative Art of Wishfulness was headed in the Dreambinders as their Day of the Elements.

Fearing another mishap akin to Nancy Dwight-Blamey's, all were early that morning asked to make their way to Tirta Empul—the water element—in pairs.

Alexandra asked Godfrey if she could ride with him. He took too long to make up an excuse and had to concede: 'I don't see why not.' Venerika and Jennifer rode together and Bradley squeezed his arms and legs around Ne'cole's much smaller frame. She had so ingrained herself with the co-facilitators that it was now she advising them on joyology, oneness, selfies. Donny rode with M.T. and as there was a trio left over Fairchild offered to hire a car for Felix and Turbot.

As Godfrey eased the brakes down the hill which led to the carpark he lifted one of Alexandra's arms from his waist and flapped it up and down in an attempt to wake her up. Her slack-jawed head stirred not from his shoulder blades. So with all the strength of his throat he yelled and jiggled the handlebars and squeezed the brakes and yelled a little more.

She woke instantly and fully. 'My God what!?'—gripped tight at Godfrey's waist and looked as a meerkat left and right—'What's happening? Did we die? Why are you yelling!?'

Godfrey cackled; they swerved as he stretched forward with laughter.

'My Godfrey, that's not funny! That's not funny at all!' She tapped him gently on the side of the head. A second tap was left unfinished—her hand running over and then through the hair behind his ear. 'I was sleeping so peacefully.'

He shook his head from her fingers and said, 'It was practically the definition of funny,' and slowed into a gap in the parallel scooters.

All gradually assembled at the ATM beside the blue and white sign reading 'Welcome to Holy Spring.' Fifteen minutes passed without the arrival of Donny and M.T.. Alexandra grew anxious at the number of tourists arriving by scooter, by taxi, by van—the Chinese by herd of bus—and amassing at the ticket hut. She had scheduled their purification ritual early so they could enjoy it as authentically as possible. If Donny and M.T. took very much longer they might have to start without them. She sent Jennifer with a soft j to line up, with instructions to buy one for everyone and said that she was sure they had just gotten a little lost and would arrive soon.

And soon it was that they did. M.T. eased a scooter very slowly towards them. She looked mortified. As she neared they could see red on her arms and a discolouration at her chin. Donny, dressed as a carrot, leaned his green stalk and encircled smile out from behind her. She parked and he helped her from her seat. As she approached with her elbows held out from her waist Alexandra said, 'Oh my God what happened?'

M.T.'s entire right arm was pink and red and brown with grazes. Her chin was split open and a cheek was packed with gravel—her right thigh almost bare of skin and a long squiggle of blood dripping at her knee. All rushed to her, Venerika foremost among them: 'Stand back, I'm a doctor!'

'Are you?' said Godfrey. 'Is she?'

'A joyologist, stand back.'

'That's not real.'

'Stand back! Are you OK? Donny, what happened?'

'We had an accident,' said M.T. in a feeble voice. She was frowning as her whole body shivered.

'My Godfrey, are you OK?' said Alexandra.

'I'm fine,' said Donny.

'M.T.?'

'I think so,' she whimpered.

'I grabbed onto her when we came off and I don't really remember what happened but I think she got most of the road. *Good* day to dress up as a carrot.'

'I was at the top of that big hill,' M.T. sniffled, 'and we'd followed your directions but we started to get unsure of where we were going.'

'*She* started to get unsure.'

'So I opened Google Maps on my phone and had that in the bike yelling directions at me and it told me to turn right, but you'd said turn left, right? At the statue?' Alexandra consulted her wrists. 'So I started to turn right, but Google was telling me to turn left and then Donny said he was scared of heights and he started yelling and I just hesitated and the handlebars wobbled and we came off.'

'Oh my God,' said Alexandra. 'Do you want to go to the hospital?'

'No, that's OK,' said Donny.

'Not you, idiot,' said Godfrey. 'M.T., do you want to go to hospital?'

'No, no, I'm OK. It just stings. I don't want to miss the purification ceremony.'

'Purification ritual,' said Alexandra.

Inside, wearing dispensed sarongs, they crossed a wide courtyard between a long swallow-tailed pavilion and a high red gate at the centre of a low wall. They passed two black-thatched bales and neared a split gate framed by distant jungle. A concentration of voices loudened ahead as running water grew audible. Splashing could soon be heard. Excitement became wide-eyed throughout the group, for all the wishful alchemists save for Ne'cole had spent the better part of adulthood wishing to see what they knew they were about to see.

Alexandra led them up to and through a low iron gate and down to the two pools of Tirta Empul. Water ran fast from round stone spouts, incense smoking among basket offerings stacked on their high ledge. At two of the spouts a queue of Balinese children smiled and laughed and splashed one another. Dispersed across most of the others were rows of overweight Western women in sarongs, flowers in their short hair, eyes closed and palms together. A rubber-matted walkway divided the smaller from the larger pool. Atop it as Godfrey was followed by a carrot to the larger, a Dutchman in a pink t-shirt pointed a phone down at his bare-chested Italian friend, hip-deep in the smaller. The Italian's hands were joined at his forehead as a stream ran down his back. The Dutchman trucked in and rotated and tapped as the Italian for a time stood still. Soon he turned from the fountain and reached up to look at the footage. He was unsatisfied. He asked his friend to try again; rejoined his palms and put them to his forehead and walked towards the ledge until the waters ran down his back.

Alexandra assembled everyone beneath the tree overhanging the larger pool.

'During yoga this morning,' she announced over the racket, 'I started singing my song of tantra—I already told Hennifer this—and it was flowing angelically through my body, like a wave I had

135

no control over. After eight or nine minutes I felt the space between my eyebrows quivering. Guys, I felt my third eye twitch. The divine flowed out of me, and I believe it was flowing because I was bringing you here.

'Tirta Empul has been used by the Balinese for thousands of years to wash away turmoil and to purify our souls of the negative karma that we acquire in our past lives. Today, after so *much* Creative Wishfulness, I want us all to get in the water together and wash away all negative conceptions of ourselves, to each claim our joy from the fastly flowing waters, to make an alchemically creative wish, and to let my divine energy flow abundantly through you. I have a prayer especially for today, if you'd like you can say it when you're under the sacred waters.' She closed her eyes and joined her hands and intoned: 'The body washed with water. The mind washed with honesty. The soul cleansed by alchemy. Reason cleansed by wishdom. ... And I've hired a guide for us, he's at the end of the pool there.' She waved at him, in red and golden Balinese dress; he smiled and waved back. 'He'll be walking around the pool taking photos of us the whole time, and he'll give me the memory card at the end so we can all remember claiming our joy forever. So let's go!'

She stood at the centre of the pool as Felix and Fairchild and Turbot stepped for the first time into the holy water, as Venerika and Jennifer with a soft j and Bradley and Ne'cole returned to it, as M.T. stepped in up to her ankles and hesitated.

'Are you OK?' said Alexandra

'Stings, stings, *stings*!' she said as a knee went under. 'Oh my fudging God it stings!' Her whole body tensed, she took another step in and clenched her fists at her shoulders then threw her hands in the air. 'It stings so gosh-darned much!'

'What are you doing?' said Alexandra to Godfrey. He was leaning fully clothed against the wall under the tree.

He held out one hand. 'Holding space. No!' He hovered his other over its palm. 'Claiming my joy. Wait! Or am I owning my awesome? *Could* I be doing all three?'

'Did Nancy's death have no effect on you?'

'It did not.'

'Get into the water.'

'No.'

'Why not?'

'Because I'm not a Hindu, I'm not a Buddhist, I'm not Balinese.

136

postcard

This is… It's not right.'

'You are a co-creator on The Creative Art of Wishfulness and I'm telling you to get into the water.' Godfrey shrugged his shoulders. 'Get in the water,' she growled from behind her teeth.

'No,' said Godfrey in a high voice.

'You *will* get in the water and you *will* cleanse your soul and make a wish!'

The bulge of her eyes and the roll of her head sent Godfrey momentarily back to the bungalow. 'Yep,' he said, and nodded and took off his shirt and shoes and shivered as his feet touched the submerged steps. Donny, unable to without assistance change out of the carrot, walked in after him. Godfrey lowered his open mouth into the pool and waited for Alexandra, in one of the three queues of wishful alchemist and co-facilitator, to turn her ear to him. Then he spat a sharp stream into it.

'Would you grow up?' said Alexandra, twitching her head.

'Eternal youth is a question—my heartbeat the answer.'

At her rebuke Donny, preparing to send a mouthful of water into M.T.'s mangled ear, swallowed.

'The body washed with water,' Alexandra whispered to remind everyone of her prayer. 'The mind washed with honesty…'

At the front of Godfrey's queue Bradley Farquwheat turned to catch the photographer. He was behind the thick balustrade at the distant end of the pool. When Bradley got his attention he pointed to himself. The photographer lifted the weight of his lense and pointed it down. Bradley bowed his tieless hair under the fount then lowered it into the water. Then in one quick snap he flicked his head up out of the pool and his brown mass of hair patted him loudly on the back. He looked to the photographer, who smiled and held up his thumb.

'Not afraid of the monkeys here?' said Alexandra back to Godfrey as Ne'cole's joined palms entered the stream.

There had been macaques near the entrance, lazing with bananas and harassing Korean tourists. Godfrey had forgotten to pretend to be scared of them. 'Are there monkeys here?' he said with new concern.

'You're not braving your truths, Godfrey.'

'Here we go. And what truths would those be, hm, that I'm failing to brave?'

'Monkeys.'

'What of them?'

'You're not afraid of them.'

'I very recently conquered my fear.'

'Conquered your what, sorry? You mean your opportunity?'

'No. You can't have an opportunity of monkeys. I'm not speaking your made up language.'

'I hope you wash your mind with honesty.'

'I hope you wash your mouth out with reason.'

'Reason cleansed by wishdom.'

'No. Reason cleansed by something that exists. Untainted by jealousy and suspicion and rage.'

'Jealousy? I'm the most open-minded and empathetic person you'll ever meet!'

'You're not, Alexandra, I'm sorry. Brave *that* truth.'

'Your art is your life and your life is your art, and I've created a life where I'm the most open-minded and empathetic person you'll ever meet.'

'You mean you've *invented* a story that *says* you're an open-minded person? That you've made up a fantastical story that——.'

'Thank you, my life is fantastic. Yours is a lie.'

'And yours is a delusion. What about *the* truth, Alexandra? D'you ever think of that?'

'*The* truth is that you never had a monkey opportunity.'

'No, I didn't. Because you can't have a monkey opportunity. I definitely had a monkey fear though.'

'Even in the monkey forest? You're able to enter a whole forest of monkeys despite your opportunity?'

'Such is Wishful Alchemy!' Godfrey yelled with his arms up.

'I can't *believe* you went there with your bimbo.'

'Farkwit,' he snapped in a whisper.

Alexandra turned in anger and found that Ne'cole had finished neatening her hair for the camera. The fount was all hers.

'Is bimbo a code word too, is it?' She put her palms together and closed her eyes and stepped slowly forward until the gushing was at her stomach. 'What's it code for then? Authenticity? No, happiness? No, that's knowledge. Freedom, it's freedom, right? I have no bimbo, because Alexandra Wishart tells me what I can and can't do. I used to have it, before the CIA started tracking me. The Central Intelligence Alexandra. Had freedom, now no freedom. Had bimbo, now no bimbo. Bimbo gone. Bimbo Baggins!' Godfrey fulminated with loose cheeks, disturbing most in the pool.

Alexandra turned her head sharply to the side. 'Do you mind?'

'Do not take me for some conjurer of cheap tricks! Cheap Trick, Alexandra, you remember them? *I want you to want me.*' Alexandra turned fully to his singing and pointed to herself. '*I need you to need me.*' She returned to the fount. 'Wait what's Venerika for Need? Guilt, right? No, control. Apple juice? Banana seven? Ah, who the fuck knows.'

'The body washed with water,' said Alexandra, and immersed her head until the water ran down her back. At the front of his own queue, Donny bowed his head until the round spout watered the entirety of his costume. He mumbled as an echo: 'The body washed with water,' as Alexandra stepped back and regathered her hair. 'The mind washed with honesty.' She looked to her right, where Jennifer with a soft j stood with eyes closed and palms joined—'The soul cleansed by alchemy,'—and to her left where Donny the waterlogged carrot was being prevented by his costume from standing straight. All three finished in desperate harmony: 'And reason cleansed by wishdom.' Alexandra reached up to the ledge behind the spout and grabbed with both hands at the white smoke wafting from the incense as Donny slipped and sank. She drew what she had grabbed to her face then waved her open hands over her head; put her palms back together and turned as Donny surfaced and gasped and sank again. She gave a calm kind of grin and tilted her head to the side and looked from Godfrey to the water. 'Your turn,' she whispered, grinning still. 'Perhaps you should cleanse your love decisions.'

Godfrey tongued at his molars as she glided to the rear of the pool. 'Cows will be held in esteem only as they supply milk and they *will* have the same value as goatsssss-a.' He hissed as he stepped towards the pouring ledge. Beneath it, he found the edifice larger than he had anticipated. The light green, almost yellow, of the offering baskets stacked on top of one another, the rising incense smoke, the stone wall behind them—all much higher than they looked when holding space and claiming joy and owning one's awesome under a tree. A calm seemed to come to him. The splash of the running water, the moss on the spout—reminded him of the wet stone at Gunung Kawi and of Or—her cheeks, her bambi hair, her front teeth inturned.

'Hm,' he said, surprised, the packed pool suddenly to him silent. His eyes moved quickly to both sides of the spout as Bradley lifted Donny by the stalk and swam him to the rear ledge. Then he thrust his neck into the stream and sang in falsetto: 'High on the hill was a lonely goatherd, lay-ee yodel-ay-ee, yodel-ay he-hoo!' Then he deepened his voice and rumbled loose cheeks—'Me-sa no like-a this,'—put his hands against the cold stone wall and slurped and drew his head back until the water ran onto his chest. 'You're bastard from a basket! A bastard from a basket!' he yelled upwards. 'Was Moses a bastard in a basket? Was Moses even a bastard, who *were* Moses' parents? Eve, and Anubis. Anubis, the head of a jackal. A jackal among ruinsssss-a! Love among the ruins, where our sheep half-asleep don't know the wolves are closing in, dressed as them. *Ravening* wolves, who you'll recognize by their fruit for wolves do oft hold cantaloupe. Beware of wolves bearing fantaloupe! *Never* look a gift fantaloupe in the wolf. All the better to see you with!' he squealed from his strained neck in a kind of Mexican.

'Is everyone watching?' said Alexandra to the group floating around her at the centre of the pool. 'Godfrey's creating here and now. Do we think it's because he has no shirt on? Bearing his soul to the gods of tomorrow? Remember what he said about creative nudity? Or is it because of the holy mountain waters? Divine madness.' She extended a demonstrative hand towards his head, shaking under the fountain. 'This, is what The Creative Art of Wishfulness can do to us if we take it fully into our brave soul lives!'

'The mind washed out with goddam soap.' Godfrey's neck was hosed by falling water. 'The soul cleansed by a backyard abortion clinic with zero qualifications and dirty tools. Bimbo Baggins spoiled by the CIA and reason stole by wishdom! You *stole* fizzy lifting drinks!! You lose, good day, sir! That land has been had, it's gone. Draaiiiiiiinage!' He tensed his neck and raised his face to the spout. 'Drainage, Godfrey, you boy. Drained dry.'

Between the Lawn of Authentic Growth and the Zone of Incredible Vibes, at the top of the Slope of Artspiration, there stood the Chamber of Alchemical Change, used for the final evening's ceremony by practically all the fifty wellness retreats which each year ran at Zen Resort.

At the centre of the long pavilion a square fire-pit with low walls blazed. Lines of red and pink flower petals ran along the narrow gradations in the slate which rose to the pit's edge. Alexandra stood alone at its western side. Her co-facilitators had hot knees at its corners as Bradley hit a drum with a leather-ended stick. The surviving wishful alchemists stood in a loose circle, from Godfrey at one end to Venerika ringing a small bell at the other.

The night was already broiling. Though waiting over rising flames had soaked his shirt to dark, Godfrey's constant face-sweating was nowhere near the evening's most severe. M.T. Dillika and Donny Vossehol both were leaking at the forehead. Her blood poisoning was coming on strongly and his e. coli infection had started very loudly to grumble. He clutched at his aching stomach as M.T. shivered and Alexandra Wishart spoke.

'Welcome to the sacred Havanam Fire Ceremony. I *am* the dragon goddess who has just realised she's not a lizard, and now I'm learning to spit fire. Fire has been used in the process of alchemy by every culture on earth, to turn base materials into the elixir of purposeful life. Fire's used to combine the ingredients that create our own organic panacea—fire, is what our souls should be on. Alchemy is you touching my arm, and it setting *fire* to my soul.

'In the very back of your Dreambinders you'll find a tearable sheet of paper called Yesterday's Nonspiration. Tonight I want us *all* to write down our pain, write down things that we did previously that did *not* make us forget to eat and sleep, and we're going to let go of them all, now, in this Chamber of Alchemical Change.' She looked to the yellow-lit ceiling and bulged her eyes and smiled. 'And once we've cleansed ourselves of pain, we're going to stand up and look each other in the eye and make a promise to Agni, the Balinese god of Fire, to start only doing things that make us forget to eat and sleep. We're *all* going to make one Resolution of Revolt. It might be the wish you made at the water temple. It might be simply to embrace uncertainty and step into the field of possibility. And we say it *loud*, because from now on we are all Wishful Alchemists together, and Wishful Alchemy is creating your art from your life and your life from your art. Who'd like to go first?'

The group seemed strangely unwilling. Donny was using most of his strength and concentration to hold in the contents of his stomach. M.T. was beginning to hallucinate. Felix felt still, despite four and a half days of exploring his bluest shortcomings, that he had only ever done things that made him forget to eat and sleep. Fairchild was filling in the last page of his Dreambinder while Turbot worked up the courage to think about beginning to do likewise.

Eventually Ne'cole stepped forward and raised a hand. 'I'll go.' She closed her eyes and threw her screwed up piece of paper into the fire then bounced onto and off her bare toes.

'Before this retreat I felt empty. And the one thing I can say of

Alexandra, and Godfrey, and Venerika, and Hennifer, is that you guys have filled me back up. There's so much authentic genuineness here, so much radical revitalizing empowerment, so *much* creative wishfulness. So my Resolution of Revolt… is…' She paused. Bradley tapped faster at his drum. Ne'cole smiled in anticipation of announcing to the group what had been for the last six hours brimming inside her. 'I'm going to start my own retreat!'

An unbeaten drum and silent bell.

'The Art of Creative Wishfulness,' she announced. Jennifer with a soft j was joined in applause by Felix and Fairchild; Donny slapped his thigh with one sweaty hand; Godfrey wrinkled his chin and nodded.

'That's amazing, Ne'cole,' said Alexandra, unwilling to look in her direction. She thought of her own branding and her own content: 'I hope it's as successful as you deserve it to be,'—her own business.

'I think I should go next,' said Venerika, turning her bell up as she raised her hand to ask.

'My God, please, yes!' said Alexandra.

Venerika stepped forward and dropped into the fire the sheet torn from her Dreambinder. 'I too, am going to start my own retreat. A writing retreat. Not just workshops anymore. It'll include Write Yourself Free, and Alexandra I hope you'll come and teach us how to rewrite our lives. I *think* it'll be called Wildspiragination. And as well as passing on the techniques of splendacious descriptiveness, I'm going to take people through the whole munimous journey of writing wildly free perfervid poet-tree.'

Ne'cole had long been applauding while jumping up and down. Donny slapped his thigh and M.T. stared at the ceiling and redoubled her efforts towards not fainting. Godfrey, with a very wrinkled chin, felt ill after Venerika's attempt at rhyme. 'Can I?'

'Do you have a resolution?' Alexandra asked, certain that he did not and expecting him to disrespect her ceremony.

'I have a revolting resolution, yes.'

'Do you really?'

'Yes,' said Godfrey, almost offended by the suspicion.

'Proceed.'

'Thank you.' He stepped forward. 'Firstly I just wanted to say how amazing an opportunity it's been to meet you all. You've all given me so much. So so much—more than you could know. But none as much as Alexandra, who's provided me with this opportunity to share my creativity techniques with the world, and who's brought me to this beautiful island. Thank you, Alexandra, sincerely.' Conceding that he might be taking seriously her ceremony she nodded once and very gratefully accepted his gratitude. 'Oh, and here,' said Godfrey, and dropped his scrunched up piece of blank paper into the fire. 'Be gone! So my revolting resolution is… to not never be so unafraid of none of all the world. To go into and out of and through it, more fullier, so that not just the most peoples than Black Hebron will see throughout and of my paintings when I display them in the national gallery of the worlds. To get out of my owned way, and from now on and henceforth hitherto to build some apart from just of my paintings, and try to not to always not be working so unalone. I thank you.' And he stepped back from the pit as though returning to formation.

Alexandra felt herself proud. She had gotten through to him after all. He had not only not made a mockery of her sacred Havanam Fire Ceremony, but had made a Resolution of Revolt swearing to all present that he had been listening to her the whole time, that the same insatiable wanderlust burned within him as with her, that he could not wait to continue their journey together, that he would build his own website. (I mean, what a soulspirational success she'd made of the boy!) 'I'll go next if you guys don't mind?' Godfrey's applause died down and the drum and bell rose again to prominence.

She closed her eyes and threw her piece of paper into the fire. She grabbed at its smoke and ran it over the top of her head. Then she spoke solemnly to the flames. 'I swear, by the moon and the stars in the skies, to stop seeing the world as I would like it to be, and,' she momentarily smiled at Godfrey, 'to start seeing the world as it *is*. Then, with wishful alchemy, to use that new audacious reality to transform my own. I soared the sky looking for birds to keep me company, and not until I sang my truth did they arrive. So I resolve to sing my truth—seen as it is, not as I would like it to be—in order to attract more birds to my song.' Godfrey's chin was very wrinkled. He had nodded with relief at her first resolution, then with exhausted acceptance at her profession of flight. Alexandra caught him nodding only at her very final resolution: 'And I resolve this year to travel to a country that I've never been to before, and to not be alone on those travels.'

He jolted to her his very not-nodding head. Hers it was that now bobbed up and down. His they were whose eyes now bulged.

'I'm ready,' said Turbot.

'Please, yes, thank you!' said Alexandra, transitioning without applause. 'This is such a huge moment for us all. Can we all feel the transformative energy? The Alchemy of Fire? We can't wait to hear your resolution, Turbot. Please.'

Turbot took half a step forward and read from the slip of paper in her hand.

'This morning at the water temple I wished for the strength to be able to exercise my right to choose whether or not my parents had a right to give birth to me. Listening to all your brave resolutions and your authentic determination, I've realised that I do have that strength.' She raised her arms from her sides and took another half step forward. The beat of Bradley's drum accelerated to its fastest yet. 'Thanks to The Creative Art of Wishfulness, I *have* the strength to choose whether or not I was born.' And Turbot Slurritrend leaned forward with her arms outstretched and leaned forward, and leaned forward—and leaned forward—until her bare toes left the slate and her throat and pelvis hit the raised edge of the fire pit.

'What the fuck?' said Godfrey as with Fairchild and Jennifer with a soft j he stepped in to pull Turbot from the flames. She very quickly tucked herself into a ball, so as to fit fully sideways into that sacred space of non-judgment—that is to say, the fire.

The final Creative Art of Wishfulness dinner was held in the Spirit Restaurant. Of the Wishful Alchemists only Ne'cole, Felix, and Fairchild were in attendance. Donny and M.T. had elected to ride in the ambulance which took Turbot to the hospital. Godfrey brought to the long table a half bottle of Balinese rum and eleven beers.

The abiding and almost tangible mood was one of apprehension. Nobody was certain that it had been a good ending to a retreat nor were any absolutely convinced that it had been a bad one. Certainly none would ever ascribe an unpositive epithet to their Creative Art of Wishfulness. Most had decided merely to profess to feeling— the co-facilitators and Ne'cole from experience—that the ending had been an unexpected one.

Before their food arrived Godfrey asked for eight shot glasses. Bradley exclaimed that he was drinking to honour fallen comrades. Jennifer with a soft j drank to everyone's speedy recovery and said that toilets are layers of exclusion. Fairchild sipped and said that he was grateful to be healthy. Felix drank and said that the rum tasted purple. Ne'cole and Venerika abstained, the latter saying, 'Recovery! That was one of my favourite words in November. A great name for a retreat, don't you think? Creative Recovery. Like rehab, but for creativity.' Alexandra took a very small sip and winced and thought about her testimonials, her branding, her business. Then with overriding joy she thought of Godfrey's resolution. Godfrey downed his shot and thought about who was most likely to leave their beers for him to drink. Then with the expectation to create lifted—all obligation to be alchemical gone and the pressure to be their best *most genuine* selves released—conversation soon came on easier and less metaphorically than it yet had done. Nobody was even forced to connect with their food before they ate it.

Felix talked of all the colours he had seen in Bali. Fairchild talked of the strength and the power of the full blood wolf moon ceremony. Alexandra added: 'I really feel the pull of Mercury in retrograde, you know?' Ne'cole explained how full each of the favourite workshops had made her. Jennifer with a soft j said that she had never seen so many people owning their awesome and that carrots used to be purple. Venerika said that some of her new favourite words were Picasso, wheelbarrow, Wishcraft, communication, and backwards. With raised eyebrows, lips, and nostrils she thanked Godfrey for giving them to her. Though they disliked, resented, and were suspicious of him, Godfrey Lackland was still an object of exploitative interest to the other facilitators. Having risen to the positions of Creativity Counsellor *and* Happiness Captain without even being a lifecoach—and having been brought to Bali to lead soulspeditions without ever designing an online course—all wanted very much to figure him out.

'How 'bout you, G-bro?' said B-rad.

'Yes!' said Venerika. 'Where to next? Where will your resolution take you?'

'India,' said Godfrey. 'India alone.'

'I've lived on the banks of the Ganges since the turn of the century,' said Jennifer with a soft j. 'I try to challenge whiteness once a day.'

'White,' said Felix and did not elaborate.

'India alone as in only India?' said Venerika.

'No, no. India alone. By myself.'

'Didn't you resolve to stop being alone?' said Ne'cole.

'One of my revolting resolutions *was* to try to not to always not

145

be working so unalone, yes. But I have six weeks in India to do one big work—my magnum opus, as Alexandra would say—and then the world's my oyster, inside a tomato, growing a midget's thumb.'

'You always work and travel alone?' said Ne'cole, seated beside him.

'I must.'

'Because you have to or you want to?'

'I have to.' Then Godfrey simpered and tilted his head down to her. 'Though I could be persuaded into making an exception for you of course.'

'Oh I have so much work to do!' said Ne'cole, spraying jubilance over the table like a waterfall onto ponchoed tourists. 'I have to build my sales page, I have to find a resort—I wonder if I should ask them here—I have to design the life design! Oh, I feel so radiantly alive!'

Perhaps it was the repeated use of the 'a' word; perhaps it was the absence of the 'I'. Alexandra pulled back that gremlinny grin which betrayed in her discomfort and slid sideways out of her chair and said, 'Excuse me,' and disappeared into the darkness of the Lawn of Authentic Growth.

All at the table stared wishfully at Godfrey. 'What?'

'Go,' said Ne'cole.

'What do you mean, go? Go where?'

'Go,' said Venerika, nodding.

'I have more crystals than friends,' said Jennifer with a soft j. 'She needs you.'

'What the hell does that mean?'

'We all know, brah. It's OK.'

'You all know what?' Godfrey lowered an eyebrow to the tablecloth.

'She wont show it, but she's fragile,' said Ne'cole. 'Go.'

'I don't want to go,' said Godfrey as a child.

'She told us.'

'Told you what?!'

'Trust us,' said Ne'cole. 'We've all been through so much together. She needs you.'

'She does not need me. She definitely needs someone, she doesn't need me.'

All eyes still fixed authentically on him, Godfrey realised that the truth was in no way any of their truths. 'God fucking damn it,' he said and took a newly opened beer with him.

146

Alexandra had walked only as far as the Zone of Incredible Vibes. Leaning back onto a palm trunk with her arms crossed, she stared with one hand cradling her cheek.

'What's your problem now?'

She threw a hand in his direction as she pushed off the tree and hurried past the Tipi of Fanatical Tolerance. Godfrey walked after her. 'What are you doing?' she yelled sideways.

'I'm stepping into the field of possibility. What does it look like I'm doing?'

'This is the Slope of Artspiration.'

'Fuck off. It's *astounding* what you don't hear, do you know that? Astounding. And what you don't listen to. And I am sure that whatever you've told those people back there is the most astounding thing of all. Will you stop walking? Hello?'

'Astounding?' She stopped and turned between the fishpond and reception. Behind her, the peaks of the bungalows rose black against the starless sky. 'Astounding? Astounding!? I'll tell you what's astounding. You don't even have the balls to admit—. Come on! *Come on*!' She smiled with bulging eyes. 'It's like... OK, here's the thing. I don't... Come on, are you serious?' she laughed. 'It's like you won't even—Like, are you *serious*!? Come on! Because *I* think it's astounding that—I don't know, I just don't know. Come on. Seriously?' she laughed.

Godfrey drank from his beer and awaited coherence.

'I just don't—. I'm not—. Come on! I don't invest this amount of energy in someone. I don't spend this time with someone unless I'm interested in... Nnnnmn. In them. You won't even—. Are you serious? Come on. Maybe not as a boyfriend,' she chuckled, 'not right now, but unless there's a bigger interest I just don't spend the time.'

'Again I ask, what are you talking about?'

'I'm alone. And any chance to do something is always welcome but logically—*logically*—I don't invest this time unless I'm interested in more. And I sit there and I listen to you say, again and again, you want to be *alone*? If it's the case I don't think it's good that we see each other anymore. Maybe it doesn't bother you because you're made of steel, but it *bothers* me! I don't feel, I just don't feel good, I don't—I'm not trying to get anything more out of you, OK? But I don't want to think anymore, I want to have fun! And I don't know, I guess you don't like me like that.' She leaned back and waved her hands in the air and shouted: 'I guess he doesn't like me like that! But I can't complain or say anything because if I complain then I'm jealous! But I'm *not* jealous!' She threw her fingertips from her forehead: 'I'm the most open-minded and understanding person you'll ever meet! Even if we *were* together and you wanted to see other people I would understand! I don't want anything serious *either*.' Her knuckles beat at her clavicle like a silverback's at its chest. 'But I put all this energy into getting to know someone, and it feels like a letdown. I don't know what it is—I just know I want sex! I don't want to talk anymore! So if you don't want to have sex with me, then we shouldn't see each other again.'

Godfrey smiled. 'That is so insulting, Alexandra. And still, I have absolutely no idea what you're talking about.'

'Of course you don't! Because you're too busy flirting to truly understand anyone, to connect. Even flirting with me to get what you want, but you don't *see* the hurt you cause. I'm not even upset right now! I'm not. I even hope we can keep this in some way. It's almost romantic. Haha! It's romantic, back and forth between us, will-they-won't-they? Walking at sunset, and riding motorbikes.' The rollercoaster was back. 'But then it comes to night time and you pretend you're asexual, or you flirt with Ne'cole while I'm sitting right across from you! Do you want *her*? Do you love her?' Alexandra hunched her shoulders and squinted. 'Do you want everyone but me?! Am I that ugly? I don't know, but then I do know because I know you do that, you have sex, you fucked your bimbo in my pool.'

'Woah,' said Godfrey in one of his parabolas. 'Here we go.'

'I don't want to be building, or investing so much *energy*, if there's not going to be any sex in it for me!' She rounded the pond and leaned over the frog and pointed at herself and growled. 'These people, they talk to me, they talk to me for a whole fucking year, and then they can't even fuck me!? And you're one of them! No, you're the worst of all, because you won't even admit it. What is all this talking for, Godfrey?'

'It's yelling, this is not talking.'

'I want to finish it! I want some fun, physical fun! I'm tired of being in my head and talking, it's boring hanging out with you if there's no chance of sex!'

'Thanks a lot.'

'I'm tired of it all, I'm so bored. It's like nothing happens at the end, you push me away—it's all conversations and no orgasms. To me it's natural to have sex! Is that not natural to you!? Can't we at least finish what we started!? Can't we fuck?'

'You can't talk to people like this, Alexandra.'

'And then we don't have to talk again! We don't have to see each other ever. But you take off at the end of the night and fuck someone else and I'm always going to bed alone!? Alone!' From a brief foray into screaming she subsided into wistfulness. 'I guess we're both so alone you can't even see it. Just two artists in a fishbowl, and our art is the fire that we light and it projects these shadows—you know?—on the wall and you think they're your friends and you start talking to them.'

'Alexandra.'

'But then someone walks in like that Jew or Ne'cole and they turn the light on and you see the shadows were just your own hands all along.'

'Alexandra.'

'What?'

'You are not an artist.'

'I need support and saving too, in my own way, and I won't ask for it unless I feel there's a desire to offer it, and I haven't felt that from you since we set foot in Bali. I felt it in Bangkok.'

'Felt what?!' Hitherto calm and somewhat enjoying the spectacle of perfect irrationality, Godfrey in a high voice almost threw the questions at her and the night. 'What are you talking about!? Huh? You met me randomly. You came up to me and said, "You're gonna think I'm weird but I just felt I *had* to talk to you." And I did think you were weird, but I didn't say anything because I was starving and I needed more cheese.'

'More cheese, that's all I am to you! Cheese and lies!' she shouted to the air high above the pool. 'Cheese and lies! Cheese and lies! The lies, Godfrey! I value truth above *everything else* and you couldn't even give me that. You lied about seeing your bimbo, you lied about being afraid of monkeys, you lied about having a girlfriend in Bangkok. From day *one* you've lied! Does your girlfriend know about your bimbo? Does your bimbo know about your girlfriend?'

'I don't have a girlfriend,' Godfrey said from behind clenched teeth.

'I *saw* you kissing her.'

'No, you stalked me and you made your own fucking conclusions. You arrived at your own truth.'

'I stalked you? Oh, yes, I stalked you! I wouldn't *have* to stalk you if you had social media, but noooo! You're too good for social media. Just like you're too good for everyone, too good for me even though you told me I was your destiny. Then to spend a whole week of nights hearing you breathe without ever opening up to me as a human being or truly communicating?'

'Woah, woah, woah—slow down there, crazy horse. When the fuck did I say you were my destiny?'

'In the taxi.' Godfrey's eyes searched fruitlessly for recall, retention, recognition. 'You said that once your destiny has been revealed there's no happiness if you don't follow it, and that there we were.'

'There is no chance in hell I said that.'

'And then you didn't remember the orchid, but—'

'What orchid!?' Godfrey thrashed. 'Are there cameras watching me? Is this an impractical goddam joke?'

'At the restaurant in Bangkok.' Alexandra tried to calm herself; swallowed deeply between phrases. 'There was an orchid on the table, and when you arrived, I was wearing a dress, with orange orchids. But you didn't remember.'

'You are lost, Alexandra. Lost. What kind of a lonely fantasyland do you live in?'

'All I wanted was for you to communicate truly. You're free to do what you want, Godfrey, but I just don't spend this much time for nothing.'

'And I don't want to spend time with you. Honestly. Spending time with you is like hanging out with a judgmental Romanian auntie. Look at yourself. Listen, to yourself! Screaming abuse at me in the middle of the night, in the middle of a resort, throwing guilt at me, just like you throw guilt at these empty guinea pigs in exchange for five thousand fucking dollars to come to Bali and be your friend!'

'I can't *believe* I paid you five thousand dollars for this,' she sighed, disappointed in her own optimism.

'Paid him what?' said Jennifer with a soft j Toogood.

Hearing from the Spirit Restaurant the tone and volume, but not the content, of their exchanges, Alexandra's co-creators had thought it best to go and see if they were both all right.

'I only got two thousand,' said Venerika Odorono.

'We get two-k and he got five?' said Bradley Farquwheat.

'Oh guys,' said Alexandra, saddened that they had found out.

'That's not fair,' declared Jennifer with a soft j. 'Does he even suffer from transgenerational trauma?'

'Guys, Godfrey gets nothing else out of the retreat. He has no other products to push to the alchemists.'

'That's less than half,' said Bradley. 'I just redid my bathroom. A.W.? I sent you a selfie in it.'

'This isn't right, Alexandra. *Five*-k?'

'Guys. This is an organic co-creation. I've said it before. You signed the agreement and were happy with what you were getting.'

'Yeah but we didn't know he'd be getting more than us,' said Venerika. 'He's not even a lifecoach.'

'We do this for love, remember? Plus all the extra components you can sell. Venerika, I heard you selling Write Yourself Free to Fairchild. Godfrey doesn't have that.'

'Already free,' said Godfrey, raising a hand to the affronted crowd. 'Throaty twinkle.'

Alexandra now seemed to return to the seriousness with which she had begun her seminar. She ran her hair behind her ears and stood up straight and became meticulously animated.

'You know how I feel about what we do. The retreat has to be a "Fuck Yes" from everyone. You should want to do it for nothing. Without a "Fuck Yes" what are we *even* doing here, you know?'

'Fuck yes, I have a mortgage,' said B-rad.

'And fuck yes I have two children,' said Jennifer with a soft j. 'If it doesn't make money it doesn't make sense.'

'Fuck yes I have my own retreat to worry about,' said Venerika.

'And Godfrey's a struggling artist.'

'So am I.'

'So am I.'

'So am I.'

'No, Godfrey's a real artist,' said Alexandra.

'So am I.' 'So am I.' 'So am I,' came almost at once.

'No, listen. Guys. Godfrey is actually a real artist.'

'Gasp, Gasp, Gasp,' came precisely all at once, followed by three, 'And what are we then?'s.

'I'm so tired.' Alexandra's bulging eyes now shined a sore red in the blue of the distant pool's light. 'So tired. Can we talk about this tomorrow?'

'You'll be hearing from my lawyers,' said Jennifer with a soft j Toogood. 'Gender is a spectrum.'

VI

As three sticks of incense were placed across three offerings at the mossy pedestal before Ganesh—and the tropical birds whooped their morning song above a young woman in a white tunic crossing dry grass in the new light of morning, bright all between the long shadows of young coconut trees—and as prayer drums frolicked through the valley behind Zen Resort and her sister waved in figure-eights a pink orchid through white incense smoke rising within the stone-carved niche of their family's spirit shrine—Godfrey Lackland had endured.

The sky seemed softer and the heat gentler, the jungle more temperate, the birds less panicked. For a moment even the chainsaws seemed to stop buzzing. Momentarily his room smelled of jasmine rather than rubbish fire. Rising without a sense of dread, he knocked on the front door of the bungalow beside his own.

He heard shuffling within but was given no answer. He knocked again. 'Alexandra?' The shuffling seemed to panic; Godfrey thought he heard it trying to open the back door. He turned the doorknob and found beside her unmade bed Fairchild McMonnies.

'What are you doing in here?'

'The moon made me do it. Nothing.'

'Made you do what?'

Godfrey looked to Fairchild's elbows. His hands were behind his back. Fairchild shook his head and lowered two MacBooks to his sides, one with a purple devanagari om stickered over its logo, the other with the Eye of Providence in a green triangle.

'What the hell are you doing?'

'The moon made me do it.'

'Get the fuck out of here, would you? Where's Alexandra?'

'Not here,' said Fairchild and attempted to leave the room.

'Give me those,' said Godfrey as Fairchild passed him with the MacBooks in hand. 'Jesus, you people.'

Staring off into space while she turned a reusable latte cup in her hand, Alexandra Wishart was at Healing Foods Café.

'You look like someone died,' said Godfrey.

152

'Apart from Nancy and Turbot?'

'I caught Fairchild trying to steal these.'

'I'll just buy more. The one definite Why I have in life is money. I gave so much of myself that my aloneness became a tunnel that nobody could enter. I need to be re-alived again. The journey to self is never lost or won and I just didn't come this far to only come this far.'

'We need to talk about last night.'

Alexandra dismissed him in three descending notes. 'No we don't.'

'We do. You can't speak to people like that. This isn't even about me. This is about how you interact with the whole world, with other people.'

'We're not people.'

'Then what are we?'

'Artists. I was sad you're leaving.'

'You were screaming at me like I was a child or an animal. Do you remember what you said?'

'I don't want to hear it.'

'Of course you don't. Because it won't fit in with your image of yourself, will it? You can't listen to your own words if they don't fit in with how you want to see yourself. That's deranged, Alexandra.'

'You're focusing on the caca. I don't have time to remember the caca.'

'The caca. Do you want to know what I prayed for yesterday at the water temple?' She stared still at the display case of vegan cakes and turned the cup. 'I prayed for you to say what you mean and for you to mean what you say. For your sake, not mine. I reserved my one wish, for you.'

'You did that for me?' For the first time since his arrival she looked him in the eyes, and smiled.

'For you to have a relationship—' Momentarily her eyes bulged with excitement. 'With the truth. Not your truth, the truth. The actual world. There's no such thing as your truth. Do you understand this?'

'My Godfrey, you still don't get it! I choose to remember the twenty times we laughed till we peed ourselves. I choose to remember the sunsets and the riverboat cruises and the music and all the dancing and all the times you made the complicated so simple, and our adventures. Today's World Eating Disorder Day. But none of it matters now. We part ways and never see each other again. It's fine.'

'Why does it jump straight to never seeing each other again?'

'I want to watch the northern lights and run with the wolves. Maybe I'll go to the mountains of Northern France to die like my heroes. I don't know where I'll go. I have no one to be anywhere for. I guess I could go back to Vancouver.'

'You're Canadian?'

'You don't know the first thing about me. You never wanted to connect, you just wanted to use me, like everyone else.'

'You're the one who uses, Alexandra. You brought me here for sex, d'you remember that? God fucking damn it. I just want to do my work as an artist, you're the one that came along and sucked all the energy out of everything.'

'I dread the aloneness waiting for me there. The thought of eating alone in a big city. I'm tired of people hiding from me and pushing me away. I don't have time for it anymore.'

'Where do you *want* to be, Alexandra? Don't worry about anyone else, or about being alone. Where do *you, want, to be*?' Her staring was beginning to anger him. 'Do you have family?

She sighed and stared and turned the latte cup faster than before. 'When one thing passes, what does a creator do?' She looked at Godfrey and answered her own question: 'She doesn't hold onto the caterpillar's corpse. She turns herself into a new creature, and becomes the butterfly that causes hurricanes.'

'You have a very profound misunderstanding of the lifecycle of a caterpillar. There are no mountains in the north of France. Where does your head exist? Honestly.'

'I've never *been* anything but worthy, and waking up to your true nature is like entering the eye of paradox, I *am* a unique storm. You can't take that away from me.'

'I don't want to take whatever the crap you just said away from you. But I definitely don't want to be a part of Hurricane Alexandra.'

'We part ways and never see each other again. I don't even know why you're here. I have to go, my taxi's here. I didn't even know I didn't have my MacBooks, that's how much you hurt me.'

Alexandra Wishart rumbled two suitcases across the paved drive to the waiting van and spun their handles to the driver. With her guitar slung at her back she turned and put her hand on top of her new fedora and looked from behind large sunglasses at the gardened jungle in front of the resort's arrival pavilion.

'I'll see you next year!' she said to it. 'Fiercely.'

Godfrey Lackland pulled a suitcase to the top of the steps. He switched the strap of a loaded duffle bag from one shoulder to the other in order to lift her third suitcase onto his thigh and cart it down the steps.

'You didn't have to help me to the taxi.' She pinned her hair back with her sunglasses. 'I know you don't want to spend time with me.' He helped her take the guitar from her back and handed it to the driver.

'I don't know why you think that, Alexandra. You act like I hate you. I just don't like being yelled at. By anyone.'

She stepped back and up into the van and mumbled, 'Mm hm.'

'I'll see you 'round?'

'You don't want to.'

Godfrey became emphatic. 'Why do you think that?! Goddam it, honestly.'

'Should I think that you do?' she said, with bulging eyes and wobbling head.

'I don't not want to see you, Alexandra.'

'You don't?' And the driver slid the van's door across.

Alexandra peeked through the window's curtains and waved and blew Godfrey a kiss. For the last time in Bali his chin wrinkled beneath his scrunched nose beneath very furrowed eyebrows.

Godfrey searched through his music player for the song he had been holding onto since the first morning of The Creative Art of Wishfulness. He pressed play. Through the dome-speaker on the balustrade came the opening cry in baritone and whine of *Free At Last*.

A pizza, ordered from the Spirit Kitchen, sweated on a plate on the glass-topped table between two chairs. Having tracked down some prosecco he stood facing the pool and shook the bottle and looked back at Or. 'You ready?'

Bradley Farquwheat bounded up the stairs to say goodbye. Godfrey turned at the sudden yelling of 'Namaste, bro!' and pushed the cork with his thumbs from the bottle's neck. Its fat end hit Bradley in the eye socket. He fell back holding his face and thumped and flopped onto the first landing.

Godfrey laughed and filled Or's glass then his own and stood on his balcony and sang in his deepest voice his favourite verse: *If I'm too young to pray I ain't too young to die. Thank God Almighty I'm free at last.'*

He drank from his glass and smacked his lips apart and gave a long hiss of deliciousness. He downed the rest in one gulp and sat beside Or as he refilled. He lifted a slice from its plate and lowered his mouth to catch its drooping end. 'There is *so much* palm oil on this pizza. Why?'

'So I looked your friend up,' said Or.

'What friend?'

'Alexandra Wishart.'

'Please don't say her name. Not yet. Way too soon'

'No, but listen. She has a *huge* following. And her posts sound insane. But everything that her followers say to her is positive, but not normal positive, like crazy *crazy* positive. "You are the most amazing this." "You are the truly enchanted goddess." "You speak rainbows of truth where others drown me with disconsolingation." I've never heard this word. I think it was weird for her to find somebody that didn't have thought she was the most amazing person, right?'

'Welcome to the real world, sister.' Godfrey folded the slice in half and spoke as he chewed: 'So I have a question for you.'

'Oh yes?'

'Come to India.'

'That is a question or a demand?'

'Which would you prefer?'

'First I have to ask you a question.' Godfrey nodded once as he swallowed. 'I am engaged.' He nodded a few more times and tongued masticated crust from his molars. 'This was supposed to be my honeymoon but I called it off at the last minute, and I say I want to go alone.'

'So you... cheated on your fiancé with me?' Godfrey could not tell if he was flattered or insulted.

'Well, no. Well, technically yes. When I met you, the day after I met you, the morning after you slept over actually, I called it completely off. For good.'

Godfrey pouted and nodded and soon said, 'India?'

'You don't care?'

'Why would I care? You're not still with the guy. Let's go to India.'

'We should go to India together?'

'Why not?'

'That's crazy.'

'Oh, it's crazy all right.'

'I have a villa in Canggu for six days. I can come next week?'

'I'll be there from tomorrow. The vanguard. I'll scope the joint out, find the best discotheques, the triangliest samosas. And we'll hang out in India for a while.'

'India together?'

'The freshest of fresh starts after a week of pure hell.'

The quiet fuzz of transferred vinyl cut to perfect silence; shortly drums were whacked and an electrified harmonica jived and trilled. Godfrey pointed to the speaker as his chin bounced. Then Little Walter sang: *'Ain't no need-a goin' no further brother...'*

'Will there be music there?'

'Ain't no need-a goin' no further man!'

'We will always have music in India.'

'And singing?'

'I should hope so.'

'Dancing?'

'Definitely not.'

'There will be no jealousy, right?'

'Zero jealousy, no fake languages, no surveillance, no expectations, zero mind games, very zero screaming matches. Just painting, you, and I, in India.'

'And will there be sex?'

'There will——. Yes. There will be that. A great deal of that.'

'Then I see you there.'

Little Walter seemed now to shout as the song ended—*'Your money's gone and your health is bad, all you can tell is the fun you had. Ain't no need-a goin' no further now.'*—and the harmonica began to fade out.

'What'll you do in India?'

Or turned her head and smirked, pushing dimples into her cheeks.

'You.'

ACT FOUR

Madurai, Athens of The East

I

Robin Williams dressed as Pan, the only god who dies, flying with his arms wide, a leash at his neck held two levels below by a fifty-armed Chinese Mahasadasiva, a phone in each of her other hands taking pictures of her twenty-five faces.

A Smurf Beyoncé riding a peacock, blue beside the sketch of a four-armed Gorky's foot on the shoulder of a cowering Larry David; a chubby Assistant Manager in full spandex, bug-eyed and cross-legged upon his bicycle seat within a flame-arched niche—and between them all as pink devas and blue guardians, rat-headed politicians wearing Nascar jackets with the logos of their sponsors stitched onto their breasts and stuck onto their visored helmets.

Godfrey Lackland penned the final curve of a baby boomer's tusk then added a zhong and a guo to each padded sleeve before allowing himself to look from his sketchbook up to its sublime model—a rajagopuram sloping sharply to its spiked and rounded top, erupting from the sparkling olive waters of the temple tank over which it towered, smashing calmly through the sandstone colonnade upon which it seemed to rest.

He had come to Madurai to look upon the many-sculpted towers of the city's renowned Meenakshi temple. He had not expected to be utterly taken by them.

Of infinite variety—the labour surely of a thousand men over a dozen centuries—he had been so fixated by this southern great gopuram that he had made its aspect his first open-air Indian studio. The city's tallest edifice, it was divided into nine tapering levels, a number which Godfrey took as a sign of the rightness of his work. The idea for his *Nine Levels of Purgatory* (hell having been abolished as too extreme) had been growing for two years and his notes were providing him with more grotesques than he could include in so small a work. But on four A4 pages he was piecing

159

together his own left half of the southern great tower—the bottom three tiers spread over facing pages, the second three on a page turned sideways, the top tiers on their slender own and less detailed.

In the shade of the colonnade which enclosed the temple tank, Godfrey put his binoculars to his eyes and inspected the ribbed trousers of a flame-haired Kali, the scrotal protrusion from her belly, and tried to make out what exactly was in each of her hands. There seemed a trowel, a wooden spoon, a bo—.

'Mr Godfrey, three o'clock, sir.'

'Already?' Godfrey said to Suman, the police officer he had taken on as tour guide and clock. 'Thank you, Superman.'

'You are welcome, sir. Today is the day, isn't it?'

'Today *is* the day, isn't it!'

'Very happy for you, sir.'

Godfrey closed his sketchbook and rolled up his pens and pencils and strolled along the stone ledge—rounded the fading flaxen vista of bronze lotus and thick golden flagpole and red-and-white striped wall and palm tree crown. The gushing of the water jets filtering the tank loudened as he neared the central coloured walkway.

A truck beeped once as it rolled past the brown wire fencing in front of the main entrance. A machine poking out from its tray buzzed as it ran a white stream of diesel smoke around the temple's perimeter.

Godfrey strode through the smoke with his forearm across his mouth. He stepped into the sunshine of the pink-and-white bricked street which encircled the temple—the orange and melon and lime stands, the men in shirtsleeves hobbling with lungis folded like diapers, the young women in short saris over trousers with jasmine strings in their hair, the older with their bellies out in full-length gold-woven dress. The smell became one of cardamom and incense as prayer music warbled in perpetual crescendo beneath the distant beeps of traffic. A hope-eyed man at his soft-serve machine amid the fabric shops and the banana stands called Godfrey over as he stepped onto and down from and onto the kerb upon which plastic-toy vendors squatted behind their wares on outspread handkerchiefs. At the corner, steel bowl after steel bowl of deep fried food was arranged upon tiered crates outside the shop to whose samosas Godfrey was becoming addicted. Then beyond the yellow steel barricades which kept the temple street relatively quiet as traffic-free, a man dodged a cow as he rounded a corner on his high-cycled cart and Godfrey's path became one of evasion and careful pacing. The street surged with a torrent of yellow auto and thin scooter and wandering cow and rumbling Royal Enfield and creaking bicycle.

'Ah, India,' Godfrey exhaled happily to himself as he froggered to his motorbike.

He slid his sketchbook and pens into the leather saddlebag over the petrol tank and squeezed the clutch as he pulled the bike back into the street. He put the key into the ignition and hoisted a leg over and found neutral with his toes—kicked the engine to running and joined the dusty river of vehicles.

He was one of three leaning against the chrome bars outside arrivals. As he waited he watched himself in widescreen in the mirrored glass overhead, the blue of his shirt pale against the concrete reflected behind him, the lenses of his sunglasses flares of red among the dull leaves of the manicured bushes at the foot of the ashen hills in the furthest distance. Soon the glass doors opened. Out came a luggage-bearing Indian. Then a family. Then a succession of families, drifting all towards taxi drivers. At last, the pale and slender figure for whom Godfrey was there.

She had on her grey skirt with the falcon feathers, her shoulders bare above a flowing white top. She looked left and found no one, scanned right and found Godfrey smiling against the rail.

'You seem happy to see me.'

He grabbed the tops of her arms, not quite her shoulders and not her biceps, and stepped in. 'More than you know.' He kissed her cheek. 'Welcome to India.'

She patted him on the back and leaned away. 'It's the emptiest airport I ever seen.'

'Empty?' Godfrey smiled. 'Hoo hoo! Just you wait. Now come here.'

Godfrey took her fingers from her suitcase handle and put them behind his back and embraced and kissed her. 'What? Oh.' She kept her mouth closed then said, 'I feel gross.'

'You do feel gross.'

'Hoi!'

'But you look amazing. Shall we?'

He wheeled her suitcase to his bike, parked in tree-shade on red dirt beside two concrete barrels, one labelled 'dustbin', the other 'dust bin'.

'The only place in the world where they actually have bins for dust,' Godfrey said as though narrating an advertisement.

'Really, they do?'

From the young trees overhead several crows cawed in triplets as Godfrey strapped Or's suitcase to the rack behind the seat.

'I guess I shouldn't have wore a skirt,' she said, contemplating sitting behind him.

'Side-saddle?'

'What? Hang on.' She looked around, then hitched up her skirt and moved a foot and a leg through the gap between Godfrey's back and her suitcase. Godfrey turned on the speaker clasped at his handlebars and hit play as he rolled out of the airport's carpark and onto the main road.

Drums tat-a-tat-tatted over a bass line and a rising and winding guitar, until a girl's voice began to lilt: '*One pill makes you larger, and one pill makes you small…*'

Flanked by fields of red dirt and plots of beige dust, they passed several cows at rest outside the faded jade-green portico of a temple as a giant wooden-wheeled cart came at them, pulled by high-horned zebu. Godfrey dodged a dog in the middle of the narrowing street as they entered a strip of houses with entire sides painted as yellow billboards for cement companies and a butcher shop with a skinned goat hanging from a bamboo beam and women sweeping dust from wet hearths and two dogs browsing a pile of rubbish next to a gutter running with bright green fluid.

Godfrey smiled and tapped his clutch hand at the grip as the voice hastened: '*Tell 'em a hookah-smoking caterpillar has given you the call…*' They passed the pink office of the communist party, white hammer-and-sickles flanking Tamil script over an assembly of people not doing any work then the high red-and-white striped walls of a palm-shaded temple. Godfrey slowed as a man in upfolded green lungi pulled two cows across the street in front of him. '*When the men on the chessboard get up and tell you where to go…*' A pack of dogs ate the rubbish around a red skip opposite a pink Shiva shrine at the corner of a vast fluorescent-green bog in which a man stood balls-deep washing his cow not very far from a man standing balls-deep in a fluorescent yellow shirt washing himself. The road came out to open land—to winding beds of bracken and mounds of landfill and plains of dust planted with crumbling bollards—'*…and your mind is moving low—go ask Aliiiiiiiiice,*'—

footpaths of dust and refuse and very briefly faded-green rice fields, two hills in the hazy distance topped by white temples, and an orange creek and scattered rubbish shaded by banyan then scrub and buildings and a right turn onto a larger road and traffic—scooter and bicycle and auto and motorbike and bus and minivan and scooter and auto—'*Whennnnn logic and proportion have fallen sloppy dead,*'—bicycle and scooter and scooter and auto, scooter, motorbike, scooter, bus.

Or moved her hands from Godfrey's thighs to his waist and held onto his shirt as they crossed a bridge which rose above a rubbish fire and a dust-lot of trucks and cows with painted horns nuzzling the rubbish beside a pile of rubbish beside an overflowing rubbish bin and a KFC and a pile of rubble inside a bus shelter between several coconut carts and a banana stand—'*Remembeeeeer, what the dormouse said!*' They moved with a dense block of small beige trucks loaded with white sacks and of rusted green buses without doors whose blaring, trilling horns frightened them both. The block seemed now to close in and to slow—'*Feed your head, feed your head!*'—until the song fell part and Godfrey's bike stopped in traffic. 'What the fuck?' said Or, unable to breathe comfortably. Wedged between two buses and stared down at, she coughed and spluttered and put her mouth to her shoulder.

'What?' said Godfrey back to her, the horns and the engines and the droning music were so near and profuse as to dampen their words to mute. Finding her shoulder covered in silt Or spat as though ejecting a mouthful of watermelon seeds. She leaned up to Godfrey's ear and said, 'What?'

'I said, What?'

'I can't breathe.'

'Why didn't you go at the airport?'

'What?' She subsided into a cough as the horns retripled as the traffic started to move.

Soon Godfrey slowed along a road whose centre barely rose above the dust. He turned into a red-gated drive and was saluted by a moustachioed guard in peaked cap and beige uniform. All seemed to calm as they rolled along a boulevard of low hedge and forest canopy, a new quiet of bamboo and poinciana leaves whooshing beside them, of fig and arjuna rustling overhead. Godfrey pulled into a plot of dust shaded by a banyan tree and turned off the bike.

'Wait'll you see this place,' he said and let Or slide out and down before him. With her thumbs and the ends of her first fingers she pushed back her hair and shook her head and coughed. 'Woah.'

'What?'

'You have a…' He hesitated in pointing to her eyebrows, made singular by dirt, and her top lip, coloured as though by a brown pencil.

She looked into one of the bike's mirrors and was frightened by her bearded self. 'My God!' She spat on the bottom corner of the front of Godfrey's shirt and with it redivided her eyebrows. 'This place is so dirty.'

'It is out there, but wait till you see where we're staying.' He led her towards the low thick-columned portico at the hotel's front.

'Mr Lackland,' said a man in mandarin collar and glasses, emerged to meet them. 'This must be the young woman you have told us so very much about.'

'Or, this is Chandan Babu. Chandan, Or.'

'You are just as beautiful as Mr Lackland have described. Please,' he said, opening a palm to the building proper.

They ascended the gentle stone slope to reception. Two desks sat in front of a bookcase to their left; a low red couch and two chairs were arranged before a carved door to their right. Godfrey led Or straight on. A thin rough-hewn pillar stood before a long and low marble bench which marked a break in a high hedge. Beyond and at some distance a colonnaded building, its roof of black-stained red tile, ran low and wide atop two tiers of silvery stone, the tiers themselves above a third, lower and wider level which subsided into waters of brightest turquoise.

'Oh wow,' said Or as they stepped over the bench and at the top of the closer steps beheld in full—so late in the day beginning to fall under shade—the still waters of the swimming pool of the Heritage Madurai. 'It's so beautiful.'

Designed, with the hotel, by Geoffrey Bawa, its descending levels of textured stone—the lowest lapped in a breeze or at bathing guest by clear and shallow water—were modelled after the temple tanks native to Tamil Nadu. Its walls pulsed and shone with dove-grey at dawn, with rippled cream in the early morning, with warmed honey at dusk. Presently the steps were the colour of shortbread, divided by veins of mercury, the blocks moisture-stained at their joins.

'Isn't it incredible?' said Godfrey astonished still each time he looked at it. 'And it's all ours, there's never anyone in it. Now come see the room.'

He rolled her suitcase past reception, under the low colonnade beside a lawn and frangipani—squirrels playing on manicured grass, everywhere the scent of jasmine—to the open-air dining area which looked out to the floating roots of a dark and enormous holy fig. Through a stone-walled passageway to a porch lined with the same rough-hewn columns, they came to the heavy wooden door of room 201.

'It's so nice!' Of polished floorboards and a large desk with a green-shaded banker's lamp, unfolded shutters halved the room and gave view from the office chair to an outdoor area. Godfrey had strewn flower petals onto the bed.

'Is that a love heart?' said Or to their arrangement.

'Too much?'

'Mm,' she mumbled high in mild agreement.

'But look.' He pointed beyond the glass walls and through the open doorway.

'This is ours?'

The pillows on the bed looked out to an enclosed area of the same worn stone, its white roof beamed—and two columns capitalled—with teak. At the enclosure's glimmering closest edge a frangipani tree was bordered on three sides by a miniature turquoise pool. Beyond a polished mahogany tête-à-tête chair a mirror and sink were at the furthest wall.

'This is amazing!' said Or, as though Godfrey did not know. She put both feet into their private pool.

'It's incredible, right? And watch this. He went inside and picked up the phone beside the bed. 'Hi, can I order room service? … Yes. … Chicken chukka. … Garlic naan. … Raita. … Yes. … Yep. …. No. … What? … Why? … No, no. … Yep. … What? No! … No, that's all. … Why? ... Whatever. … Yep, thanks.' He hung up and smiled and nodded at Or; scooped up a handful of petals from the bed and flung them into the pool.

'I've never seen someone so happy from ordering room service. I thought you were on a budget.'

'We're celebrating! You're in India, we're in India together! And the room's not that expensive, that's the most amazing thing. They were so amazed that anyone wanted to stay here longer than two nights that they gave it to me for eighty dollars a day. And if you pay half, right? That's seventeen-fifty for six weeks, of this! Only twenty-eight percent of the retreat money for a roof over our heads, and a fine roof at that—and that desk, that pool, and *this* pool! Look at this thing! And come round here,' he said and led her to the outdoor shower. 'The other one's over the toilet so do you want right and I'll take left?'

'Can't they be unasex?'

'You mean we both shower in both showers? Revolutionary.'

'No, we both shower in the same shower,' she said, and lifted the lever to send cool water over her head.

'Not at the same time, surely.'

'Only at the same time.'

'And don't call me Shirley.'

'What?'

'Nothing.' Godfrey put his head under the shower and kissed her. She ran her fingertips back through the weight of her wet hair and lifted her head to have her neck kissed. When Godfrey had moved his mouth so far down that he was sucking she groaned and turned and lifted her skirt over her waist and put her forearms against the shower's cold stone wall.

They were in towels when the doorbell chimed. Godfrey had the boy take the tray out to the plunge pool. Or was shown and had announced its contents as Godfrey brought from the bar fridge a Kingfisher and two glasses.

'Thank you,' he said to the boy as he walked backwards into and out of the room. 'Oh, wait.' Godfrey went inside and found the lights to the pool then brought out his speaker. 'Always music, right? Stones?'

'Always Stones,' said Or, paddling her feet in the electric blue of the white-lit water.

Shortly a guitar riff and a snare whack and an, 'Oh yeah,' sounded as Godfrey poured beer and reclined at the pool's edge.

'Lechaim?'

'Lechaim,' Or smiled over her glass.

'If I were a rich man,' he sang. 'Isn't this all very rich-manny?' He inserted his finger into the knot at Or's chest and pulled. Her towel came undone. 'Is that so?' she said as she repositioned it across her hips.

'That is so.'

'Well, you too.'

'I'm already topless.'

'Then be bottomless.'

'It's weird to eat when a penis is visible.'

'How do you know this?'

'It's a hunch.' He tore off a piece of bread and lay it on his plate then stirred the chicken dish with a spoon. Taking the piece of bread back up, he folded it and filled it with chicken and onion then covered it with raita.

'Is it good?' said Or, her eyes widening with anticipatory delight.

'So goddam good,' he said, and offered the uneaten handful to her.

'Oh,' she said, surprised, and lowered her mouth to it. 'My God,' she mumbled as she chewed. 'That's the best thing I ever tasted.'

'It's so good, right?'

'So good. Can we stay in here the whole time? It's so much nicer than out there.'

'What would we do in here for all that time?'

'Eat this. Listen to music. Drink beer. And each other.'

'Drink each other?'

'You *are* naughty. Do each other?'

'How might we *do* that?'

'Well there is the sink I can see, and the mirror out here. And a very large bed in there. And a desk I saw. And a chair...'

As the music hastened and Mick Jagger yelled that the sunshine bored the daylights out of him, Or pushed aside the tray of food and removed the towel from her thigh and slunk down into the pool. She pushed her back into its lowest step as she turned to face the bedroom. 'There is this pool too,' she said almost as a question. Slowly she drew her legs towards her body. Very slowly she opened them.

'There *is* this pool,' said Godfrey, suddenly nervous. He downed his beer and conveyed a mouthful from the bottle to Or's tongue. He put his fingers into her hair and squeezed her scalp then scaled her closest knee with his hips.

They spent most of the night making tremble the locations in the room which Or had listed, then the early morning dreaming up a new list and making it tremble too.

The hotel's breakfast was a buffet divided between what Indian chefs thought Westerners ate for breakfast and what Indians actually ate for breakfast. Most of the food lay on a bench encircling a large square column in the restaurant's centre. Trays of fruit elsewhere unpresentable withered beside two towers filled with unheard-of combinations of juice and one filled with a smoothie which poured suspiciously like yoghurt. To their right ran a row of electric food warmers, sitting like openable turtles, filled one with thick brown liquid, one with a kind of rice porridge, one with a thinner browner liquid. Rounding the next corner, three large bowls of chutney—each morning a rotation either of coconut, coriander, mint, tomato, or peanut—and then the western turtles: reconstituted scrambled eggs, soggy cubes of potato, small chicken sausages which gave most who ate them asthma attacks. At the wall furthest from the folding glass doors which looked out to the lawn, beside the two men frying things on demand, the bread—white, sliced, and stale—which Godfrey sometimes inserted into a conveyor toaster that took so long to do its work that he began to reconsider whether or not he actually wanted, or even cared for, toast.

'I can barely walk,' said Or as she brought outside a plate of browning watermelon and glass of pseudo-smoothie. 'Last night was amazing. You were amazing.'

'I was amazing, wasn't I?' Or grinned and shook her head. 'I mean, that was sex. I stepped it up. Everything. You were moaning, you were writhing—screaming at one stage.'

'I was worried in Bali.'

'About what?'

'You were always ah… elsewhere, you know? But now you are liberated, so you can fuck like who you are. Agadah.'

Godfrey nodded and thought and soon said, 'That's a good theory. Only when we're free from worry and stress can we… make sex like who we actually are.'

'Making sex? You don't can say this in English, right?'

'You don't can, no. Making love.'

'That was *not* making love, that was fucking.'

'You can only fuck when you're free. *Very* interesting.'

A waiter came to their table. 'Good morning, sir.'

'Sanjay! Good morning, Sanjay. This is Or.' Godfrey pronounced fully, and correctly, her long 'r'.

'Your wife, sir?'

'Not my wife, no.'

'Very good, sir, your friend, sir. Godfrey's friend, would you liking coffee?'

'I would like coffee, yes.'

'Black coffee?'

'White.'

168

'Milk coffee or coffee with milk, madame?'

Or scrunched her nose and looked at Godfrey. 'Hm?'

'You are wanting milk coffee or coffee with milk?'

'I don't know what you are asking me,' she smiled. 'So I'm going to say, coffee with milk.'

'Just like Mr Godfrey sir, madame.'

As Sanjay went inside to retrieve the coffee Godfrey's breakfast was brought out. A thin twice-folded pancake, its edges overhanging its plate, he unfolded it to show Or the chopped red onions spread over its inside. 'Dosa,' he said, and refolded it and sliced its end with a knife and fork.

'Is it good?'

'Oh, they're good. Crispy like crepes, but with flavour because of the dipping sauce.' He dipped his forkful into a pool of mint chutney. 'You just eat fruit for breakfast? What *do* Israelis eat for breakfast? All I know about is hummus.'

'Israeli breakfast is the greatest breakfast there ever was.'

'All right, calm down.'

Or laughed. 'What do you mean, calm down?'

'You having hummus withdrawals? It's been five days no hummus,' said Godfrey in his imitation of Eddie Murphy's Old Jew.

'My God, you sound like my grandfather Moshe,' said Or, bending forward and smiling. 'What we are doing today? We are tourists?'

'Or Dayan, I am yours and you are mine for the rest of the weekend. We can hang around here, swim in the pool. But I do have to do just a bit of work this afternoon, then we can sightsee. Will you meet me there at four?'

'I can meet you there at four.'

'Excellent.'

'I have only one question.'

'And what's that?'

'Where is there?'

'What?'

'You haven't told me where to meet you.'

Late in the afternoon Godfrey was on cold stone under the edge of the colonnade, looking again and again over the dull green water of the temple tank, and up with abiding awe to its southern great gopuram.

He was drawing above the chubby assistant manager in lycra on his bicycle—in place and imitation of Siva upon Nandi—a dwarapala, gatekeeper, in place and imitation of its green-skinned model. Once moustachioed and flame-haired, his 16 hands bearing spears and bows and daggers, Godfrey's adapted guardian was bespectacled, androgynous, purple-haired—wielding a latte, a test tube, a degree in gender studies, a head of broccoli, an iPhone doubling as a vibrator.

Lowering his binoculars from his face, as he bowed again to his sketchbook he saw a figure gentle and slender among the squared edges of the columns and the blobs of the saris. In a white dress printed with a kind of oversized orange and maroon paisley, tied at her neck and belted at her waist, Or came to the top of the opposite corner of the tank. Godfrey watched her search the steps, where he had told her she would find him, and gave a kind of comfortably grinning, 'Hm,' before returning to his work.

When she found him hunched over the sketchbook on his knees, she lowered her head and made her way through the crowded central walkway.

'You would not believe what I had to go through to come here,' she said, solemn and irate.

'Good afternoon, Miss Dayan! Have a seat.'

'Where have you brought me?' Now she seemed offended.

'What do you mean?'

'I have never seen nowhere so disgusting in my life.'

'What?' Godfrey chirped. 'Look where you are! Look up, look out. This place is incredible. Y'ever seen a view like that?'

'But to get to this view! Godfrey, it's like a Palestinian funeral out there.'

'What do you mean? The traffic?'

'Traffic! I have seen traffic. That was not traffic. And I had to walk half the way. Do you *know* what I did have walked through!?'

'It's too hot for walking, why'd you walk?'

'I got into a tuk tuk and I tell him this temple, but the driver will not take me past some bridge so I have to walk. Do you *know* what the first thing I see when he push me out of the tuk tuk? Two men taking shits. Not one, Godfrey. Two men next to each other, on a bridge, like the bridge is a kind of an unspoken toilet. Toilets should not be unspoken. Toilets are spoken, otherwise they are not toilets! They wear diapers already, why don't they take shits in them? And so hot, Godfrey. It's *so* hot! I'm sweating, look—I don't sweat. I wore uniform in the desert with a rifle and pack and I did not have sweated once. It's hotter than the Negev here. And people live in it? Trillions of them?'

'It is warm. You'll acclimatise.'

'And after the bridge!' she said extending a rigid hand towards the top of the gopuram. 'I'm nearly killed by motorbikes and buses and cows—cows, Godfrey! What the fuck? They are everywhere, moving the traffic *at me*. And the rubbish! Mixed with stones and concrete and people like part of the sidewalk? In Israel we have grass on the side of the street. Here they have rubbish and men making shits? And I'm followed by eight guys, fat guys with red eyes like crack-men, I have to turn around and tell them fuck off while I'm crazy from the noise, the horns—the bippidy-beep-beep and the err-err, blairrrrhhhh!' She questioned him at last with a mild kind of smile. 'Godfrey, to where have you brought me?'

'So you did *not* enjoy the walk here?'

'I'm not walking anywhere again. I go with you or I don't go.'

'It's alive out there, no?'

'Alive? I'm alive,' she tapped at her sternum. 'I don't make shits on a bridge.'

Godfrey chuckled and said in a high voice: 'Come. I want to show you something.'

He rolled up his pens and stood and offered Or his hand. She took it and stood and he said, 'You look beautiful, I like that dress,' and kissed her cheek. 'You *are* sweating.' He strolled with her through the colonnade, the stone cool under bare feet, women in saris at the edge of the steps, sitting and talking in pairs and young families eating from plates of banana leaf, cymbals and drums and 'Om naya shivaya,' gurgling softly within. Overhead, large painted lotus flowers with petals alternating in red and yellow or pink and white or blue and magenta, decorated the ceiling between the columns against dark green, each surrounded or borne by emerald parakeets.

At the central walkway, where a long and thick queue of people waited among steel railings to enter a sanctum, a woman knelt then lay down in front of them. Another lay beside her, then beside them a father and his boy. Or looked to the direction of their extended arms and joined hands.

'What are they doing? They're praying to a fire extinguisher and a handrail? Godfrey, they are praying to a handrail.'

'I never really know what they're doing when they pray. You should see them pray to Ganesh, but at least they're praying, right? They're pious. I prefer the pious to the impious.'

'The what?'

'The impious. The not pious.'

'This is idolatry. What are *they* doing!?'

At the corner of the temple tank at which Or had entered there stood a white statuette in a basin of chalk. Several men and women were leaning down to it, taking each a handful of powder and sprinkling it onto the mound on the figure's head before smearing their own foreheads and reaching under their shirts to smear their bodies. Then each crossed their arms and put the backs of their hands to their ears and bobbed up and down at the knees.

'*That's* praying to Ganesh.'

'They look insane.'

'Is it different from rocking back and forth at the Wailing Wall?'

'Yes, because now they're spinning around in circles with their hands on their heads, Godfrey! For a pile of white powder?'

'And the tank,' Godfrey said, and turned to it. 'Is said to be a true judge of literature. You throw your work in, and if it floats it's good and if it sinks it stinks.'

'You really like it here.'

Resting his forearm on a column, his ankles crossed, Godfrey smiled as he stared admiringly out over the water, to the trees green and brown at the thousand-coloured bases of the eastern towers, smaller gopurams like stern and colourful sentries guarding the inner keep and its candy-striped walls. 'I do like it here. Everything has… it has meaning.'

'It does?' she said retracting her features into their face.

'It's like a system I'm trying to work out. The colours, the symbols, the gods.'

They came out to the path enclosed by the inner and outer walls of the temple. Around its first corner an elephant stood swaying, its ears and the end of its trunk pink, forehead painted in white with a sharp teardrop below three lines. A loose chain was hung with bells around its neck, jingling as the animal rocked from one front leg to the other. 'My god, it stinks.'

Godfrey smiled. 'You see an elephant this close up, inside a temple, and all you say is it stinks?'

'What, I should drop my pants and fire a rocket? The poor animal. It's chained like a slave. My people sympathise with slaves, we don't gawgle at them.'

A family of three approached its rocking head. The mother urged the daughter to step forward and hold up some cash. The elephant grabbed the bills with the end of its trunk and passed them back to its mahout, who deposited them in a basket. The animal lifted its chained foot then raised its trunk to touch the top of the daughter's bowed head. Then the father held out a 100-rupee note and bowed and the elephant passed the money back to the mahout and swayed and rocked and touched the father.

'Pious, right?' said Or as the mother offered the elephant money and too was blessed.

Godfrey needed to pick up a shirt from the market, up the street from the eastern entrance. They descended through an open fence of pointed steel bars into a dark hall of square columns capitalled with chubby open-mouthed lions. At most of its corners stood dozen-armed gods sculpted in shining black granite. Stalls selling fabric faced sewing machines at which old men sat in white singlets; racks of dresses and mobiles of handbags and vendors on stools crowded and narrowed an already crowded and narrow walkway.

'There are so many people,' said Or as though in summary. 'They're just everywhere. All the time.'

Godfrey sidestepped to the stall that had his shirt and reached over the crowd to take a bag from its salesman, whom he thanked before shuffling back the way they had come. 'You could disappear here very easily if you wanted to,' he called ahead.

'No you can't, we are the only white people. Oh wait, except for her.' Or pointed to the distance at Godfrey's back. 'That's Alexandra, right? Is that Alexandra?'

'What!?' said Godfrey, with an instant sternness. 'Are you—.'

'Hi!' Or said, and waved a hand over Godfrey's head. He whipped to look behind him then snapped his face back. Or was grinning. 'You should see your face! You're actually afraid.'

'Please don't do that again,' he smiled, and shook his head.

Back up through the steel fence they were released from the confines of the crowd and walked beside one another. The sun had almost set. Floodlights over the stalls beneath an arch lit white the street around the temple, the dusty rainbow of the statues in its niches outshone by the long eastern entrance opposite. Godfrey spun as he strolled, marvelling at the detail. A small crowd of people stood praying at the entrance's rollable gate as overhead, cherubs danced on the curved ceiling beneath painted gold-hemmed green and red curtains; Shiva and Parvati in the tympanum; flanked by Ganesh and Meenakshi—as a single male voice gurgled prayers from beyond the pink ceiling and the Hall of Ubiquitous Goddesses within.

'I think you and her would have made a nice couple,' said Or as they strolled on.

'What!?'

'Think about it.'

'I've not once thought about it.'

'You are better suited to each other than me and you.'

'How!?' Godfrey squinted. 'She's insane.'

'And I'm Israeli. You don't know what you're in for here.'

'Do your worst, Jew.'

'You know I'm trained in psychological warfare?'

'I do, but what does that mean?'

'It means I can make you doubt whether or not you even exist.' Leaning up and across to Godfrey, she seemed proud of the ability. He leaned down and over to her and their foreheads met with their eyes. 'Plus she travels all the time, you travel all the time. You're older than me, she's old.'

'Oh!' Godfrey chimed, pleased at the jibe.

'See?'

'But she's insane.'

'So are you.'

'I'm not insane, I'm obsessed. And maybe you're right, I'll give her a call. You and I have done everything we could possibly do together, right? She was, after all, an artist. You're just a civilian.'

'I can't *believe* you said this.'

'Why not?' Godfrey smirked.

'I'm the artist in this competition, thank you.'

'How?'

'You don't know, because you don't ask me about me. You *are* obsessed, with you.'

'Oh!' Godfrey chimed again. 'Is that so? Well what do I know about you, Or Dayan? You're very good looking, your smile charms fear from my heart. You're a trained soldier, in psychological warfare no less. You sold soap in Japan, and you haven't eaten hummus in a week.'

'You don't know.'

'I don't know what?'

'That I am a soprano.'

'Opera?'

'I told you I sang when I was young. I trained from fifteen to

174

sing opera, all through my IDF as well.'

'And now?'

'I have the training and the voice but no desire.'

'Then you're not an artist. To an artist, the desire is everything.'

'What's your desire?'

'To paint. To hang one day on a pillar in the Third Temple. Misunderstood now, anonymous till death, I just have to ensure that the work endures and that I have another season to p— come on, *that's* pretty cool.' As they turned the corner the street seemed almost to have emptied. Godfrey pointed ahead, to the sun lingering on the horizon, glowing beside the southern gopuram's stone base, the tower's enormous silhouette half obscured by trees and rising high over gold, with just-discernable ornament and almost-muted colours, to its jagged crown and pointed top. 'Come on.'

'I mean… if I ignore the portable toilets right there and pretend they don't stink like fucking piss. And if that guy had legs and wasn't about to beg me for money, and this hairy gypsy wolf child wasn't here, and down that alley a cow was not eating rubbish, and the crows like death, then maybe, I might say it looks kind of nice?'

'You are impossible to please.'

'Uh huh.'

With stone and a hedge high behind them and crickets whirring on the lawn in darkness, Godfrey and Or paddled their feet at the corner of the pool closest to the restaurant, turning the long reflections of the lights under the wide pavilion into yellow squiggles across a warm and watery blackness.

'Kinda skinny for an opera singer, no?'

'I wasn't always so skinny.'

'Chubby Or. That I would like to see. And you *lost* the desire?'

'I can't sing Freya in Israel, so yes.'

'Freya?'

'Wagner. And if my own country don't let me practise my art, why should I be an artist for it? That's fascist.'

'Art has to be fascist.'

'What?!'

'Art requires subordination, of the self and the will, to something beyond yourself, to a life-allowing totality.'

'You sound pretentious and dumb. This means you're a fascist?

'An easygoing one I think.'

'That was quick!' said Or as their dinner was brought down on a large tray. Sanjay put it on the low table between two sun lounges and introduced it to them—chicken chukka in a brass bowl, two garlic naans, a cucumber salad, raita.

In swimming shorts and a bikini Godfrey and Or hunched over the tray in the soft grey of the lights embedded in the stone beside them. He tore off a piece of bread then transferred slices of cucumber to the empty half of his plate.

'Is it good?' said Or, widening her eyes and almost smiling.

'I haven't tried it yet.'

She almost sang: 'So I just wanted to say… that I am very happy I came here.'

'Ah, I'm happy you came too. Your first full day in India. How was it?'

'I am glad that I am here with you.'

'I'm glad that you're here with me too.'

With a foot between their noses, she leaned up from the sun lounge and kissed him and smiled then with a knife and fork sliced through curry-smeared bread. 'My God, try this.' She cut off another length and put her fork almost to Godfrey's lips.

'I'm eating the same thing as you.'

'This is the perfect combination. Try it, it's good?'

Godfrey stared into her very excited eyes and hesitated to open his mouth. He squinted and wiped the sweat from his forehead. When eventually he ate her offering and told her it was good he said, 'So Monday I have to start work properly.'

'What do you mean?'

'I worked a half-day yesterday to pick you up from the airport and today only a couple of hours so this is my weekend. But Monday I have to get back into it or I'll lose it. Six paintings in six weeks, and after seven days I'm only halfway through the first one.'

'You are quite brilliant, Godfrey Lackland.'

'Well, we'll see about that.'

II

A tract of dust, a corrugated shack, an interval of rubble.

Piles of dirt and a field of sand and a mound of dirt—sometimes in the distance a plain of pale scrub—a dry river bed covered in rubbish, two gatherings of brick and the side of a house painted as a yellow billboard for a cement company. A cow eating a dusty rainbow of rubbish beside a steel skip and an apple cart in front of a gated tract of dust and a cow eating rubbish from a smouldering pile—occasionally, the crumbling walls and peeling paint of a palm-shaded temple. A tall frame of rusting transformer behind a hill of gravel and a patch of scrub and a longer interval of rubble, a cow munching at a pile of pressed sugarcane—an open gutter of dried rubbish—two yellow steel frames as roadblocks to slow the traffic; a corrugated shack, a tract of dust and a wandering goat and the cloudless sky pale with heat, invasive and scorching even within the constant wind of riding.

With little to see as they drove, Or kept for most of the trip her head resting between Godfrey's shoulder blades. With less traffic to deal with, Godfrey stroked for most of the ride his hand at Or's bare thigh.

They came to and drove through a wide statue-topped arch. After rounding a bend of dry and pointy scrub littered or hung—they could not tell which—with clothing, they wound and ascended a hilltop, the road cut out of cactus-sprung red rock. The forest became dense and the canopy soon closed over and loitering monkeys began to appear at the corners—sometimes solitary and one-eyed on rubbish, sometimes in families blocking a lane—always devious. The motorbike followed a riverbed of black sludge pecked at by chickens before men began walking out of the forest from God-knows-what pursuit and the roadside turned to one of rubbish among bramble or bramble among rubbish—they could not tell which—and the monkeys thickened on the ground, stalking in gangs upon the rocks of dry riverbeds and making whole trees bounce and picking insects from one another's crotches.

Godfrey sensed a parking lot among an expanse of dirt opposite an open shack; he pulled the bike in and switched off its engine.

'This,' said Or, smiling, 'is where you invite me for romance?'

177

'You don't think it's romantic?'

'That was the ugliest drive I've ever been, and I once drove through Lebanon.' Beside the shack, opposite a slope of dirt and weed and litter, a low and wide roof was sunk into the hillside, its awning of painted pink and jade. A forested mountain of no great height rose and fell behind it. At its centre a small faded gopuram stood almost without ornament, its but two guardians merely four-armed. Three shirtless men talked at the entrance of peeling blue paint, their sagging breasts resting almost on their bellies. 'Where have you brought me for romantic daytrip?'

'This, is an Abode of Murugan.'

'What is a murugan?'

'Murugan is the Hindu god of love, and youth, and war.'

'So he is my God.'

'How d'you figure that?'

'You are only one of these things. I am a soldier. I am young. I am in love.'

'You're in love?'

'Of course, you moose.'

'With who?!'

'Idiot, why else I am here?' They slid off their flip-flops in front of the old woman squatting between the shack and the gopurams. 'In this extremely romantic location, surrounded with rubbish and monkeys.' Godfrey took off his sunglasses as he and Or ducked and descended through the doorway. 'You are agadah.'

'I'm what?'

'Agadah.'

'I don't know the word you're saying.'

'Agadah means … If you will it, it's *not* a dream. Agadah it means that you don't just dream things, you make them happen—whatever is in your mind you just make it happen. So you are agadah.'

'I'm agadah?'

'Agadah in life, agadah in bed. Agadah.' Columns painted with gold then pink then blue rose to a ceiling sectioned with trios of variegated pink, yellow, magenta flowers against green, vermillion, purple, indigo—the whole colourful complex guarded and divided atop the inner and outer walls by round chrome bars. Both flanks had a floor-to-ceiling gate, open and loitering with monkeys. 'And what is an abode?'

'It means it's one of his homes.'

'Well I hate to tell him this…' She spoke as though to the ceiling:

'Murugan, you choose to live in a shit-hole.'

'And Japan *after* your engagement?' Godfrey whispered as they ambled over the marble. 'No, during?'

'During,' said Or at full volume.

Godfrey's voice rose to a median. 'For how long?'

'One year.'

'Working at Soapland to make money to go back to Israel to start a business.' Since sitting blissfully down to a late breakfast Godfrey had been constructing the purposeful narrative so far absent from his conception of her. 'And things didn't work out with your fiancé because…'

'Why do you want to talk about this?'

'I'm trying to find out who I'm in love with.'

'But so unnatural… ly. Like, what is your height? I don't need to know because I see you here. Who am I? You're talking to me.'

'Oo, you're gonna get it,' said Godfrey and, in a way that was becoming their own, he leaned over on his bare toes as she rose onto hers and they bumped foreheads and stared blurredly, irately, excitedly, into one another's eyes.

She responded according to the new ritual: 'Only if I get it from you,' and they returned to gazing at all the colour. 'But we can say that you have spent more time in me than he did.'

'Gross.'

'You are so a prude.'

'Such a prude, and yes. I probably am.'

The marble floor at the rear of the mandapam was flooded. 'Such gross,' said Or, the error intentional and made with a smile as her toes became wet. 'Can't these people keep one surface clean *and* dry? Everything is either dirty or wet, these mooses!'

'Meese.'

'What?'

'Nothing. Love, huh? That I did not expect.'

In the centre of the complex, beyond a low maze of chrome railings, a dozen Indians had gathered at two open doorways, wherein a small bell rattled among smoke beginning to appear. Godfrey and Or approached the noise and the crowd. The bare-breasted priests who had been talking outside were bedecking three idols in dark niches, sprinkling water onto the ground, splashing the statues, ringing a bell. The flabbiest had a bronze plate in one hand; upon it the flaming wick of a lamp danced with oily smoke. In his other he held by the knob-handle a thin round-bottomed cone of embossed bronze. One by one the crowd stepped through one doorway, stood before the first niche, prayed—moved along to the second. At the third they placed money onto the plate and pushed the lamp-smoke to their faces. As they did so the largest priest circled his cone above their heads then cupped it over one of his breasts.

'This is amazing,' Godfrey whispered. 'It feels ancient, does that make sense?' He jostled his head to get a better look from outside the sanctum. 'At the Meenakshi temple, non-Hindus aren't allowed to get this close, but...' He turned to—.

Or was outside. One of the open gates led out to a red-paved courtyard, both ends of which looked up to the mountains in whose valley the abode was ensconced.

'Did you see that?' said Godfrey, calling across the courtyard. She stood at a red-and-white-striped wall beside a row of plastic taps.

She called back: 'No, but maybe you want to see this?'

When Godfrey came to her side he, as she, looked upon a descending slope of rubbish—of paper plates and empty bottles and plastic wrappers and plastic bags and torn woven mats and discarded clothing, plastic wrappers and waxed cups and plastic bags—some of it charred—of squares and strips and circles and lengths and crumples and tears and bunches and discs—of green and cream and blue and red and plastic and white and yellow and plastic. Swarming with flies, its length and depth ran down to a dry riverbed, foraged as far as their four eyes could see by monkeys—pulling fabric over their heads and tasting from beneath squashed bottles and pushing paper aside to rifle through layer after layer, to turn within lumps and bumps of refuse—scrambling to a high bough or jumping onto the wall and sprinting across the courtyard whenever they uncovered something edible—and jade and indigo, and plastic and azure, and brown and pink and leaf and rotting garland—of wrinkled newspaper and square-cut banana leaf and stinking ash.

'Well?'

'Well what?'

'What do you think of your India now?'

'Look at that.' Godfrey pointed back to the temple.

'Look at this, come on!'

'You come on! You can't come all the way out here and say this is all you saw.'

'It's disgusting.'

'Yes, but that's not what's here. You're at an Abode of Murugan, Or. You can't see only this.'

'I didn't see only this, but if I see this *and* that, I remember this.'

'I told you about India. You have to look past the outer surface.'

'I can look past it, but I can't smell past it.'

'And if you look beyond the appearance, and think of the internal, you see the divine soul is in everything—including the appearance.'

'This genormous sea of rubbish, it has divine soul?'

'Of course, and I'll use it in a painting. But I'm not going to focus only on this and let it define the experience of walking, Or, through an Abode of Murugan, of seeing people pray to the god of war, and love, and youth—beside my love. Look past the appearance.'

'I'm a Jew, I don't have to look past the outside to see the inside. God looks after our inside and outside, whether we like it or not. And if you say that divine soul is in this rubbish river, I don't want one.'

'Well you have one. And it's blacker than this smouldering pile of monkey-garbage.'

'You are calling me black?'

'Grrr,' said Godfrey and turned and rose to his tiptoes.

'I am not Ethiopian Jew,' said Or with alike aggression and put her forehead up to his. 'Now you're the one that's gonna get it.'

'Only, if I can get it from you.' And they snarled and subsided into a kiss which had them temporarily ignore the smell. Soon Or whispered: 'We're kissing beside a river of monkey garbage.'

'Uh huh.'

'You're lucky I am unromantic.'

'But in love?'

'Waiting for you to drop your pants and fire a rocket.'

Back at the statue-topped arch they stood at the bike and shared a warm Bovonto. They stared out over a kind of roundabout formed by a circle of dry weeds.

'It's like Indian Dr Pepper,' said Godfrey, rereading the label. 'Dr Pepper isn't it?' he said in an Indian accent. 'Dr Pepper and Sergeant Pepper, the two qualified peppers. Peter Piper picked a peck of qualified peppers. What if they're the same person, Or?! You ever think about that? Dr and Sergeant Pepper, the same guy. Pepper's a medic! Peter Pan, the god who dies, picked a peck of pickled medics. What is a peck? Don't listen to him, peck! Peck!

Stupid fat daikini!'

'It's too hot for your brain right now.'

'It's so fucking hot.'

They listened to the sound of bickering monkeys and yelping dogs and cawing crows, smelt the dust and the cow dung and the frying oil and the cumin and the burning rope and the dust, and sweated profusely in unison. Or handed the bottle back to Godfrey and he drank its last hot mouthful before mounting the bike and letting Or slide in behind him. They rolled around the roundabout and Godfrey kicked the bike into second gear as they returned to the road for Madurai.

Tired, Or nestled into his back and stared at the passing dust on the other side of the street. From the first alley that came onto the asphalt in front of them, a man emerged on a scooter, around which the steel frame of his food-cart had been welded. Ahead, a man on a motorbike seemed to be in a hurry to get to the Abode of Murugan. The steel frame rattled as the scooter crossed the unpaved gap between alley and road. Wanting to turn right he looked only left. The motorbike horn sounded. The motorbike horn was unheeded. The moment the motorbike's front tyre touched the scooter the rider's bare forehead hit a crossbar and his body went limp. He flew feet-first into the frame, his torso bending backwards, his legs dangling through the bars until his knees stuck into the road and his face smashed down after them. The scooter's brakes now fully applied, its rider and frame stopped in a cloud of dust. The plastic of the motorbike's fairings and the glass of its mirrors skidded and shattered across the asphalt. Godfrey and Or, already slowing, pulled over in shock.

'Holy fucking hell,' said Or, her hands shaking and whole body tingling. 'What did I just see?'

'Jesus Christ,' said Godfrey, as they with open mouths turned their faces from the body and its creeping pool of blood.

'I can't believe I see this,' she said feebly into her hand.

'He died instantly and… Ergh. He folded through the frame like—. Argh. Like a sheet of paper through a printing press. A human body.'

'We're wearing helmets from now on,' said Or, almost in tears. 'I don't care what you say about freedom.'

'Mmmmm,' said Or when Godfrey had pulled out and rolled over. 'Breakfast?'

'Mmmmm,' said Godfrey, barely able to speak. He lay with his legs open and put the pillow that had been under Or's pelvis behind his head. He watched her slink out of the bedroom and stalk past the rough stone of the columns beside the plunge pool, her bare cheeks barely rising and not at all wobbling as she disappeared around the wall of the shower.

He was still grinning when she brought out, grinning, a plate of sliced fruit from the breakfast buffet. 'I've never been licked like that.'

Godfrey shook both hands at the sides of his head. 'Vot, shtill no hummus?'

'I've seen chickpeas in food. But no tahini, no lemons. Indians are lime people. Lime people cannot make hummus. Yours is good?' she said as milk coffee was poured for them both.

Godfrey looked down at his shrivelled sausage and fried egg sandwich. 'Haven't tasted it yet.'

'So I think I've found a Pilates studio.'

'Here? Well it is India. There's gotta be yoga somewhere.'

'Donkeyclown, Pilates is not yoga!' Or laughed. 'And there are even two, so I think today I check them both out and see what one is best.'

'*Two* yoga studios!? Let me guess. One's called Wishful Alchemy, and the other's called Abundance Through Authenticity.'

'No. Thank you,' she smiled. 'One is the Liberation Movement Studio and the other is Mind Body Motion. And Mind Body Motion has a vegan café, I think is my best shot for hummus. So maybe while you're working today I can go to there? And I will research I think some ways to make money online.'

'Online? What the hell for?'

'I don't love love it here, but I think Israel is not where I want to be right now.'

'No more yoga dojo?' Godfrey smirked.

'Don't call it a yoga dojo.'

'Pilates and krav maga. Yoga and karate. It's a yoga dojo.'

'You love to make fun, huh?'

'Only of you.'

'I was going to ask if you can take me to there? I'm not walking here again. Two men shitting on a bridge is enough. What would be today, four men pissing in a tunnel?'

Godfrey laughed and said, 'Of course I'll take you. Give me a kiss.' And she did.

'Now before you run off to do your doodles, we need to talk about one thing.'

'My doodle?'

'I prefer to sit on that, not to talk about it. We need to talk about your messifulness.'

'My messiness?' he said, surprised by what was already an accusation. 'What are you, a clean freak?'

'Our room is a crack den.'

'It is not! It's—. I mean… it's a *bit* untidy but we have housekeeping.'

'Yes, and until they come to clean I have to live in it. It's OK for you, you run off to work. But until three I live in your monkey garbage.'

'Monkey garbage,' Godfrey laughed again. 'So why don't you—. Wait, no.'

'What?' she said, already offended.

Godfrey shook his head as though refusing pie. 'Nothing.'

'It's your mess!'

'Not all of it! What about your creams and your bottles?'

'You mean the ones on the bathroom sink?'

'There are some on the bedside table.'

'That's coconut oil, and we know what that is for. And I have night cream there because my skin dries out when you have to sleep with the air-conditioner. You could be just a little tidier and cleaner?'

'I'll tell you what, you've been here a week. If you transfer the money for the room—and I don't mean to nag—I'll keep it tidier. Deal?'

'Oh my God, I forgot, I'm so sorry! That must have been annoying at you, right?' She looked to the beamed roof and worked out the process: 'I have to send it from the Japanese account to the Israeli account, that will take a few days, and then I think from *that*—what day is it?—I can send it to you as soon as possible. OK?'

'And I'll try not to have my boxer shorts lying around.'

'And the beer bottles and the scraps of paper?'

'And the beer bottles and the scraps of paper.'

'We should be wearing helmets.'

'No!' said Godfrey, dismissing the idea with the adamance of a child.

184

'We should be wearing helmets.'

At the largest intersection between the Heritage and the city, Godfrey put his feet to the paved road and watched through a gap between two buses as a wind-blown woman in a jade and brown sari attempted to navigate the violent torrents of traffic which, when they were allowed to, rolled through and over and around a pile of rubble that served as a kind of desert-storm's eye. An afternoon haze bathed everything in khaki light made edible by a swirling swarm of dirt, the desiccate concrete frames of the faded houses beyond her all the paler for the wakes of dust which followed each new torrent. Or had her feet on the bike's rear pegs. She watched a gypsy hawk to the auto passengers clay frying pans stacked on her head.

Apparently given a green light, their own torrent began to stampede and Godfrey clicked down to first and leaned around the eye. A front of concrete mixer and dump truck and auto and motorbike and car and rusted brown bus watched as they turned. Or looked through the occasional foliage of a tree—past the green skips surrounded by rubbish and between the cows grazing on refuse—beyond the strip of dirt which separated the road from the shop-lined street. They passed a four-storey supermarket and a fabric shop and a luggage emporium and an underwear store and a KFC, an optometrist's—then between the top of a steep wall of dirt and the bare canopy of a tree, Or saw a word in plain black lettering against a fiery background.

'Woah, woah, woah,' she said as they passed it. She tapped Godfrey on the shoulder and pointed. 'Does that say what I think it says?'

'What the hell?' Godfrey smiled. He checked his shoulder for speeding traffic and pulled the bike in and turned it around. As he braked to a stop Or's disbelief turned to fury. The word was on the awning of a shopfront which occupied the lowest floor of a crumbling building whose side was painted as a yellow billboard for a concrete company. Below the word, small white text read: 'Exclusive Men's Wear Garments.' Not only was the word in large black letters above but too it was printed below in red-fading-to-blue capitals and followed by, 'Garments,' this strange pairing flanked by candles and greetings of 'Happy Diwali!'

Godfrey's forehead was furrowed as his head darted suspiciously around, for there the word—of all the words—was. Unmistakably and unashamedly it took up the entirety of a fiery billboard: Hitler.

'OK, what the fuck?' Two cardboard rectangles were stuck between the awning and the ground, both printed with the price of the store's shirts, their jeans, their pants. Its glass door was flanked on one side by a fully clothed male model on a curved plaque and on the other by—. 'I don't fucking understand!' said Or at volume. 'Can you explain this to me!?' Her hand was extended as fully as possible in the direction of the shopfront, her fingers stiff and stacked. 'Is this a joke? What is this fucking place!?' She hit Godfrey's back with her forearm. 'Can you tell me what is going on here? Where do you bring me?'

'I have absolutely no idea what's going on.'

'It's not like they just like the word and don't know what it means. Because the motherfucker's picture is there!'

The other curved side of the entrance was a portrait of the Führer, staring off into the distance, conspiring either to invade Poland or give a deeper discount on jeans—they could not tell which—his moustache as narrow and as bushy as the day he was made Reichskanzler.

'Enough, India! Fucking hell! OK? Enough!'

A man in grey jeans and purple shirt walked in circles outside the entrance, flicking a hand towel as he talked on his phone.

'This is so strange.'

'Strange!? Get me out of here. Take me to Pilates before I hurt someone.'

Godfrey's '*Nine Levels of Purgatory, or the Southern Rajagopuram*' was now but a single uncoloured sketch from done. Its three top levels, on a sheet of portrait-facing paper, had been filled with repeated, barely discernable, statues—raping football players from every code and musicians in barbarian dress and actors in pulpits and journalists typing out opinions they thought were their own—minor figures all of modern mythology. Its middle three, on their own landscape-turned page had now their Moroccan centaur kidnapping a Valkyrie, their Singer-Songwriter with star-framed glasses and enormous overbite, a stand-up comedian simpering behind a microphone, an emaciate pair of crackheads beating their infant child, a female soccer player boring people to life, a pimply blob-Cartman staring as though into a computer screen. The lower tiers, across two pages drawn in finest detail and coloured with greatest enthusiasm—with their fifty-armed blue Chinese Mahasadasiva restraining Pan and the bug-eyed Assistant Manager on his hobby; with their green-skinned cardinal with children kneeling in the folds of a cassock raised by ten fondling hands and Gorky's fangs slobbering over Larry David and dozens of rat-politicians-with-sponsors—were all complete and the work painted in faded jades and powdery blues and bleached yellows and earthen reds and orange. Godfrey had only to add the curled Tamil word for 'Tomorrow' onto the rounded top of the tower. He finished the cross-hatching under which the symbols would be drawn then from his book of musical notation began transcribing and transforming the elaborate 'h' and the Tamil squiggles into thick-bordered script.

'Almost done?' said Or, so loudly and near his ear that his pen ran with fright to the edge of the page.

'Are you fucking serious?'

'Woah! Calm down.'

'Yes, calm down. You literally almost ruined an entire goddam painting—two weeks of work, Or, and I'll calm down.' He took one slow breath—'I'm sorry,'—and waited until his temper allowed the injection of kindness. 'Please don't do that again.'

'I won't, *I'm* sorry. I didn't think.'

'Oo, you're gonna get it.'

'Only if I get it from you.' And they kissed.

'How are you?'

'I've had enough.'

'Of me?'

'Of India!'

'What now?'

'This place, it gets busier and dirtier every day, it's horrible, Godfrey. I have to start wearing a surgical mask, like a Japanese girl. You can't breathe, the air is toxic. I don't like it, honestly. I think I hate it, is that bad? The streets they smell like fart factories, and there are Hitler clothing stores, Godfrey! Hitler! It's just—. It's a piece of shit. India is a piece of shit.'

'The Hitler store is weird. I'll look into it.'

'The walk from Pilates was seven minutes to here. And I saw a woman with a leg that was like huge and melted? Like a blob and she was sitting, she was begging and the dogs are all around her disguuuu-ssting, and I'm followed again by rapists, I can feel dirt in my teeth crunching when I yell at them and the piles of rubbish! The smell! My God!'

'What are they?' A large black bulb dangled by a chinstrap in each of her hands.

'I got us helmets.'

'Why would you get us helmets?'

'We are wearing them.'

'Well, we'll see.'

'No we won't.'

Or felt a tug at her dress. She turned and found two little girls smiling up at her, one offering a garland of jasmine in the palm of her hand. 'This is for you.'

'Oh, thank you so much!'

'What is your name?' said the girl holding the flowers.

'My name is Or. What's your name?'

'My name is Jumana.'

'And you?'

'I am Nilashri.'

'Thank you for the flowers! What do I do with them?'

'In your hair,' said Nilashri, turning at the waist with her hands behind her back.

'In my hair? How do I put them in my hair?'

'Like this,' said Jumana, twisting to show the garland in her own.

'All right Jupiter, Natashally. Take the flowers over there,' Godfrey ended up saying to Or.

'What's wrong with you, grumpy man?'

'I am *this* close to finishing this painting. It's taken me two weeks, and now I have to somehow erase this thick black line. I'm not getting enough work done.'

'All you do is work.'

'And kids have been bothering me all day, asking about cricket. Cricket! I need to get this done. Could you, please—I'm begging you—take the girls over there and leave me for twenty minutes and I'll be finished.'

The sun was low over the temple's roof, its orange glow already burning among a palm tree and about to turn the early evening sky into a vast wash of grey and purple thistle. 'He's angry, isn't he?' said Or to the girls then walked with them to the other end of the temple tank. She sat on a lower step and let them tie her hair so the jasmine hung in two loops at her neck. She thanked them very much and stood and looked across at Godfrey, his head jolting freakishly sideways over his sketchbook. He stuck his tongue to the outside of his mouth and contorted his shoulders as his elbows arced back and forth. She turned and ascended and strolled into the main part of the temple.

A man beating a drum at his hip followed her to the southern entrance of the hall which surrounded the inner sanctum. A crowd prayed to a nine-foot-high granite Ganesh, a priest draping it with green foliage and robing it in white. The ceiling lights were on, the whole stone-cut complex a kind of ordered white-lit cavern, its roof of blue and green and pink and yellow-lion capitals on peach pedestals—all looming high over a floor and countless columns of cold dark stone. Or stopped and let the drummer pass behind her; stood among men in polo shirts and beige trousers and women in saris, all arms crossed and fingers at earlobes before approaching the priest. He leaned down to mark their foreheads with white as they dropped cash onto his tray.

Deep music echoed in the dark and columned distance. Or walked with the crowd that seemed all to be drawn in the same direction, her head pitching and yawing as she took in the height, the colour, the imposing vastness—every fourth column carved with a rearing Yali—half horse, half elephant—unaware that slowly her mouth was opening. At the hall's first corner a middle-aged woman in crimson sari had a surbahar—larger and deeper than a sitar—across her knees. She plucked it slowly and slid her curled hand up and down its neck. Or gave a high still-not-impressed, 'Hmph.' To her left, a kind of gallery of deities upon columns flanked the eastern entrance, all dozen-handed and armed with spears upon high pedestals, life-sized and robed in saffron and aproned in white and garlanded with strings of magenta and yellow flower and green leaf, foreheads dotted with orange and smeared from ear to ear with chalk. She was tall among the crowd of people praying before them. She looked down at the women, some pot-bellied, one albino, sitting on the stone and pulling from shopping bags a metal tray onto which they offered half a coconut and a handful of bananas.

'Everything they see,' she muttered, then turned again. Watched over by the statues, a square porch of columns had each outer surface carved with an avatar of dancing—guarding—reposing—Siva, their inside shining with amber and surrounding a floor-to-ceiling pole of carved gold. Distant beyond the dark and heavy porch a shower of bells began to sound, then a kind of raw trumpet to blare. The worshippers looking up at the gallery shuffled towards the new music. Or followed until it formed a line of crowd at the hall's next corner.

189

She looked down the length of a long colonnade, vast and empty of people. The music was coming from its end: a frantic drum started up and the squeaky trumpet convulsed as a procession came round the distant corner. Or pushed a finger at the protrusion in her left ear to muffle the noise. As it plodded, the head of a white cow became discernible, as did the man walking beside it, bashing—one-two, one-two—the drum which the animal bore at its side. Behind the cow there lumbered an elephant, its white-lined forehead and pink-edged ears obvious among the angles of the columns. Her eyebrows instantly raised; she took the finger from her ear as the procession neared—could see at its centre a thicker group of people surrounding an idol in a green niche, borne upon shoulders—one-two, one-two, spasming trumpet, bells—but she could not for long take her eyes off the elephant. The cow passed before her and the elephant shortly came within reaching distance. It was the garland at its neck that was sprinkling everywhere the sound of bells. It had at its sides two long carpets tied at its spine, fringed with yellow and embroidered with blue leaves and yellow flowers and white cockerels and flecked through with woven silver. The one-two and the trumpet fell silent as the elephant turned the corner beside her. It was followed by torches then two shirtless men bearing a wooden casket on long poles. At last, two beams upon shoulders carrying a kind of palanquin upon which rested an idol shrouded in emerald-green fabric within a rounded arch of bronze, flaming and pinched at the sides. A thin priest rung a single bell not a metre from Or's enthralled eyes as he waited for the palanquin to turn the corner. Met by a shirtless man holding a trishula to his shoulder, the raised green shroud approached and the priest turned to lead the procession and the crowd of Hindus awaiting it off in the direction of the woman still plucking the surbahar.

The spectacle was over. Or stared at the shorter colonnade of white-lit ceiling—green and painted over with pink and yellow flowers—at the golden pole and its dark porch glowing with molten amber beyond the high columns.

She said, 'Woah,' and looked left and right to see if there were any foreigners to whom she might remark upon the intensity of her wonder.

'Goddam *finished*!' said Godfrey as they crossed the rooftop of the Madurai Residency. 'You have no idea how good this feeling is, it's almost why I do it. This is the high. This is the I-just-made-a-million-dollars-in-four-seconds.'

Shown to one of the curved plastic arches at the rooftop's edge, Godfrey moved his seat to beside Or's. 'Congratulations? Is that what you say when you finish a painting?'

'I don't know, I've never been in anybody's company while I'm working. One down, five to go. I just have to step up the work rate a little.'

'Hm?'

Their view over the railing was of the end of the bridge upon which Or had seen two men jettisoning themselves. The traffic below was incessant—a school of headlights waiting to come off the bridge, a convoy of brake lights rounding a neon church onto it—and very distinctly loud: truck horn over bus horn drowning out a background of unceasing bips and beeps and blares.

'I said I'll just have to work a little bit harder, to get the next five paintings done.'

'You will work more than already?'

'Hm?'

'You said you will work more than you already do?'

'I think so, yeah. Five paintings in four weeks I have to do now.'

'What!?'

Three huge air-conditioning units, resting on a ledge over the terrace's entrance, sent loud hot air out and down into the already gushing breeze. An ambulance siren interrupted the train horn that was being punctuated by truck horns.

'I said it's five paintings in four weeks now.' Godfrey leaned the cover of the menu against his forearm and said, 'Shall we order the usual?'

'No, something different. Too much wet food.'

'The traffic's so loud! I was even having trouble concentrating from the chatter in the temple today, the drums and the, "om nay shiva, om nay shiva." It's like these people have never heard of quiet.'

'Good evening, sir,' said an arrived waiter.

'Hello!' Godfrey yelled, 'Beer! We want beer. Kingfisher, two bottles. And something dry, not a wet curry. Which one is dry? Dry?'

'All curries can be made dry if you're liking, sir.'

'You like spicy?'

'What?'

191

'Do you like spicy food?' Godfrey annunciated across to her.

'Yes!'

'Can we get chicken chettinad, dry,' Godfrey almost yelled. 'With extra onion, and—'

'No!'

'No?'

'No more extra onion. It's like kissing tabboulleh now.'

'Two garlic naans and raita.'

'Plain naan, one,' Or said past him to the waiter. Then she pointed at her menu. 'And can I also have aloo gobi?'

'Aloo gobi, yes, madame. Dry also?' Or nodded and the waiter took his notepad into the kitchen.

'You've seen the elephant procession in the temple?'

'Pardon?'

'Have you seen the elephant procession in the temple?'

'They do that every night,' Godfrey shouted.

'It's kind of amazing, right?'

'Yes! This place is amazing.'

'Why we are here? I can't hear you?'

'It's the only rooftop restaurant in the city.'

'But the view is a piece of shit!' said Or as their beers arrived. As Godfrey poured his into a glass she said, 'Is it good?'

'Huh?'

'Is it good?'

'Is what good?'

'Your beer.'

'I haven't… I was just pouring it. Are you asking if Kingfisher's good, or if this glass of beer is good?' Or shrugged her shoulders. 'Do you realise you always ask me how my food is before I've tasted it?!'

'I can't hear you. What?'

'Do you realise that you always ask me how my food is before I've tasted it?'

'No,' she smirked.

'Always. And I think, How can I tell if it's good if I haven't tasted it yet?'

'I do? Ha ha,' Or laughed, and tried, and failed, to recall ever having asked him how his food was. 'Anyway, cheers. Lechaim!'

'I realise of course it's no shame to be poor,' Godfrey said in baritone. 'But it's no great honour either.'

'Every time with you,' Or smiled and leaned onto the table. 'You are a gentile fiddler on the roof. Hey, and we are on a roof!'

Shortly their food was brought and the dishes arrayed on their table. Godfrey surveyed them before spooning curry onto his plate. He tore off a piece of his bread.

'And I'm not going to ask you if it's good or not, right?'

'You can ask,' Godfrey said with an exhaled smile. 'It just struck me as odd.'

Or rearranged the plates so that the cauliflower was in front of her. She tore off a corner of naan and used it to pick up a fried floret. Godfrey reached his fork over and transferred two pieces to his plate. Or stopped mid-chew and leaned back in her chair.

'So you liked the elephant procession, uh? What's wrong?'

'What?'

'What's the matter?'

'Nothing, why?'

'You look bored. Or furious.' Still leaning back from the table, she glowered down at the traffic. 'What the hell's wrong?'

'It's nothing. I just—.' She turned a piece of cauliflower over with her fork.

'Tell me.'

'I don't love it when people take food from my plate.'

'Ha. I'm sorry. Are we not sharing? We've shared every meal since you got here.'

'That's why I order this separate.'

'Ah, I am sorry. Is it good? I'm kidding. Here,' and he returned the cauliflower to her plate.

'No don't—' she said and closed her eyes. About to tell him she also disliked having food put onto her plate, she dropped her fork and turned from staring at the traffic to stare at Godfrey. He lifted his chin and squinted at her. Shortly he whispered: 'So I guess that means you *don't* like people taking food from your plate?'

'What!? I can't hear you, fuck!'

III

When first light bounced off the plunge pool, orange and blue through the bedroom windows, Or's eyes cracked open and she was excited to find Godfrey lying beside her. She reached over his bare shoulder and took up the air conditioner's remote and pointed it at the unit behind her and turned it off. She shuffled her hips towards his body; ran her hand over the front of his boxer shorts; kissed his shoulder blade and the centre of his back then pressed a little harder.

'What's happening?' Godfrey said as though exhaling a puff of dust. 'Hm? Why's the air conditioner off?' Or put her hand to Godfrey's stomach and pressed down as she slid her fingers under his elastic waist. 'What are you doing?' he puffed again.

'It's time for the rooster to wake up.'

'I'm so tired. What time is it? Don't call my penis a chicken.' She moved her hand down until she could squeeze everything. 'What time is it?'

'Time for this.'

'No, no,' Godfrey moaned without consonants. 'I only just got to bed.'

'Yesterday was the first day that we didn't have had sex.'

'Mm,' said Godfrey, and turned the air-conditioner on.

'Don't you think that's bad?'

'I don't think it's anything.'

She stretched her neck up to his ear and whispered 'Don't you want to feel my mouth around you?'

'Of course, later though,' he said in nothing but vowels and h's. 'I feel like I've been hit by a truck.'

'All you do is work, you know this?'

'No, I just didn't get any work done the day before. The sun sits in front of that hill all afternoon, I can only stay there for a short while. Look at my forehead, it's crispy.'

'Wear a hat.'

'You're a hat.'

'If you go back to sleep you'll miss breakfast again.'

'Hm? Mm, the samosas are twelve cents each across the street, I'll just eat them.'

194

She shuffled up the bed and curled over his shoulder. 'So we are not going to eat breakfast together anymore? I love sitting there with you. I thought you liked it too, the squirrels and the pool and the birds. Come to breakfast, what if I set an alarm? And I do some Pilates and work and you come for the end of breakfast.'

'Yoga dojo.'

'I feel like I haven't seen you at all from the last few days.'

'I like that idea.'

Or tapped topless at her phone. 'You get ninety minutes more sleep, OK?'

'Heavenly. Night night.'

'I love you,' she said and kissed him on the cheek and went outside to shower.

'Huv you hoo,' he breathed.

Mid-morning the stone of the pool was the colour of strawberry-stained cheesecake, its slowly bending waters low as though rising naturally in pure cyan from the earth. The quickly warming air sung with whirps and chip-chips and the strange calls of unseeable birds in the high trees of dry green surrounding and springing from the grounds. Godfrey spotted Or's laptop on a table on the lawn beside the covered dining area; he kicked his feet through the crunchy leaves and frangipani flowers. She was on the furthest lawn, sideways in front of the end of the long red-roofed pavilion which overlooked the pool. Her right hand and knee were stuck into a thin blue mat on the ground, her left hand behind her head. She raised her left leg then sent it backwards then brought its bent knee forwards to point her toes at Godfrey. He stood over the table and tilted his head until his face was parallel with hers—raised his eyebrows and pouted and nodded. She shook her head and smiled and looked away as she lost control of her breathing.

Godfrey asked for coffee with milk then for fun said that he changed his mind to milk coffee then went inside and built a plate of sweating cheese and chopped onion and asthma sausages.

'Morning yoga?' he said as Or came to the glass-topped table with her blue mat rolled under her arm. 'How Indian.'

'Pilates!' Sweat had stuck short curls of hair to her forehead.

'There's definitely no difference, that was yoga.'

She put her hand behind his ear as they sat. 'You have no idea what you're talking about, my love.'

'I rarely do.' He put his cheek to her forearm then took her hand from his ear and kissed the inside of her wrist.

'Did you have a nice sleep-in?'

'It's nine-thirty in the morning, that's not a sleep-in.'

'You know you work too much, right?'

'No! That's like saying I live too much.'

'Don't you want to live your life?'

'My life *is* my work. D'you already eat?'

'And what if the woman you love tells you she doesn't love you staying in the bar after dinner to draw until I have to come to get you?'

'I'd tell her that she should find a passion equal to my own, and pursue it also to the point of neglect.'

'Neglect! That's what you do to me! You neglect me.'

'I assure you, as I have done, that every spare moment I have is yours. But I *am* here to work.'

'And I? And me? What I am here for?'

'To get to know me?'

'To have fun! But there's no fun here. Maybe I come to work with you? We'll have the drive together and the time between sketching, yes?'

'Do you think that's a good idea?'

'Why couldn't it be?'

'Because when I'm working I'm working.'

'So I do Pilates while you work.'

'Yoga dojo.'

Godfrey straddled his bike while he waited in the patch of dirt beside reception. Or emerged from reception wearing a small backpack and handed him a helmet then put on her own.

'What's this?'

'Kasda.'

'What?'

'Your hel-*met*,' she said, buckling hers at her chin.

Gently he laughed. 'I'm not wearing this.'

'You are. You said we're driving half an hour, that's as far as the monkey temple. You know what we saw there.'

With the adamance of a child, 'No.'

Impatience of a mother, 'Yes.'

Godfrey lowered his head to the petrol tank. 'I don't want to wear it.'

'And I want you to wear it. Just today, for me. Then tonight I wear for you whatever you want. Deal?'

Godfrey tongued the front of his bottom lip then stretched it with his cheeks as far back as they would go. He inhaled a kind of barely audible hiss.

'Come on!' said Or as though the whole thing were a trifle. 'It's just once.'

He looked into the thing and disliked immediately its cloth and foam interior. He turned it over in his hands—a matte-black dome without visor, the plastic clips of its chinstrap clicking against the sides that would encage his cheeks. 'Once turns into twice,' he sang in a high and cautionary voice. 'And twice turns into me never enjoying myself again!'

'Look, my love. I am the most easygoing person you will ever meet, but you have here two choices. You can freely do what I ask you to do, or I can manipulate you into doing what I want you to do.'

He frowned at the gas tank then twisted his neck around until in the furthest corner of his eye he saw Or happily and impatiently staring at him. 'That's fucked up.'

'Mm hm.'

Godfrey sighed; eventually he straightened the helmet upside down and slowly raised it until its bottom edges touched his hair. With his hands above his head he paused. 'Come on,' she said as though to a dachshund. He squeezed the helmet down and fiddled to enjoin the male and female clips. 'That wasn't so hard.'

Godfrey lifted a hand in a gesture of joyless acknowledgment to the moustachioed guard at the gate. Or shuffled in closer to him and put her arms around his waist and clunked the side of her helmet against the bottom of his and rested her head at his back. The smell changed from dust to onions to dust to gasoline to mould to camphor to sandalwood to cumin and cardamom to dust to rubbish fire to wet backpack and dust to pickled armpit then rubbish fire to black exhaust smoke to unlit charcoal to forsaken chicken coop to dust. His drooping face and rigid jaw were exhausted and seething as they rode beyond Madurai and drove the gentle rise of an overpass between a flooded lake and the hunch of tree-veined rock upon which he would soon be painting.

Parked at concrete steps which rose to the beginning of the path to the hilltop, Or took off her helmet and shook her head to loosen her hair. 'See, that wasn't so bad.'

'I loathed every minute of it,' Godfrey smiled, and put his helmet over a mirror. 'It takes *all* the fun out of riding a motorbike.'

'It's exactly the same,' Or moaned.

'We go up.'

Between a tin bucket of dung cakes resting on a wall of cinder blocks and a dilapidated palm-thatched portico, Godfrey took his sketchbook and roll of pens and pencils from the saddlebag and pocketed the keys. Five old men in orange robes were asleep on the shaded concrete floor of the arch at the start of the ascent. A red path littered with straw rose before Godfrey and Or in the midday sun.

Amid the smell of plastic-fire and the mooing of cows the straw turned to dry leaves as slow music echoed from somewhere in the dropping distance, punctuated by auto horns. The climb turned to a path between parched bracken and dead thorn and red dirt and desert grass. Godfrey and Or puffed and dripped with sweat; crows seemed to fly in and rearrange themselves on bare branches. He stopped to take off his shirt and pointed back to the view over the flooded plain and the overpass.

'I learned a word yesterday,' said Or. 'Bleak.'

'Still not impressed?'

'It's *so* ugly,' she smiled.

The sky was cloudless over the path rising and turning at right-angles on itself. The view to the east was of tiny three-storey block-houses on a plain of dark green scrub—the furthest distance Madurai and the four gopurams of the Meenakshi temple. At last, overhead, as the crows cawed and kahhed, were the beige domes of two concrete shrines, the higher facing the smaller as the path turned from red and grey paving stones to dirt and rocks. To the left of the hilltop blackening brick steps rose high between red-and-white-striped walls to a white porch. Or followed Godfrey up onto a polished platform, where a black granite peacock on a slab of red-tiled stone faced locked wooden doors.

'This is the vahana of Murugan.'

'It is indeed,' said Godfrey. 'How'd you know that?'

'There's a lot you don't know that I know.' The porch looked beyond crumbling low walls over the city. As they returned to the dirt Or said, 'What *is* this place?'

'I actually don't know, I've never seen anybody up here. But it's holy somehow.'

'It's like after the apocalypse.'

'It is eerie.'

'What you are even painting?'

'This,' said Godfrey, pointing beyond the shrines. They crossed the hilltop, passed the first structure of small wooden doors encased in concrete under a single unpainted tier, and touched a reclining Nandi surrounded by litter. The dirt path lined with rubbish led around dead bushes and shrivelled weeds to the rocky edge of the hill. Godfrey stepped carefully in his flip flops over the mass of orange boulders, turned to offer Or his hand, brought her out to the stony clearing upon which he had for the last four days been working. The deranged music ceased to be an echo and now could be heard—high-pitched trumpets and trilling male voice and rattling drums—rising loud and crisp out and over the entire view. Looking across to the larger and higher rock, itself overlooking houses as cubes of peach, of mint, of white, and beige—the square dome of a gopuram jutted out at the foot of the hill as if to mediate between striking and indifferent mountain and sprawling and grovelling settlement.

'It's at least an interesting view?' said Or.

'Why's the music so loud?'

'This is maybe their Masada.'

'That's another Abode of Murugan.'

'I should drop my pants and fire a rocket? It's forty-five degrees, Godfrey. The hottest.'

'All the way up here and we're still surrounded by rubbish.'

'They are colourful, the houses. What you are painting?'

Godfrey stepped up onto the furthest ledge and gesticulated as though he were composing and manipulating. 'I'm enlarging the houses and shrinking the rock.' He grabbed with his fingers here and twisted with his wrist there. 'And have you seen everywhere the sides of the houses painted with billboards for concrete companies?'

'Mm.'

'Here each house has a picture of what's causing its inhabitants to become wretched. It's a landscape, basically an Age of Kali and a Garden of Earthly Delights, ruled over by honourless men and vindictive women.'

'Oh, a happy painting.'

'As must it be. You're doing Pilates?'

'I go up there,' she said, pointing with her thumb to the raised pavilion and reposed peacock. 'And try not to feel like the world has ended. Have a nice day at work?'

'Have a nice day at... Pilates?'

Godfrey knelt down and unfurled his pens and pencils and took up a 2B as he returned to standing. Or unrolled her blue mat behind the peacock and in the sunless and breezeless heat she poised herself as a beetle on its back. He opened his sketchbook and rested its spine on his right forearm, his fingers at its top keeping it open, and took up where he had yesterday—when the sun seemed too near his face and the heat became disorientating and the music far too loud—left off: at the barren Disney elephant graveyard, with Ganesh and Airavata and the carpeted elephant from the Meenakshi temple—elephantine forms of religion—lying on their sides and beginning to decompose.

The music—it was the same song, though fifteen minutes had passed since it had taken alarming precedence in the order of Indian noise—was suddenly switched off. 'Thank fucking God,' said Godfrey as the crows and the distant horn-beeps became the greatest disturbances with which his concentration had to contend.

He worked at the animation-styled figures of a withered Mufasa and skeletal Dumbo and soon could hear behind him the whooshing of strained human breath. He ignored the forceful inhaling as he fossilized two large ears—thought that Or must have been swinging a leg with particular vigour. He sat, and moved his pencil to the facing page, where in fingers and hair he had been working on a Modern Kali—not modest, not maternal, not helpful, but aggrieved, vindictive, insidious. Long struggling with what to put into her four hands, he knew only that she was to hold the instruments by which she imposed her resentment. An hour ago he had been given her second: a motorcycle helmet. As he sketched the thing he grew conscious of the relative silence of the crows, usually his ominous only companions, and the relative volume of the air coming from Or's cheeks. His pencil stopped moving over the paper. He turned an ear to the pavilion high across the hilltop. The breathing seemed to hush; he returned to the helmet. When its outline was drawn he added a few drops of blood to the severed uncircumcised penis in one of Kali's upper hands then adjusted the length of the test tube that was her earring. Then he moved over to the facing page, and drew on the outside of a house a soldier dressed as a carrot watching television in an armchair, Godfrey's adaptation of homes ruled by cowardice, a line he had found in the Bhagavad Purana. He noticed between pencil strokes that the audible breathing had started again. Its regularity distracted him from the remembered logo of a television station; again he turned. Or was on her back, oscillating her arms and kicking out her legs and struggling to breathe. And in struggling, amplifying.

'Yoga,' he said, and returned to his sketchbook with shoulders hunched like an aggrieved goblin. He focused on the gopuram between the rock and the town, much enlarged on paper compared to his view beyond the ledge and about to be stomped on by Kali, its decoration a miniature replica of his *Nine Levels of Purgatory*. Re-sketching his Robin-Williams-Pan, the collection and release of air between tiling and roof seemed now to redouble in intensity. Godfrey threw his pencil into the spine of his book and clapped it shut. Or's butt was in the air and her legs pointing back behind her head, her feet almost at the ground as though she wanted to kiss her knees. She huffed as she released the pose, puffed as she returned a single leg to the mat—huffed again as she pointed the other at the ceiling.

'Oi!' Godfrey called out. Or circled her raised leg one way then whistled a gust of air as she wound it the other. 'Or!'

'Yes?' she called out and grabbed an ankle with both hands.

'Can you be quiet?'

'What?' she said, as she put her forehead to her shin.

Godfrey called across the hilltop: 'I can't concentrate.'

'What?!' and Or eased back to prostrate.

'I can't, fucking, concentrate!' Godfrey yelled.

She stood from her mat and came out to the top of the brick steps. 'What is the matter?'

'Your breathing.'

'What about it?'

'You're breathing so loudly. I can't concentrate.'

'Oh, I'm sorry,' she said with her hands at her hips. 'Should I stop breathing?'

'I didn't say that. But do you have to do it so loudly? It's like you're trying to keep a hot air balloon up.'

'It's not easy these sequences,' Or called down as she descended. 'I'd like to see you do one of them. And I'm *so* sorry for breathing.'

'I've been breathing, that wasn't breathing. It's like you're opening and closing the vents of a tunnel.'

'Well I'm sorry that I'm here to spend time with you.'

'Can't you just breathe a bit quieter? I don't want to sound like an a-hole, but I can't hear anything over you touching your toes.'

'You can't hear me over the noise!'

'I can't hear the noise over you. Oo, you're gonna get it,'

Godfrey said with clenched teeth. He leaned to crash his forehead against hers. 'Nope,' she said and lunged away from him. 'How it's going?'

Godfrey reopened his sketchbook and tapped the nib of his pencil at the gopuram. 'Still sketching.'

'Jesus, scary! And it's…? Right?'

'Yep.'

'So scary. The temple is the same as the last one. Have you been inside here?'

'I haven't, no. I've just been up here.'

'Should we go down to have a look?'

'Really?'

'Why not?'

Godfrey looked at Or's blotchy face then out to the sun. High overhead, it seemed to be attacking his forehead, melting his sketchbook, trying very hard to cook him from the ground up. 'I guess so,' he sighed. 'You gonna complain and point out all the rubbish?'

'Are you going to let me breathe?'

The street which led to the temple's entrance looked as though it were erected as the set of a Western film. The concrete facades, flat and square, led to a peach and teal gopuram over the dark hall of the temple's entrance; the rock towering behind the whole crude and khaki view, veined with bushes, its hard slopes covered in hot sunlight. A man in a white shirt and orange lungi pulled a blue-metal cart of green and yellow coconuts ahead of Godfrey and Or as women in saris swept the dust from the footpath with brooms of tied twigs. Music played through the street from a bassless speaker, the woman's voice a witch's sweetness luring children with deep-fried candy. Someone yelled for a coconut and the cart-puller drew to a stop; he hacked with his machete as an auto came around the corner and careened through yellow barricades to splutter and rumble at them.

The columns of the porch were rearing horses painted as though by children; Godfrey and Or kicked off their flip flops at the side of its steps. At the end of a long hall lined with shops—some open and selling trinkets and calendars and bottled cow urine, some shuttered with steel plates—a red-draped Siva and chalk-covered Ganesh greeted them as they passed towards high iron-framed doors bolted open. The entrance smelled of guano, the crowd following behind them larger than that walking ahead. Through open sunlight into a dark hall—of stone and sculpted columns, this figure smeared entirely in orange, this with red, this in white and robed with green.

Sections of chrome fencing led them to the right of the temple, up a flight of steps and over large geometric shapes painted onto the ground in red and yellow and blue and green. The last, before a larger enclosed hall, had a pentagram at its centre. 'Star of David!' said Or under her breath and poked Godfrey.

Through open doors bolted with brass latches embossed with peacocks, they entered a higher, still larger hall. Its barricades led them out to a wing whose halogen lights combined with the sunlight of a metal gate to give the passage a blue and medical tinge. A drum began to sound above and ahead. A nadaswaram started up, its note-bursts shrieking and random between the deep beats of the metallic drum and the ringing of a tiny bell. Rounding the passage, they returned to the larger hall and walked along its upper tier, daylight replaced entirely by electric white.

'I think we're inside the rock,' Godfrey whispered as they stepped onto another staircase. 'That we could see from the hilltop.'

'It's pretty cool in here,' Or whispered, her head rolling as she ascended, impressed by the growing height and moved by the isolation of walking on and in and up.

'Temperature cool?'

'No.'

'There's no rubbish, right?'

'I don't know. It feels different.'

At the top of the stone steps, the longest and steepest yet, Godfrey and Or together looked back to the depth of the hall—their heads almost touching the blue ceiling, eye level with the teal-and-magenta flowers and purple cornices and lion capitals at the roof. Chanted prayers joined the startling music, all of it sounding loudly from two open doorways above.

A shirtless priest unlocked and rearranged panels of chrome fencing. Godfrey and Or now found themselves as the rear of a queue of people, in saris and singlets and trousers and shirtsleeves, rounding to another flight of steps not rising forwards but inwards, into the smaller and darker hall above. Ceiling fans wobbled quickly overhead as Godfrey and Or stepped onto the rising stone. Soon they had ascended to what was the temple's final room—

smallest, lowest-ceilinged, darkest—its metallic railings so numerous and narrowly spaced as to seem as though they were for penning sheep.

'Should we be here?' Or whispered.

'Why not?'

'They're praying. I don't want to pray.'

The drum-beat and the trumpet screams had ceased. At the front of the room scissor gating had been pulled back from three doorways. At the first, the queue stopped to pray with hands clasped before waddling towards the chanting and the bell-ringing. 'We can't go back.' The narrowness of the railings and the thickness of the crowd behind them meant their only way out was through. 'We'll just walk past and shake our heads.'

'Doesn't head-shaking mean yes?'

'That's head-wobbling. I think shaking's universal.'

They shuffled on among the crowd—black stone flickering with white light, ceiling fans whirling and buzzing—and shortly came to the final turn in the barricades. They moved with the old women, the middle-aged men, the small children—the queue tightening at its front as some took longer to pray and those behind grew impatient and pushed. At the first doorway Godfrey and Or waited in a four-deep crowd to glimpse the wall ahead. The high-pitched voice of the chanting priest became almost deafening as it echoed through the columned gallery. At a stone balustrade they now stood in pitch black before an idol of Ganesh, his painted trunk and waist draped in white cloth alone discernible in electric candlelight. Waddling through the passageway, squeezed into one another by people, they came to the second doorway, its square niche unlit but for a single lamp flickering on the ledge before it. The tiny man behind Or said, 'Siva.'

'Siva?' she whispered.

'Siva.' They had to walk back out into the light of the hall to get around to the final doorway. At its far wall a bald and bespectacled priest stood with a necklace and no shirt. Its niche was the deepest of the three and red-lit by electric candles. A small black idol was tied across and garlanded and draped—with white cloth and strings of blue flower and lengths of green leaf. Godfrey looked over the steel bar which kept everyone from it, looked down to his left and to his right at the deposits of oil and turmeric. Or leaned in behind him. 'Which one is this?'

'Murugan,' Godfrey whispered then turned away. He lifted a

declining hand to the priest, waiting with a long flame beside his bowl of white chalk. Or looked back up at the idol and down to her left and to her right—wet stone and clothed idol—listened to the chanting that sounded almost like a hum and the sweetly ringing bell which seemed a presage—inhaled the shroud of incense rising through the cavern. She turned to follow Godfrey and came face to face with the priest. He had just finished a short prayer before smearing the forehead of the Hindu before her. Without breaking rhythm he wiped his covered thumb across Or's forehead then was handed fifty rupees by the man behind her and wiped his forehead too.

Or stepped out and down into the next uncrowded room and sighed with a feeling of release. 'What just happened?'

'You were seen.'

'Seen?'

'By Murugan. The paint's to show that you've been seen by a god.'

'Oh yeah? I think they should be painted for being seen by me.'

Godfrey laughed and they walked on, back down through the mirrored half of their inward journey.

'It was intense in there,' said Or as they stepped over the bat-stinking doorway.

'The whole country's intense. But the temples do do something to you. The darkness, the fire, the music, it feels ancient and mysterious. And the participation.'

'The participation?' said Or and touched her fingers at her forehead. She looked at their tips and saw white chalk. 'It feels stupid to have this, right? Like a tourist.'

'You look insane.'

They came out to the sunshine of the street. Or stepped down from the porch and put her forearm to her head and slid it from elbow to wrist across her eyebrows. She looked at Godfrey as she turned to her waiting sandals. 'Is it gone?'

'Mm hm.'

She put one foot forward and wiggled it into a flip flop. When she stepped fully towards the pile of chappals a sharp bark yapped below, accompanied by a sharp pain. Or screamed and jolted from all the shoes. A three-legged dog hopped backwards with its teeth showing and hackles raised. A line of blood already dripped at her shin. 'Oh my God, Godfrey!'

'What?'

'That dog just bit me.'

205

'What dog?' said Godfrey. Or looked up from her shin and too found it gone. 'Are you OK?'

'My God, it hurts.'

'Let me have a look.' Godfrey took his handkerchief from his pocket and kneeled down and wiped the line of blood from her leg.

'Ah! What the hell?!'

'What?'

'It fucking hurts!'

'All right, I'm just taking a look. Aren't you a soldier? Toughen up.'

'Where the fuck is the dog? I need to see if it had rapies.'

'It didn't have rabies.'

'How do you know? It only had three legs and looked dirty. Can you find it? Can you see it? I looked down and it was gone. Fucking India. Godfrey, it hurts so much.'

'Just stay calm. Let me get a bottle of water and I'll clean you up.'

'We go to the hospital.'

'We don't need to go to the hospital, it's just a dog bite.'

'I don't have all my rapies shots, we don't have rapies in Israel. We go to the hospital, now.'

'We've—.' Godfrey sighed then almost continued: 'I only jus—.'

'What? … What!? I'm bitten by a rapid dog and you are thinking about your pictures?!'

'Rabid.'

'What?'

'A rabid dog, not rapid. You weren't bitten by a fast dog.'

'You think this is time for jokes? If you thought I was crazy now, you see me with rapies. I will *eat* you.'

'Jesus.'

'We go to the hospital. Now.'

'Stay here and I'll get the bike.'

'Run.'

'I'll walk rabidly.'

'Run!'

'Yep, running,' and off Godfrey hopped, jogging up the Western street to the foot of the hill upon which he felt he should be sketching. He sped back and snaked through the yellow barricades and braked hard outside the temple's porch.

'Helmet,' Or said as she limped to him.

'How's your leg?'

'Put your helmet on.' She unclipped hers from the handle behind the seat.

'I'm not putting my helmet on, just get on the bike.'

'Put your fucking helmet on!'

'Jesus.'

'Now hurry.'

'It's not as dirty in here as I have thought. Thanks for staying on my side.' The plastic mattress crunched under its bedsheet as Or shifted her weight.

'Of course.'

'OK, Madame,' said the doctor, returning to the consultation room with a tin tray. She placed it beside Or's hip; on it two long cardboard boxes were beside two very long-needled syringes. 'We have two treatments available after being bitten by the dog. One is local treatment, called PCE vaccination made in India. PCE is purified chicken embryo. Or we have HDC vaccine, called human diploid cell vaccine and made in Israel.'

'HDC,' Or shouted. 'You give me the circumcised needle.'

'I have to tell you there is significant difference in cost between the treatments and—'

'I don't care. I don't want to have dead chicken inside me. Give me the Israeli one, whatever it costs.'

'First I have to ask if you're having travel insurance, or how you will be paying for the vaccination because the cost difference is quite significant.'

'We don't care about cost. Just give me Israeli needle.'

'What's the cost difference?' asked Godfrey, standing at her side.

'We don't care!' said Or and very firmly squeezed his hand.

'The Indian vaccination is costing forty-five US dollar. The Israel-made vaccine is costing seven hundred US dollar. As you can see the cost difference is quite significant.'

'That is significant, yes.'

'Pay her.'

'What?'

'I didn't bring my purse. Give the doctor your wallet. Doctor, we take the Israeli one, OK?'

'Wait, can I just ask?'

'There's nothing to ask.'

'What if the chicken one's more effective?'

'You think a fifty-dollar Indian chicken needle can be better than Israeli?'

'She is right,' said the doctor. 'Both are perfectly effective for

207

vaccination but PCE is requiring injection today, and again in four days and then again in two weeks. HDC is only once.'

'Just pay her,' said Or behind grinding teeth.

'I am a doctor, Madame,' she smiled. 'I don't carry credit card machine.'

'We're able to pay. He's able.' Or looked up at Godfrey and placed her hand around his and now affectionately squeezed. 'Aren't you?'

'Yes,' Godfrey said, bowing his head. 'We can pay for the Israeli one. Seven hundred US dollars, which is... a thousand Australian.'

'Now you give me the circumcised needle!'

Godfrey waited outside while Or was given painkillers and had a watch-list of symptoms explained to her. Lakshmana Multispecialty Hospital—a thin eight-storey building of light and dark blue blocks—stood on the main road halfway between Madurai and Murugan's second Abode. On maps delineated, the road was in reality a long boulevard made indistinct by the dust which spilled in from its outer lanes and ran out to strips of dirt used for parking by trucks and buses, and mounds of dirt between green skips surrounded by white powder and fenced-off frames of electricity transformer and trees giving shade to coconut carts and sadhus. On both sides of the road a narrow lane was kept somewhat clear beyond all this, the dirt quickly reappearing at the concrete steps outside the shopfronts of KFCs and fabric and luggage and concrete and underwear shops and Domino's pizzas and optometrists and Vodafone shops and shops whose wares could not by their English signs be precisely derived—'medicals', 'self-creation media', 'power systems'.

Standing at the top of the steps outside the hospital, beside an ambulance parked in its steep driveway, an alley came out to the road at Godfrey's right. The point at which its smaller gutter met the road's larger had either caved or been smashed in. Triangles of concrete jutted out of a t-junction of green-glowing sludge, litter and dirt for some time accumulating therein. A man stood over it, his lungi folded like a diaper, scraping his teeth with a stick. The preeminent smell was of a vinegar fermented not from ethanol or grapes or even onions—but from bin juice. And it all seemed to Godfrey to be rather tiresome.

The whole dirt-washed panorama was now a too-familiar sight. The roads seldom changed, Godfrey realised, not even in configuration let alone detail. On some streets the buildings were narrower, yes, and on some there were greater accumulations of parked motorbike and on some more cows—he could presently see only four—and some streets did have a mosque instead of a church. But even beyond the city limits—and only apart from the inside of the temples and within the grounds of the Heritage—this khaki and broiling townscape was all Godfrey could remember of India.

'This is India,' he thought, then admitted. 'This?' he exhaled, and turned from the man spitting into the sludge. As his face met the road—rattling and beeping with cars, with autos and motorbikes, thundering and screaming with trucks and buses—an auto bumping along below cracked a billow of black smoke directly at him. He coughed and spluttered and turned his head as a breeze came off either the sludge or the rubbish beside it. He breathed in deeply to recover the air lost to exhaust; the hot bouquet invaded instantly his nasal passage. He gagged, coughed, hunched, and retched. He put his palm to his mouth and at his cheeks felt his fingers textured. He pulled them from his face. Sweat had turned whatever had been on his hand to thin blobs of mud. He ran both palms down the front of his shirt, slowly but perceptibly turning from baby blue to a kind of green. 'What the fuck?' he said as he looked down at the tawny smears coming off his hands.

This was it. India had been systematized, rationalized, worked out.

And this, was it.

To his left, across another alley and beyond a dust-covered awning hung from rusted scaffolding he found a four-storey supermarket, Day-One, its closer entrance set back from a storey of rubbish piled in plastic bags behind three overflowing wheel-bins. Half a dozen inserted shopping trolleys rested beside the automatic glass doors of the further entrance, from which now emerged a slender feminine figure, immediately recognisable as not Indian. The young woman stood at the top of the steps and puffed out her bony chest and stood on her tiptoes and smiled as she raised large sunglasses to the daylight. She gazed briefly to her right before taking an armful of coconut water and a bag of avocados down to the lane. Thinking that the figure seemed suspiciously familiar, Godfrey leaned back from the street. Realising why it seemed disconcertingly so, he stepped back up the hospital steps and concealed his body behind its polished black doorway.

'What the fuck?' He leaned forwards to look again at the woman, now attempting to hail an auto. Godfrey flagged the first person to walk out of the hospital's glass doors. 'You speak English?'

'Yes, sir,' said the man, wobbling his head.

'Do me a favour. Can you see a Western woman out on the street? Down there?' He curved his wrist and index finger from the cover of the doorway.

The man stepped out from the shade of the entrance and said, 'Down there, sir?'

'Yes. Is there a woman holding a bag of avocados. With sunglasses. Waving for an auto?'

'Hello, Madame!' The man called out. 'Madame?'

'What the fuck are you doing, don't do that!'

The man smiled and looked back and reassured him. 'There is nobody there, sir.'

'Really?' Godfrey leaned forward and poked the top half of his head out. She was gone, if in fact she had ever been there.

'Hm?' he said to himself then, 'Hm. Nandri,' he said to the man, who seemed to be awaiting further instruction. He wobbled his head and walked down the steps. Godfrey looked again to the supermarket rubbish before going back inside to wait among air-conditioning.

'Nnnnn, my leg,' came around another groan from the bed. During Or's last relapse into pained sleep Godfrey had closed the shutters which gave view over the bed, the plunge pool, the tête-à-tête. All day working in fits and starts—absolutely the least productive way for him to do so—and creating as he drew, each of her interruptions meant another five minutes lost to preparation. The painted side of a house now taking shape as an image of government trying to get people to love themselves—one rat-headed politician handing out copies of that book by Glovindria— Godfrey replaced the sponsors on a second's jumpsuit with the sewn-on offer of free hugs.

'Nnnnn,' sounded again from the doorway. 'Godfrey?' said Or in a feeble voice. 'Can I have more tea?'

'More tea?'

'Is that OK?'

'That's a lot of tea.'

'I'm sorry, is it too much tea?'

'I have no knowledge of an upper critical limit to tea consumption.'

'What?'

'Give me a second.' And he gave up on being able to work on this non-mechanical side of his art. Almost out of spite he ran his pen over the outline of a jackal among the background of foundations in ruins. He slid out his chair and turned on the electric kettle and sat on the side of the bed.

'This is difficult for you?' Or said, the groan absent from her voice.

'Is what difficult?'

'Making me tea and looking after me when I'm sick?'

''Tis the easiest thing in the world.'

'Then why don't you be better at it?'

'Huh?'

'Stop complaining when I ask for more tea. I'm sick. I was bitten by a rapid dog.'

'Rabid.'

'I don't care fuck how you say it. I was bitten by a dog with rapies. Where's the tea?'

Godfrey yelled in tone but not volume: 'The water's boiling!' and returned to the kettle.

'I have made a theory,' Or called out.

Godfrey scrunched his nose and flapped his mouth as he mimed her words to the wall. He dropped a teabag into her mug and said, 'Hit me.'

'Do you think maybe I was bitten by the dog because I did have wiped the chalk from my forehead? Like I am punished for turning away from God?'

'Because? No. Succession is not causation.'

'What?'

'The wiping didn't cause the biting,' he yelled as he brought through the mug.

'But I feel sort of different.'

'You feel different because you were given a rabies vaccination, d'you know what that is? It's a tiny bit of rabies in your system.'

'Is it?'

'It is.'

She moaned and said, 'I'm sorry I didn't have come to breakfast again. My leg still tingles when I'm walking. You think I can have more painkillers?'

'You can have as many as you'd like, it's paracetamol.'

'And when you've finished your picture you can clean a bit?'

'Huh?'

'Your mess. So much frumpled clothings on the floor.'

'You're not moving from the bed.'

'I can see it.'

'So clean it up.'

'It's your mess and I am in pain!' Godfrey went back to his desk. 'I also have made a question.'

Adding a shaking head to his scrunched nose and flapping mouth he mimed again: 'I also have made a question. ... What is it, darling?'

'I think you hesitate when I said can we go to the hospital.'

'Hesitated? Not at all.'

'You did, you hesitate and now you are neglecting.'

The scrunch, the flap, the shaking head. Then, 'How 'bout you stop busting my balls for ten minutes?'

'Busting your balls?'

'I'm trying to work here and you're calling me every ten minutes for tea, which is fine, but when I bring it to you don't tell me to clean up and interrogate me.'

'I am not busting your balls, my love.' She smiled at the miniature pool with only the bottom half of her face and called out: 'But if you want to see ball-busting, I will put them in a vice and turn them into blintzes.'

'You know you brag of your capacity for torturing people, right?'

'Thank you for judging my personality some more!'

Godfrey leaned on the doorway between desk and bed. 'I wasn't judging, I'm just pointing it out.'

'You said arrangement is judgment. What you choose to tell is the telling, right? Lately you are choosing too much to arrange me. God forbid someone did arrange the facts of you, huh? Walking with your high head. You think being a painter,' she said, deriding the vocation with a wobble of her shoulders, 'puts you above everything?' She extended her arm and stiffened her hand then put it to her chest. 'Including taking care when she's sick of the woman you *love*?'

'It doesn't put me above anything,' Godfrey calmly said. 'But I do think that what I do is greater than most people's work.'

'Great? You are doing paintings.'

'You don't do paintings, you create them.'

'Oh yes, I forget, Godfrey the great creator!' Her stiffened hand began to flail and to whirl. 'Watch out everybody, the great creator wants to paint! But don't be sick, because you'll have to ask for help from Godfrey the Great!'

'Godfrey the Great? I like that.'

'You are arrogant I think.'

'You're the one calling me great. I don't think I'm great at all, I just want to do my work as an artist.'

'You think a little bit you're a god. Go and make your paintings in the city.'

'I don't want to go out there. I think I'm afraid of India, it's insanity out there. It's like uncontrolled mayhem.'

'Go then to the bar, I don't want you here.'

Next day, Or's leg had ceased to tingle and she could walk without pain. As Godfrey gathered his pens and pencils from his desk she said in a kindly voice that she would walk him to his bike. 'Do you think you will finish today?'

'No, it's still a few days from done.'

'These things take longer than you think, huh?'

'They seem to. In Bangkok I could work for six hours straight, no breaks. I can't get to that here.'

'Helmet?' Or said at Godfrey's side.

He toed the clutch pedal. 'What about it?'

'Put it on please.'

'No.'

'Yes.'

'How about, I wear the helmet when you're on the bike, but when I'm alone I'm allowed to enjoy myself?'

'How about, you wear your helmet so you don't get brain damage and leave me alone in India.'

'How about I drive like I always do, safely, and I'll be fine, because I've made a special deal with the big man.'

'As long as egotism veils the heart, God cannot shine upon it. He does not make deals with stupidity.'

'Where the hell'd you get that from?'

'I was reading your Bhagavad Gita. Unveil your heart, wear your helmet. Please.'

He kickstarted the bike and said, 'I really don't want to.'

'And I really want you to. I'm the most easygoing person you'll ever meet, but I just want this one thing from you. Please wear a helmet.'

Godfrey shook his head as he lifted the helmet from its

impalement on his mirror and squeezed it down over his ears.
'Happy?'

'Kiss?'

'Gotta go!' and the bike lunged forward and he drove off. As he
approached the second bend in the road he took off the helmet
and rested it on his lap. On his side of a y-intersection a deep
concrete gutter ran with sludge and overgrew with creeping weeds.
As he passed it he looked down into the milky-blue fluid which
trickled over its bed of rocks and rubbish. 'Not symbolic enough,'
he thought. When shortly he came to the bridge upon which Or
had been introduced to India he readied his hand at its chinstrap
and made sure there was nobody coming up beside him. With one
arc of his left arm he threw the helmet over and off the bridge.

The sides of almost all the houses were not only sketched, but
painted, with what was causing the wretchedness of their
inhabitants. Godfrey had only to finalise what Kali would hold in
her fourth hand, to colour her clothing, to finish off the severed
crotch of the honourless man who mirrored her in size and
symbolism—and had to personalise her eyes. Then, at last, his
second India painting—tentatively titled in his book of musical
notation as *The Garden of Earthly Delights in the Age of Kali*—would be
finished.

A depiction of that which had recently been biographed on a
Balinese ridge, Godfrey had spent hours trying to decide whether
merely to de-penis the cacao-drinking Viking or to take away his
testes as well. Normally determining impulse more valuable than
reflection, Godfrey slid his sketchbook onto his knee and turned
the page blacklettered with 'ABITE NUMMI' and changed the
Honourless Man's crotch from one under which he had tucked
everything to one which bore no trace at all of a genital.

Sitting upon the rock and overlooking the hill, the sun making
the ink run fast from his pens, the crows cawing in the dead trees
behind him—auto horns jiggling below and Tamil music pounding
and piercing the midday air—he for a time wondered why genitals
were always in the plural, and could you have just a genital? Then
he returned to Kali's final empty hand. He had decided that the
fourth instrument by which she would impose her resentment
would be an alembic, an apparatus used in alchemy to sublimate
mercury—whatever that meant. He placed it in the hand at the end
of the flaming arm then wrapped her fingers around it.

214

He took his shirt off and wiped with it the sweat from his face. Standing on one foot and flailing her elbows, Godfrey filled in the floral pattern on the tank top above her distended belly then coloured the stripes of her yoga pants. At last came the remainder of her face. Already wild-haired with her tongue poking out between persimmon lips, Godfrey had left her eyes until very last, reasoning that the ultimate tone of the painting would determine how widely bulged they would be. The sun grilling his lowered neck, he twisted his shirt into a rope and hung it over his shoulders. He drew very lightly the bottom of one eye but decided it would end up too narrow for "barren despair". He drew a thicker line below it before curving across and around to complete the organ. With brow as distant from lid as was anatomically possible, its looked vain, lascivious, admonitory. He relaxed his hunch, shook out his right hand then wiped its sweat with his shirt. A single eye, then he could paint the top half of her face. So soon would the work be finished.

An anxiety began to grip him as he returned to his sketchbook. Making them wide-set, he put his pen to her left tear duct. It went low on the eyelid as a curved shadow appeared on the bottom of the facing page. He came to the eye's pointed outer corner then came back and went high on the upper eyelid; descended to join the line with the tear duct as the silhouette rose to darken the Honourless Man's ungenitalled crotch. Soon a full half of the work was enshadowed; Godfrey's pen stopped halfway through the first side of her iris.

'I can't *believe* you're actually here.'

His neck twisted to the darkened page.

'You're like a desert hermit sacrificing yourself for your art, giving radical permission for the world to say yes to *so* much.'

His face drained of tension and most of its colour. His head rose from his sketchbook and his eyes bulged. That voice, that accent— he was too frightened to turn.

'I like her eyes, who *is* that?'

Standing on a rock behind Godfrey Lackland, Alexandra Wishart put a palm on the ground and lowered herself to sit beside him. His eyes like tennis balls in concrete, Godfrey turned his head and dared not to look upon her till his twisting neck and frozen stare had forced him to. She smiled with persimmon lips and grateful eyes. He reached across and put his fingertips at her forehead.

'Are you here?' She put a cheek to the back of his hand and

215

smiled. He poked at her nose. 'How are you here?'

'I've been asking around for days, a couple of locals said they'd seen an artist coming up here to paint. That's Durga? The fierce warrior goddess? This is so amazing, Godfrey, I can't *imagine* the blood and the sweat and the soul you've put into it. Artists are like—'

'What a—' The desire for disbelief numbed and almost muted him. 'What are you here? Why are you doing here? When? Ha ha! What? But no. How?'

'I have nowhere else to be in the world. You're working here alone and I'm working alone, it doesn't make sense for us to not work alone together!'

Godfrey felt a sense of purpose that was, outside of his work, extremely rare. 'It's horrible here, Alexandra. The dirt, the dust, the noise, traffic, cows—the cow shit. There are people everywhere. The gang rapes. It's not safe at all for you to be in Madurai.'

'My hotel is *so* nice, you should *see* it. Where are you staying?'

'In a horrible, horrible place. With cockroaches and cold water. What are you doing here?'

'Tell me what you're painting! This is *so* amazing—I'm in India sitting next to a painter *while* he paints!' She unlocked her phone and lifted it high and leaned her head to Godfrey and smiled up at it. 'Why is she holding a cucumber? Is that a cucumber with ketchup? Gross. I like her lipstick, it matches mine.'

'Why have you come to India?' Godfrey asked, unable to recall a satisfactory explanation.

'I just spent two weeks in Malaysia, I went there to meet a guy I'd been messaging, a photographer, but he turned into a giant weirdo. He kept saying all this stuff about how deep his heart was and I just kept thinking, your heart is this big—right?—it has a finite size, it can't be that deep. I think I got that from you, your authenticity's contagious. India's been on my bucket list for *years* and you're working here alone and I work alone so why shouldn't we work alone together? And your creativity lecture, my Godfrey! Everyone asked for it specifically but I had to tell them you don't write anything down because you're a genius. A Jesus genius, you're like Jesus up here aren't you? Sweating, dying from the sun, covered in blood and tears, just to *paint*. This is your Sermon on the Mount *and* your Crucifixion! Artists are the only people who keep the world sane, don't you think? We save the world, like doctors. We're the world-soul's psychiatrists.'

Godfrey stared into her bulging eyes and remembered that he had had no water since breakfast. Perhaps he was hallucinating—hopefully, he was hallucinating. He reached across again and put his fingertips on her face, scraped them from her forehead to her chin. 'You miss the human connection as well, I know how you feel. Connection's so important.'

'I was just about to leave.'

'Oh you were?'

'And to celebrate with alcohol.' He rolled up his pens and pencils and wiped his shirt over most of his body.

She rubbed her palms together to dislodge the stones embedded in them. 'I love celebrating! What are we celebrating? You should *see* my hotel. It has a huge pool and it overlooks the city and there are peacocks—peacocks!— walking around.'

'How long are you here for?' The path underfoot changed to concrete-slathered brick then to red and grey paving stones.

'I hope a really long time, I need the stillness. I feel *so* great here. I want to use my anger *only* against wrong and be violent for liberation, to destroy in order to empower others to create, does that make sense? I even found a yoga studio called The Liberation Movement—isn't that a cool name?—they have the most intense hummus, though I couldn't find my amino profile powder. Oh, it's one of my *dreams* to move to India and open up a health-food store! We are *definitely* getting inked here, my Godfrey! For every milestone we reach we get a tattoo, don't you think? You should come and stay at my hotel, will you stay at my hotel?'

'What? No.'

'You can't be your best self if you're staying in a hotel with cockroaches.'

'I'm all right. Thank you.'

'You *totally* should! I can pay for it, it'll be a tax write-off through my new artist's foundation. I've just started building it—the view up here is so gorgeous—to give artists the freedom to create, like a secret society of patronage. You can be our first Living Wishfully artist! Yes!'

'I'm going to another city tomorrow. Trichy. For another painting.'

'Oh, Trichy, I've heard of that place! I've always wanted to visit, there's a yoga centre that's supposed to be amazing.'

They walked between sadhus through the concrete arch and descended the last of the steps. Godfrey put his sketchbook and pens into his saddlebag and the key in the ignition.

'This is yours? It's beautiful. I'm so happy you could use the Bali money for something that makes you happy. Have you heard the Hungarian word, "eletmüvesz?" It means life-artist, someone who lives their life as though it's a work of art. That's so you. I was thinking this morning I'd *love* for you to be real and to be here so I can feel like there's someone working in the background, even if it's on a faraway mountain.' Godfrey held in the clutch and toed into gear and kicked it. 'Even the feeling that someone's there in the background, that's enough for me.'

'I'll see you round, Alexandra.'

'Have dinner with me?'

'What?'

'Will you have dinner with me?' Godfrey turned the key back. The gateway between the bucket of dung cakes and the palm-thatch portico was silent but for birdsong and insect-hum. 'Every day I dread the aloneness of eating by myself.'

Godfrey blinked once, long and slow. 'When?'

'Now. Tonight. I understand though if you have plans with someone else.'

'Who!? Else!? Where does your brain go, Alexandra? Why—.' He looked at her, in strap sandals and white dress bursting with violet columbines—her neck longer than it seemed it should be, her lips unnaturally smooth in so coarse a climate, her eyes dark, large, and sad—her gaunt figure hopeful, vulnerable, alone. He thought upon spending his evening having to boil water and make sarcastic faces while defending himself. 'You want to have dinner?'

'Unless you have other plans?'

The bike reached the end of the winding forest road which rose and turned between dry shrubs and bougainvillea to Alexandra's hotel. Godfrey looked back at her, resting with closed eyes between his shoulder blades, and slowed and pulled in under the hanging roots of one of dozens of sacred fig. He woke her up and was struck by the grandeur of her hotel.

Above and below, thin walkways rose and descended to white-walled hotel rooms, their rooves stalked by peacocks. A little up the hill, a wide path terraced down to a sunken plastic fountain and a lawn before a beige balustrade topped with white globes. With the hotel's restaurant behind them and the fountain trickling at their left they overlooked the whole dry and sprawling city, a panorama of square lego blocks peach and taupe and beige, stuck everywhere below into a dark green plain of intermittent treetops, the gopurams of the Meenakshi temple highest in the flat and smokey distance.

'Isn't it incredible,' said Alexandra. 'Me in India. Looking out over her city like a queen of old, ruling my people from my high sanctuary, blessing the inhabitants with my royal peacocks in attendance.'

Tables were brought out and set up around them as two peacocks foraged in the shrubs at the base of the restaurant's yellow columns.

'Are you hungry?'

'I am actually starving.'

'And we're celebrating?'

'What are we celebrating?'

'You're here!' she said, as they sat at a table in the deepening gold of early evening. 'Both of us here working alone! Order anything you want. I do want to apologise for how Bali ended by the way. I think both of us needed, from that first misunderstanding, to own our roles more, to accept the strength of our respective signals. That confusion's why the retreat didn't end as well as I needed it to.'

'It didn't?'

'Four deaths is unheard of. And I only got two video testimonials and they're not great. I should have put your seminar later so people were inspired at the end. And Venerika hacked my email and stole my entire format for her retreat.'

'She what?'

'It happens. Ne'cole's paid to have her search rankings higher than mine too. People google The Creative Art of Wishfulness but they get The Art of Creative Wishfulness. You can't compete with search rankings. So now I'm building a new course, something they couldn't *possibly* create because I'm the genius.' Alexandra raised her wine glass and announced: 'Your Year of Living Wishfully!'

'What's a year of living wishfully?' Godfrey clinked his poured beer against her water.

'*Your* Year of Living Wishfully. A year-long guided journey of self-recovery and ingenious life design. Once it's built I won't have to work anymore, just the launches each year. A passive income, a real salary, for the first time—peace of mind, freedom! So much space to breathe and create, so much. And part of the reason I'm *here* here is I want you to do the creativity modules for it.'

Godfrey croaked like a toad: 'The what?'

'I can create the self-creation stuff, that's my art and my life, but I want you to create Wishfolios telling people *how* to access creativity and *how* to focus it into one big project.'

'No.'

'No?'

'How can you possibly want me to work for you after what happened?'

'I can't focus on that!' she said, dismissing in an instant all that she knew Godfrey was talking about. 'I choose to focus on what you brought the alchemists, what you contributed to the journey— I've never *seen* such a reaction to content. And you'll be giving them so much more, *all* the creativity secrets to alchemise their artistic vision and rekindle their soul fires.'

'Can you hear yourself yet? Still. You haven't—'

'When people see tangible results at the end the testimonials go through the roof! Every day here you're going through the very creative process itself, it's fresh and hot in your mind, and if that bimbo isn't here to distract you from your work you only have to transcribe what you're already doing into goal-oriented modules!'

'And which bimbo would that be?'

'Have you forgotten her already?'

'No, I remember her. But you sound like a bitch when you talk about her like that.'

'She was a bimbo, come on!'

'She wasn't a bimbo at all, Alexandra. I'm sorry, but green does not look good on you.' Godfrey made a mental note to repaint Kali's skin from blue. 'She is a very interesting person. Literally a soldier, and trained in psychological warfare. And an opera singer.'

'Bleh, opera?'

'Blergh?'

'Opera's gross, so old-fashioned. Nobody loves to the point of suicide. She was a bimbo. And what's psychological warfare? She knows how to mess with people's heads?'

'She?'

'Why would you train in something like that but go to peaceful Bali on vacation? It doesn't make sense, *she* doesn't make sense. She was a liar and a bimbo and you fell for her like a stupid old boy and you were distracted so our neurons got crossed. But your queen forgives you, because your seminar was so *good*. Surrender what you do to her and she'll release you from fear—and we'll build this course together and you can do the creativity modules, right?'

'No! I don't have time. I have three weeks left here and three paintings still to do—more actually, the first two need to be finished. I'm already working from waking till sleeping and like I said, I'm leaving tomorrow for a week then I don't know when I'll be back. And I don't like what you do, Alexandra. I'm sorry to say, but Bali was interesting only as a dip into the wider world of people's minds. It was exposure to symptoms of a disease that I don't want. I just—. I don't have time. I simply want to do my work as an artist. Plus, that bimbo is—'

'Please don't talk about her. The important thing is that you're here working alone and I'm here working alone.'

'Yes, but I'm n—'

'I'll pay you ten thousand dollars.'

Godfrey turned the key in the door to their hotel room and called out as he pushed in: 'Hello?'

'Hi,' Or called from outside. Godfrey put his sketchbook and his pens onto the desk. She was paddling her heels in the plunge pool. 'Where have you been?'

His eyes wide with dread, Godfrey said in monotone and with raised eyebrows, 'You're not going to believe this.'

'Believe what?' she said, twisting to smile up at him.

'Ale—. Why is your face painted?'

'I went to the Meenakshi temple for darshan. It was such a beautiful ceremony, truly. You look terrified, are you OK?'

'Alexandra's here.'

'What do you mean?'

'I just had dinner with Alexandra. She's in India. Alexandra's *here*.'

221

IV

'"The Oxford of South India." Doesn't that sound nice?'

Or squashed her smaller backpack onto Godfrey's, already flat on the back of the motorbike. 'What is Oxford?'

'It's a university city.' Godfrey ran an octopus strap over and under both and hooked its other end to the rack. 'Ruskin and Burne-Jones went there.'

'I don't know who they are. In Australia?'

'England.'

'Never heared of it.' She straddled between Godfrey and the luggage. 'Why do you care if it's in England? Helmet?' Godfrey found neutral with his foot and turned the ignition. 'Helmet.'

'It got stolen.'

Her own already clipped, she put her hands at Godfrey's shoulders. 'It what? When?'

'Yesterday at the hilltop. One of the homeless dudes in the orange robes took it I think.'

'Well we buy another one on the way,' she said as she readied her feet on the pillion pegs.

'Well we don't.'

'Well we will.'

'No we won't.'

'You will see.'

'You'll see.'

'OK,' she said and flapped her hands once on Godfrey's shoulders.

'OK what?'

'We can go.'

Having successfully avoided pulling over for the entirety of the four-hour ride, Godfrey grinned as he pulled into the sloping gravel car park of the L'Americaine Hotel. He stood and turned and recoiled from Or's dirt moustache.

Its high lobby was walled and desked with mahogany laminate; unread English-language newspapers were fanned out on a coffee table among red pleather couches. Checked in, the steps to the elevator led them past a kind of gift shop wherein a seated woman was surrounded by racks of M&Ms and Peanut Butter Cups and Hershey bars—shelves of Doritos and Cheetos and Ruffles beside a refrigerator of Snapple and A&W and—. 'Thank you,' said Godfrey to no one and took a Dr Pepper from the fridge.

They waited a very long time for a very slow elevator to take them to the fourth floor. Halfway along an unlit corridor of open doors and dust they found their room. Godfrey threw their bags onto the bed and took off his boots and shirt.

'*How* does this work?' Or called from the bathroom.

A rusting metal cone sticking out of the wall shot two needles of water—one at the ceiling, one at the window of opaque glass slats.

'Do you use the tap to fill the bucket?' said Godfrey. 'And the ladle thing to pour water on yourself?'

'Why have a shower if this what you have? And mosquitoes,' she said, and slapped one against the aqua tiling.

'But there is a balcony.' Godfrey unlocked and slid open its door. 'What the,' he coughed, as a gust of hot dirt fled past him and made for the room, 'fuck?'

Directly below him, the scent of spit-soaked sweatsock evaporated from knots of rubbish white and beige flowing around scrub and growing through weeds. A kind of path had been tamped into the dirt; old women with bunches of sticks rearranged its surface. A cluster of thatched rooves without walls preceded the beginning of concrete buildings, the first's side painted in yellow and blue as a four-storey billboard for Ramco Cement.

Opposite and to the horizon ran facing street-fronts of crumbling mint and peeling salmon, squeezed buildings all possessed of a sunken riverbed of rubbish for a nature strip, crossed in places by bridges of prostrate doors. And in the centre of it all, the street—a concrete wall not really dividing its direction or its lanes—careening with doorless buses, smoke rising in no less than seven plumes, a fire raging at the corner of a four-way intersection of hobo, tractor, and motorbike—the hot afternoon filled with rubber smoke and screeching music and the clown-horns of scurrying autos.

'It looks like an Intifada down here. Why would you put a balcony outside this window? Can you tell me that? The Oxford of my arse.'

'There are no towels in the room,' Or called from the bed, drenched and shivering from the plastic buckets.

'I mean, this is the view and you think anyone wants to look at it? Maybe—yes! Again! India's the future of the world, Or. You're forced to look at what's ugly, told that it's beautiful, and guilted into it being a privilege to be able to do so.'

She came naked to the balcony and put one foot outside. 'I kind of like it.'

'What do you like about it?'

'All right, calm down.'

'What do you like about this view? Tell me. The spotfires? The mounds of rubbish? The pack of wild dogs?'

'Is that what they are?'

'Yes. Dragging a water buffalo skeleton over a pile of trash.'

'I don't know. It's… It's alive.'

'Alive?'

'It's life.'

'You can't replace life.'

'Why we are here again, in this Oxford of India?'

'Alexandra's in Madurai and thinks we're in Trichy. And there's a temple here that looks incredible, twelfth century. The entire thing's made out of stone and I thought I could use it for the next painting. Shall we go take a look at it?'

'Yes, but we are walking.'

'Walking?'

'You're not riding motorbike without a helmet.'

'What the hell have you done in here?'

As though visited by a putrid tooth fairy, black footprints ran from the bathroom to the bed and back again. 'There are no towels, I told you, and the floor is dirty.' Or jumped onto the bed and slapped a wet hand against the wall. She grinned and showed Godfrey the dead mosquito and blood smear, inflicted and incurred.

Turning into a narrow street hedged with dirt they passed a steel gate covered with glued-on posters, a hammer and sickle at every corner. At their feet a shallow gutter oozed with lime green fluid, plastic bags and water bottles resting therein as sliced fruit in jelly. Both Or and Godfrey had long learned the necessity of mouth-breathing. Not even that could save them here. Mouldy, algal, fluorescent—their dry retching was synchronized as the smell of hot and rotting entrails invaded their faces in one rising rancid assault.

Blue security bars and chrome queue barriers at the porch of a small temple; an abandoned litter of blind and squeaking puppies. A cow munched at green leaves on the ground beside a man pouring coffee high from a steel cup into paper, and out onto sunlit concrete strangely almost dirtless. It was a boulevard encircling a vast tank of gherkin water, fenced off entirely by a pointed steel fence the colour of bronze. Multicoloured mandapams stood at intervals over its banks, plain concrete steps leading everywhere down to a meandering oily film. Faded gopurams towered over the opposite, distant, bank—matched in height and exoticism by high palm trees above the low horizon of crumbling buildings.

'This is incredible,' said Or, tapping her fingertips along the fence.

'I think we should leave India.'

'What? Look at this place.'

'In the three-minute stroll it took to get here we saw a dead human on the side of the road, Or, covered in flies. A goat's severed head on the back of a motorbike. I can—' He sniffed her dress. 'I can smell the gutter we just walked past. You literally smell like an oyster fart. Inside a tomato growing a midget's thumb. We've fallen into the bog of eternal stench, did you think that was possible? And all the women look like Hoggle. Why don't we go to Cambodia? It's cheap—it's not cheap here. I can switch half the paintings to Cambodian temples, Angkor Wat and whatnot. If Grieve liked it it must be cool, right? This place is filthy. I thought maybe just Madurai was gross, like I'd accidentally picked the worst city in India. I think I picked the cleanest. This place is a shithole, it's like everything's about to end, the whole world, just heating up and ready to implode. Every moo from a street cow is like they're saying, 'Beware,' Godfrey mooed. 'Bewaaaare! And I know I need that for the paintings, but three weeks is enough. I've smelt enough to last a lifetime. This is a new notebook, I've already filled up my old one just with India. Can we go to Cambodia? Have you been?'

'I like it here.'

'You like it here? Since when?' They rounded a corner of the tank and were given the sight of a middle-aged man's back.

'Once you look past the bad stuff, and think of the internal, you really do begin to—. This place feeds my soul I think.'

'It feeds your soul?' Sitting atop the first step on the other side of the fence, the man's sleeves were rolled up and his legs spread. 'How can it fee—. What the fuck?' He was leaning back on his left hand as his right jiggled up and down in his lap. 'This, feeds your soul?' Godfrey raised his voice rather: 'There is a man masturbating not five feet from you, and this place feeds your soul?'

'You don't think if you walk down the street in Australia there are people jacking off in their homes?'

'In their homes, Elaine! Not on the street, overlooking a man-made puddle of dirty water. What is he even flapping off to? Does he have a filthy water fetish? Give it a rest, buddy!' Godfrey shook the fence and flailed his head: 'India's a fucking prison! The most modern prison there is, why? Because nobody knows it's one and it's fifty years before it's time and everybody thinks it's fucking fantastic. This, is Milton's Brave New World. People have been convinced, I don't know how, that hell is actually heaven.'

'You are losing it, huh?'

'Oh, I'm losing it!'

'Is that Alexandra?' Injecting alarm into her voice Or pointed at the corner to which they were walking.

'What!?' Or smiled as Godfrey hid behind her; she threw her head back with laughter. 'That's not funny!'

'It's funny, come on! Where is your sense of fun, agadah? You're looking at life the wrong way. What did happen to looking past the surface and being in India together? Remember? You have to think of the internal, Godfrey, and see the divine soul in everything.'

'Are you fucking kidding me?'

A dry river bed seemed to mark the city limits. The streets narrowed and the buildings shrunk to huts. They strolled a road covered in dust, crossing to walk in hut-shade whenever turns exposed them to the sun. They passed several men lifting their lungis like children their t-shirts to pee—four tractors hauling trailers of rubble—two bicycles pulling each a flat-cart of rotting carrots. The smell was mostly of a yoghurt fermented from off camel's milk that had itself gone bad. At one miniature corner the huts were of concrete and newly painted—bold green, brightest cyan, smoothest magenta. A flute playing somewhere from a speaker was joined by a kind of witch's voice chanting a rollercoaster of a cackle. A poster was hung on the outside wall of a coral-painted snack kiosk. Cackle, *cackle*, cackle. On it a stone face was garlanded in pink and white flowers, obviously an idol, cackle, its forehead dotted with red and smeared with turmeric. Its nose was flat and its lips bulbous and its bug-eyes—cackle—painted white then lined and cackled with black.

'What the fuck is that?' said Godfrey. 'That is creepy.'

'It's so interesting!'

'It's not interesting, it's creepy. This is what they worship, Or, do you see? What is that thing? It's creeping me the goddam hell out.'

'I think it's cute.'

'Cute? No! The whole place is colourful animism and idol worship. People fall for the colours and they see exotic animals, and they think it's amazing I've figured this place out.'

'We worship our bank accounts. You said this. We fall for consumer things. What is more gross?'

'You *are* kidding me, right?'

Eventually they came to manicured lawns stuck with sugar and coconut palms. Schoolgirls sat in shaded circles as goats frolicked among them. High sandstone walls guarded the complex which Godfrey sensed was the temple and his destination. A pathway cut out of one of the lawns sank to a doorway through one of the longer walls. Halfway down, the path was submerged in opaque water.

Godfrey descended and took off his flip flops and put them on the lawn beside him. He rolled up the hem of his trousers and stepped ankle-deep through the doorway; slowed and stared and could not but say, 'Holy…'

Directly in front of him a porch, its square columns worn almost to round, had as its base a tiny stone mandapam behind which stairs rose to the unlit entrance of a raised temple. To his left a huge pyramid soared, covered entirely with statuettes and round arches—all of it in the same golden stone—and crowned with a dragon-scaled dome. And the entire ornate panorama was flooded from wall to wall.

'You've got to see this.'

Flocks of pigeon circled overhead—palm tree to stone niche to palm tree—as a priest in an orange robe came out of the darkness and leaned a bare arm against the column at the entrance beneath the pyramid. To Godfrey's right a stone elephant seemed to be swimming. It was the carved bottom of a balustrade which rose to a dark porch entirely of columns, jutting out from the temple's long and low middle. The corners of its smooth roof were topped by resting Nandis at both ends—the whole complex reflected in waves of translucent pear bending in the olive floodwater which seemed to keep it afloat.

Standing in the gap of a stone platform higher than their heads, Or held her dress out of the water as she came to Godfrey's side. 'It's gorgeous.'

'It's incredible. I can see the painting already. Two pages longways, one upright for the pyramid. What do we worship? Carved in place of Siva, Ganesh, Durga, Murugan—our system of belief. It's just a shame we can't go inside. I wonder how long it takes for the water to drain.'

'Why can't we go inside?'

'It's flooded.'

'So walk through it. There are people up there, look.'

Three generations of one family were strolling through the massed columns of the protruding porch.

'The water's gross.' Shimmering in the sunlight, swirls of muck and streaks of oil rocked back and forth upon the flood.

'Gross? Come on, agadah. What happened to you? You are such a baby now.'

'You have an open wound on your leg, Or. A dog bite no less.'

'I will always be fine.'

'What do you mean, fine? The water's filthy. If that gets into your body...'

'Godfrey. The great sufferings vanish for those who pray.' Or closed her eyes and joined her palms and slid them up until her fingertips touched her chin. 'Praise be to the lord who abides in our heart, source of all existence. Hail, divine illumination, form transcending experience.'

'Hail? Heil? Or, what the fuck are you talking about? What's happened to you?'

'It's a prayer, to Murugan.'

Godfrey threw his eyebrows upwards and thrust his bottom jaw as far forward as it would go. 'A prayer?'

'So I know I'm being taken care of.'

He drew back the corners of his mouth and rubbed his bottom teeth at his top lip. 'By a psychiatric nurse?' From within the pyramid there came the blaring of a spongey brass horn. It was a nadaswaram, slow and deep bursts sounding like a call. 'What the hell is that noise?'

The notes grew more frequent and more adamant and rose in pitch and echo over the water. Or lifted up her dress and without look or word waded to the furthest stone staircase. Godfrey looked down into the water and thought of the dead dog in the canal and Alexandra vomiting overboard. He squirmed as Or traversed and ascended. Eventually he rolled up his trousers as far as they would go and followed. The trumpet shrieked high and dipped low and halted all over the place as he raised a wet foot onto a first dry step; blared and trilled as he rose to the covered porch. He could see through the temple to other wall of the complex, turned and beheld the colonnades high above the water, the nearby Sivas wearing in the niches of the pyramid, stone darkened where restorative hands could rarely reach.

Or was behind the nadaswaram player. He was cross-legged beside a white-draped granite nandi, elbows out and lifting and lowering the length of his wooden trumpet as his notes flitted and squealed, stopped and screamed. Shirtless priests came out of the inner sanctum and asked for fifty rupees on their trays. Then without warning or slowing the nadaswaram went silent. The final echo streaked through and out of the entire temple, its end visible in the tiny square of daylight distant through the darkness of the elephant-drawn porch.

Or's eyes were closed and her joined hands at her throat. 'I love it here.'

'I mean, right here, maybe. But not India. No more India.'

'Praise be to the lord who abides in our heart,' she said as though reminding him. 'Source of all existence, Godfrey. Form transcending experience.'

'Won't Yahweh be pissed if you start praying to Murugan?'

'Not praying, praising.'

'Isn't he a jealous God? I feel like I read that somewhere.'

'Jealousy comes from insecurity. If God is insecure then he's not worth worshipping. But if he is worth worshipping, it means he is not jealous.'

'I think that's illogical, but I can't prove it.'

'Really,' she said looking again around the room. 'This place so reminds me of the hostess bars. I miss Japan.'

Having asked for beers at L'Americaine's reception, Godfrey was told that of the three hotels in Kumbakonam that were not dumps only The Sangam had a bar. Underground and admitted to in whispers, Godfrey and Or found the unsigned room and beyond its heavy door and black-out curtain sat in dim lighting on art-deco swivel chairs. The bar itself squared off a sunken floor wherein two men tended in bowties; the mirror and the shelves of liquor behind them were framed by red columns and a black lintel modelled on the Itsukushima gate. The tops of elongated paper lanterns were stuck awkwardly onto the walls whose main features were the televisions playing Tamil music videos between pixellated posters of Yoshitoshi battlescapes.

They had been drinking solidly for an hour, opening the session with a large Kingfisher and a gin and tonic before switching to neat Old Monks.

'So I have a question for you.'

'Mmmmm,' said Or, her whole head rising with her intonation.

'Are you really trained in psychological warfare?'

'Mmmmm,' and she swung her had back down. 'My last boyfriend called it psychological Or-fare.'

'Your fiancée?'

'No.'

'Your boyfriend before your fiancée?'

'No.'

'Where does the boyfriend fit in?'

'Bali.'

'Huh? Before you met me?'

'Iiiii… met him the day after I met you, I think. No! The day after we have slept together.'

When Godfrey had made a mild attempt at piecing things together he stopped squinting. 'You had a boyfriend *and* a fiancée while we were in Bali?'

'We didn't have really discussed it in terms of concrete. I think more he thought I was his girlfriend than he was my boyfriend. I told you I had a villa in Canggu for a week when you left.'

'Yeah but… you didn't tell me it was with another dude.'

'What, you are jealous?'

'Please. It's just strange.'

'You're strange.'

'Kiss me, stranger.'

'Oo, you're gonna get it.' She kissed him as their foreheads met. She put a hand on his knee then her chin on his shoulder. He nuzzled his cheek into the softness of her hair. 'Look at this!' Godfrey turned to the television screen about which she was excited.

A podgy man with a goatee, in a white singlet and camouflage trousers, was stomping his feet into a hill and grunting. A hand-tapped drum the only music beneath him, he spun and wiggled his shoulders, surrounded by an army in full uniform. The drum fell silent and four Sikhs bent their necks twice in a kind of sideways peck. Then the man in the singlet made a butterfly with his joined thumbs and smiled at the camera and sang: '*Ding-a ding ga-ding ga-dinga ding-a dong-a ding-a dong-a ding ga-ding ga ding ding.*' The drum returned and he put one hand behind his back and one in front— and with his feet stepped as though riding a hobby-horse around a nursery. '*Ding-a ding ga-ding ga-dinga ding-a dong-a ding-a dong-a ding ga-ding ga ding ding,*' then the grinning army made butterflies with all of their thumbs and sang in a higher voice around him: '*Ding-a ding ga-ding ga-dinga ding-a dong-a ding-a dong-a ding ga-ding ga ding ding.*'

'You can't laugh at this!' said Or as Godfrey squeezed his eyes shut and put his fingers to the bridge of his nose.

'I know I can't,' he convulsed. 'I just... I can't figure out if India's some kind of joke. A childish joke. The colours, the sounds. The gods. It's like little kids were given a box of crayons and told to invent a culture, ding-a ding.'

'You are so racist.'

'How's that racist? It has nothing to do with race, it's the culture. I mean, I like it in here, and this is India. But out there... Hooph!' He looked from the television to the three white panels of Takamori in snow. 'I have always wanted to go to Japan. And now I've added Soapland to my itinerary.'

'You could not afford Soapland, my love.'

'How much is a ticket?'

'A ticket?'

'Does it include all the rides?'

'Let's just say you would have to buy more than a beer to get in.'

'Two beers? Can we have two more beers?' he said to the bartenders. 'Three?'

'A bottle of whiskey and table fee to start. Then the hostess fee.'

'What's a hostess fee?'

'To choose your girl.'

'Hm? To go on the waterslides with?'

'No,' Or smiled. 'The girl that sits at your table.'

'Woah, woah, woah—back it up, crazy horse. What do you mean, you choose the girl that sits at your table?'

'You don't know what a hostess bar is, do you?'

'Soapland, Land of Soap.'

She grinned. 'Do you want to know?'

His smile was gone. 'I don't know. Do I? What's a hostess bar?'

'It's a bar where men pay you to spend time with them.'

Godfrey blinked a few times then looked momentarily with a raised eyebrow to the bartenders. 'Are you a prostitute?'

'Excuse me! How fucking dare you!'

'What? You just said men paid you to spend time with them!'

'Yes, not to fuck them.'

'What, you just hang out and play Nintendo?'

231

'You are their friend kind of. I made one good friend actually.'

'No doubt you did. I want people to pay me to be their friend.'

'Who would pay you to be their friend? You're a asshole.'

'I am an arsehole,' he laughed. 'So you made a butt-load of money from Japanese men paying you to be their "friend"?'

'Don't say it like that! My friend there was sad, he was so rich but he have nothing to do. His father have invented the lids of the things that sit in the ground—what they're called? Metal circles, big ones, that lead to under the street?'

'Sewers?'

'Yes! His father have made the company that make these lids of Tokyo, so he was so rich but he had all this money and no friends. And he come into the bar and we just talk, conversation.'

'He'd give you money to be his friend?'

'After a few months we were close. He knew my dream and I told him about the studio and he want to help.'

'And no jiggy jiggy? I don't want to speak for Japanese men, not the manliest of fellows, but there's no way in hell someone spends time with someone, someone who looks like you, and they don't want to bang them.'

'Maybe he did. But he never gotted to.'

'I'm getting the fuck out of here,' Godfrey strained to announced. 'Can we have the bill please?'

'You don't believe me?'

'People pay you to be their friend?'

The rum, drunk in haste, completed its work as they walked through dirt—camel yoghurt and pickled armpit—back to L'Americaine. Having eaten only bar snacks, Or took from the lobby's strange store a bag each of Doritos and peanut M&Ms. 'You shouldn't eat that stuff,' said Godfrey as they stood waiting for the elevator.

'Why I should not?'

'It has palm oil in it.'

'So what is this?'

'There's five floors in this building, why does the goddam elevator take so long? I'm taking the stairs.' Or emerged from the elevator as Godfrey reached their floor. She offered him a chip from the open bag. 'No thanks.'

'You have to be hungry.'

'I am, but they have palm oil in them.'

'What is palm oil?!'

'Oil made from palm trees.'

'And these trees hurt you in some way? Did they call you a prostitute? No! They try to make you wear a helmet!'

Godfrey smirked as Or jumped backwards onto the bed. 'You're a smartarse, you know that?'

'Mm hm. Look.' She opened the M&Ms and put one between two corn chips. 'Palm oil sandwich. I *like* palm oil.'

'That's disgusting, first of all. And palm oil, Or, is single-handedly responsible for making the Orangutan extinct.'

'They are allergic to it? Why do they eat it then? I've never seen a rangatang eat Doritos.'

'Their habitat was destroyed to make way for palm oil plantations.'

'Uh huh.'

'You don't care about the environment?'

'You haved a can of Dr Pepper. That doesn't have rangatang oil?'

'Orangutan. And no it doesn't.'

'How many flights do you take in a month? Flying kills environment too. You paint on paper using trees. Where are they growed?'

'Grown. I use sustainable paper, thank you.'

'Maybe these M&Ms have sustainable palm oil.'

'There's no such thing.'

'I am sorry for the rangatangs, but...' She crunched a corn chip between her teeth. 'Sorry, rangatangs.'

'Orangutan.'

'I'm hungry, sorry rangatangs. Kiss me.'

'Orang-utan.'

'Sorry to them guys. Kiss me, stranger. I want to fuck.' She slid the straps of her dress off and pulled it down to below her breasts.

'You have Dorito dust in the corners of your mouth, you think I'm going to kiss you like that?'

She read the flavour on the bag. 'You don't like Nacho Cheese? Kiss me then here,' she said pointing to a nipple. 'We didn't had sex for four days now.'

'I'm covered in sweat and you're a Dorito.'

'You're a rangatang.'

'I'm taking a shower.'

Or was asleep—M&Ms melting under her arm and shards of Dorito on her bare chest—by the time he had figured out how to wash himself using the buckets.

In the darkness of deep night, as Godfrey and Or slept semi-clothed on top of the bedsheets—stirring constantly at the buzz of a mosquito too close to an ear—the nowhere-near-silence outside was shattered by a speaker blaring the words, 'Allahu akhbar.' Dogs could be heard barking in the distance as the speaker quickly returned to silent. Then it started up again, louder and longer, an amplified voice streaming into their room, clicking and crackling as though played from a record—trilling and wafting and cresendoeing the same slow phrase again and again: 'Allahu akhbar.' Or's eyes shot open; she sucked in a hiss as she woke. 'Eima! Eima'le!!' She stood on the dusty floor and darted her head left and right.

'What's wrong?' said Godfrey, slightly calmer. 'What the fuck is that noise?'

'It's the adhan.'

'The what? Why is it so loud? What time is it? Am I awake?'

'I thought they are Hindus.'

Now sounding as though the speaker were inside their room, the voice droned the word, 'Muhammad,' at redoubled volume. Godfrey too startled from prostrate. 'What the hell's going on?' The voice shrieked and wailed as though its testicles were squeezed tighter and tighter as it joined the dozens of syllables in the word, 'Allah.'

'That noise, I hate it—it have memories for me.'

Both stood wide-legged beside the bed, their hands ready at their sides, waiting for an attack or for the noise to stop. When eventually the hiss of the loudspeaker clicked off the traffic took its place—jiggling clown horns, constant scooter beeps, screaming buses, howling trucks—as Indian day at four in the morning began.

Standing in almost darkness Godfrey confessed: 'We can't go back to the Heritage.'

'Why not?'

'I'm out of money.'

'Because I have only paid half? Why do you keep bringing it up? I told you—'

'No, not because of that. It's just more expensive here than I thought. This hotel was forty dollars a night. The Intifada Inn. But I do really need you to transfer that money, my bank account's disappearing fast.'

'Yes, I keep forgetting. I remember in the morning but after Pilates I start to studying and forget. I told, it's hard to get money out of a Israeli bank account.'

Persephone Enthroned.

Atop a porch of columns carved instead of yalis with pangolins, tigers, rhinos, whales—a vast lintel made of straw supported the work's central figure of Persephone Enthroned, flanked by a pomegranate tree and a spinning wheel. A thin man in a David Bowie t-shirt knelt under the tree, begging Persephone to spin all the world's straw into smartphones. An apple and a two-tailed fox rested at the ends of the pile of straw, in place on paper of the stone Nandis lying before Godfrey's sweating eyes.

His new *Epic of Limitless Consumption* ran down to the water and from right to left across the temple and his pages. In the frieze beneath the columns of extinct species, Rumpelstiltskin promised Persephone, promised Kore, promised Proserpina, that he would turn the straw into smartphones in exchange for their past, their fertility, their future.

A miniature church, a mosque, a comintern, a gopuram— alternated as the merlons atop the structure of the central page, the temple's long main body the façade for five-and-a-half niches, wherein five granite women toiled in a modern Labours of the Months. At the windows of the niches, blue men and red men and yellow, blue and green and red men—the Six New Heresies—held tin cans between the columns and their ears, listened to the consumer prejudices and social preferences of those working for the construction of the pyramid at the painting's Western end.

Cloudless, Godfrey looked upon shimmering lime-coloured water under a bright blue sky, the long temple floating before him in cream, in silver, in russet and khaki and umber and smokey stone. The sweltering afternoon was quiet, flecked with the cooing of birds and occasionally the echo of a Tamil voice in the porch before him. Too, the water gently lapped in the hot breeze between the wall and the temple—but that was it. It was, Godfrey realised, too quiet.

In the shade of the colonnade at the platform's end, Or sat with her legs crossed not as Godfrey could sit, but with one leg folded back on itself and the other draped across it, both knees pointing at him while her ankles lay flat on a mat. Her hands were behind her back—one arm over her shoulder, the other reaching behind her waist. In Madurai her Pilates had been accompanied by grunts and exhalations. Here she was making not a sound. But Godfrey couldn't worry about it. Four weeks into India and only two paintings almost complete.

235

So the pyramid crumbled.

Its furthest sketched corner sinking into the ground, eroded by the mining of its surroundings and foundations—Indian and Chinese villagers dove from boats into an ocean of plastic to raise its sand before sailing back through palm oil plantations to the body of the temple, where the sand was used in the construction of the sixth office-niche—that in which a David Bowie t-shirt wearing a David Bowie t-shirt sat over smartphones at its desk.

As it crumbled, the Norman figures on the pyramid scrambled to ascend—the plastic surgeons, child molesters, the grown-men-in-playsuits and eighty-five-year-old lead singers, the flocks of Syrian men, Jezebel Dulrich and Dippy the Chug, Jareth and Hoggle—climbed over one another as they salivated at the thought of reaching the top, there to dethrone Icarus, despondent with rebar frames for wings, one leg folded back on itself and the other draped across it, the son of Daedalus leaning sideways to counter the tilt of the structure beneath him.

Godfrey moved his binoculars from the dragon-scaled dome to the frieze just over the waterline below him. Its kalis and hanumans encircled by vines, its ridden and rearing elephants with trunks crossed, its pairs of lion and armies of warring spirits—still he could hear but the shallows, glimmering chartreuse between the angles and curves of stone. He unpressed them from his eyes and looked again along to Or.

In bright pink singlet and tie-dyed blue leggings, she was balancing on the palms of her hands. Leaning forward with her elbows pressed to the sides of her knees, her hair was an almond bouquet on one side of her closed eyes. Very slowly she extended one leg back and held it as her head quivered. She brought the leg back in, stilled herself, extended the other—quivered.

Surely this was yoga, Godfrey thought. But did he prefer interruptions and not-yoga or silence and yoga? Or rather, silence, and the girl with whom he was in India doing yoga? No, he had to work—and concentration was to Godfrey like the levitating of something very heavy to a great height, and holding it there. Momentarily he could break the trance, the X-Wing returning slowly to the earth. But if he lapsed too long and its wheels stuck into Dagobah swamp, he could not raise it that day again.

Or bent over straight-legged until her fingers touched the mat, her bunched hair flopping out into the sunlight. She stepped her right foot back then wrapped the inside of her forearm around her left calf. She took a deep breath and leaned forward, lifted her right toes from the mat. When one leg had almost formed a straight line with the other she crept her right hand towards her planted foot and wrapped it around her ankle.

Surely this was yoga.

Their bags tied down at the rear of the bike, Or returned from a quick walk down the hellish street and chimed: 'Ready.'

'You already have a helmet.'

'This is yours.'

'I'm not wearing a helmet, Or.'

'Then I'm not riding back with you.'

'What's your problem?'

'What's yours? The woman you love wants you to wear a helmet, is that not enough?'

'You want me to wear a helmet?'

'I want you to wear a helmet.'

'Then so I shall.' He put in on and clipped it at his chin and said, 'Let's go,' as Or readied herself behind him. He fiddled at his speaker and hit play as he rolled out onto Intifada road. The song that had been stopped upon their arrival started up again—a parlour guitar and the slurring voice of C.W. Stoneking: *Nothing... Nothing can be right, when everything is wrong.'*

They crossed the bridge and the buildings shrunk to huts. Soon the two-lane road became a narrow path through forest of bamboo leaf and vine-choked sugar palm. *'Nothing can be wrong when I'm walking with my baby—I wish that I was!'* As the cornet wandered the road ran out past bracken and dry thicket to open fields of beige chaff, the searing horizon of low brown mountains. Godfrey reached up to his cheek and unclipped the strap and peeled it off his head and threw it into a ditch.

'What are you doing?'

'What?'

'Your helmet!'

'I told you I'd wear it. You didn't say how long for though. I wore a helmet, you happy?'

'Pull over.'

'No.'

'Pull. Over.'

'No.'

'I am asking you to pull over.'

237

'You're telling me to pull over.'

'Will you pull over, please? My God.'

'Nah.'

'Why do you be like this? If you don't pull over I will scream.'

'Scream away, my dear.'

And she did. He put up with the unbroken howl for a few hundred metres, smiling as he drove with it in his ear. Then the scream turned into words. She shrieked that she wanted to get off the bike and threatened to jump off right now in order to do so. Godfrey pulled over under leafless trees.

'What the fuck is your problem?!' Or lifted her leg over and stepped back from him and the bike.

He kicked down its stand and sat with his feet planted. 'You know what my problem is. Stop trying to make me wear a goddam helmet. Why are you so fixated on controlling me?'

'Controlling you!?' Or yelled among plumes of noxious smoke. 'How am I controlling you? I just want you to be safe.'

The roadside had been cleared of greenery and covered with rubbish. A fire had been lit at the bottom of its slope, black char and smouldering plastic creeping up the dirt to the road.

'I'm perfectly safe as I am. I was here a week before you, I'm a good driver and I don't go that fast. Just relax.'

'It's not you, it's the buses that don't look and the trucks that try to hit you. You cannot control them.'

'And you can't control me.'

'I don't want to control you!'

'Then shut the fuck up about the helmet. Trust that I'll be fine, get on the bike, and let's go home.'

'You will be fine? Who do you think you are? You think you are a god?'

'Huh?'

'You think you are invincible? Why can you be fine without a helmet? Because you're invincible? If you're invincible you must be a god, right? Do you think you're a god?'

'I do not think I am a god.'

'Then wear a helmet, please! I want you to be safe. I worry when you don't wear one. Do you want the girl you love to be worried?'

'Nope,' said Godfrey without patience.

'And I worry when you don't wear a helmet, so either you do want me to worry or you're lying.'

'You *are* trained in psychological warfare.'

'Oh, this is not psychological warfare—this is the woman who loves you, you're not a god!'

Godfrey clenched his teeth. 'I know I'm not a goddam god! I just don't want to wear a helmet, I don't see what the big deal is. I don't make you do anything, why are you trying to tell me what to do?'

'I'm not telling you what to do, I am telling you what I want. Why can't you respect what I want? It's like when you hesitate to take me to hospital. I want to go and all you can think of is yourself. Do you want to make me happy?'

'Do you respect what makes me happy?'

'What makes you happy is dangerous and comes from thinking you are better than everyone else. You are not, Godfrey. You're the same as everyone, and everyone wears helmet.'

'Tsss.'

'What?'

'Helmets, plural. And the Indians don't wear them.'

'You want to be like the Indians?'

'No.'

'You are going to eat with your hands too?'

'Are you? Why are you wearing a helmet if they don't? You love it here so much, assimilate to that.'

'I wear a helmet because I don't think I'm better than everyone. Egotism does not veil my heart, I don't think I'm a god. You think you're invincible, but I could break you in one second.'

'Why would you want to break me?'

'Come back to earth, little boy! You are not a god!'

'Listen, sugar tits, if—'

'What did you call me? Why are you smiling? This is a joke to you, right? Life is one big joke? Ha ha? You don't take nothing seriously, not even the happiness of the woman you love. Come back down to earth, Godfrey!'

'And you're the one to bring me down, right? The woman who loves me, is the one to bring me down?'

'Bring you down to earth because you think you are a God? Yes.'

'It's such an extreme conclusion, Or. Why do you think I think I'm God?'

'Oh, you think you're *the* God, not *a* god? You are God-frey now?' She threw her fists down at her sides and screamed: 'Just wear a fucking helmet!'

'I don't goddam want to.'

'Come back down to earth, fuck! You think you're a god, I'm

239

not going to worship you.'

'I don't want you to worship me! Where have you gotten this from? What the hell is going on!?'

'Come back to down earth! You are not a god! I'm not going to worship you!'

V

'You're like my royal genius-in-waiting, but a dashing creativity pirate at the same time! How *do* you know so much fascinating stuff about stuff that feels *so* important? Your thirst for knowledge, it fills me with life.'

'Mai tais are so good!'

Godfrey crossed his ankles on a sun lounge and sipped at his second, savouring the flavour of grenadine, hitherto unknown to him. On the far side of the hilltop upon which Alexandra's hotel stood, a steep steel stairway led down through scrub and wandering peacocks to a pool. He had just finished explaining to her the Venetian through Byzantine through Greek derivation of the meaning of that bird in Western art.

'Even I could drink these,' said Alexandra. 'You really know how to suck out the marrow of life, how to live deliberately *and* purposefully. It's so inspiring to see someone who creates but who *lives* at the same time. A real eletmüvesz, a life-artist. It's so rare, at least for me.'

Flanked by the hotel's wellness spa and a two-storey block of hotel rooms, the view beyond the pool and across a lawn was of the hilltops upon and from which Godfrey had two weeks ago been working. They rose on the horizon, from the expanse of bland-green tree and square concrete house, like a kingly ascent to a rock-throne.

'Will you include symbolisms in your modules?'

'Uuummm... no, symbolism's a style of working. It's not a method of creating or a path to artspiration.'

'You've been thinking about this a lot, ay?'

'I always dedicate myself to the task at hand.'

'It's going to be so amazing! I made some notes while we were reading, you wanna hear them?'

'Of course. But!'

'What?'

'Can we order two more of these?'

'Definitely.' Alexandra waved at the waiter, standing behind rolled blue towels in a bamboo hut. The only guests at the pool (and from what Godfrey could tell, the only at the hotel), he had been watching them for half an hour and was all too glad for something to do. Godfrey held up two fingers to him and he rushed off to make and fetch them.

Reclined on the lounge beside him, Alexandra took up her crimped and dog-eared and pink-highlighted copy of *She The Warrior* and opened to the page kept by her pencil. She alternated between two voices, one an inspired narrator, one her casual own.

'So. Your Year of Living Wishfully. I was at rock bottom. My life was becoming a disasterpiece and I *needed* something to save me—and all through the videos and the emails I hint that what I would have needed was something exactly like the Year of Living Wishfully—And then slowly the truth hit me—while I invented this course, that I had *lived* the journey that would save me—and I make it obvious that if they live the course they'll be saved too, right?—This, was the process of learning to love myself back to life—which is the grand narrative of the whole course—I was so low on the self-love spectrum, I needed an infusion of destruction to make way for the regenerative fire of self-creation.'

'Wait,' said Godfrey, confused by the voices. 'The course saved you, or you made the course based on what did save you?'

'No, the money will save me. But I have to get them to buy it, and they'll buy it because it's the course that saved me.'

'That's circular logic.'

'It's logical, right? People are so lost and they'll pay a *fortune* to find themselves again.

'But you're lost.'

'I'm not lost!' she smiled. 'Look at where I'm staying! Why do you think I'm lost? I love how you don't care what you say, even if it's offensive and untrue. You just blurt out what you're thinking, right, it's authentic. I guess that's what makes a good creator? You *have* to translate that into your creativity modules. So…'

'So you're lying to them.'

'What?! How?'

'Twice. First you're saying this course saved you. Which it couldn't have because it didn't exist when you were lost. And then you're saying that this course saved you, which it hasn't, because you're still lost.'

'I'm not lost, my God! You're looking at things the wrong way, Sir Godfrey! Mr Free-cheese-in-Bangkok, who's the lost one?'

The waiter returned and transferred their cocktails and a bowl of bhuja to the low sidetable between them. Again he handed the bill to Godfrey. Again Alexandra intercepted and signed it.

'With all kindness, Alexandra. This sounds evil.'

'Evil? My God! I'm the most genuine and well-meaning person you'll ever *meet*. I'm *fighting* to save and empower my people. Online wellness is the new Wild West.'

'Fighting as a cowboy or an Indian?'

'Which one's are good?'

'You tell me.'

'See! I *believe* in the transformative power of this course, because I've lived it. And I've *seen* it, and I offer them salvation and if they want to buy it, they buy it.'

'But you're lying to them about where the salvation came from *and* to where it leads.'

'You don't understand! I've lived this course, Godfrey, it's been my life for five years, and all I'm doing is turning my life into my art and my art into a sustainable soul business. I used to have the same self-doubt as you, it's called impostor syndrome. But the second you get real evidence, the second someone emails you to tell you that your course, something *you* created, stopped that person from committing suicide? The self-doubt disappears.'

'This course stopped someone from killing themselves?'

'Several people.'

'So suicidal people sign up?'

'And they love it! We are saving lives, Godfrey. This is creative surgery on every area of life. Regular surgeons can fix a broken arm, but we creative surgeons, we bring people back to life! We're Doctor-freaking-Frankenstein!'

'You really have some kind of spin on what you do.'

'And I do so much! People won't even have to leave their laptops—everything's sent straight to their inboxes, it's all automated. A hundred k, and the lifestyle I deserve. I can buy you all the mai tais you can drink, you alcoholic.'

'Wait, you don't actually do any work?'

'I'm doing the work now, all of it. *We're* doing the work. And once it's in the platform it's automated: from day one the Wishfolios go out and they're in their online group, and they repurpose their journeys together.'

'First of all, what the fuck is a Wishfolio?'

'It's a registered trademark, it's what you'll be writing—the worksheets for the emails.'

'And second of all, there is no reward without work.'

'Do you *know* how much I work? My God, all I do is work! Which reminds me! Where were you last week? I went to Trichy and asked all over but I couldn't find you anywhere.'

'You went to Trichy?'

'Uh huh. I thought we could work alone together. Where were you working? Srirangam? The rock fort? I went to both everyday, I figured you'd be at one, but I gave up and came back, I couldn't find you.'

'I was around. I got ah… kind of sick so I had to stay in my room a lot.'

'So I got you a present.'

'You what?' She passed it over from her handbag. 'What is this a flip phone? I feel like Dwight Schrute.' He unflipped it and put it to the side of his head.

'Who?'

'Dwight from The Office.'

'Oh, I used to work in an office doing marketing. It was awful.'

'Why do I want a flip phone?'

'You can't not have a phone, Godfrey. It's 2019, it makes no sense. Even terrorists have phones. And if we're working together on this Year I'd like to call you, and you can call me if you have questions about your modules. And if you're around maybe we can hang out in town, even have dinner one night a week? Just one night. Every day I dread the aloneness of eating alone. And you can tell me more about peacocks and history and what you've been working on and make me laugh and turn the complicated simple and recount to me more of your Indiana Jones adventures across the seven galaxies!'

'You haven't seen the Meenakshi temple, right?'

'I haven't seen any temples, I've just been working. I've barely had time to selfie here.'

'Remember the painting I showed you? That tower's modelled on the one in the main temple. I should show you it to you, it's sublime.'

'My God, would you?'

Godfrey parked his bike in the garage underneath Hotel Vijay and took the elevator up. Walking the narrow white-lit hallway, its walls and ceilings of flaking bone paint, the rattling drums and shrieking voices of Tamil music came loudly out and in from all directions. Most of the other rooms' doors were open. Within, lone men in towels sat on the ends of their beds and pointed their remotes at their televisions and groups of men sat in singlets and trousers in wooden chairs and pointed their remotes at their televisions. Godfrey looked back and across in confusion as he unbuttoned his greening darkened shirt and came to the floor's only closed door.

Inside, the music and a great deal of noise besides turned instantly more intense. Past a bathroom the colour of bloodied milk and a bed that smelt of ski boots, Or was at the open window with her legs on a second chair and a book open at her knees.

'What are you wearing?' Godfrey smiled.

'Agadah! Do you like it?'

'Stand up?' She rose and smiled and twirled. The orange and green edges of a sari, printed with bunches of purple milkwort, shimmered as the fabric floated with her.

'It actually looks good on you,' Godfrey threw his sketchbook and his pens and pencils onto the bed and unbuttoned his trousers.

'It does, right? And it's so much cooler than our clothes. I think you should wear a lungi.'

'Not in a million goddam years, my love. And the ah... the forehead?'

'Darshan.'

'Meenakshi?'

'Uh huh.'

'Come 'ere,' he said and pulled her body into his. She smelled of turmeric and camphor. 'I'm just going to get rid of this.'

She jerked her forehead away from his hand. 'No! Why?'

'Come on,' said Godfrey, his palm raised still. 'I can deal with the sari, you look hot in it. But I'm not taking you to bed with that on your forehead.'

'Wiping away the tilaka denies the power within the three forms of self.'

He dropped his arm from the small of her back. 'And where have you gotten that one from?' He was tired of her assertions, which were recitations. He went to the window. The sixth-floor hovel overlooked a dry temple tank, its silted bed filling with weeds, its centerpiece a white kind of concrete altar topped with a yellow dome. Surrounding it in two squares were the backs of innumerable uneven shanties, their rooves of rusting corrugated iron, and the high facades of a hodgepodge of buildings: taupe balconies and powder blue windows and pink awnings and pee-coloured sides and asparagus-stained cages.

'From here.' Or picked up the booklet that had been at her knees. A yellow-bound collection of coarse pages, its soft cover was printed with a painting of six-headed Murugan on his peacock and entitled *What Do Hindus Believe?*

'And that's what this little book says?'

'It was because I wiped it away, because I denied the three forms of self, that I was bitten by that dog.'

'And where precisely does it say that?'

'I just know it. If you purify the spectacles of your mind you can *see* the world is God.'

'Of course you can.'

'How was work?'

'It's awful out there. The worst location yet, worse than the hilltop. What the fuck is that?' Godfrey used the windowsill to jump from the floor. 'Was that another cockroach?'

'Agadah, grow up! So what a cockroach? They're a part of nature.'

'I goddam hate it here.'

Below, at the barren tank's corner, three steel skips stood as the radius of a half-circle of rubbish, grazed all of it by three cows, beside which three men sat with silver trays on their knees, rearranging yellow moisture with their hands and fingering it into their mouths. Music was playing from several of the shanties, male voices shouting down female screeching down male, most of them shops selling parts for televisions, stereos, speakers. Horns were held down at maddening length as standstill autos waited to pass through the narrow passage left by two-deep rows of parked motorbike.

'And the painting? How it goes? Can I see it?'

'I hate it so much. No, I never show unfinished work. But it'll be ready in a few days.' He re-embraced her. 'How does this thing come undone?'

'It take me twenty minutes to put on. Maybe just lift it up?'

'Oh, I can lift it up,' he said, and began to. 'And we can get rid of the face paint?'

'Turn me around?'

'Indeed,' and she let him.

Afterwards they lay next to one another with his arm under her head, his fingertip circling at her shoulder, staring both at the creeping brown stains on the ceiling.

'Do you feel like things have been off with us lately?'

'Yeah. I think it's because I'm working so much. And I'm getting bored here. I get frustrated just working with no downtime. You can't exercise because the air's toxic so I'm getting fat. The toxic air's making me sick, I have a sore throat you wouldn't believe. I just… India's not for me.'

'You should explore the culture more.'

'Oh I've explored it plenty. And I just don't like it. I'll get these paintings done and we can get the fuck outta here. How about— ooh, I have an idea. How about tomorrow we go to The Heritage for a swim?'

The thin quiet of bamboo leaves and a breeze shaking clusters of scarlet flower; bookcases behind the busy reception opposite the ornate door, the rough-hewn pillar with the rolled up screen and the marble bench looking out to the wide pavilion, its burgundy tiles shadeless under the high trees behind it. And in the morning sunshine the stones of the sunken Heritage pool as blocks of champagne, its waters stillest turquoise. So early in the day they would still be cold, Godfrey thought as he stepped over the bench. Between the hedges they beheld the pool entire, its long steps descending slowly at both ends to water made—'

'Mr Luckland, so good to see you again!'

One foot lower than the other, Godfrey turned onto the higher. 'Chandan Babu, hello!'

'So nice to see you, sir. How can I help?'

'Well, we were wondering, Chandan, you remember Miss Dayan?'

'Of course, Miss Dayan, how are you madame?'

'Hello again.'

'We were thinking we'd love to take a dip in the pool. We're in Madurai only for the day and we thought it'd be nice to swim one last time, in the most beautiful pool we've ever seen.'

Chandan Babu clasped his hands together in gratitude and tilted his head. 'Thank you so much for saying so, Mr Godfrey.'

Godfrey took a further sideways step down. 'So that's all right?'

'I'm sorry, Mr Godfrey.'

'Hm?'

'Pool is for hotel guest only.'

'Ah. What about previous guests? Who stayed here for three weeks? The longest anyone's ever stayed, remember?'

'Yes, Mr Godfrey. Pool is for hotel guest only.'

'Can we pay to swim? Just for an hour. How much is that?'

'Mr Godfrey, yes, sorry. Pool is for hotel guest only.'

Godfrey and Or had gravitated back to the hedge. Chandan Babu smiled and watched, waiting for them to comprehend precisely for whom alone was the pool and quickly thereafter to leave. On he clasped his hands beneath his smile.

'What do we now?'

'I guess I go to Pilates.'

'I guess I'll go to work?'

Godfrey took a final wistful look at the champagne stone, the sweet glacial water, and was farewelled at his motorbike by Chandan Babu.

With his back against the far side of the pool, Godfrey watched Alexandra on the southern lawn of her hotel. As the girl in the nighty covered with glittery swastikas, she turned upon her toes and tilted her head as one hand reached high to take photos of herself with her phone.

When eventually she returned to the red tiles of the pool she asked Godfrey if he would take a picture of her.

'On one condition.'

'What?'

'That I can do it from right here.'

She handed him her phone and took from her sun lounge a towel and her copy of *She The Warrior* and lay at the pool's edge.

'Now just make sure that—see how the screen has gridlines?— make sure there's equal amounts of water and sky. Can you do that?' She raised the knee furthest from the camera and held the book open and pretended to read a right-side page with the book's cover facing the phone. 'I'm going to run my hand through the water so just take a bunch and I'll pick which one's best.' She lowered her left hand into the water and ran it back and forth as she sweated in the sun. 'Come closer as you take them. Yep.' When the phone had made a sufficient number of shutter sounds she said, 'Show me? … No! See this? I need to be centred longways as well, and the tiles underneath me have to be straight with these gridlines. See? How can you know so much about painting and so little about photography?'

'So I have a question,' Godfrey said as he returned to sabotaging her photos.

'Mm hm?' she said and pretended to read.

'There you go, I'm not taking anymore. How, if you haven't

gotten this 100-k thing off the ground yet, how do you stay in hotels like this? That apartment in Bangkok, it must have been hundreds of dollars a night.'

'I'll tell you a secret?'

'If you have to.'

'It's me.'

'What's you?'

She reached her arm out over the pool and flapped with a finger the book's front cover. 'Glovindria.'

'Huh?'

'I'm Glovindria. It's one of my old handles, before The Creative Art of Wishfulness took off. I wrote these blog posts years ago and somehow they went viral. I don't tell anyone though because I made Glovindria a wild warrior woman who runs with the wolves, I want to keep her like that.'

'You wrote that book?'

'Mm hm.'

'The book you read for advice. You wrote it?'

'It doesn't make *that much* money, but it's still an income while I work on my abundance journey. My agent's talking about turning it into a film, can you imagine? Oo, you know what? Maybe I could show your art to my agent. I don't really know how that world works, are there agents for painting?'

'Art agents.'

'I wonder if my agent knows any.'

'Don't bother. I've submitted my portfolio to every reputable art agent in Australia, New York *and* London. I didn't even get rejections, I got silence. Modernity greets me with silence but I don't paint for them, I paint for eternity.' He switched to a seldom-used bogan: 'So fuck 'em.'

'You should *have* social media!'

'No, I shouldn't!'

'My Godfrey, you're so stubborn. If you put your art on social media do you *know* how many people will see it!?'

'All I have to do, Alexandra, is make sure I have more time to paint. Another season through which to work—which means money, pure and simple. Do you know what Michelangelo said about art? "To carry out one's art three things are necessary—money, money, and yet more money."'

'Money, money money, I know what you mean. But the money I give you helps, right? Another season maybe? You know, the only definite I have in my life is money? People come and go, but money allows *me* to come and go. I read somewhere that your following times three is what your income should be from social media. Your Year of Living Wishfully is going for double that. Double! Oo, why does business turn me on so much? I hope you don't think I'm obsessed with money. Because I am. And Your Year of Living Wishfully is everything people need to turn their pain into purpose and purpose into self-recreation and I feel *good* about it, and about working with you. We're creative warriors you and I, and we the creative warriors save the world by saving ourselves. Do you ever think that? Oo, could you take notes while I think?'

'I already was.'

'She turns people's pain into business,' was the thought that got him out of the pool to dry his hands and take up his pen and return to his new notebook. 'She acknowledges it without acknowledging it—put that pain porpoise and the depression dolphin in Seaworld,' he wrote, remembering a grotesque from Bali that he still hadn't used. 'Their cage-fights as water-tank-fights watched by applauding tourists.' And once again Godfrey's notes accumulated as Alexandra paced back and forth in her bikini between his crossed ankles and the pool.

'Superman standing over the earth, not saving himself but shaving, the curls of his chest hair falling into city streets, each one righting a wrong—cleaning an ocean, executing a Christian. Delacroix's *Liberty Leading the People*, Marianne pulling the spine out of Marie Antoinette Mortal Kombat style—she said backbone right?—the dead bodies at her feet either herself or other Marie Antoinettes with Raiden holding a musket behind her and a young Sub-Zero with a flintlock pistol. The tricoleur? Just yellow, the cover of Glovindria's book painted as a billboard for a cement company—I can't believe she reads her own spiritual advice for spiritual advice. Wild's not a noun, lady. You can't have a wild and neither can I—what does that mean?—a Wild Thing on a leash? Da der der *der* der—you make my heart sing! Thing playing the drums—no what's his name? Animal! Unbind your Animal. 'Unbind your Animal from the Muppets,'—his arms tied behind his head, legs dangling like a prisoner in a Roman dungeon. 'You lucky, lucky bastard!' Fields of corn with babies growing at the tops of the stalks, a farmer ejaculating into the soil—No! A lake of lily pads growing over the temple tank in Kumbakonam, the farmer sitting on the step overlooking his lily pads and jiggling his wrist in his lap, yes!—cultivating the water with himself. Ha ha. What would a creative middle finger look like? The middle finger *looks* creative, or it *is* creative? Like a large hand with its middle finger raised, the entire thing tattooed with the symbols of vanity, vanitas vanitatum—*or*, a chimp finger-painting only with its middle finger, on an easel drawing Siva, creation and destruction, blue with his consort a smurf Beyoncé riding a peacock. You make my heart sing! A shitload of cocaine in Wendy & Michael's bedroom—on mirrors, in plastic-wrapped bricks—Peter Pan, the only god who dies, chasing his shadow, footprints in the coke dust and outline marked on the walls, Wendy following to snort from its footprints. A human heart already sliced in two by Mel Gibson as Braveheart—'Your heart is free, William; have the soulspiration to follow it,'—the organ half-painted blue and offered to Wile. E. Coyote, licking his lips with a knife and fork in hand and a throaty twinkle. 'The narrative you choose to believe'? She didn't take a *thing* on board from Bali. What if the narrative you *choose* to believe is told by Borat singing about potassium in—'

'Can I see the notes?'

'Hm?' said Godfrey, the change in her tone from impassioned narration to casual inquiry startling him from the levitation.

'Can I see the notes?'

'What'd you say?'

'The notes, can I see them?'

'Oh, the notes. … I'll umm… I'll type them up and email them to you. I write in a kind of shorthand, you won't understand it, should we head to the temple?'

'Yes! Can you give me twenty minutes, I have to get changed?'

An hour later, in a white sari printed with clusters of white and yellow angel's trumpets, Alexandra descended the angles of red steps which led up to her second-storey room.

'You're going the full India hog, uh?'

'Do you like it?'

'It looks kind of racist.'

'What!?'

'You're not Indian. You look like you've gone off your rocker and are about to start Bollywood dancing.'

'Oh, I love those videos.'

'Helmet?'

'No, I love that you don't wear one. Bukowski said that above all

251

we should live dangerously and build our houses on Vesuvius! Oh, I miss volcanoes.'

And with her head resting on his back and the small bend of a smile on her face they drove the twenty minutes into town.

'So you can't take your handbag in,' Godfrey said as he walked her through traffic from his usual parking spot, 'and you can't take phones or cameras.'

'No phones? That's ridiculous! Why not?'

'I don't know. Maybe because it's a holy place.'

'My phone is my connection to my world, what's holier than connection? *Only* connect.'

'You leave it up there with them and we go in through here.'

He pointed to the booth thronged by—bin juice!—by people leaving their chappals, their bags, their phones with women in saris. Alexandra took Godfrey's flip flops up with her. They and her own and her bag were exchanged for a number and deposited in a pigeon-hole. In separate queues for men and women, Godfrey and Alexandra stood on a wooden box in a long cage and were metal-detected, patted down, felt up.

Inside she had no desire to conceal or restrain her excitement. She twirled beneath the ceiling of painted lotus flower and emerald parakeet; told Godfrey she had stopped breathing while looking out over the temple tank; screamed, 'Art is the fire by which we see each other's souls!' while staring at the southern gopuram erupting through the colonnade. She lay face-down and reached beside the men and women reaching for the fire extinguisher and the handrail; with one hand against a yali-carved column she put the other to her chest and asked Godfrey to join her in auscultating eternity.

'I cried, did you see? I can't believe I'm here in Mother India. I think I was Indian in another life. Yes! And I threw myself onto the funeral pyre after my husband was murdered by the British Empire. Oh, I hope I was, can you imagine? I want to come here every morning and thank the gods of yesterday for their sacrifice. And pray here every evening to the gods of wild tomorrows. Everything has so much meaning, I know it! Can you explain it all to me?'

'All of it?'

'In good time, Sir Godfrey, in good time. Can you believe this is where we're creating right now!?'

'You can smell the elephant shit?'

'You think there are elephants here!?' she said with bulging eyes and lifted heels. She bulged further: 'Oh my God, can we pray inside the temple?'

He led her into the white-lit sanctum, its roof of blue and green and pink and yellow, its yellow lions on peach pedestals—looming high atop the countless columns of dark stone. When she had passed the huge garlanded Ganesh she stopped walking and put a hand to her chest and held her breath. 'Oh my God.'

'What?'

'I feel burdened. All the beauty here. But it's a liberating burden, like a turtle shell.' She closed her eyes. 'Fierce goddess, protect us both from fear and bless us with good fortune, looks, success, and fame. Fierce mother goddess, wash the mind with honesty and deterge the soul by alchemy.'

They walked beneath the height, the colour, the columned vastness. Godfrey slowed whenever she stopped to catch her breath, stared whenever she held her hand to something, waited whenever she flapped her fingers at her face to stop herself from crying. Standing among the cold grey columns at the sanctum's first corner, looking round to the warming amber of the twenty-four forms of Siva—the beating drum and sprinkling bells and screeching and halting nadaswaram of a procession loudened as it neared.

'There *is* an elephant!' she said and grabbed his arm.

The procession halted to allow the palanquin and its emerald-shrouded idol to be taken into the sanctum sanctorum. Godfrey leaned onto his toes to look over the crowd around the elephant, red carpets tied at its back and bells softly sprinkling as it nodded in waiting.

'This is the most amazing thing I've ever seen,' Alexandra whispered. 'It's so non-inauthentic.'

'It's pretty fucking cool, I'll give you that.' Godfrey looked across at her. 'Do you want to know what—. What are you doing?'

'I'm recording,' she whispered. Her phone was upright at her stomach.

'You can't have phones in here, Alexandra. How did you get that in here?'

'I stuck it between my legs.'

'How far up?! Put it away.'

'That doesn't apply to us. We're creators.'

'It does apply to us, put it away.'

'My followers will love this, it's *so* instaperfect. My God, I feel like I'm looking straight through the outer world and seeing the divine soul in everything. It's like the beginning of the soul's journey to creative freedom—can you feel it?'

'Excuse me, madame,' said a thick-mustached and beige-uniformed police officer.

'Oh,' she said, and tucked her phone into a fold of her sari.

'You leave now, madame,' said his beige-uniformed and thick-ponytailed partner.

'No, I'm sorry. I didn't know.'

'You knew. Please, this way.' The officers raised each an arm towards the high gallery of dozen-handed gods. 'Meenakshi temple is sacred place.'

'Sorry, Superman,' said Godfrey, 'she's—'. But they were escorted in silence through the Hall of Ubiquitous Goddesses out to the eastern entrance. 'I told ya.'

'Can I come to work with you today?'

'You do *not* want to spend time where I'm having to spend time right now.'

'I know you sayed it's gross, but we haven't have been having time together.'

'There are literally stray dogs everywhere. It's worse than the hilltop. No shade, it fucking stinks.'

'Time with you is more important to me than these.'

His fourth open-air Indian studio was a bridge overlooking a vast riverbed, dry except for festering puddles of bright green algae. Lengths of broken concrete and slabs of blackening polystyrene lay strewn near the banks and around the bridge's pylons. In a few higher spots laundry was being dried, rectangles of maroon and orange cloth stretched on wooden easels and raised slightly from the mud. If Godfrey leaned out far enough he could suck in fully the smell of burnt turkey necks swirling in a broth of dehydrated people's urine—see bare feet protruding from makeshift shelters and the ashes of bonfires piling everywhere anew with tied bags of rubbish, pecked open by birds, contents spread like desiccate vomit from pierced stomachs. Beneath him stained skips had been wheeled into place, each one licked or used as a scratching pole by several starving cows.

Or put her hand on his shoulder and kissed him on the cheek as he readied his notebook, his roll of pens and pencils, his sketchbook—on the concrete ledge of the bridge. Five metres down from him she set up her own morning's things and put her elbows on the ledge and looked out over the riverscape.

Godfrey opened his notebook and slid it aside then opened his sketchbook and returned to the facing pages of his *Reign of Mahishasura, or Ever-Changing Evil.* A narrative in mud, from the top left to the bottom right would soon run from bank to bank a succession of manipulations and deceits, spiritual and temporal, all in the name of money. At its top was already a circus made of bread inside a colosseum, gladiators walking on baguette stilts and emperors in top hats taming loaves of pumpernickel. In the Forum beside it, Vladislav Surkov was shapeshifting from the head of a People's Commissariat to an executive officer for a non-profit to a spokesperson for a corporate sponsor. At the bottom of the right-hand page, a rough sketch of Mowgli as a vulture in a three-piece suit, working as an equine psychiatrist at curing a lone white horse of low self-esteem.

Truck horns blared from the roads running in both directions along the river. To Godfrey's distant right Tamil music screeched gently from the concrete houses. He whacked at his jaw and checked his fingers for bloody success; cracked his neck and shook his head and returned to sketching an oompa loompa trying to catch an oyster in a tomato. He had left space in the work's centre for his own Temple of Antoninus and Faustina, an adaptation of the Greek-looking temple which stood crumbling between his own bridge and the next, its steps descending to rubble and roof caved in, a lone white horse grazing in the shade of the single tree which grew before it. Godfrey took up his binoculars and inspected its columns. They were carved as though a small block were placed upon a larger upon a smaller upon a larger, paint so faded that they appeared rubbed with green and pink chalk. A new song began from somewhere. Instantly it was clearer than the others. Very soon it was also louder as much nearer. It was that rattling and stomping song from the television in The Sangam's bar. Godfrey's looked to the noise. His dome speaker was under Or's open book. 'Or,' he called across to her, but was unheard. 'Or!'

'Mm?' She turned from the book, happy to hear his voice.

'Can you?'

'Can I what?'

'Turn the music off.'

'Huh?' She closed the book on her finger and came over to him. 'What's the matter?'

'Can you turn the music off? There are four hundred people playing the same goddam thing, do you have to listen to it right now and right here?'

'You don't like it?' she teased.

'No,' he smiled. 'They guy's literally just saying ding-a ding-a ding.'

'Music is a divine form of the Hindu understanding of the universe.'

'Please don't start with that shit. He is just saying dinga ding ding. It's pop music, Indian pop music. It's not deep, ga-ding. And I cannot concentrate when it's playing, ga-ding, ga-ding.'

'Well, I'm sorry.' She went and turned off the song. 'What you are painting today?'

'Still sketching.'

'I thought you have finished sketching.'

'Not yet, it's getting more complicated as I go.'

'You have hardly touched it,' she said looking over his arm to the sketchbook.

'What do you mean?'

'Since Monday, you've barely done a thing on it.'

'How do you know?'

'Look…' She pulled her phone from her sari and showed him a picture that looked very much like his sunlit double page.

'What's that?'

'I took a photo on Monday. You said you were working on it yesterday, and the day before. But you've…' She inspected the paper from corner to corner. 'You've put just three tiny people.'

'What are you, monitoring my work?'

'A friend asked what you painted so I send him a picture.'

'Please don't do that, this is private. And a work in progress. That's not cool.'

'I'm sorry, he was curious. You are working so slowly though.'

'Yes. Because whenever I try to get work done, people play music all around me and bust my balls about how much work I'm getting done ga-ding.'

'I'm sorry I want to come and spend time with you today. I'll go and read in silence?'

'What Hindus Believe? Tell me, what do they believe about silence? Never heard of it, have they?'

'No, I got a book yesterday from the book exchange at Pilates.' She held it up and turned its cover to Godfrey.

'No! Or, you should not be reading that. Or, do not read that book!'

'You are telling me what to read?'

'That book is nonsense. Do you know who wrote it?'

'She sounds interesting. I readed—read—her biography inside the cover. She is a priestess.'

'Whoever Glovindria is, is a deranged psychopath with no qualifications to be giving any advice to anyone.'

'How do you know this?'

'Everyone on the goddam retreat was reading that book.'

'So you're telling me what to listen to and what I can and can't read? Who is controlling who?' Then his phone rang. He hurried to reach into his pocket and silence it. 'I thought you didn't have had a phone.'

'Yeah I bought it the other day. It was like twelve dollars, to keep track of Alexandra. She texts me where she's going for dinner, and I know that you and I can have dinner somewhere else.'

'She knows I'm here, right?'

'Why do you keep asking that?'

'Because I trust you.'

'If you trusted me you wouldn't ask.'

'I don't like you spending time with her.'

'What? Why not?'

'She hates me. You should not spend time with someone that hates me. Living beings are deluded by hate, but we don't know it's not un-indistinct from love, and whoever seeks one alone crosses that illusion. Alexandra is not seeking to cross over, she hates me.'

'Is that Hinduism or is that in that book?'

'It makes sense, right?'

'It doesn't make any goddam sense at all. The world doesn't not know that it isn't not un-indistinct. It's just negative things until it sounds positive, it's bullshit. Please put the book down, it's genuinely nonsense. Give it to me?'

'No,' she smiled and held it as far back from his as her arm would extend.

'Give it to me,' he warned.

'You're going to throw it to the river.'

'Yes, I'm going to throw it in the river. It is nonsense, it comes from that book, and whoever wrote it is unwell.'

'Thank you for all the extra life. I get nervous about new doors and old patterns, but your presence makes me feel like a ferocious fairytale, do you know what I mean? Like I'm the good witch that can't be burnt?'

Godfrey was staring down a peacock. Hoping to scavenge some bhuja, it had dared to come close enough for him to inspect—to admire the luminescent blue and tropical-ocean green of its neck feathers, undulating as it jerked and lowered its head. Arriving to find Alexandra reading by her pool, he told her he needed an hour to finalise the ideas for his modules. She said she was going get a massage today anyway. It took him fifteen minutes to make them up. She emerged from the hotel's wellness spa in a bathrobe, bursting to thank him for three of the dozen revelations she had had during her ninety-minute sukharogya rub-down.

'Aren't they so beautiful? I saw one with its tail out yesterday. The most beautiful things are the most superfluous, d'you ever think that? Did you hear what I said?' He was inspecting at length the curve of its beak and trying to figure out what the white around its eyes was made of. 'Godfrey?'

'Hm?'

'I said thank you.'

'For what?'

'Just thank you. Know that I'm grateful. Should we get to work?'

'Yes! Work.'

'I need to get changed. Come to my room and talk me through what you're thinking?'

Up the steep steel stairway and up again beneath the roots of a holy fig, faded crimson steps led to her room. A mahogany four-post bed without canopy stood against the back wall. It was flanked by brass desk lamps on matching nightstands. Two deep armchairs stood beneath antique floor lamps.

'Jesus Christ, Alexandra, this room!'

'It's pretty nice, ay?'

He jumped down into a couch and bounced on its springs. He stood and knocked on the heavy table at the French windows which opened to the balcony. 'A man could get a lot of work done here.'

'I'm gonna take a shower. The shower's so huge, do you wanna come in?'

'Come in?'

'Mm hm.'

'To the shower?'

'Do you wanna take a look at it?'

'I've seen a shower. I'll be on the balcony.'

'OK then,' she said and slid off her bathrobe a moment too late.

Godfrey had already turned his back. 'I can't wait to hear what you've come up with.'

Half an hour later she came out in her blue dress printed with orange orchids to overlook with him the city. 'Isn't the view gorgeous?'

'Meh. India's gross. I gotta get outta here. Hey, I know that dress. The orchids.'

'You remembered! I *love* living out of a suitcase, don't you? We live other people's dreams, do you ever think that? We make the impossible likely. Oh, I feel so serene here,' she said with a popped foot and her hands on the balustrade.

'Serene? This is the most stressful place I can imaginate.'

'I know I'm acting out of necessity here, for the liberation of the people who depend on me. And even more serene when you're around, just the presence of another creator makes me feel at ease. At easel.' She pointed to him. 'You should write something about that, being at your ease-el. Being in Mother India it's like the universe has stopped contracting for a moment. Our moment. Should we go to the lawn and you can have a drink and give me your presentation?'

'Presentation?'

A single table had been set close to the beige balustrade and its white globes. With the onset of dusk the flat lego panorama began to glow beneath a hazy kind of pink. A waiter came out and Godfrey ordered beers and mai tais.

'So what have you come up with? Wow me some more.'

'You want a progression, right? Four weeks, so I have four modules.'

'Wishfolios.'

'Exactly. Four. You wanna hear 'em?'

'Absoblessedly.'

'Week one: How to Attract Lightning.'

'Oo, I love it! What does it mean?'

'For any idea, any really big idea, you need to be hit by a lightning bolt, that's what I call them. And you can't sit down and invent these ideas, you have to be struck by them, like lightning. But there are methods that I think can help you attract the lightning.'

'Attract the lightning. I love it! Oo, it reminds me!' she sang.

'What reminds you?'

'I have a proposition for you.'

259

'What now?'

'Have you been to Venice?'

'Italy? No.'

'Well! How would you... You ready for this?' A second table was placed beside theirs, brought across by two waiters with its tablecloth clamped in place, then a third. 'The Creative Art of Wishfulness Venice, 2020. Would you? Will you? Teach your School of Wishcraft and Creativity, in Venice!? It came to me this morning when I was watching The Tourist. Art therapy and ingenious life design in Venice! Gondolas! The Renaissance!'

Godfrey boomed: 'Do you not remember Bali?'

'That was so long ago! We'll have grown so much by then, and my God, Venice will sell itself! Bali was seven people, this'll be twice that. I can write off your flight to Europe, we can learn Italian, and you and I could go a week earlier and have all that peaceful creative energy to ourselves.'

'Alexandra. Do you not remember? Screaming at me. For hours. Twice. Rolling your head around like a serial killer. Abusing me? Calling me horrific names,' he laughed. 'Do you not—'

'Sir Godfrey, that's not important now!'

'It is important now, and it'll be important then.'

'You always focus on the caca.'

'Yes, I do.'

'I'll pay you five thousand dollars.'

'Fuck! Ga-ding-a ding.'

She leaned in and grinned and shook her head and reassured him: 'You can bring girls back, don't worry.'

Godfrey pressed his forearms into the edge of the table and grinned as well. 'What girls, Alexandra? I don't understand where this obsession with me bringing girls back has come from.'

A grill was wheeled onto the lawn and placed in the centre of the six assembled tables. Three steel trays followed after it, laden one with raw seafood on ice, one with metal skewers of marinated vegetables, one with stacks of lamb chops. Godfrey's neck shot up like a meerkat's. 'That's lamb. I friggen love lamb, I haven't had it in a year.'

'Venice is something to think about, now what's week two?'

'Week two! Unleashing The Crazy.'

'Oh, I love it *so* much!' Four potted coconut palms were brought across and placed at the corners of all the seating. Strings of fairy-lights, nailed into their trunks, were pulled out and hooked in to form a ring as dusk disappeared and orange-speckled night arose. 'Tell me more? Give me the elevator pitch?'

'Once you've been hit by lightning and you have that idea, you have to crazify it. Disney calls it Imagineering—you take it to as crazy as your imagination can go, then you engineer it back down to what's possible.'

'You're so so good at this, you'd make a *fortune* if you ran a creativity retreat! I could build and launch the whole thing for you! Yes!' The fairy-lights were turned on and a chef came out to light the grill. He rearranged his utensils and scraped the hotplate as banquet menus were handed to Godfrey and Alexandra, the only guests on the terrace. 'Should we order wine? Wine makes me do crazy things. Imagine drinking wine in Venice! Italy, my God! Venice will so sell itself, you just have to say the word, show people a few pictures! Oo that reminds me! I got you a present.'

'Why do you keep getting me presents?'

'Think of this as down payment. Now…' She readied her handbag on her lap and straightened her back. 'I figure you're a painter, which means you love images, right? And you travel so much to *all* these beautiful places, and you really should be taking photos. If not for content, then at least to remember them.'

'OK.'

'So I got you this.' She slid a wrapped rectangle across the table.

'What is it? What have you gotten me?' He almost smiled. 'Please stop getting me presents. … Alexandra this is too much.'

'It's nothing. They're so cheap here and I bought a new one and this is my old one. I figure you have an eye for composition so you'd take really good photos, and you deserve it. Think of it as an advance on the Wishfolios. How to Attract Lighting. How to *Be* A Lightning Rod. I love it, *they'll* love it. Plus you'll need the phone for Venice! Think of all the photos you'll want to take. Can you imagine? The Renaissance, the costumes the masks—and the pizza! Oh, and we'll definitely get there a few weeks earlier, we can watch every sunset together. And we are *totally* get inked in Venice!'

'It's so I can take photos.'

'Yesterday you are complaining about money and now you are buying a new iPhone?'

'Newish. They're cheap here, and I don't want to spend much longer in India and I'm not going to finish all the paintings— photos are the best way I can record everything to work from later.

I don't know why I never thought of this before.'

'She bought it for you.'

'What's that?'

'She bought it for you.'

'She?'

'You know.'

''Fraid I don't.'

'Alexandra.'

'What about her?'

'She bought it for you.'

'What makes you say that?'

'Did she?'

'No.'

'What, she's your sugarmama now?'

'Where d'you learn that word?'

'Don't make fun to my vocabulary. You think I'm *so* dumb, but I can see what's going on. You have a sugarmama, Godfrey, staying in a fancy hotel, and she gives you money and buying you gifts, but it's only because she wants to fuck you.'

'Ey! That's not nice.'

'Give me the phone, I want to call her.'

'Are you crazy, she hates you.'

'She does hate me?'

'She doesn't want to get a phone call from you.'

'I want to call her, I want to tell her to stop being your sugarmama.'

'Please don't call her that, it's weird.'

'That's what she is. And you like spending time with her more than me, right?'

'Are you serious? I spend time with her because I'm working for her.'

'She's your sugarmama and she worships you. Godfrey, yes! This is why, this is why you like her—because she worships you! And now she's your sugarmama also?! I don't want you talking to her anymore.'

'Well it's not for you to decide who I do and do not talk to.'

'You cannot spend time with someone that hates me and who gives you money because they want to fuck you.'

'She doesn't want to goddam fuck me! I've told her several times, to her face, that I am only interested in working for her. That is it.'

'There's no way someone spends so much time with someone and doesn't want to fuck them. Do you know who said this?'

'Gandhi.'

'You. You are *not* Gandhi. You are not a god.'

'So you keep telling me. Without Alexandra, Or, I wouldn't even be in India. We, wouldn't be in India. She has given me months, almost a year, of time to work, time to paint. That's invaluable, and she's the only person who's ever done that for me.'

'So you're using her for money? Under a disguising of being grateful that she already did have gived you money. This is up fucked, Godfrey. Who even are you?'

'Who the fuck are you?'

'I'm someone who works for my money.'

'As a prostitute.'

'Fuck you! What are you?'

'Not a prostitute.'

'No?' Long raised, Or's voice now went all in. Her hand with fingers stacks reached high outside their window. And she yelled. 'You just admit to me that you spend time with her because she gives you money! What does this sound like to you?'

'Sounds like you.'

'You're not spending time with her anymore. That's it. You are delusional. She's your sugarmama, she worships you, and you are not spending time with her anymore.'

'Listen, sugar tits. If—'

'Don't you say this to me! You will not talk to me like this! Who the fuck you think you are? You are not a God!'

It took them an afternoon of separation to calm down.

'I love you so much.'

'Yeah, you still do?'

'Of course, you are agadah.'

'Sorry I called you a prostitute.'

'I am sorry I called you a prostitute.'

'Just because my boss used to have a crush on me doesn't mean she's in love with me. You'd never call your boss your sugardaddy, right?'

'I'm sorry, I know. I just, we have argued a lot in Kumbakonam and then we came back to here, obviously this is not as good as Heritage and you are working so much, I'm amazed by what you do. I guess… I'm scared of losing you?'

'Let's do something special tonight. Fancy dinner?'

The waters of the pool were soaked black with night, reflecting as still and darkest crystal the white lights of the low pavilion behind it—the frangipani trees lit pink and green from below, the rapid pulsating of crickets, and restaurant crowded and bronze beyond glass. Between rough-hewn pillars grey and warm in the evening heat, Godfrey held out Or's seat. They told Sanjay they already knew what they wanted.

'With extra onion.'

'Really?'

'Of course,' said Or. 'Let's go nuts!'

When their beers arrived Godfrey held up his glass. 'Lechaim,' Or said and met it with her own. 'To Mahishasura.'

Always surprised by the attention others paid to his work, Godfrey smiled and said, 'Really?'

'I think it will be your best painting yet. And it has the best theme of any you have showed me. I'm sorry, really, for stopping you the other day. I should have been more sensitive to your job.'

'If I had an office job would you come to work with me?'

'Exactly.'

'And, to you. Cheers. I'm glad you've found something you're passionate about. I like watching you explore the culture, it's refreshing. Makes me feel younger.'

'It's *so* fascinating once you scratch the surface and look in the inside. I'm surprised you hate it so much, when we got here you *loved* it.'

'I don't know what happened. The place just became like a horrible gross nuisance. Like everything's designed to prevent me from doing my work as an artist.'

In the backseat of the car that she had requested from her hotel's reception, Alexandra Wishart hunched over her phone. At dinner she had posted one of the photos that Godfrey had taken of her. She recommenced the deleting of what misaligned with how she wished herself to appear, with responding to those containing questions, affirmations, congratulations. When eventually all the attributions of divinity had been liked she pressed the home button and swiped right and searched and swiped again and found between two of her banking apps the radar icon for which she was looking.

Still the blue dot on her screen had not moved. She leaned forward and showed its white brightness to the driver. 'Can you take me here?' He knew of the destination and after three times repeating its name as a question said, 'Taking you there, OK, Madame.'

Their dinner was brought out on a large tray. Godfrey unfurled his napkin and placed his cutlery on the table as Or spooned chicken chukka and rice onto her plate.

'Bete'avon.'

'What's that?'

'Hebrew for bon appetit. He has come with his soul's desire to the place that God has chosen.'

'Wordy. Is that *What Hindus Believe*?'

'It's Hebrew too, from the Torah.'

'So many holy books. How do you keep up?'

Godfrey folded his torn bread over his chicken and sliced tomato and cut off the new triangle's closest edge. He skewered it with his fork and dipped it into the bowl of raita at the side of the table.

'Is it good?' Godfrey froze. 'What?' said Or, the differing height of his eyebrows perplexing her. He considered for a moment that she might be joking. 'Oh, I'm so sorry! Ha ha! I didn't even realise. Eat, eat! Bete'avon!'

He did, and closed his eyes and raised his chin. 'So goddam good.'

'Is it good like I remember?' With her thumb she slid wet brown chicken over to her rice then lowered over her plate her entire hand like the claw of an arcade game. She squeezed the new combination into a kind of rounded cube. Then she picked it up and put it in her mouth.

'What the hell are you doing?'

'What?'

He considered for a moment that she might be antagonizing him. 'You're eating with your hands?'

She used the ends of three fingers to shift rice across her plate. 'Our fingers are extensions of the five elements. When you eat with your hands you create a physical connection with your food, and also a spiritual connection.'

He considered for rather a longer moment that she might be pre-psychoanalytic, unable to self-reflect—agadah. 'What the hell is with people forming connections with their food, honestly? Are you kidding me, Or? Why don't you just eat it?'

'I am eating it.'

'With a knife and fork!'

265

'I thought you might like to know that Godfrey said he was in India alone.'

Or's claw dangled in mid-air. Godfrey said, 'What are you doing here?'

'And that tonight he was working. I see that he's still calling his bimbo his work.'

Or looked up from her handheld dinner. 'You did not know that I am here?'

Godfrey put an elbow on the table and scratched his eyebrow with his ring finger. 'Or, she made it clear from the start that being paid was dependent on being here alone. So I—'

'So you choose money over admitting that I exist?'

'He told you he was at my hotel today?'

'I can't fucking believe you.'

'And drinking cocktails at my pool.'

'So that is why you're not doing any work. Did he pay for them?'

'Or, you—'

'Did he pay for them?' she said over him. 'And he tells you he calls working for you 'psychopath management'?'

'Hemingway said that action is character. I gave you another chance and you've shown me your true character.'

'Are you fucking serious? I gave *you* a second chance. You behaved like a goddam psychopath in Bali and I told you I wanted to come here alone.'

'Yet you're here with your bimbo.'

'Yes, I didn't want to come here with you. And this is why. The great vengeful vacuum of a priestess, Glovindria! How are you here? You said you were having dinner at the Residency.'

'I can't believe I bought you an iPhone.'

'I knew it!' said Or and wiped her fingers of curry.

'If you hate me so much, Godfrey, why do you want to work with me?'

'Or, will you—'

She had upped from the table and very hastily made for the entrance. Godfrey twisted to rise from his seat but turned back and pressed at the inside corners of his eyes.

'I can't believe I fell for it again. All the talking, always talking, and spending all this time together. But you're just using me.' She sighed. 'Are you sure this is what you want?'

'And off we go. *You* are using *me,* Alexandra! You insert yourself into my life because you're lonely, and you think we're going to end up together.'

'Are you sure this is what you want?'

'What I want, is to not be with you. I mm not attracted to you, I think you are insane. And you've done little since Bangkok but teach me the meaning of fear.'

'Where the fuck are you going?'

Or had almost finished gathering and stuffing her things into her suitcase. 'Where you are not. You make me sick, get the fuck out of here.'

'Why do I make you sick?'

'I don't want to talk to you, get out of here.'

'I'm paying for the room, remember? I'm not leaving.'

'Oh, yes, money, money, money—your whole life is money. But rely for money on a woman who wants to sleep with you, your fucking sugarmama who takes care of you, and you lie to her about me existing? I don't know you. I don't know who you are. You make me sick just thinking about you. And when I do think, I see a fascist—a pathetic loser fascist obsessed with money. You're here because I haven't paid you for Heritage, that's all. Fuck you.'

'Or, that is entirely untrue. I'm here because I would like to talk to you about what's happened. She said—'

'Too fucking late, you idiot. You're a pathetic liar, I hate liars. I will never believe another more word you say. Do you know where liars go, Godfrey? Into your paintings. You're a hypocrite. You pretend you are God to compensate for your lies, the same lies you put in your paintings. You judge, because you're covering up your lies and you *know* it. *You* are the green Smurf Beyoncé whatever-the-fuck! Get out of my way.'

'Where are you going?'

'Get out my way you helpless little liar. You sad, disgusting, lonely narcissist—look at you, you can't even take care of yourself.'

'So this is fear. Why are you so cruel?'

'I'm not cruel, I'm telling you the truth for the first time, because no one else will—because you surround yourself with people who worship you. "You're so brilliant, My Godfrey! You're so much talented." You're not brilliant, you're a moose! Why don't you get a job like everyone else instead of lying to rich lonely women and leading on your sugarmama for money? Oh, you make me sick. It's because that you think you're a God—divine—you are the chosen one. "I don't need to wear a helmet! I'm too good to work!"

Everyone works, Godfrey!'

'Not you.'

'I work for my money thank you.'

'As a prostitute.'

'Get out of my fucking way.'

Still in the doorway, Godfrey put a palm against the door frame and tensed his outstretched arm. 'No.'

'Get out of my way, now.'

'I don't want you to leave, I want to talk to you.'

'I don't want to talk to you! Don't you understand? You make me sick, you're a pathetic narcissist!' She extended her hand, fingers stiff and stacked, over his elbow towards the elevators. 'Go back to your sugarmama! She can stroke your ego and pay for your life, you pathetic idiot! Get used to being alone. You're a narcissist. You think you're the centre of the world, but you'll always be alone because everything to you is money. You don't even deserve to be in the same room as me, who do you think you are?! You pathetic person and disgusting liar. I don't even hate you, I nothing you. Get out of my way. This is your last warning.'

'Yeah, or fucking what?'

And she swung her left arm to his wrist and put her right behind his elbow and with a twist of her shoulders broke his arm.

'Morning :)

'So I just wanted to say that some of your choices have unsettled and disappointed me deeply. You were here for weeks with your bimbo while I thought that I was here with you. None of this is cool or acceptable to the narrative I choose to want to have of my life.

'Personal comments aside, I've been reading articles on the price-ceilings forming now around online courses and I have to change the cost of YYLW. Combined with the number of sign-ups I expect to get, this means that the course doesn't lend itself to extra payments. I'm paying B-rad 2k for his Spirituality Wishfolios and with what you got for Bali it wouldn't be fair to the other co-creators to pay you as much as initially discussed. For the sake of not changing the sales page and the course program I'm still totally down for you to do the Creative Wishfolios—if you agree to do them without payment.'

With his arm freshly cast, Godfrey awaited the preparation of his bill in the hospital bed in which Or had been vaccinated against rapies. Too painful to hold the phone with both hands, he laboured to reach one thumb across its overly large screen in order to tap out his reply.

'Huh? You want me to do the Wishfolios for nothing?'

Then appeared instantly, as it had been drafted on one of her laptops and copied and pasted to her phone:

'This is an organic co-creation and an alchemisation of the birth-pains that we've endured together. But I feel like I'm fighting alone on the barricades of this western front, as I have been from the start. I'm *not* a business or a corporation, I'm a person who fights around the clock and enjoys connecting with friends while giving *and* receiving value. If any collab became an inconvenience or felt like an obligation, Godfrey, why do it?! Know what I mean? :)

'I'm sure as an artist you'll understand—you paint for the joy, right? Joy comes first? Spare me any collab or relationship that isn't a joyful Fuck Yes! because without the Fuck Yes! what are we even doing here? :) I'm deep in the trenches up here trying to get everything ready for the launch, but I need you to tell me the truth for the first time ever, and tell me if your Wishfolios are not a Fuck Yes! for you.

'If they're not, for whatever reason, then please—I'm the first who doesn't want you to do them and you're absolutely free and no hard feelings. :)

'Iron your cape, Godfrey. Who knows... you might just fly.'

Godfrey locked his phone and threw it onto the crunchy fitted sheet over the plastic mattress and thought on how fleeting were the pleasures of the earth, how costly its treasures, brittle its rewards.

'Ding ga-ding, ga-ding-a ding. Fuck.'

ACT FIVE

Their Year of Living Wishfully

I

Through an unparted sea of vagrant, beggar, and homeless—of amputee, driver, and porter—the hot smell of composting vomit beneath incense in dusty manure—wild and mange-bare dog and painted and rubbish-fed cow and emaciate hysterical chicken— Godfrey Lackland walked with his right arm bent by plaster and his backpack strapped down tight at his shoulders.

Come to stand upon dusty tiles in a bare new hall, he deduced the location of the ticketing window by its densest concentration of brawling people. When quickly he realised that the queues were approximations of force rather than organisations of patience, he pushed his way through and leaned down to the semi-circle cut out of a window and waited for an old man at his computer screen to swivel his chair to greet him.

When after a time he'd swivelled not Godfrey said, 'Wanakkam. ... Hello. ... Bangalore. I need a ticket to Bangalore?'

At last the swivel. 'Bengaluru, Sir?'

'Bengaluru, yes.'

'First or second class?'

'Second class. No, wait. How much is first class?'

'First class ticket very nice carriage. A/C soft seat. One hundred fifty rupees.'

'A hundred and fifty rupees?' said Godfrey to himself. 'That's three dollars. For first class, with air-conditioning? A hundred and fifty rupees?'

'Yes, Sir, one hundred fifty rupees, very nice carriage, A/C soft seat. Please you are filling out this form.' He slid out a carbon-copy slip.

'How long's the train ride?'

'Very fast train, Sir. A/C soft seat, twelve hours.'

'Twelve hours? For three dollars?' Godfrey mumbled. His

270

monetary autism kicked in. Three divided by twelve was point-two-five. 25 cents. '25 cents an hour?' he said to himself. He leaned further down and forward: 'That's very affordable.'

'Very nice train, Sir. A/C soft seat.'

Along a red-and-white platform in new morning, pink reflecting in the polished concrete from neon information boards, Godfrey listened for his own details in the slow echo of the tripartite announcements. When his train was announced in English for platform seven he took from his pocket the music player whose silver body flashed him back to Laotian plumeria and the pool with its raised ledge all day in the sun and the robed monk reading in front of The Orange Temple. He pressed play. There sounded in his ears only the rustle of transferred vinyl then the deep rising and falling of an acoustic guitar: up, up, up, up—down, down. Shortly Huddie Ledbetter's unmistakable holler: '*I'm Alabama bound,*' rose and fell in the guitar's melody and was returned in higher chorus: '*I'm Alabama bound! ... I'm Alabama bound—*'

Godfrey turned at the bent arrow which—urine!—directed him to his platform. He ascended a covered flight of steps whose fronts alternated underfoot between painted yellow and a slogan in Tamil, painted yellow and a slogan in Hindi, painted yellow and English. The chorus and Lead Belly together: '*And if the train don't stop and turn around, I'm Alabama bound—I'm Alabama bound!*'

'One medicine for all diseases: cleanliness,' read the third step, in capitals and white paint against a dusty blue background.

'*Now don't you leave me here—Now don't you leave me here!*'

A slogan in Hindi; a slogan in Tamil; and, 'Let your environment be as clean as your home.'

'*And if you will go anyhow, leave me a dime for bail—leave me a dime for bail.*'

A slogan in Hindi; a slogan in Tamil; and, 'They who embrace the Self, know neither within nor without.'

'*I'm Alabama bound—I'm Alabama bound!*'

Hindi; Tamil; and, 'Purify the spectacles of your mind to see the world is God.'

'*And if the train don't stop and turn around, I'm Alabama-bound.*'

Hindi; Tamil; 'Your art is your life, your life is your—'

No, it didn't say that. But imagine if it did.

The painted white stripe running the length of the train was cleaner than the dark carriage-blue above and below it. Inside, long padded seats and a floor of riveted steel—rusting chrome luggage racks and halogen lights—and fixed to the ceiling dozens, strangely dozens, of caged fans, silent though all whirred as they failed to cool the morning.

The only person on the train, Godfrey swung his backpack overhead and slid across a seat to a wooden window shutter, barred on the outside by four horizontal lengths of dented steel. Shortly someone stepped up off the platform and checked the wall-numbering against his ticket. He slid his yellow fabric bag down to Godfrey's calf and lowered himself onto the aisle-edge of the seat.

'*You can turn your good heart, just whiskey boy, and let that King Kong be.*'

And another, then another—then many, many—many—others, lifted themselves off the platform and found their seats. The four men now at Godfrey's plaster-casted elbow, in lungis and chappals and shirtsleeves, took plastic containers of wet food and rice from their fabric bags and cracked open their lids and ate with their fingers.

'*…Alabama bound—I'm Alabama bound!*'

Godfrey turned onto his left butt-cheek and looked out the window, through the open doors of the train beside his to the next platform across, where a woman with a wreath of jasmine in her braid swept a concrete bench with a bunch of twigs.

'*The preachers in the stand… Pass his hat around… Singing brothers and sisters shoot your money to me, I'm Alabama bound—*'

He pulled from his trousers a new pocket-sized book of musical notation and placed it on his thigh. He uncapped a pen with his teeth and opened its cover—looked upon the blackletter words of its title page: 'VENIT NOX', for the night was coming, when no man can do his work as an artist.

'*I'm Alabama bound—I'm Alabama bound.*'

With the side of his hand he held open the staves and wrote down his bank balance—$2020—which gave him no confidence.

'*I'm Alabama bound!—I'm Alabama bound!*
'*And if the train don't stop and turn around…*'

II

Alexandra Wishart in large sunglasses ran her fingertips over the last vestige of plaster crumbling to sea-soaked brick on the side of a home. As she stepped up onto a bridge she caught sight of a treetop and the tacked-on façade of the Gesuiti, its Baroque Virgin in the very act of assuming opposite the potted chimneys which overlooked their campo.

At the height of the bridge an African man in blue jeans and red t-shirt stood over an array of handbags on a white sheet.

'Nice lady, come here please.' Grabbed by the arm, Alexandra had little choice but to look at what the man was offering.

'What are they?'

'Real authentic,' said the man, and pointed to the arrangement at his feet. 'Gucci, Louis Vuitton, Coco Chanel. How much you pay for Gucci?' He handed one to her. 'For you today, nice lady my first customer, very special price. Gucci just for you... normally five thousand dollars, for you today one hundred euros OK?'

Alexandra beheld the bag in both hands. 'This is a hundred euros? It's Gucci! My God, how is it so cheap?'

'Just for you, Madame, special price for a nice lady. Don't you feel you need it? Looks *very* good on you I say. Imagine, new husband from new handbag. Take it now, OK: eighty-five euros.'

'You said it's authentic?'

'Of course authentic! Look at the stitching.' He unzipped the bag and pressed out its lining; turned it upside down and showed Alexandra its seamless bottom. 'OK for you *eighty* euros, but this is my final price today only. You are very beautiful, Madame, can I tell you?'

'Well thank you. Thank you a lot, I——. Wait, I don't think I need another——'

'Madame, look at the stitching. See? Genuine real. Authentic *authentic* Gucci, just for you. Normal price five thousand dollar!' he said, smiling as he tried to inspire her. Then he relented: 'OK, seventy-five euros. Take it now, I give to you, here.' He zipped it back up and offered it to her.

'Seventy-five euros for authentic Gucci? My God! OK. Ummm...'

273

She stepped down onto the Fondamenta Zen and after consulting her wrists strolled beside a chalky-green canal flowing with stems of seaweed. The shadows from the windowsills were long and low on a coral-pink house, its chimney in relief and green shutters folded back over beds of cascading flower. Alexandra raised the camera dangling at her neck and photographed the façade. She strolled and ran her fingers along the underside of jasmine overgrowing from a concealed garden; leaned a bare shoulder against salt-brick between high windows and looked across to the pointed arches of a porta d'acqua, held in place by rods of rusted iron. Though she could not read Italian a stone plaque on a bricked-up window said that it was once the house of 'L'ALCHIMISTA MAMVGNA BRAGADIN,' and she told people that she really wanted to learn.

Approaching the fondamenta's final steep and short bridge she saw low at a break in the wall a blank page. As she neared she saw that it was in fact an open book. Then that it was being written in. At last she discovered that it was held by a young man in a blue oxford shirt, rolled at the sleeves. His strangely trousered legs were out along the first dry step, ankles crossed—the crimson front of one matching the rear of the other and vice versa in gold. His back was against the white stone of the break in the wall.

For a time Alexandra looked at him, conjecturing as to what he might be doing. 'Wait, writing,' she thought, then realised: 'A writer!' She took off her sunglasses and spoke: 'You're going to think this sounds strange, but I just had a feeling I *had* to talk to you.'

Frustrated by the frequency of strange interruptions here, the young man squinted up from his notebook. 'What?'

'Are you a writer?'

'Are you a cop?'

'Huh?' She inspected his clothing and noticed instantly the collar fraying at his neck. 'You're a writer, right?'

'I might be,' he snapped, now impatient of her. 'Why?'

She angled her nose until her head was parallel with his book's spine and looked down at his pages. They were covered with unlined cursive, filled at all angles with scribble, crammed with tiny paragraphs. His fingertips were blotched with green ink. Her eyes bulged. 'My God, you *are* a writer.' She redoubled their bulge and stood at his calves and smiled. 'What do you write?'

'Obituaries.'

274

'This is so amazing, you have no idea. What are the *chances*? Another writer in Venice!' She put a hand to her chest. 'I'm a writer, and I meet you here in the inspirational home of Hemingway and Picasso and the Renaissance?! My name's Alexandra.' She patted down the breeze-blown wrinkles of her white dress bursting with violet columbines and lowered a stiff palm for him to shake. 'Do you ever suspect it's your dark side that keeps you whole? I just bought twenty acres on the moon but I asked for it to be on the dark side—why, do you think?'

'What the fuck are you talking about, lady?'

'Oh, I'm sorry. ... What's your name?'

'Octavian.'

'That's not your name!' she smiled, always glad to be flirted with.

'It is.'

'I'm a writer too, an artistpreneur actually. I'd love to read your prose, what are you working on right now?'

'If you talk about you lose it.'

She gasped as her eyes became larger than all ever. Barely able to breathe she quickly worked up the courage to ask: 'Could I read something you've written?'

'No. Why?'

'I haven't danced with words in so long. Writers heal the world, don't you think? We embrocate its soul with the aching beauty of our truth. Nothing is impossible when *you* become possible.'

'What the *fuck* are you talking about?'

'Have you ever taught creativity?'

Octavian looked to the urns on the top of the high wall across the water—those to which he had for some time been meaning to write an elegy—and wished very much that the woman would go away.

'Have you?'

'Have I what?'

'Ever taught creativity?'

'Creativity can't be taught.'

'No but it can! *Could* I read your prose?'

'Why?' he almost yelled. 'Who are you?'

'*Ding-a ding ga-ding ga-ding ga-ding ga-dong-a ding-a dong-a ding ga-ding ga ding ding.*'

'After last year's Bali retreat exploded my heart and tattooed a rainbow on my soul, I knew I had to come back for The Creative Art of Wishfulness in Venice!'

275

'*Ding-a ding ga-ding ga-ding ga-ding ga-ding ga-dong-a ding-a dong-a ding ga-ding ga ding ding.*'

Orange light glaring in from the side towards the Rialto bridge, the 1080 x 1080 image saturated and filtered until the Grand Canal was turquoise: 'Fuel your brave soul life. Free your authentic mind. Ensorcell your awakened heart.'

'*Ding ga-ding ga-ding ga-ding ga-ding ga-ding ga-dong-a ding-a dong-a ding ga-ding ga ding-a ding.*'

A full-width image of the Salute at sunset from the Accademia—gondolas floating down a river of mercury, water taxis motoring up with silvery wakes—and across it light grey text against strips of red:

'Kiss life on the mouth. Have a sordid love affair with your purpose. Fall madly in lust with your vision! *Honour* your hunger—*reclaim* your superpowers from the Gods of Tomorrow—*alchemise* the ammunition of your happiness!!'

'*Ding ga-ding ga-ding ga-ding ga-ding ga-ding ga-dong-a ding-a dong-a ding ga-ding ga ding-a ding.*'

The high mosaics of St Mark's glinting in full daylight, its gothic baldachins frozen in lament, domes bulbous as though choked—families feeding a plague of pigeons and Chinese tourists in shiny puffy vests clustered at closed umbrellas beside:

'Would you LOVE to connect in person with kindred troublemakers from all over the world for an ENTIRE WEEK of art therapy and yoga, nutrition and meditation, and ingenious life design? To be led by world-renowned life coaches, dieticians, New York Times Bestselling wordspirationalists and professors of Joyology? All while in Venice?! The home of gondolas, the Renaissance, and all-time epicentre of European alchemy!

'What exactly *is* The Creative Art of Wishfulness®?'

'*Ding-a ding ga-ding ga-ding ga-ding ga-dong-a ding-a dong-a ding ga-ding ga ding ding.*'

A full-width excerpt from Veronese's *Wedding at Cana*, its chubby marble balusters behind a banquet of jewels and jesters and Jews, its Suleiman and daggered Turk in emerald green, the bearded midget bearing a parakeet—the painter himself in a white tunic at a viola before the Virgin—all over:

'The Creative Art of Wishfulness® unleashes your genius and liberates the purposeful narratives of your dreams. It sits you in front of the easel of fearlessness and empowers you to repaint your greatest work of art: your life. Like no other self-creation experience™, The Creative Art of Wishfulness® is a wild soulspedition© into non-inauthenticity™ that gives YOU the secrets to alchemise your heartistic vision™.'

'*Ding-a ding ga-ding ga-ding ga-ding ga-dong-a ding-a dong-a ding ga-ding ga ding ding.*'

'On our amazing week of art therapy and yoga, nutrition and meditation and ingenious life design, you'll:

'PENETRATE the void of your becoming; REWILD your brave soul life; DETERGE the limits of your awesome™—all while harnessing the benevolent divine destruction that empowers real, genuine, actionable soul-self-recreation™!'

'*Ding-a ding ga-ding ga-ding ga-ding ga-dong-a ding-a dong-a ding ga-ding ga ding ding.*'

'Places are VERY limited and early-bird sign-ups close TONIGHT!

'Click _HERE_ to begin your own personal Renaissance, and join us on a 1000-year gondola-ride through agrestal artspiration™ that begins with one simple Authentic Demandment©:

'Love Thyself.'

'*Ding ga-ding ga-ding ga-ding ga-ding ga-ding ga-dong-a ding-a dong-a ding ga-ding ga ding-a ding.*'

·venit nox·

45013746R00171

Printed in Poland
by Amazon Fulfillment
Poland Sp. z o.o., Wrocław